Steal You Away

Niccolò Ammaniti was born in Rome in 1966. He has written three novels and a collection of short stories. He won the prestigious Italian Viareggio-Repaci Prize for Fiction with his bestselling novel *I'm Not Scared*, which has been translated into thirty-five languages.

Jonathan Hunt currently divides his time between Italy and Britain. His translations include Niccolò Ammaniti, *I'm Not Scared* and Tommaso Pincio, *Love Shaped Story*.

Also by Niccolò Ammaniti

I'm Not Scared

Steal You Away

Niccolò Ammaniti

Translated from the Italian by Jonathan Hunt

CANONGATE
Edinburgh · New York · Melbourne

First published in Great Britain in 2006 by
Canongate Books Ltd, 14 High Street,
Edinburgh EH1 1TE

This paperback edition published by Canongate Books in 2007

1

First published in Italy as *Ti Prendo e ti porto via*
by Mondadori Editore s.p.a.

This English translation was supported by
the Italian Cultural Institute, Edinburgh

British Library Cataloguing-in-Publication Data
A catalogue record for this book is available on
request from the British Library

ISBN 978 1 84195 932 0

Typeset in Sabon by
Palimpsest Book Production Limited, Grangemouth, Stirlingshire
Printed and bound by Clays Ltd, St Ives plc

www.canongate.co.uk

To Nora

. . . and I remembered the days when I was innocent, and the red light of coral lit my hair, when starry-eyed and vain I would gaze into the moon and force her to tell me you're beautiful . . .

Sei bellissima, Loredana Berté

Why is the mandoline no more in fashion?
Why do we never hear the strummed guitar?

Guapparia, Rodolfo Falvo

Alegría es cosa buena.

La macarena

18th June 199. . .

1

It's over.

Holidays. Holidays. Holidays.

For three months. An eternity.

The beach. Swimming. Bike rides with Gloria. And the little streams of warm brackish water among the reeds. Wading knee-deep, looking for minnows, tadpoles, newts and maggots.

Pietro Moroni leans his bike against the wall and looks around.

He's twelve years old, but small for his age.

He's thin. Suntanned. A mosquito bite on his forehead. Black hair cut short, in rough-and-ready fashion, by his mother. A snub nose and large hazel eyes. He's wearing a white World Cup T-shirt, a pair of frayed denim shorts and translucent rubber sandals, the kind that make a black mush form between your toes.

Where's Gloria? he wonders.

He threads his way through the crowded tables of the Bar Segafredo.

All his schoolmates are there.

All waiting, eating ice creams, trying to find a patch of shade.

It's very warm.

For the past week the wind seems to have disappeared, moved off somewhere else taking all the clouds with it and leaving behind a huge incandescent sun that boils your brain inside your skull.

It's eleven o'clock in the morning and the thermometer shows thirty-seven degrees Celsius.

The cicadas chirp away obsessively on the pines behind the

volleyball court. And somewhere, not far away, an animal must have died, because now and again you catch a sickly whiff of carrion.

The school gate is closed.

The results aren't up yet.

A slight fear moves furtively in his belly, pushes against his diaphragm and restricts his breathing.

He goes out of the bar.

There she is!

Gloria is sitting on a low wall. On the other side of the street. He goes across. She pats him on the shoulder and asks: 'Are you scared?'

'A bit.'

'So am I.'

'Come off it,' says Pietro. 'You've passed. You know you have.'

'What are you going to do afterwards?'

'I don't know. How about you?'

'I don't know. Shall we do something together?'

'Okay.'

They sit there in silence on the wall, and while on the one hand Pietro thinks she looks even prettier than usual in that light-blue towelling T-shirt, on the other he feels his panic growing.

If he considers the matter rationally he knows there's nothing to worry about, everything was sorted out in the end.

But his belly is not of the same opinion.

He wants to go to the bathroom.

There's a bustle in front of the bar.

Everyone comes to life, crosses the road and throngs around the locked gate.

Italo, the school caretaker, comes across the yard, keys in hand, shouting: 'Don't push! Don't shove! You'll hurt yourselves.'

'Come on.' Gloria heads for the gate.

Pietro feels as if he has two ice cubes under his armpits. He can't move.

Meanwhile they're all pushing to get in.

You've failed! says a little voice.

(*What?*)

You've failed!

It's true. Not a presentiment. Not a suspicion. It's true.

(*Why?*)

It just is.

There are some things you just know and there's no point in wondering why.

How could he have imagined he'd passed?

Go and look, what are you waiting for? Go on. Move.

At last he breaks out of his paralysis and joins the crowd. His heart beats a frantic little march under his breastbone.

He uses his elbows. 'Let me through . . . I want to get through, please.'

'Take it easy! Are you crazy?'

'Keep calm, you idiot. Where do you think you're going?'

He receives a couple of shoves. He tries to get through the gate, but because he's so small the bigger pupils just throw him back. He drops down on all fours and crawls between their legs, circumventing the blockage.

'Calm down! Calm down! Don't push . . . Keep back, for Chr . . .' Italo is standing beside the gate and when he sees Pietro the words die in his mouth.

You've failed . . .

It's written in the caretaker's eyes.

Pietro stares at him for a moment, then runs forward again, towards the steps.

He bounds up them three at a time and enters.

At the other end of the entrance hall, beside a bronze bust of Michelangelo, is the noticeboard with the results.

Something strange is happening.

There's this boy, I think he's in 2A, his name is . . . I can't remember his name, who was going out and he saw me and stopped, as if it wasn't me standing in front of him but some kind of Martian, and now he's looking at me and nudging another guy, called Giampaolo Rana, his name I do remember, and he's saying something to him and Giampaolo has turned round too and is looking at me, but now he's looking at the noticeboards and now he's looking at me again and speaking to another boy who's looking at me and another boy's looking at me and everyone's looking at me and everything's gone quiet . . .

Everything has gone quiet.

The crowd opens out, leaving him a clear path through to the class lists. His legs take him forward, between two wings of schoolmates. He goes on till he finds himself a few inches from the noticeboard, being pushed by the kids arriving after him.

Read it.

He looks for his section.

B! Where is it? B? Section B? One B, Two B. There it is!

It's the last sheet on the right.

Abate. Altieri. Bart . . .

He scans the list from the top downwards.

One name is written in red.

Somebody's failed.

About halfway down. Somewhere around M, N, O, P.

It's Pierini.

Moroni.

He shuts his eyes tight and when he opens them again everything around him is blurred and wavy.

He reads the name again.

MORONI PIETRO FAILED

He reads it again.

MORONI PIETRO FAILED

What's the matter, can't you read?

He reads it yet again.

M-O-R-O-N-I. MORONI. Moroni. Mor . . . M . . .

A voice echoes in his brain. *What's your name?*

(*Sorry? What did you say?*)

What's your name?

(*Who? Me . . . ? Er . . . Pietro. Moroni. Moroni Pietro.*)

And up there it says Moroni Pietro. And right next to it, in red, in capitals, in big capital letters, FAILED.

So that feeling was right.

And there he was hoping it was just the usual sickening feeling he gets when he's due to have a piece of classwork returned and he's ninety-nine per cent sure he's done really badly. A feeling which always turns out to be unjustified because, as he knows, that microscopic one per cent is worth far more than all the rest.

The others! Look at the others.

PIERINI FEDERICO	PASSED
BACCI ANDREA	PASSED
RONCA STEFANO	PASSED

He looks for traces of red on any of the other sheets, but they're all solid blue.

I can't be the only one in the whole school who's failed. Miss Palmieri told me I'd pass. She said everything would be fine. She prom . . .

(*No.*)

He mustn't think about it.

He must just leave.

Why did they pass Pierini, Ronca and Bacci and not me?

Here it comes.

The lump in the throat.

A spy in his brain tells him: *Pietro, old pal, you'd better get out of here quick, you're going to burst into tears. And you don't want to do that in front of everyone, do you?*

'Pietro! Pietro! What does it say?'

He turns round.

Gloria.

'Have I passed?'

Her face bobs up at the back of the crowd.

Pietro looks for Celani.

Blue.

Like all the others.

He tries to tell her, but can't. He has a funny taste in his mouth. Copper. Acid. He takes a deep breath and swallows.

I'm going to throw up.

'Well? Have I passed?'

Pietro nods.

'Yesss! I've passed! I've passed!' Gloria shrieks and starts hugging the kids around her.

Why is she making such a fuss about it?

'Hey, and what about you?'

Answer her, go on.

He feels sick. Some hornets seem to be trying to get into his ears. His legs are limp and his cheeks are on fire.

'Pietro! What's the matter? Pietro!'

Nothing. I've only failed, that's all, he feels like answering. He leans back against the wall and slides slowly down to the floor.

'Pietro, what's the matter? Aren't you well?' she asks him and looks at the lists.

'Didn't you pa . . . ?'

'No . . .'

'What about the others?'

'Y . . .'

And Pietro Moroni realises that everyone is staring at him and crowding around him, that he, sitting there in the middle, is the jester, the black sheep (red sheep) and that Gloria is on the other side too, now, with all the others, and it doesn't matter, it doesn't matter at all, that she's looking at him with those Bambi-like eyes.

SIX MONTHS EARLIER . . .

9th December

2

On 9th December, at six twenty in the morning, while a storm of rain and wind lashed the countryside, a black Fiat Uno Turbo GTI (a relic of an age when, for a few lire more than the basic model, you could buy a motorised coffin that ran like a Porsche, guzzled like a Cadillac and crumpled like a can of Coca-Cola) turned off the Via Aurelia at the exit for Ischiano Scalo and went along a two-lane road that cut across the muddy fields. It passed the sports centre and the big farmers' club building and entered the village.

The short main street, Corso Italia, was covered with earth washed down by the rainwater. The poster of the Ivana Zampetti Beauty Farm had been torn off by the wind and dumped in the middle of the road.

There wasn't a soul around, except for a mangy mutt with more breeds in its bloodline than teeth in its head, which was rooting among the rubbish spilled from an overturned bin.

The Uno evaded the mongrel, cruised past the lowered blinds of Marconi the butcher's, the tobacconist's-cum-parfumerie and the bank, and entered Piazza XXV Aprile, the heart of the village.

Waste paper, plastic bags, newspapers and rain scudded across the station square. The yellowing leaves of the old palm, in the middle of the little garden, were all folded over to one side. The door of the little station, a squat grey building, was closed, but the red sign of the Station Bar was lit up, indicating that it was already open.

The car stopped by the war memorial and stood there with its engine running. Its exhaust pipe belched out dense black fumes. Its darkened windows made it impossible to see inside.

Then, at last, the driver's door opened with a metallic creak.

Out came a blast of *Volare* in the flamenco version by the Gipsy Kings, and closely followed by a big, burly man with long blond hair, bug-eye sunglasses and a brown leather jacket with an Apache eagle embroidered in pearls on the back.

His name was Graziano Biglia.

He stretched his arms, yawned, loosened up his legs, took out a packet of Camels and lit one.

Home again.

The Albatross and the Go-Go Girl

To understand why Graziano Biglia decided to return on precisely 9th December, after an absence of two years, to Ischiano Scalo, the place of his birth, we'll have to go back a bit in time.

Not all that far. Seven months. And we'll have to hop over to the other side of Italy, onto the eastern coast. The part of it known as the Romagna Riviera.

The summer is just beginning.

It's Friday evening and we are at the Carillon del Mare, a cheap little restaurant on the beach, a few kilometres from Riccione, specializing in seafood and bacterial gastroenteritis.

The weather is very warm, but a light sea breeze makes everything more bearable.

The restaurant is crowded. Mainly foreigners, German and Dutch couples, people from the North.

And there stands Graziano Biglia. Leaning against the bar, drinking his third margarita.

Pablo Gutierrez, a dark lad with a fringe and a carp tattoo on his back, enters the restaurant and comes over to him.

'Shall we start?' the Spaniard asks.

'Okay.' Graziano casts a knowing look at the barman, who

reaches down under the bar, pulls out a guitar and hands it to him.

This evening, for the first time in a long while, he's in the mood for playing. He feels inspired.

Maybe it's the two margaritas he's just drunk, maybe it's the breeze, maybe it's the intimate, friendly atmosphere in that rotunda by the sea, who knows?

He sits down on a stool in the middle of the small dance floor, which is lit by warm red lights. He opens the leather case and draws out his guitar like a samurai unsheathing his katana.

A Spanish guitar made by the famous Barcelona luthier Xavier Martinez specially for Graziano. He tunes it and has the impression that a magic fluid flows between him and his instrument, fusing them into a single entity, capable of producing wondrous chords. He glances at Pablo. He is standing behind two conga drums.

A spark of mutual understanding ignites in their eyes.

And without more ado they strike up with a piece by Paco de Lucia, then move on to Santana, a couple of John McLaughlin pieces and, to end with, the immortal Gipsy Kings.

Graziano's hands run deftly up and down the neck of the guitar as if possessed by the spirit of the great Andrès Segovia.

The audience love it. Applause. Cheers. Whistles of approval.

He holds them in the palm of his hand. Especially the female department. He can hear them squealing like rabbits on heat.

This has something to do with the magic of Spanish music and a lot to do with his looks.

It's difficult not to fall for a guy like Graziano.

The blond mane of shoulder-length hair. The massive chest covered by a soft brown carpet. The dark, Omar Sharif-like eyes. The jeans, faded and torn at the knees. The necklace of turquoise. The tribal tattoo on his bulging biceps. The bare feet. The whole conspires to shatter the hearts of his female listeners.

When the set is over, after the umpteenth encore of *Samba pa ti*, after the umpteenth kiss blown at the sunburnt German girl, Graziano takes his leave of Pablo and heads for the toilets to empty his bladder and recharge his batteries with a nice lungful of Bolivian snow.

He is about re-emerge when a tall brunette tanned as brown as a chocolate biscuit, a bit long in the tooth but with tits the size of balloons, enters the bathroom.

'It's the men's . . .' Graziano says, pointing at the door.

She stops him with one hand. 'I'd like to give you a blow job, do you mind?'

Has anyone ever refused a blow job?

'Be my guest,' says Graziano, indicating the toilet.

'But first I want to show you something,' says the brunette. 'Look over there, in the middle of the room. You see that guy in the Hawaiian shirt? He's my husband. We're from Milan . . .'

Her husband, a slightly built man with slicked-back hair, is stuffing himself with peppered mussels.

'Wave to him.'

Graziano does so. The man raises his champagne glass, then claps his hands.

'He thinks you're great. Says you play divinely. That you have the gift.'

She pushes him into the toilet. Shuts the door. Sits on the seat. Unbuttons his jeans and says: 'But now we're going to cheat on him.'

Graziano leans back against the wall, closes his eyes.

And time vanishes.

Such was Graziano Biglia's life in those days.

Life in the fast lane, as a song title might put it. A life of encounters, pleasant surprises, positive energies and flows. A life to the tune of a merengue.

What could be better than the bitter taste of the drug numbing your mouth and a billion molecules whirling in your brain like a wind that rages yet does no harm? Of a strange tongue caressing your pecker?

What?

* * *

The brunette invites him to join them for dinner.

Champagne. Fried calamari. Mussels.

The husband has a pet-food factory in Cinisello Balsamo and a Ferrari Testarossa in the restaurant car park.

I wonder if they take drugs? Graziano thinks to himself.

If he can sell them a few grams and make a few lire, this already promising evening could become magical.

'You must have an amazing life: all sex, drugs and rock'n'roll, eh?' asks the brunette, a lobster pincer between her teeth.

It depresses Graziano when people say things like that.

Why do they open their mouths and spew out words, useless words?

Sex, drugs and rock'n'roll . . . The same old line.

But over dinner he continues to muse on it.

Actually, it's true in a way.

His life is sex, drugs and . . . no, you can't really call it rock-'n'roll . . . and flamenco.

But what's wrong with that?

Sure, many people would hate a life like mine. Drifting. Rootless. But I like it, and I don't give a damn what anyone else thinks.

Once a Belgian guy, sitting in meditation on a flight of steps in Benares, had told him: 'I feel like an albatross borne on the currents of air. On positive currents which I control with a gentle flap of my wings.'

Graziano, too, felt like an albatross.

An albatross with one great commitment: not to harm others or himself.

According to some people pushing drugs is harmful.

According to Graziano it depends how you do it.

If you do it to make ends meet and you're not trying to get rich, it's okay. If you sell to friends, it's okay. If you sell quality drugs and not crap, it's okay.

If he could make a living just from playing the guitar, he'd give up pushing on the spot.

According to some people taking drugs is harmful. According

to Graziano it depends how you do it. If you overdo it, if you let the drugs freak you out, it's not okay. He doesn't need doctors and priests to tell him that the white stuff has unpleasant side-effects. But if you only take the occasional toot, there's nothing wrong with it at all.

And what about sex?

Sex? Sure, I get a lot of it, but how can I help it if women like me and I like them? (I'm not into men, let's get that quite clear.) It takes two to have sex. Sex is the most beautiful thing in the world if you do it in the right way, without any complications. (Graziano has never reflected much on the obviousness of this statement)

And what else does Graziano like?

Latino music, playing the guitar in restaurants (*as long as I get paid!*), sunbathing on the beach, fooling about with his friends in front of a huge orange sun as it sinks into the sea and . . .

. . . *and that's about it.*

Don't believe those people who say that if you want to appreciate the good things of life you have to work your butt off. It's not true. They're trying to con you. Pleasure is a religion and the body is its temple.

And Graziano had organised his life accordingly.

He lived in a studio flat in the centre of Riccione from June to August, in September he moved to Ibiza and in November he went to Jamaica for the winter.

At forty-four years of age, Graziano Biglia felt like a professional gipsy, a vagabond of the dharma, a migrant soul in search of its karma.

That's how he described himself, at least until that evening, that fateful June evening when his life intertwined with that of Erica Trettel, the go-go dancer.

And here is the professional gipsy two hours after the feast at the Carillon del Mare.

He is sitting in the gallery of the Hangover, slumped over a table, as if some thief had stolen his backbone. Eyes reduced to slits. Mouth half-open. In his hand he holds a Cuba libre which he can't drink.

'God, am I wasted,' he keeps repeating.

The mix of coke, ecstasy, wine and fried seafood has done for him.

The pet-food manufacturer and his wife are sitting beside him.

The discotheque is crammed fuller than a supermarket shelf.

He has the impression that he's on a cruise ship because the discotheque keeps rolling from side to side. The place where they're sitting is lousy, though it's supposed to be the VIP area. A huge speaker, hanging above his head, is shattering his nervous system. But he'd rather have his right foot amputated than get up and look for another place.

The pet-food manufacturer keeps yelling things in his ear. Things Graziano doesn't understand.

He looks down.

The dance floor is swarming like an anthill.

All that's left in his head is simple truths.

It's a madhouse. It's Friday. And Friday's always a madhouse.

He turns his head slowly, like a Fresian bull grazing in Swiss mountain pastures.

And he sees her.

She's dancing.

Dancing naked on a cube in the middle of the anthill.

He knows the usual dancers of the Hangover. But he's never seen her before.

She must be new. Wow, she's a real fox. And can she dance.

The speakers vomit out drum'n'bass over a carpet of bodies and heads and arms and she is up there, as remote and unattainable as the goddess Kali.

The strobe lights freeze her in an infinite sequence of plastic sensual poses.

He observes her with the fixed gaze typical of substance abuse.

She's the sexiest woman he's ever seen.

Imagine being her man . . . Having a girl like that beside you. Imagine how they'd envy you. But who is she?

He'd like to ask someone. The barman, perhaps. But he can't get up. His legs are paralysed. Besides, he can't take his eyes off her.

She must be something really special because normally the young heifers (that's what he calls them . . .) don't interest Graziano.

A communication problem.

He usually hunts more seasoned game. He prefers the mature, voluptuous woman, who can appreciate a sunset or a moonlight serenade, who isn't full of hang-ups like a twenty-year-old and who can have a good fuck without burdening it with paranoia and expectations.

But in this case every distinction, every category goes down the can.

A girl like that would make a poof turn straight.

Imagine screwing her.

A faded image of making love on a white beach on a desert island goes through his mind. And as if by magic his cock begins to stiffen.

Who is she? Who is she? Where did she come from?

God, Buddha, Krishna, First Principle, whoever you are, you've materialised her on that cube to give me a sign of your existence.

She's perfect.

Not that the other go-go girls, around the sides of the dance floor, aren't perfect too. They all have firm buttocks and shapely legs, full rounded breasts and flat muscular stomachs. But none of them is like her, she has something special, something Graziano can't put into words, something animal, something he's only ever seen in the black girls of Cuba.

This girl's body doesn't react to music, it is music. The physical expression of music. Her movements are as slow and precise as those of a t'ai chi master. She can stand immobile on one leg, wiggling her pelvis and sinuously moving her arms. The other girls are spastics compared to her.

Amazing.

And the incredible thing is that no one in the disco seems to notice. Those fools keep moving around and talking when a miracle is taking place before their very eyes.

Suddenly, as if Graziano had sent her a beam of telepathic waves, the girl stops and turns towards him. Graziano is sure she is looking at him. She stands quite still, there, on the cube, and looks straight at him, him in the midst of that mayhem, him in the midst of those milling masses, him and nobody else.

At last he sees her face. With that short hair, those lips, those green eyes (he can even see the colour of her eyes!) and that perfect oval, she's the spitting image of an actress . . . an actress whose name is on the tip of Graziano's tongue . . .

What's her name? The one who starred in Ghost?

How grateful he would be if someone could prompt him: Demi Moore.

But Graziano is in no state to ask anyone, he's mesmerised, like a cobra before a snake charmer. He stretches out his fingers towards her and ten little orange-coloured rays are released from their tips. The rays join together and trace a wavy path like an electric flashover across the disco, above the oblivious masses, and reach her, in the middle of the dance floor, enter her navel and make her shine like a Byzantine Madonna.

Graziano starts trembling.

He and she are linked by an electric arc which fuses their identities, transforms them into imperfect halves of one complete being. Only together will they be happy. Like one-winged angels, from their embrace will come flight and paradise.

Graziano is about to burst into tears.

He is overwhelmed by a boundless love, such as he has never felt before, a love that is not vulgar lust but the purest of emotions, a love that impels a man to reproduce, to defend his woman from external dangers, to build a den to raise children in.

He reaches out his hands seeking an ideal contact with the girl.

The Milanese couple gaze at him in amazement.

But Graziano can't see them.

The discotheque is no longer there. The voices, the music, the confusion, have all been swallowed up by the mist.

And then gradually the greyness disperses to reveal a jeans shop.

Yes, a jeans shop.

Not a trashy little jeans shop like the ones in Riccione, but one that resembles in every way and every detail the stores he's seen in Vermont, with neat piles of Norwegian fishermen's sweaters, rows of Virginian miners' boots and drawers full of socks hand-knitted by the old women of Lipari and jars of Welsh marmalade and Rapala lures and there are he and the go-go girl, now his wife, very obviously pregnant behind the counter, which is in fact not a counter but a surfboard. And this jeans shop is in Ischiano Scalo, in place of his mother's haberdashery. And everyone who passes by stops, comes in and sees his wife and envies him and buys moccasins with penny buttons and Gore-tex parkas.

'The jeans shop,' whispers Graziano ecstatically, his eyes closed.

That's what the future holds for him!

He has seen it.

A jeans shop.

That woman.

A family.

And no more of this footloose life, with all its trendy nonsense, no more loveless sex, no more drugs.

Redemption.

Now he has a mission in life: to meet that girl and take her home with him because he loves her. And she loves him.

'She loves me,' sighs Graziano, and he gets up from his chair and leans over the rail with arms outstretched to reach her. Luckily the Milanese guy is there to grab him by the shirt and stop him pitching over and breaking his neck.

'Are you out of your mind?' the woman asks him.

'He fancied that little tart down there in the middle.' The pet-food manufacturer bursts out laughing. 'He wanted to kill himself for her. Can you believe it? Can you believe it?'

Graziano is on his feet. He is open-mouthed. He is speechless.

Who are these two monsters? And how dare they? Above all, what are they laughing about? Why are they mocking a pure, fragile love that has blossomed despite all the ugliness and filth of this corrupt society?

The husband looks as if he's going to die laughing at any moment.

Now this son-of-a-bitch dies. Graziano grabs him by the neck of his Hawaiian shirt and the man stops laughing at once and puts on a smile with too many teeth. 'I'm sorry, I do apologise . . . I really am sorry. I didn't mean . . .'

Graziano is about to punch him on the nose, but then thinks better of it. This is the night of redemption, there is no place for violence and Graziano Biglia is a new man.

A man in love.

'What do you understand, you . . . you heartless creatures,' he mutters under his breath, and staggers off towards his beloved.

His love affair with Erica Trettel, the go-go dancer from the Hangover, proved to be one of the most disastrous episodes in Graziano Biglia's life. Perhaps that mix of cocaine, ecstasy, seafood and Lancers that he had ingested at the Carillon del Mare was the immediate cause of the coup de foudre that short-circuited Biglia's mind, but the remote causes were obstinacy and congenital blindness.

Normally, when you wake up after a night of over-indulgence in alcohol and psychotropic substances, you have a hard time even remembering your name, and indeed Graziano had erased from his memory the successes of the Carillon, the pet-food manufacturers, and . . .

No!

Not the girl who had danced on the cube.

He hadn't forgotten her.

When Graziano opened his eyes next day, the image of him and her in the jeans shop had nested, octopus-like, among his neurons and, like Orion Quest inside Grandizer, continued to pilot his mind and body all summer.

For throughout that ill-omened summer Graziano was blind and deaf, he refused to see or hear that he and Erica weren't suited. He refused to understand that his fixation was irrational and would bring only pain and unhappiness.

Erica Trettel was twenty-one and stunningly beautiful.

She came from Castello Tesino, a village near Trento. She had won a beauty contest sponsored by a salami factory and run off with a member of the jury. She had worked at the Bologna Motor Show as an Opel girl. A few photographs for the catalogue of a swimming-costume manufacturer in Castellamare di Stabia. And a course in belly-dancing.

When she danced on that cube at the Hangover she could concentrate, give of her very best, blend in with the music, for positive images kept flashing, like Christmas-tree lights, in her mind: her in the dancing troupe of *Sunday Live*, photographs in *Novella 2000* of her coming out of a restaurant with a guy resembling Matt Weyland, and the big quiz show and TV commercials for the Moulinex stainless steel grater.

Television!

That was where her future lay.

Erica Trettel's desires were simple and concrete.

And when she met Graziano Biglia, she tried to explain this to him.

She explained that these desires did not include getting married to a superannuated rocker who was obsessed with the Gipsy Kings and who looked like Sandy Marton at the end of the Paris–Dakar rally, much less ruining her waistline by giving birth to screaming brats, and even less opening a jeans shop in Ischiano Scalo.

But Graziano just would not understand and explained to her, like a teacher to an obstinate pupil, the world of television is a kind of mafia. He knew this only too well. He had played on *Planet Bar* a couple of times. He told her that success on TV was ephemeral.

'Erica, you must grow up, you must understand that human beings weren't created in order to make a show of themselves, but to find a space where they can live in harmony with heaven and earth.'

And that space was Ischiano Scalo.

He also had a recipe for getting *Sunday Live* out of her head: leaving for Jamaica. He argued that a holiday in the Caribbean would do her good – it was a place where people enjoyed themselves and chilled out, where all the stress of this crappy society counted for nothing, where friendship was all that mattered and you just lay on the beach and did fuck all.

He would teach her everything there was to learn about life.

All this garbage might have made some impression on a girl who was into Bob Marley or the liberalisation of soft drugs, but not on Erica Trettel.

The two of them had about as much in common as a pair of ski boots and a Greek island.

Why, then, did Erica lead him on?

This snatch of a conversation between Erica Trettel and Mariapia Mancuso, another go-go girl from the Hangover, as they were getting ready in the dressing rooms, may help us to understand.

'This rumour about you going out with Graziano, is it just baloney?' Mariapia asked as she tweezed out a superfluous hair that had planted itself next to the areola of her right nipple.

'Who told you that?' Erica is doing some stretching in the middle of the room.

'Everybody's saying it.'

'Oh . . . are they?'

Mariapia inspects her right eyebrow in the mirror, then attacks it with the tweezers. 'Is it true?'

'What?'

'That you and he are an item.'

'Well, sort of. Let's say we're seeing each other.'

'How do you mean?'

Erica snorts. 'What a pain you are! Graziano loves me. He really does. Not like that shit Tony.'

Tony Dawson, the English deejay at the Anthrax, had had a brief fling with Erica before ditching her for the lead singer of Funeral Strike, a death-metal band from the Marche.

'And do you love him?'

'Yes. He doesn't create any problems. He's a straightforward kind of guy.'

'That's true,' Mariapia agrees.

'Do you know he gave me a puppy? It's really cute. A fila brasileiro.'

'What's that?'

'A special breed, very rare. They used to use them in Brazil to hunt down the slaves who escaped from the plantations. He looks after it, though – I can't be bothered. I've called it Antoine.'

'After the hairdresser?'

'That's right.'

'And what's all this about you getting married and going to live in his home town and opening a clothes shop?'

'Are you crazy? No, it's just that the other evening we were on the beach and he starts going on about his home town, this jeans shop selling Norwegian sweaters, his mother's haberdashery shop, saying he wants to have children and marry me. I told him it was a nice idea . . .'

'Nice?'

'Hold on a minute. You know how it is when you say things just for the sake of saying something. Right then and there it seemed like a nice idea. But he can't get it out of his head. I must tell him not to go around telling everybody about it. It makes me look stupid. I'm going to get really angry if he goes on.'

'You tell him.'

'I certainly will.'

Mariapia switched to the other eyebrow. 'And are you in love with him?'

'It's hard to say . . . Like I said, he's very kind. He's a really nice person. Ten times better than that bastard Tony. But he's too superficial. And all this talk about the jeans shop . . . If I'm not working at Christmas he says he'll take me to Jamaica. That'd be cool, wouldn't it?'

'And . . . do you give him any pussy?'

Erica got to her feet and stretched. 'What kind of a question's that? No. Not usually. But he keeps on pestering me, so every now and then, in the end . . . I give it to him . . . What's the word?'

'The word for what?'

'When you give something but not all that much of it, you give it but you're a bit reluctant.'

'I don't know . . . Gradually?'

'Not gradually, stupid. What's the word, now? Come on, help me.'

'Stingily?'

'No!'

'Sparingly?'

'That's the word! Sparingly. I give it to him sparingly.'

Graziano in his courtship of Erica abased himself as never before, he cut a ridiculous figure waiting for her for hours on end in places where everyone knew she would never go, he was eternally glued to his mobile searching for her in Riccione and the surrounding area, he had the wool pulled over his eyes by Mariapia who covered for her friend when she went out with that bastard of a deejay, and he ran up huge debts to buy her a fila brasileiro pup, a superlight canoe, an American apparatus for doing passive gymnastics, a tattoo on her right buttock, an inflatable dinghy with a twenty-five horsepower outboard motor, a Bang & Olufsen stereo, heaps of designer clothes and shoes with eight-inch heels and an indefinite quantity of CDs.

People who were fond of him told him to stop it, that it was pathetic. That that girl would wipe the floor with him.

But Graziano wouldn't listen. He stopped screwing old slappers and playing the guitar, and stubbornly persisted, though he no longer mentioned it because it got on Erica's nerves, in believing in the jeans shop and that sooner or later he'd change her, that he'd uproot from her head that malignant weed that was television. It wasn't him who had decided all this, fate had decreed it, that night when it had placed Erica on a cube in the Hangover.

And there was a time when it all seemed, as if by magic, to be coming true.

In October the two of them are in Rome.

In a rented studio flat at Rocca Verde. A tiny little place on the eighth floor of a tower block squeezed in between the eastern bypass and the orbital.

Erica has persuaded Graziano to come with her. Without him she'd feel lost in the metropolis. He must help her find work.

There are lots of things to do: finding a good photographer for her portfolio. A smart agent with the right contacts. An elocutionist to get rid of that harsh Trento accent and a drama teacher to loosen her up a bit.

And auditions.

They go out early in the morning, spend the day doing the rounds of Cinecittà, casting offices and film production companies, and return home in the evening, exhausted.

Sometimes, while Erica is having lessons, Graziano puts Antoine in the car and drives to Villa Borghese. He walks across the deer park to Piazza di Siena and then down towards the Pincio. He walks fast. He enjoys these rambles in the park.

Antoine limps along behind him. With those great big paws he finds it hard to keep up. Graziano pulls him by the lead. 'Come on, keep moving. You lazy mutt. Hurry up!' But to no avail. So he sits down on a bench and smokes a cigarette and Antoine starts chewing at his shoes.

Graziano no longer resembles the Latin lover of the Carillon del Mare. The guy who made the German girls swoon.

He looks ten years older. He's pale, with bags under his eyes, black roots in his hair, a tracksuit, a bristly white beard, and he is unhappy.

Desperately unhappy.

It's all going wrong.

Erica doesn't love him.

The only reason she stays with him is that he pays for her lessons, the rent, her clothes, the photographer, everything. Because he chauffeurs her around. Because in the evenings he goes to get the fried chicken from the takeaway.

Erica doesn't love him and she never will.

She doesn't give a shit about him, let's be honest.

What am I doing here? I hate this town. I hate this traffic. I hate Erica. I've got to get out of here. I've got to get out of here. I've got to get out of here. It's a kind of mantra which he repeats obsessively.

So why doesn't he do it?

There's nothing difficult about it, all you have to do is get on a plane. And away you go.

If only he could.

There's a problem: if he stays away from Erica for half a day, he feels sick. He gets gastritis. Can't breathe. Starts burping.

How wonderful it would be to be able to press a button and wipe his brain clean. Get those soft lips, that fine hair, those wicked, bewitching eyes out of his head. A complete brainwashing. If Erica were in his brain.

But that's not where she is.

She has lodged like a fragment of glass in his stomach.

He's in love with a spoiled child.

She's a bitch. And completely devoid of talent. She may be good at dancing, but she's hopeless at acting, at standing in front of a TV camera. She fluffs her lines. The words die in her mouth.

In three months all she's been given is a couple of walk-on appearances in a TV film.

But Graziano loves her even though she's a failure. Even though she's the worst actress in the world.

Shit . . .

And worst of all, the more of a bitch she is, the more he loves her.

When there are no auditions to do, Erica spends the whole day in front of the TV eating frozen pizzas and Algida Viennettas. She doesn't want to do anything. Doesn't want to go out. Doesn't want to see anyone. She's too depressed, she says, to go out.

The house is a mess.

The heaps of dirty clothes thrown to one side. Rubbish. Piles of plates encrusted with sauce. Antoine pissing and crapping on the carpet. Erica seems to be in her element in filth. Graziano isn't, he loses his temper, shouts that he's fed up with living this way, like a bum, that that's it, he's off to Jamaica, but instead he takes the dog for a walk in the park.

How could anyone live with her? She'd try the patience of a Zen monk. She cries over nothing. And flies into rages. And when she's angry terrible things come out of her mouth. Projectiles that sink into Graziano's heart as if it were butter. She's bursting with poison and as soon as she gets a chance she spits it out.

You're a shit. You disgust me! I don't love you, can't you get that into your head? Do you want to know why I stay with you? Out of pity. That's why. I hate you. And do you know why I hate you? Because you hope I'm going to fail.

This is true.

Every time an audition goes badly Graziano secretly rejoices. It is one small step towards Ischiano Scalo. But then he feels guilty.

They don't have sex.

He points this out to her. She opens her legs and arms and says: 'Help yourself. Fuck me like this, if you want.' And a couple of times, in desperation, he does, and it's like screwing a corpse. A warm corpse which every now and then, when there's a commercial break, picks up the remote control and changes channel.

All this lasts until 8th December.

On 8th December Antoine dies.

Erica is in a parfumerie with Antoine. The shop assistant tells her dogs are not admitted. Erica leaves him outside, she has to buy some lipstick, she'll only be a minute. But a minute is long enough for Antoine to see a German shepherd on the opposite pavement, run across the street and get knocked down by a car.

Erica goes home in tears. She tells Graziano she didn't have the courage to go and see. The dog is still there. Graziano rushes out.

He finds him at the side of the road. In a pool of blood. Hardly breathing. A trickle of dark blood runs out of his nostrils and mouth. He takes him to the vet, who puts him to sleep with an injection.

Graziano returns home.

He can't bring himself to talk. He loved that dog. He was a funny old creature. And they kept each other company.

Erica says it wasn't her fault. She had only been a minute buying the lipstick. And the bastard driving the car hadn't braked.

Graziano goes out again. He takes the Uno and, to calm himself down, does a complete circuit of the orbital at a hundred and eighty kilometres an hour.

It was a mistake to come to Rome.

A terrible mistake.

He's made a complete mess of things. She's not a woman, she's a plague sent by God to destroy his life.

In the past month they've quarrelled almost every day.

Graziano can't believe the things she says to him. She wounds him deeply. Sometimes attacks him so violently that he can't defend himself. Give tit for tat. Tell her she couldn't act to save her life.

The other day, for example, she accused him of jinxing her and said that if Madonna had been saddled with a guy like him she'd still be just plain Madonna Louise Veronica Ciccone. And she added that in Riccione everyone said he was a crap guitar player and that all he was good for was selling stale pills. And finally, to cap it all, she said the Gipsy Kings were a bunch of poofs.

That does it! I'm leaving her.

He must succeed in doing it.

It won't kill him. He'll survive. Even junkies survive without drugs. You do cold turkey, you go through hell, you think you'll never make it, but in the end you do and you're clean.

At least Antoine's death has served to bring him to his senses.

He must leave her. And the best way to do it is with a calm, detached speech, without any anger, the speech of a strong man with a broken heart. Like Robert De Niro in *Love Letters* when he dumps Jane Fonda.

Yes, that's all that's needed.

He goes home. Erica is watching *Lupin III* and eating a cheese sandwich.

'Do you mind turning off the TV?'

Erica does so.

Graziano sits down, clears his throat and begins. 'I've got something to say to you. I think it's time you and I called it a day. You know it and I know it. Let's be honest.'

Erica looks at him.

Graziano resumes. 'I give up on this relationship. I believed in it. I really did. But I can't go on. I haven't got a lira left. We quarrel all day long. And I've had all I can take of Rome. It disgusts me, it depresses me. I'm like the seagulls, if I don't migrate, I die. At this poi . . .'

'Seagulls don't migrate.'

'Okay. Like the fucking swallows, does that make you any happier? I should have been in Jamaica by this time. Tomorrow I'm going to Ischiano. I'm going to borrow some money, then I'm leaving. And we'll never see each other again. I'm sorry things . . .' Here the De Niro-style speech dies.

Erica listens in silence.

How is Graziano talking?

What a strange tone there is in his voice. Usually he kicks up a row, shouts, raves. Not now, he's cold, resigned. He sounds like an American actor. Antoine's death must have really upset him.

All at once she suspects that he's not just making the usual melodramatic scene. That this time he means it.

If he leaves, what will happen?

It'll be a holy mess.

Everything looks black to Erica. A future without him is something she can't even imagine. Life sucks as it is, but without Graziano it would be shit. Who will pay the rent for the flat? Who'll go and buy the chicken at the takeaway? Who'll pay the fees for the drama course?

Besides, she's no longer so sure that she's really going to make it. All the signs seem to be that she hasn't got a chance. Since she arrived in Rome she's done dozens of auditions and never landed a decent part. Maybe Graziano's right. She's not cut out for TV. She hasn't got what it takes.

She feels a pressure below her throat, a prelude to tears.

Without a lira she'd be forced to return to Castello Tesino, and rather than go back to that icy cold place with those parents of hers, she'd go on the street.

She tries to swallow a mouthful of sandwich. But it remains there, in her mouth, as bitter as gall. 'Do you mean it?'

'Yes.'

'You're leaving?'

'Yes.'

'What am I going to do?'

'I really don't know.'

Silence.

'Have you made up your mind?'

'Yes.'

'Really?'

'Yes.'

Erica starts crying. Very quietly. The sandwich between her teeth. The tears dissolving her make-up.

Graziano toys with his cigarette lighter. He flicks it on and off. 'I'm sorry. But it's much better this way. At least we'll have pleasant mem . . .'

'I wa . . . wa . . . want to co . . . come with you,' Erica sobs.

'What?'

'I wa . . . want to come with you.'

'Where?'

'To Ischiano.'

'What the hell for? Didn't you say you loathed the idea?'

'I want to meet your mother.'

'You want to meet my mother?' Graziano repeats, parrot-fashion.

'Yes, I want to meet Gina. But then we'll go to Jamaica for a holiday.'

Graziano says nothing.

'Don't you want me to come?'

'No. I'd rather you didn't.'

'Graziano, don't leave me. Please.' She grasps his hand.

'It's better this way . . . You know it yourself . . . It's no use . . .'

'You can't leave me in Rome, Grazi.'

Graziano feels his innards melting. *What does she want?*

She can't do this. It's not fair. Now she wants to go with him.

'Graziano, come here,' says Erica in a sad, sad little voice.

Graziano gets up. He sits down beside her. She kisses his hands and clings to him. She rests her face on his chest. And starts crying again.

Graziano now feels his guts reviving. A boa constrictor has come out of hibernation. His windpipe is suddenly unblocked. He breathes in and out.

He puts his arms round her.

She sobs. 'I'm sorry. I'm sorry.'

She's so small. Defenceless. Like a little girl. A little girl who needs him. The most beautiful little girl in the world. His little girl. 'Okay. All right. Let's get out of this damned city. I won't leave you. Don't worry. Come away with me.'

'Yes, Graziano . . . Take me with you.'

They kiss. Saliva and tears. He wipes away her dripping mascara with his T-shirt.

'Yes, we'll leave tomorrow morning. But I must call my mother. So she can get the room ready.'

Erica smiles. 'Okay.' Then her face clouds over. 'Yes, let's go . . . Oh, but wait a minute, the day after tomorrow, shit, I've got to do something.'

Graziano is instantly suspicious. 'What?'

'An audition.'

'Erica, it's the same old . . .'

'Wait! Listen. I promised my agent I'd go. He needs some of the girls on his books to go through the motions of doing an audition, the director has already decided who he's going to choose, a girl with influential backers, but it's all got to seem fair and above board. The usual bullshit.'

'Don't go. Tell him to get lost, the bastard.'

'I must go. I've promised. After all he's done for me.'

'What has he done for you? Nothing. He's tapped us for money. Tell him to get lost. We've got to go.'

Erica takes both his hands. 'Listen, let's do this. You leave tomorrow. I'll go to the audition, lock up the flat, pack our bags and join you the next day.'

'Wouldn't you like me to wait for you?'

'No, you go. Rome has stressed you out. I'll come up by train. So by the time I get there you'll have prepared everything. Make sure you buy lots of fish. I love fish.'

'Okay. Do you like toad's tail?'

'I don't know. Is it good?'

'Delicious. What about clams, shall I get some of those?'

'Clams, Grazi. Pasta with clams. I love them.' Erica gives a smile that lights up the whole flat.

'That's one of my mother's specialities. You'll see. We'll be well looked after.'

Erica leaps into his arms.

That night they make love.

And for the first time since they have been together, Erica goes down on him.

Graziano is lying on that unmade bed strewn with sweaters, smelly T-shirts, CD sleeves and breadcrumbs and watches Erica there, between his legs, sucking his pecker.

Why has she decided to go down on him?

She's always said she found it disgusting.

What is she trying to tell him?

Simple. That she loves you.

Graziano is overcome by emotion and comes.

Erica falls asleep naked in his arms. Graziano, keeping quite still so as not to wake her, holds her in his arms and can't believe that this beautiful girl is really his.

His eyes never tire of looking at her, his hands of caressing her or his nose of smelling her.

How often he has wondered how such a perfect creature could have been born in that godforsaken little village. She's a miracle of nature.

And that miracle is his. Despite their rows, despite Erica's character, despite their different outlooks on life, despite Graziano's faults. They are linked together. Linked by a bond that will never break.

Okay, he was wrong, he was weak, indecisive, cowardly, he humoured Erica in all her whims, he let the situation deteriorate to the point where it was unbearable, but this outburst of rage of his had been providential. It had swept away the cobwebs that had been suffocating them.

Erica felt that she was going to lose him for ever, that this time he wasn't just pretending. And she didn't allow him to leave.

Graziano's heart is overflowing with love. He kisses her on the neck.

Erica murmurs: 'Graziano, will you bring me a glass of water?'

He fetches the water. She sits up, and with eyes closed, holding the glass in both hands, drinks greedily, dribbling onto her chin.

'Erica, tell me something, do you really love me?' he asks, getting back into bed.

'Yes,' she replies, and snuggles up against him again.

'Really?'

'Yes, really.'

'And . . . will you marry me?' he hears himself say. As if an evil spirit had put those dreadful words in his mouth. A spirit that was intent on fucking things up.

Erica curls up more tightly, pulls the duvet further up and says: 'Yes.'

'You will?'

For a moment Graziano is lost for words, overcome. He puts his hand over his mouth and shuts his eyes.

What did she say? Did she say she would marry him?

'Really?'

'Yes.' Erica mumbles drowsily.

'When?'

'When we get to Jamaica.'

'Right. When we get to Jamaica. On the beach. We'll get married on the cliffs of Edward Beach. It's a beautiful spot.'

That is why Graziano Biglia left Rome on 9th December at

five o'clock in the morning, despite the thunderstorm, bound for Ischiano Scalo.

Bearing all his worldly belongings and some good news for his mother.

3

A traveller armed with binoculars on board a hot-air balloon would be better placed than anyone else to view the setting of our story.

He would at once notice a long black scar that cuts across the plain. That's the Aurelia, the state highway that comes up from Rome and continues northward to Genoa and beyond. It goes as straight as an airport runway for fifteen kilometres, then curves gradually round to the left and links up with the small town of Orbano, which overlooks the lagoon.

The first thing your mother teaches you around here is not 'never accept sweets from strangers' but 'be careful on the Aurelia'. You have to look right and left at least twice before crossing, whether you're on foot or in a vehicle (and if your engine stalls half-way across, God help you). The cars streak past like arrows. And there have been all too many fatal accidents in recent years. Now they've put up signs setting a 90 kpm speed limit, and speed cameras as well, but nobody takes a blind bit of notice.

At the weekend when the weather's fine, and especially during the summer, tailbacks several kilometres long are liable to form on this road. It's the people from the capital travelling to and from the seaside resorts further north.

If our traveller were now to turn his binoculars to the left he'd see the beach of Castrone. The waves come rolling in from the open sea here, and in stormy weather the sand piles up on the waterline and you have to climb over dunes to reach the water. There are no bathing establishments. (Well, there is one a few kilometres further south, but the locals never go there, because it's full of flash Romans eating linguine in lobster sauce and drinking

Falanghina.) No beach umbrellas. No deck-chairs. No pedalos. Not even in August.

Strange, eh?

The reason for this is that the area is a reserve for the reintroduction of migratory avifauna. A bird sanctuary, to you and me.

In twenty kilometres of shoreline there are only three points of access to the sea. Around them in summer there are the usual swarms of bathers, but you only have to walk three hundred metres and as if by magic there's no one in sight.

Just behind the beach there's a long green strip. It's a tangle of brambles, thorns, flowers, prickles, and hardy weeds rooted in the sand. Going through it is impossible unless you want to end up like St Sebastian. Immediately behind it the cultivated fields begin (wheat, maize, sunflowers, in rotation according to the year).

If our traveller were now to turn his binoculars to the right, he would see a long, bean-shaped saltwater lake separated from the sea by a narrow strip of land. That is Torcelli lagoon. It's fenced off, and hunting is banned. In spring the exhausted birds arrive here from Africa. It's a swamp, full of vicious mosquitoes, sandflies, watersnakes, fish, herons, coots, rodents, newts, frogs, toads and thousands of other little creatures that have adapted to living among reeds, aquatic plants and seaweed. The railway passes close by, it runs parallel to the Aurelia and links Genoa with Rome. In the daytime, about once an hour, the Eurostar comes hurtling through.

And there, finally, beside the lagoon, is Ischiano Scalo.

Yes, it's small, I know.

It has grown up over the last thirty years around that little station where a train stops twice a day.

A church. A piazza. A main street. A chemist's (always closed). A grocer's. A bank (complete with cashpoint). A butcher's. A haberdasher's. A newsagent's. The farmers' club. A bar. A school. A sports centre. And about fifty little stone-roofed two-storey blocks of flats, inhabited by a thousand or so people.

Until not so long ago there was nothing here but marshes and malaria, then the Duce reclaimed the land.

If our intrepid traveller should now let the wind carry him across to the other side of the Aurelia, he would see more cultivated fields, olive groves and meadows, and a tiny hamlet of four or five houses called Serra. From here begins a white road which leads towards the hills and the woods of Acquasparta, famed for their wild boars, long-horned cattle and, in good years, porcini.

So that is Ischiano Scalo.

It's a strange place, the sea is so close but seems miles away. That's because the fields repel it beyond that barrier of thorns. Now and then its smell and sand waft over on the wind.

This is probably why the tourist industry has always steered clear of Ischiano Scalo.

There's nothing to do here – no houses to rent, no air-conditioned hotels, no esplanade to walk along, no cafés to sit in drinking of an evening. In the summer the plain gets as hot as a gridiron and in winter an icy wind stings your ears.

And now could our traveller go down a bit lower, to get a better view of the modern building behind that industrial warehouse?

That is the Michelangelo Buonarroti junior high school. There's a class doing PE in the playground. Everyone's playing volleyball and basketball, except for a group of girls perched on a low wall chatting and a small boy sitting alone, cross-legged on the ground in a patch of sun, reading a book.

He is Pietro Moroni, the real protagonist of this story.

4

Pietro didn't like playing basketball or volleyball, and soccer he positively loathed.

It wasn't that he hadn't tried playing those sports. He had tried, as hard as he could, but there seemed to be a communication problem between him and the ball. He would want the ball to do one thing but it would do the exact opposite.

And in Pietro's opinion, when you discovered that there was a communication problem between you and something, it was best to avoid it. Besides, there were other things he did like.

Cycling, for example. He liked cycling along the woodland paths. And he loved animals. Not all. Just some.

The ones other people found disgusting, he was very keen on. Snakes, frogs, salamanders, insects, that kind of creature. And if they lived in water, so much the better.

Take the weever, for instance. True, its sting hurts like hell, it has an ugly face and lives hidden away in the sand, but the idea that its mysterious, unidentified poison could paralyse your foot appealed to him.

Yes, if he had to choose between being a tiger or a weever, he would definitely opt for the latter.

He also liked mosquitoes.

They were everywhere. And they were something you couldn't just ignore.

That's why he had chosen them as the subject of the science project that he was doing with Gloria. Malaria and the mosquito. And that afternoon he was due to go with her to Orbano to see a doctor friend of her father's, to interview him about malaria.

Now he was reading a book about dinosaurs. Mosquitoes were mentioned there, too. Thanks to them, scientists would one day be able to recreate the dinosaurs. They had found some mosquito fossils, had extracted from them the blood that the mosquitoes had sucked from the dinosaurs, and so discovered the dinosaurs' genetic code. In short, though he didn't understand all the details, what it boiled down to was: no mosquitoes, no *Jurassic Park*.

Pietro was pleased, because that day the PE teacher hadn't made him play with the others.

'Well? Have you decided what we need to ask Colsanti?'

Pietro looked up.

It was Gloria. She was holding a ball, and gasping for breath.

'I think so. More or less.'

'Good. Because I haven't got a clue.' Gloria punched the ball and ran back towards the volleyball court.

Gloria Celani was Pietro's best friend. His only friend, to be honest.

He'd tried to make friends with boys, but had never really succeeded. He'd played with Paolino Anselmi, the tobacconist's son, a couple of times. They'd gone to the big field to do cyclo-cross. But it hadn't been a success.

Paolino insisted on racing, and Pietro didn't like racing. They'd had a few races and Paolino had won them all. And that was the last time they'd played together.

How could he help it? Racing was another thing he loathed.

Because even when he was ahead as they neared the end of the course, flashing along towards victory, a victory he thoroughly deserved, having led all the way from the starting line, he couldn't help looking back and then he would see it behind him, that creature pursuing him with gritted teeth, and then his legs would give way and he'd let the other boy catch up, overtake him and win.

With Gloria you didn't have to race. You didn't have to act tough. You just felt good and that was it.

In Pietro's opinion, and in many other boys' opinions too, Gloria was the prettiest girl in the school. There were a couple of others who weren't bad looking, for example that girl in 3B with long black hair that reached down to her bottom, or that one in 2A, Amanda, who was going out with Flame.

But in Pietro's opinion those two weren't even worthy to lick her feet, compared to Gloria they were weevers. He would never have said as much to her, but he was sure that when Gloria grew up she would appear in those fashion magazines or win Miss Italy.

And yet she did her level best to look plainer than she was. She wore her hair short, like a boy's. She went around in dirty, faded dungarees, old checked shirts and battered Adidases. She always had grazed knees and plasters covering other wounds she'd got climbing trees or scrambling over walls. She wasn't scared to fight any of the boys, even that fat slob Bacci.

Pietro had only ever seen her dressed like a girl a couple of times in his life.

The older boys, the ones in the third year (and sometimes older ones still, the lads who hung around in front of the bar), used to play the fool with her. They tried to chat her up. They asked her out and gave her presents and offered her lifts home on their motor scooters, but she didn't want to know.

She didn't give a shit about them.

How come the fairest of them all, the much-courted Gloria, the despair of all the boys in Ischiano, she who had never sunk lower than third place in the league table of the most fuckable girls in the school carved on the door of the boys' toilet, was best friends with Pietro, the born loser, the last in line, the friendless little shrimp?

There was a reason.

Their friendship had not originated in the classroom.

In that school there was a system of closed castes (and I bet there was in your school too), rather like in India. The scum (*Chickenshits Wankers Wimps Shitfaces Pansies Niggers and so on*). The straights. And the cools.

Straights could sink down into the mud and turn into scum, or rise up and be transformed into cools, it was up to them. But if on the first day of school someone grabbed your backpack and threw it out of the window and hid pieces of chalk in your sandwich, then there were no two ways about it, you were scum, and would remain so for the next three years (and if you didn't watch out, for the next sixty years after that as well), and could forget any idea of becoming a straight.

That was how things worked.

Pietro and Gloria had met when they were five years old.

Pietro's mother used to go to the Celanis' villa three times a week to do the cleaning, and she always took her son with her. She'd give him a sheet of paper and some felt-tip pens and tell him to sit there at the kitchen table. 'Stay there and be good, do you hear? Let me get on with my work, and we'll soon be able to go back home.'

And Pietro would sit there quietly for two hours scribbling

away. The cook, an old spinster from Livorno who had lived in the villa for many years, could hardly believe it. 'An angel from heaven, that's what you are.'

The little mite was so well brought-up, he wouldn't even accept a slice of tart unless his mother said he could.

What a contrast to the daughter of the house. A spoiled minx who could do with a good spanking. The toys in that house had an average lifespan of two days. The little brat's way of telling you she was tired of chocolate mousse was to throw it on the floor at your feet.

When little Gloria had discovered that there was a living toy, made of flesh of blood, called Pietro, in the kitchen, she had been thrilled to bits. She had taken him by the hand and led him to her bedroom. To play with her. At first she had been a bit rough (MAMAA! MAMAA! Gloria stuck her finger in my eye!), but gradually she had learned to treat him like a human being.

Dr Celani was so happy. 'Thank heaven for Pietro. Gloria has quietened down a bit. Poor little thing, what she needs is a baby brother.'

But there was one little problem: Mrs Celani no longer had a uterus, so that was that. They wouldn't hear of adoption, and anyway now they had Pietro, the angel from heaven.

In short, the two children began to spend every day of their lives together, just like brother and sister.

And when Mariagrazia Moroni, Pietro's mother, began to be unwell, to suffer from a strange, inexplicable condition that left her feeling weak and listless ('it's as if . . . I don't know, as if my batteries were flat'), from something the doctor called depression and which Mr Moroni called being bone idle and finding cleaning the villa too much like hard work, Dr Mauro Celani, the manager of the Orbano branch of the Bank of Rome and president of Chiarenzano sailing club, had stepped in and drafted a plan with his wife Ada:

1) Poor Mariagrazia needs help. She must see a specialist immediately. 'I'll call Professor Candela tomorrow . . . What

do you mean Professor who? The consultant at the Villa dei Fiori clinic in Civitavecchia, surely you remember . . . ? The guy with that beautiful twelve-metre yacht.'

2) Pietro couldn't stay with his mother all day. 'It's not good for him or for her. He must come here and spend the day with Gloria after school.'
3) Pietro's father was an alcoholic, a convicted criminal, a bully who was ruining the lives of that poor woman and their adorable son. 'Let's hope he doesn't cause any trouble. If he does, he can forget about getting a mortgage.'

And the plan had worked to perfection.

Poor Mariagrazia had been taken under the protective wing of Professor Candela. This luminary had prescribed a powerful cocktail of psychotropic drugs all ending in 'il' (Anafranil, Tofranil, Nardil, etc) which had introduced her to the magical world of monoamine oxidase inhibitors. An opaque and comfortable world of pastel colours and grey expanses, of mumbled, unfinished sentences, of constantly repeating, 'Oh dear, I can't remember what I was going to cook for dinner.'

Pietro had been taken under the maternal wing of Mrs Celani and had continued to go to the villa every afternoon.

Strange to relate, even Mr Moroni had been taken under a wing, the large rapacious wing of the Bank of Rome.

Pietro and Gloria had attended the same primary school, but not in the same class. And everything had been fine. Now that they were in junior high, and in the same class, things had got more complicated.

They belonged to different castes.

Their friendship had adapted to the situation. It became like an underground river which flows unseen and constricted beneath the rocks, but which as soon as it finds an opening, a crack, gushes out in all its awesome power.

In the same way, at first sight you might have thought the two of them were complete strangers, but you'd have had to be blind not to notice how they were always looking for each other, always passing close to each other and how during breaktime they would sit whispering in a corner like a couple of spies, and how, strangely, when school was over Pietro would wait there at the end of the street till he saw Gloria take her bike and follow him.

5

Gina Biglia, Graziano's mother, suffered from hypertension. Her blood pressure was never below a hundred and twenty-eight and sometimes rose as high as a hundred and eighty. It only took the slightest anxiety or excitement and she would have palpitations, giddiness, cold sweats and fainting fits.

Usually, when her son came home, Gina was so joyful that she felt ill and had to retire to bed for a couple of hours. But when, that winter, Graziano arrived from Rome, after two years without a visit or even a phone call, announcing that he had met a girl from the North and that he wanted to marry her and come back to live in Ischiano, her heart leaped in her chest like a jack-in-a-box and the poor woman, who was making fettuccine, fainted and crashed to the floor, pulling table, flour and rolling pin down with her.

When she came round, she couldn't talk.

She lay on the floor like a capsized tortoise among the fettuccine, making incomprehensible mumbling noises as if she'd become a deaf mute or worse.

A stroke, thought Graziano in a panic. Her heart had stopped beating for a second and she'd suffered brain damage.

He rushed into the living room to call an ambulance, but when he returned he found his mother as right as rain. She was washing the kitchen floor with Cif and when she saw him she handed him a piece of paper on which she had written:

I'm not ill. I made a vow to the Madonnina of Civitavecchia that if you got married I wouldn't speak for a month. The Madonnina in her infinite mercy has answered my prayers and now I mustn't speak for a month.

Graziano read the note and threw himself disconsolately onto a chair. 'But Mama, this is ridiculous. Don't you see? How are you going to work? And what am I going to do about Erica? What's she going to think, that you're raving mad? Stop it. Please.'

Gina wrote:

Don't worry. I'll explain to your fiancée. When's she coming?

'Tomorrow. But do stop it, now, Mama, please. We haven't fixed the wedding day yet. Pack it in, please.'

Gina suddenly started rushing round the kitchen like a hysterical goblin, yelping and digging her fingers into the voluminous perm on her head. She was a small, round woman, with bright eyes and a mouth like a chicken's sphincter.

Graziano ran after her, trying to catch her. 'Mama! Mama! Stop, please. What the hell's got into you?'

Gina sat down at the table and wrote again:

The house is a mess. I must clean it from top to bottom. I must take the curtains to the laundry. Wax the living room floor. And then I'll have to go shopping. Go away. Let me work.

She put on her mink coat, hoisted a bag full of curtains onto her shoulder and went out.

No operating theatre in the local hospital was as clean as Gina's kitchen. Even if you'd examined it with an electronic microscope you wouldn't have found a dust mite or a speck of dirt. You could eat off the floors of the Biglia household and safely drink from the toilet. Every ornament had its doily, every shape of pasta its jar, every corner of the house received a daily check and vacuuming. As a child, Graziano had been forbidden to sit on the sofas because it spoiled them: he'd had to walk around in overshoes and sit on a dining chair to watch TV.

Mrs Biglia's first obsession was hygiene. Her second, religion. Her third and most serious of all, cooking.

She would prepare industrial quantities of gourmet food. Maccheroni timbales. Three days' supply of ragù. Game. Aubergines alla parmigiana. Rice sartùs as high as panettoni. Broccoli-cheese-and-mortadella pizzas. Artichoke and béchamel pies. Foil-baked fish. Stewed calamari. And Livornese cacciucco. Since she lived on her own (her husband had died five years earlier), all these delicacies were either stored in the freezers (there were three of them, all crammed full) or given away to her customers.

At Christmas, Easter, the New Year and any other festival that merited a special meal, she would go berserk and shut herself up in the kitchen for thirteen hours a day, ladelling, greasing baking-tins and shelling peas. Purple in the face, with a crazed look in her eyes and a bonnet to keep the grease out of her hair, she would whistle, sing along with the radio and whisk eggs like a woman possessed. During the meal she would never sit down, but gallop back and forth like a Burmese tapir between the dining room and kitchen, sweating, panting and washing dishes, and everyone would tense up because it's not pleasant to eat with a madwoman who watches every expression of your face to see if you like the lasagne, who refills your plate before you've even finished eating and who you know, in her condition, is liable to have an apoplectic fit at any moment.

No, it's not pleasant.

And it was hard to understand why she behaved like that, what the nature of this culinary frenzy that tormented her was. The guests, by the time they got to the twelfth course, would ask one another under their breath what she was trying to do, what was her purpose. Did she want to kill them? Cook for the whole world? Feed the starving millions on risotto with cheese and grated truffles, linguine al pesto and ossobuco with purée?

No, Mrs Biglia wasn't interested in that.

Mrs Biglia didn't give a damn about the Third World, the children of Biafra and the parish poor. She vented all her pitiless fury on relatives, friends and acquaintances. All she wanted was for someone to say to her: 'Gina, dear, nobody makes Sorrento-style gnocchi like you do, even in Sorrento.'

Then she would go all shy like a little girl, stammer out her thanks, bow her head like a great conductor after a triumphant performance and take a container full of gnocchi out of the freezer, saying: 'Here you are, mind you don't put them straight in the water or they won't be good. Take them out at least a couple of hours beforehand.'

She would stuff you mercilessly, and if you begged her to stop she'd think you were just being polite, and wouldn't take no for an answer. You would stagger out of her home, groggy, with your flies unbuttoned and feeling in need of a trip to the health spa at Chianciano for a detox.

Every time Graziano came home he put on at least five kilos in a week. His mother would make him sautéed lamb's kidneys with garlic and parsley (his favourite!) and since he had a hearty appetite she would sit in ecstasy and watch him eating. She had to ask him, she'd die if she didn't. 'Graziano, tell me the truth, how are the sautéed kidneys?'

And Graziano: 'Delicious, Mama.'

'Is there anyone who makes them better than I do?'

'No, Mama, you know that. Your sautéed kidneys are the best in the world.'

Deliriously happy, she would return to the kitchen and start doing the washing-up by hand because she didn't trust machines.

You can just imagine what kind of banquet she was preparing to cook for her future daughter-in-law.

For waif-like Erica Trettel, who weighed forty-six kilos and said she was a horrible fat lump and who when she was feeling cheerful ate cottage cheese, spelt and Energy Bars and when she was depressed devoured Algida Viennetta ice creams and takeaway chicken.

6

Graziano spent the morning feeling at peace with himself and with the world.

He went out for a walk.

The sky was overcast. It was cold. The rain had stopped but some big black clouds boded ill for the afternoon. Graziano didn't care. He was glad to be home at last.

Ischiano seemed more beautiful and welcoming than ever.

A little old-fashioned world. An unspoiled rural community.

It was market day. The vendors had put up their stalls in the car park in front of the bank. The village women with their baskets and umbrellas were doing the shopping. Mothers were pushing prams. A van, which had pulled up in front of the newsagent's, was delivering bundles of magazines. Giovanna, the tobacconist, was feeding some obese, pampered cats. A group of hunters had gathered in front of the war memorial. The hounds on the leash were shifting about excitedly. And the old men sitting at the tables outside the Station Bar were trying, like arthritic reptiles, to catch a ray of that sun which was so reluctant to come out. From the primary school came the shouts of children playing in the playground. The air was filled with the delicious smell of burned wood and of the fresh cod laid out on the fishmonger's stall.

This was the place where he'd been born.

Simple.

Ignorant, perhaps.

But real.

He was proud to be part of that small God-fearing community and proud of his own humble occupation. And to think that until recently he had felt ashamed of the place, and when asked where he came from had always replied: 'The Maremma. Near Siena.' It sounded cooler. Nobler. More sophisticated.

What a fool I was. Ischiano's a wonderful place. A guy should be happy to have been born here. And at the age of forty-four he was beginning to understand this. Maybe all that globe-trotting, all those discotheques, all those nights spent playing in clubs had helped him understand, restored his desire to be a true Ischianese. You have to go away from a place in order to find it again. Peasant blood flowed in his veins. His grandparents had slaved their lives away working that hard barren soil.

He passed his mother's haberdashery.

A modest little shop. Tights and knickers neatly arrayed in the window. A glass door. A sign.

This was where his jeans shop would be.

He could see it now.

The pride of the village.

He must start thinking about how to furnish it. Perhaps he would need an architect, someone from Milan or even America to help him create the best possible effect. He would spare no expense. He must discuss it with Mama. Persuade her to take out a mortgage.

Erica would help him, too. She had very good taste.

After these positive thoughts, he got out the Uno and drove it to the carwash. He ran it through the brushes, then vacuumed the inside, removing stubs of joints, receipts, left-over French fries and other assorted rubbish that had collected under the seats.

He looked at himself for a moment in the rear-view mirror and realised that he hadn't obeyed the first law: 'Treat your body as a temple.'

Physically he was a wreck.

The months in Rome had affected his looks. He had stopped taking care of his appearance and now resembled a caveman, with that stubbly beard and that bristly mop of hair. He really spruced himself up before Erica arrived.

He got back into the car, drove out onto the Aurelia and after seven kilometres stopped outside the Ivana Zampetti Beauty Farm, a large concrete building by the side of the road, between a garden centre and a store that sells handmade furniture.

7

Ivana Zampetti, the owner, was a large woman, all curves and bosom, with black, Liz Taylor-like hair, a zip of a mouth, gappy incisors, a remodelled nose and greedy eyes. She went around in a white coat which allowed glimpses of firm flesh and lace, and a pair of Dr Hermann sandals. And she was constantly enveloped in a cloud of sweat and deodorant.

Ivana had moved to Orbano from Fiano Romano in the mid-Seventies and got a job there as a manicurist in a beauty parlour. Within a year she had succeeded in marrying the old barber who owned it and had taken over the running of the place. She had turned it into a hairdressing salon, renewing the furniture, stripping off that ugly wallpaper and replacing it with mirrors and marble and adding washbasins and perming hoods. Two years later, her husband had died in the middle of Orbano high street, struck down by a heart attack. Ivana had sold the houses he had left her in San Folco and opened two more hairdressing salons in the area, one in Casale del Bra and the other in Borgo Carini. One summer in the late Eighties she had gone to visit some distant relatives who had emigrated to Orlando and there she had seen the American fitness centres. Temples of health and beauty. Superbly equipped clinics that treated the whole body, from the tip of your toes to the topmost hair of your head. Mud baths. Solar beds. Massage. Hydrotherapy. Lymphatic drainage. Peeling. Gymnastics. Stretching and weights.

She had returned with her head full of grand ideas which she immediately put into effect. She had sold off the three hairdressing salons and bought a warehouse on the Aurelia that sold agricultural machinery and turned it into a multi-specialised centre for the care and health of the body. Now she had a staff of ten, including instructors, aestheticians and paramedics. She had become immensely rich and much sought after by local bachelors. But she said she was faithful to the memory of the old barber.

8

When Graziano entered, Ivana welcomed him joyfully, hugged him to her large perfumed bosom and told him he looked like a corpse. She would put him to rights. She drew up a programme for him. First a course of massage, bath in toning seaweed, total sunbed, hair-dying, manicure and pedicure, and, to round it all off, what she called her recreative-revitalising therapy.

Whenever Graziano returned to Ischiano, he always liked to undergo Ivana's therapy.

A series of massages of her own devising, which she performed only after hours and on people she deemed worthy of the privilege. Massages which tended to revitalise and reawaken very specific organs of the body and which left you feeling, for a couple of days afterwards, like Lazarus when he rose from the grave.

On this occasion, however, Graziano declined the offer. 'I'm sorry, Ivana, but I'm about to get married. You know how it is.'

Ivana gave him a hug and wished him a happy life and lots of children.

Three hours later, he emerged from the centre and drove to the Scottish House in Orbano to buy a few items of clothing that would make him feel more in harmony with the country life on which he was preparing to embark.

He spent nine hundred and thirty thousand lire.

And here he was at last, our hero, outside the doors of the Station Bar.

He was ready.

His hair, glossy, frizzy and savannah-coloured, smelled of conditioner. His shaven jaw smelled of Egoiste. His eyes were dark and bright. His skin had regained its melanine and at last had that colour, halfway between hazel and bronze, which drove the Scandinavian girls wild.

He looked like a Devonshire gentleman fresh from a holiday in the Maldives. Green flannel shirt. Brown wide-cord trousers. Scottish short-sleeved pullover with the tartan of the Dundee clan (the shop assistant had told him that). A tweed jacket with elbow-patches. And chunky Timberland shoes.

Graziano pushed the door open and took two slow, measured, John Wayne-type steps towards the bar.

Barbara, the twenty-year-old bartender, nearly fainted when she saw him appear. Just like that, on an ordinary day. With no trumpets or fanfares to announce him. No heralds to warn of his impending arrival.

Biglia!

He was back.

The ladykiller was back.

The sex symbol of Ischiano was here. Here to rekindle never-extinguished erotic obsessions, to reignite jealousies, to set tongues wagging.

After his performances in Riccione, Goa, Port France, Battipaglia and Ibiza, he was here again.

The man who had been invited on to the *Maurizio Costanzo Show* to talk about his experiences as a Latin lover. The man who had won the Casanova Cup. The man who had played on *Planet Bar* with the Rodriguez brothers. The man who had bedded the actress Marina Delia (the page torn out of *Novella 2000* with photographs of Graziano on Riccione beach massaging Marina Delia's back and kissing her neck had hung beside the pinball machine for six months, and still reigned supreme in Roscio's workshop among the nude-model calendars). The man who had beaten the great Peppone pulling record (three hundred scores in one summer, the papers said). He was here again.

More flourishing and in better shape than ever.

His contemporaries, who had become husbands and fathers, worn out by a dreary, humdrum life, resembled mangy, greying bulldogs, whereas Graziano . . .

(*What on earth can his secret be?*)

. . . grew more handsome and attractive by the year. How well that hint of a pot belly suited him. And those crow's feet round his eyes, those wrinkles at the sides of his mouth, that slightly receding hairline, gave him a certain je ne sais quoi . . .

'Graziano! When did you get b . . .' said bartender Barbara, going as red as a pepper.

Graziano put his finger to his lips, picked up a cup, banged it on the counter and shouted: 'What's wrong with this place? Aren't you going to welcome back an old villager? Barbara! Drinks all round.'

The old men playing cards, the little boys at the videogames, the hunters and the carabinieri, all turned round together.

His friends were there too. His bosom pals. His old fellow-roisterers. Roscio, the Franceschini brothers and Ottavio Battilocchi were sitting at a table doing the football pools and reading the *Corriere dello Sport*, and when they saw him they jumped to their feet, hugged him, kissed him, ruffled his hair and gave him a chorus of 'For he's a jolly good fellow'. And other more colourful and ribald songs which are best passed over in silence.

That is how people celebrate, in those parts, the return of the prodigal son.

And here he was, half an hour later, in the restaurant area of the Station Bar.

The restaurant area was a square room at the back of the bar. With a low ceiling. A long neon light. A few tables. A window overlooking the railway track. On the walls, lithographs of old steam trains.

He was sitting at a table with Roscio, the two Franceschini brothers and young Bruno Miele, who had come along specially. The only one missing was Battilocchi, who had had to take his daughter to the dentist's in Civitavecchia.

In front of them were five big steaming dishes of tagliatelle in hare sauce. A jug of red wine. And a plate of cold meat and olives.

'This is what I call living, boys. You've no idea how much I've missed this stuff,' said Graziano, pointing at the pasta with his fork.

'Well, what's it to be this time? The usual lightning visit? When are you off again?' asked Roscio, filling his glass.

Since childhood, Roscio had been Graziano's best friend. Back then he had been a skinny little boy with a helmet of carrot-coloured hair, slow of tongue but quick as a ferret with his hands. His father had a junk yard on the Aurelia and sold stolen spares. Roscio lived among those mountains of metal, dismantling and reassembling engines. At thirteen he was riding round in the saddle of a Guzzi one thousand and at sixteen he was racing on the viaduct at the Pratoni. At seventeen, he had had a horrendous accident one night, his motorbike had stalled and bucked at a hundred and sixty kilometres an hour and he had been launched off the viaduct like a missile. Without a helmet. They'd found him next day, five metres below the road, in a drainage outflow from the sewers, more dead than alive and looking like an ant that's had a dictionary dropped on it. He had been in traction for months with twenty bones either broken or dislocated and more than four hundred stitches on various parts of his anatomy. Six months in a wheelchair and six more on crutches. At twenty he walked with a pronounced limp and could no longer bend one arm properly. At twenty-one he had got a Pitigliano girl pregnant and married her. Now he had three children and after his father's death he had taken over the business and set up a workshop as well. And probably, like his father, he did some shady deals. Graziano hadn't found him so easy to get on with since the accident. His character had changed, he'd become edgy and was given to sudden fits of anger, he drank, and the word in the village was that he beat his wife.

'Who are you going with now, you old letch? Still hanging around with that foxy actress . . . ?' Bruno Miele was talking with his mouth full. 'What's her name? Marina Delia? Hasn't she just made a new film?'

Bruno Miele had grown up during Graziano's two years away and was now in the police force. Who would have thought it? A notorious tearaway like Miele settling down and becoming a guardian of the law? Life moved on in Ischiano Scalo, slowly but surely, even without Graziano.

Miele had idolised him ever since he'd learned of his affair with a famous actress.

But that story was an embarrassment to poor Graziano. The

photographs in *Novella 2000* had been very useful to him, they had turned him into a local legend, but at the same time they made him feel rather guilty. In the first place, he had never actually gone out with Delia. She had been sunbathing at the Aurora bathing establishment at Riccione and when she had seen a paparazzo from *Novella 2000* prowling around on the beach searching for VIPs, she had gone frantic. She had immediately whipped off her bra and started shouting. She was alone. The minor French actor she was dating at the time was confined to their hotel with a temperature of thirty-nine as a result of food poisoning. Only a fool of a young Frenchman would pick the mussels off the mooring lines of Riccione harbour and eat them raw, saying that his father was a Breton fisherman. It served him right. But now Marina was in a fix. She had to find someone to be her beau, and quickly. She had run along the seashore looking for a good-looking male to pose with. Rapidly scanning all the beefcakes, hunks and lifeguards on the beach she had finally settled on Graziano. She had asked him if he would mind rubbing cream on her breasts and kissing her when that little man over there, the one with the camera, passed in front of them.

That was the story behind the famous photographs.

And it would probably have ended there if Marina Delia hadn't become, after a film she had made with a Tuscan comic, one of the most popular film stars in Italy and hadn't decided never again to reveal a single speck of skin even for a million dollars. Those were the only available photographs of Delia's breasts. Graziano had dined off the tale for a couple of years at least, describing how he had pleasured her fore and aft, in the lift and in the Jacuzzi, come rain, come shine. But now enough was enough. Five years had passed. And yet every time he returned to Ischiano they all started going on about Marina Delia and what a slag she was.

What a bore!

'I read somewhere that she was going out with some jerk of a footballer,' went on Miele, his head buried in the fettuccine.

'She ditched you for a Sampdoria midfielder. Sampdoria of all teams! Can you believe it?' guffawed Giovanni, the elder of the two Franceschini brothers.

'She might at least have chosen a Lazio player,' echoed Elio, the younger.

The Franceschini brothers owned a bass farm in Orbano lagoon. The Franceschinis' bass were instantly recognisable because they were all twenty centimetres long, weighed six hundred grams, had opaque eyes and tasted like farmed trout.

The two of them were inseparable, they lived in a mosquito-infested farmhouse near the tanks with their wives and children and nobody could ever remember which wife and which children were whose. They made enough to live on from the bass, but they certainly can't have got rich on it since they were reduced to squabbling over the van whenever they wanted to go out for a beer in the evening.

Graziano decided that the time had come to liquidate Delia.

He wasn't sure how much to tell his friends about his future plans. Better not mention the jeans shop. People are always out to steal your ideas. News travels fast in a village, and some son-of-a-bitch might beat him to it. First he must get everything organised and call in the Milanese architect, only then would he be able to talk about it in public. But the other news, the best part, why shouldn't he tell them about that? Weren't they his friends? 'Listen, boys, I've got something to tell y . . .'

'Let's hear it. Who're you screwing now? Are you going to tell us or do we have to read about it in the papers?' Roscio interrupted him, filling his glass to the brim with that deceptively strong local wine that slipped down as easily as fizzy pop but later grabbed your head and squeezed it like a lemon.

'I bet he's been fucking Simona Raggi. Or, let's see, who else could it have been?' said Franceschini junior.

'No, I reckon Andrea Mantovani's more likely. Poofs are the in thing at the moment,' concluded his elder brother, waving his hand.

And everyone roared with laughter.

'Could you all be quiet for a moment?' Graziano, who was getting irritated, hammered his fork on the table. 'Stop talking crap.

Listen to me. The time of starlets and records is over. It's all in the past.'

Raspberries. Guffaws. Nudges in ribs.

'I'm forty-four now, I'm not a kid any more. Okay, I've had some good times, I've travelled the world, I've slept with so many women I can't even remember the faces of most of them.'

'I bet you can remember their arses, though,' said Miele, delighted with this brilliant witticism he had thought up.

More raspberries. More guffaws. More nudges.

Graziano was beginning to get really angry. You couldn't have a serious conversation with these idiots. Right. He was going to have to tell them straight out. Without beating about the bush. 'Boys, I'm getting married.'

There was a burst of applause. Chants. Whistles. Other people came in from the bar and were instantly informed. For a quarter of an hour there was pandemonium.

Graziano getting married? Impossible! Ridiculous!

The news flew out of the bar and spread like a virus, and within half an hour the whole village knew that Biglia was getting hitched.

Then, at last, after the kisses, the hugs and the toasts, things quietened down.

There were just the five of them again and Graziano was able to resume his interrupted story. 'Her name's Erica. Erica Trettel. No, don't worry, she's not German, she comes from near Trento. She's a dancer. She's coming here tomorrow, she says she doesn't like villages, but she doesn't know Ischiano Scalo. I'm sure she'll like it. I want her to feel at home, at her ease. So I'm counting on you guys, you've got to help me . . .'

'What do you want us to do?' asked the Franceschini brothers in chorus.

'Well . . . For example, we could organise something special for tomorrow evening.'

'Like what?' asked Roscio, bewildered.

That was one of the problems with that place, whenever you tried to do anything that was actually fun, you fell under a kind of spell, your mind went blank and your IQ dropped several degrees.

The truth was that there was fuck all to do in Ischiano Scalo.

A disturbing silence fell over the group, everyone was absorbed in his own mental vacuum.

What could we do? It'll have to be something really good, thought Graziano, *something Erica would like.*

He was about to say they could go to the usual shitty Old Wagon Pizzeria, when suddenly he had a vision, an intoxicating vision.

It is night.

He and Erica step out of the Uno. He in a Sandek windsurfing costume, she in a skimpy orange bikini. Both tall, both athletic, both as beautiful as Greek gods. More lissom than the lifeguards on *Baywatch*. They walk across the muddy piazza. Hand in hand. It's cold but they don't mind. There's smoke in the air. A smell of sulphur. They enter the pools and immerse themselves in the warm water. They kiss. They touch. He slips off her top. She slips off his Sandek.

Everyone is watching them. They don't care.

Quite the opposite.

And then they do it, in front of everyone.

Quite shamelessly.

That was what they must do.

Saturnia.

Yes.

In the pools of sulphurous water. Erica had never been there. *She'll love it, bathing by night under that boiling-hot waterfall, and remember, it's good for the skin, too*. And how the others will cringe with envy.

When they see Erica's cover-girl curves, when they compare their own consorts' cellulitic loins with Erica's smooth, firm buttocks, when they set their own women's flaccid breasts alongside Erica's marble boobs, when they contrast Erica's gazelle-like legs with their own drabs' stumpy pins, when they see him mount that young filly, in front of them all, they'll feel like worms and understand, once and for all, why Graziano Biglia had decided to get married.

Right?

'Boys, I've just had a great idea. We could have dinner at the

Three Roosters, that tavern near Saturnia, then go for a bathe at the falls. What do you say?' he suggested enthusiastically, in the same tone in which he might have announced an all-expenses-paid holiday in the Tropics. 'Wouldn't it be great?'

But the response did not come up to his expectations.

The Franceschini brothers looked dubious. Miele just uttered a sceptical 'Hm!' and Roscio, after looking at the others, said: 'I don't know, it doesn't sound such a great idea to me. It's cold.'

'And it's raining,' added Miele, peeling an apple.

'You've turned into a bunch of fucking zombies! You eat, you sleep and you work. Is that all you do? You're corpses. Layabouts. Don't you remember those fantastic evenings we used to have driving around the countryside getting drunk and then going to throw bombs into the artificial lake at Pitigliano and finishing up with a bathe under the waterfall . . .'

'Wasn't it great . . .' said Giovanni Franceschini with his eyes on the ceiling. His face had softened and his eyes were dreamy. 'Do you remember when Lambertelli hit his head diving into one of the pools? What a laugh. And I picked up a girl from Florence.'

'That was no girl, that was a guy,' his brother said. 'His name was Saverio.'

'And do you remember when we pelted those Germans' minibus with stones and then pushed it over the cliff?' Miele reminisced, ecstatically.

They all laughed, carried away by the whirlwind of happy memories of youth.

Graziano knew that this was the moment to press home his point, not to let up. 'Well, why don't we do it, then? Tomorrow night we'll take the cars and drive to Saturnia. We'll get drunk at the Three Roosters, then we'll all go for a bathe.'

'But it costs the earth, that place,' objected Miele.

'Oh, come on, am I getting married or aren't I? You stingy bastards!'

'All right, just this once we'll splash out,' said the Franceschinis.

'But you must bring your wives and girlfriends, okay? We can't turn up like a bunch of poofs, Erica might get the wrong idea.'

'But my wife gets sciatica . . .' said Roscio. 'She might drown.'

'And Giuditta's just had a hernia operation,' added Elio Franceschini worriedly.

'Look, just grab your women and force them to come. Who wears the trousers at home, you or them?'

It was agreed that the party would set off from the piazza at eight o'clock the following evening. And no one could drop out at the last moment, for as Miele rightly observed: 'Only a heel backs out of a deal.'

Graziano set off homeward, slightly drunk and as happy as a child at Eurodisney.

'Thank God I got out of that awful city. Thank God. Rome, I hate you. You stink,' he repeated out loud.

How wonderful life was in Ischiano Scalo and what marvellous friends he had. He'd been a fool not to keep in touch with them for all those years. He felt a tide of affection rising within him. Perhaps they had aged a bit, but he would put them back on their feet. At that moment he felt ready to do anything for that village. After the jeans shop, he might open a British-style pub, and then . . . And then there were lots of other things to do.

He climbed the front steps, holding on to the banister, and entered the house.

There was a smell of onions pungent enough to make your hair stand on end.

'Christ, what a smell, Ma. What are you doing in there?' He looked into the kitchen.

Mrs Biglia, carving knife in hand, was quartering a gnu, or a donkey, since the carcass would hardly fit on the marble-topped table.

'Awaaaaaawaaaaa,' moaned his mother.

'What did you say? I can't understand a word you're saying, Ma. I really can't,' said Graziano, leaning against the door jamb. Then he remembered. 'Oh, yes. The vow.' He turned round and trudged off to his room. He collapsed on his bed and before going to sleep decided that next day he would go and see Father Costanzo (*I wonder if he's still around? He might be dead by now*) to discuss his mother's vow. Maybe the priest could dissolve it. He mustn't let Erica see his mother in that state. Then he told himself that there was no real harm in it – his mother was a practising Catholic and he'd believed in God himself when he'd been a child.

Erica would understand.

He fell asleep.

And he slept the sleep of the just beneath a poster of John Travolta in his *Saturday Night Fever* days. Feet sticking out of the little bed. Mouth wide open.

9

Go. Go. Go.

Go, it's late.

Go, and never stop.

And Pietro went. Down the slope. He could see nothing but darkness, *but what the hell*, he pedalled in the gloom, mouth open. The feeble lamp of his bike wasn't much use.

He leaned over, put his foot on the ground and sideslipped round the bend, then straightened up and, wheels spinning free, started to pedal again. The wind whistled in his ears and made his eyes water.

He knew the road by heart. Every bend. Every pothole. He could have ridden along it even without a lamp, with his eyes closed.

There was a record to beat, he had set it three months earlier and never since matched it. How on earth had he done it that day? God knows.

A rocket. Eighteen minutes twenty-eight seconds from Gloria's villa to home.

Was it because I'd changed the back tyre?

He had ridden so hard that when he'd reached home he'd felt sick and had vomited in the middle of the farmyard.

This evening, however, he wasn't going so fast to beat that record or because he felt like it, but because it was ten past eight and he was very late. He hadn't shut Zagor in his pen and hadn't taken the rubbish to the bin and hadn't turned off the pump in the vegetable garden, and . . .

. . . and Papa will kill me.

Go. Go. Go.

And as usual, it's all Gloria's fault.

She would never let him leave. 'You can see it looks awful like that. At least help me paint the letters . . . It'll only take a minute. You're such a bore . . .' she would say.

And so Pietro had set about painting the letters and then making the blue frame for the photograph of the mosquito sucking blood, and hadn't noticed that meanwhile time was passing.

Certainly the malaria poster had come out really well.

Miss Rovi would be bound to hang it in the corridor.

It had been a wonderful day, though.

After school, Pietro had gone to Gloria's for lunch.

At the red villa on the hill.

Pasta with courgettes and eggs. Schnitzel. And chips. Oh yes, and a cream dessert.

He liked everything about the place: the dining room with the french windows through which you could see the well-mown lawn, and further off the fields of wheat, and the sea in the background, and the bulky furniture and that picture of the Battle of Lepanto with the burning ships. And the maid serving you dinner.

But what he liked most of all was the laid table. Like those in a restaurant. The spotlessly white and newly washed tablecloth. The dishes. The basket full of rolls, focaccia and black bread. The carafe of sparkling water.

All perfect.

And it came naturally to him to eat properly, politely, with his mouth closed. No elbows on the table. No mopping up the sauce with his bread.

At home, Pietro had to fetch the food from the fridge, or the leftover pasta from the top of the cooker.

You take your plate and glass and sit at the kitchen table in front of the television and eat.

And when Mimmo, his brother, was there, he couldn't even watch cartoons, because that bully took the remote control and watched those soap operas that Pietro detested.

'Eat up and shut up,' Mimmo would say.

'At Gloria's house everyone eats together,' Pietro had told his parents once, when he was feeling more talkative than usual. 'Sitting at the table. Like in the TV series about the Bradford family. They wait till Gloria's father comes back from work before starting. You always have to wash your hands. Everyone has their own place and Gloria's mama always asks me how things are going at school and says I'm too shy and gets cross with Gloria for talking so much and not letting me get a word in. Once Gloria told them how that moron Bacci stuck pieces of snot in Tregiani's exercise book and her father told her off because you mustn't talk about filth at the table.'

'It's all right for them, they have nothing to do all day,' his father had said, as he guzzled away. 'We'd like to have a maid too. And remember, your mother used to do the cleaning in that house. You're closer to the maid than to them.'

'Why don't you go and live there, if you like it so much?' Mimmo had added.

And Pietro had realised that it was far better to avoid the subject of Gloria's family in his own home.

But today had been special because after lunch they had gone to Orbano with Gloria's father.

In the Range Rover!

With the stereo and the lovely smell of leather seats. Gloria sang like Pavarotti, putting on a deep voice.

Pietro sat in the back. Hands clasped together. Head against the window with the Aurelia flashing past. He looked out. The petrol pumps. The small ponds of the bass farm. The lagoon.

He wished he could go on like that, never stopping, all the way to Genoa. Where, he had heard, there was the largest aquarium in Europe (they even had dolphins). But Mr Celani had flicked the indicator and turned off towards Orbano. In Piazza Risorgimento he had double-parked the off-roader, nonchalantly, as if he owned the whole piazza, right in front of the bank.

'Let me know if I'm in anyone's way, Maria,' he'd said to the traffic warden, and she had nodded.

His father said Mr Celani was an absolute shit. 'Always so polite. Full of chit-chat. A true gentleman. Do sit down . . . how are you? Would you like a coffee? What a nice boy your son Pietro is. He's become such good friends with Gloria. Sure . . . Sure . . . The bastard! He's bled me dry with that mortgage. I won't have finished paying him even when I'm dead. Those people would suck the shit out of your arse given half a chance . . .'

Pietro really couldn't imagine Mr Celani sucking the shit out of his father's arse. He liked Gloria's father.

He's kind. He gives me money to buy pizza. And he's promised to take me to Rome one day . . .

Pietro and Gloria had gone to the hospital to see Dr Colasanti.

The hospital was a three-storey redbrick building right on the lagoon. With a small garden, and two large palms flanking the entrance.

He had been there once before, in the accident department. When Mimmo had taken a fall doing motocross behind the Marchi Spring and had started cursing and swearing in the waiting room because he had bent the fork of his bike.

Dr Colasanti was a tall gentleman with a grey beard and thick black eyebrows.

He was sitting at the desk in his ward. 'So you want to know all about the notorious Anopheles?' he had said, lighting his pipe.

He had talked for a long time and Gloria had recorded him. Pietro had learned that it wasn't mosquitoes that gave you malaria but micro-organisms that lived in their saliva, which they injected into you when they sucked your blood. Microbe-like things that got into your red corpuscles and multiplied there. It was strange to think that mosquitoes had malaria too.

With all this information they couldn't fail to make a good impression in class.

* * *

Dark and cold.

The wind swept the fields and pushed the bicycle off course and Pietro had trouble keeping it straight and, when a gap opened among the clouds, the moon cast a yellow glow over the fields which stretched far away, right down to the Aurelia. Black shadows chased one another across the silver grass.

Pietro pedalled, breathed in and sang between his teeth: 'Bir-dy bir-dy do not fly away! Ta ra . . .'

He turned right, went down a rough track across the fields and entered Serra, a little hamlet.

He shot through it.

At night he didn't like that place at all. It was scary.

Serra: six ramshackle old houses. A warehouse that was turned into a farmers' club a few years ago. The farm labourers and shepherds of the area go there to pickle their livers and play briscola. There's a shop, too, but it's always empty. And a church that was built in the Seventies. A parallelepiped of reinforced concrete with slits instead of windows and a silo-like bell tower at the side. On the façade a mosaic of the risen Christ is crumbling to pieces and the steps below the door are strewn with gilded tesserae. Kids use them as ammunition for their catapults. A dim lamp in the middle of the square, another on the street and the two windows of the farmers' club. Such are the illuminations of Serra.

'Lit-tle phea-sant do not fly away . . . Na na na . . .'

It was a like a ghost town in a Western.

Those narrow lanes and the shadows of the houses looming menacingly over the road, that gate banging in the wind and a dog barking itself hoarse behind another gate.

He cut across the square and came out onto the road again. He changed gear and pushed harder on the pedals, breathing rhythmically in and out. The light from his lamp lit a few metres of road, and then there was only darkness and sounds: the wind in the olive trees, his own breathing and the tyres on the wet asphalt.

He'd soon be home now.

He should be able to get there before his father did and avoid a scolding. He only hoped he didn't meet him driving home on the tractor. When he was too drunk he would stay at the club till closing time, snoring on a plastic chair by the pinball machine, then climb onto his tractor and drive home.

In the distance, about a hundred metres away, three dim lights were zigzagging towards him. They vanished and reappeared.

The sound of laughter.

Bicycles.

'Lit-tle wild . . .'

Who can it be, at this time of night?

He slowed down.

'. . . boar do not run . . .'

Nobody goes out cycling at this time, except . . .

'. . . away . . .'

. . . them.

Goodbye record.

No. It's not them . . .

They were advancing slowly. Calmly.

'HEH HEH HEEEEEH HEH HEH HEEEEEH HEH HEH HEH'

It's them.

That stupid laugh, as piercing as a fingernail on a blackboard and as stuttering as the bray of a donkey, odious, out of place and forced . . .

Bacci . . .

His breath died in his throat.

. . . Bacci.

Only that idiot Bacci laughed like that. Because to laugh like that you had to be an idiot like him.

It's them. Oh shit . . .

Pierini.

Bacci.

Ronca.

The last thing in the world he needed at that moment.

Those three wanted to see him dead. And the ridiculous thing was that Pietro didn't know why.

Why do they hate me? I've haven't done anything to them.

If he'd known what reincarnation was, he might have believed that those three boys were evil spirits punishing him for some wrong he had committed in another life. But Pietro had learned not to worry too much about why misfortune dogged him so persistently.

After all, it makes no difference in the end. If you're going to take a beating, you take it and that's that.

At the age of twelve Pietro had decided not to waste too much time wondering about the reason for things. It only made things worse. Wild boar don't wonder why woods burn and pheasants don't wonder why hunters shoot.

They just run.

It's the only thing to do. In cases like this you have to get away faster than the speed of light and if you can't, if they corner you, then you have to curl up like a hedgehog and let them vent their fury on you till it abates, like the hail when it catches you out walking in the country.

But what do I do now?

He rapidly considered the various possibilities.

Hiding and letting them go by.

Sure, he could hide in the fields and wait.

Wouldn't it be great to be invisible. Like the woman in The Fantastic Four. *They pass by and don't see you. You just stand there and they don't see you. Amazing. Or, even better, not to exist at all. Never to have been born.*

(*Stop daydreaming. Think!*)

I'll hide in the field.

No, that was a stupid idea. They'd see him. *And if they catch you hiding like a coward you're in real trouble. If you let them know you're scared, you've had it.*

Perhaps the best thing was to turn back. To flee as far as the farmers' club. No. They'd give chase. Just as he had seen their lamps, so they had seen his. And for those mental retards nothing was more entertaining than a nice nocturnal game of hunt-the-dickhead.

It would make their day.

What about making a dash for it?

He knew he was fast. Faster than anyone else in the school, but whenever he tried to race he lost. And now he was exhausted anyway.

He wouldn't be able to keep going for long. He'd slacken off and then . . .

There was nothing for it but to ride on, trying to look calm, pass by, greet them and hope they left him in peace.

Yes, that's what I must do.

Now they were only fifty metres away. They advancing relaxedly, talking and laughing, and probably wondering who was on that approaching bike. Now he heard Pierini's deep voice, Ronca's shriller tones and Bacci's laugh.

All three of them.

In battle formation.

Where were they heading?

For the bar in Ischiano Scalo, definitely. Where else could they go?

10

Pietro had guessed right, that was exactly where they were going.

What else could they do? Pinch each other to death, have a headbutting contest, play grandmother's footsteps, do their homework? The only thing to do was to go down to the bar, watch the older guys playing pool and try to filch some tokens from behind the counter so that they could get in a couple of games of Mortal Kombat.

No doubt about it.

All three of them were in agreement.

The trouble was that only Federico Pierini could really do as he pleased, tell his father to piss off, not go home and stay out till late at night. Andrea Bacci and Stefano Ronca had a slighter harder time handling the parent–child relationship, but gritting their teeth and taking bawl-outs and kicks in the arse, they followed their natural leader.

They advanced in line abreast, through the darkness, pedalling slowly, in the middle of the road.

As calm as a pack of young hunting dogs in search of prey.

The hunting dogs of the African savannah live in packs. But the young ones form separate groups, outside the family unit. When hunting they help and support each other, but they have a strict hierarchy, established by ritual fights. The leader, the biggest and boldest (alpha), and under him the subordinates. They maraud across the grasslands in search of food. They never attack the healthiest animals. Only sick, old or small ones. They surround the gnu, bewilder him with their barking, then all of them tear at him with their powerful jaws and sharp teeth till he falls down and, unlike big cats, which break the backbone first, they eat him alive.

Federico Pierini, the alpha hunting dog, was fourteen.

He was still in the second year of junior high school, having failed his end-of-year assessment twice.

A group of American neurophysiologists did some research on the prison populations of the USA. They took the meanest, most violent individuals (thugs, rapists, murderers, etc) and analysed the graphs of their electroencephalograms. They didn't use an ordinary electroencephalograph (which analyses the average electrical activity of the brain), but a more sophisticated one, capable of recording the electrical activity specific to each cortical region. They covered the prisoners' skulls with electrodes and then showed them a documentary on the industrial production of tennis shoes.

The neurophysiologists noted that in most cases the activity of the frontal zone of these individuals was low, and weaker than that of normal (good) people.

The frontal zone of the brain is used for the absorption of information from the outside world. In other words, it is the seat of the ability to concentrate – for example to sit down to watch a film and, even if it's a total yawn, to follow it from beginning to end without getting distracted or fidgety or starting to disturb your neighbour, but at the very most to breathe hard with exasperation and cast the occasional glance at your watch.

This research led them to formulate the theory that violent people have a poor capacity for concentration, and that this correlates to some extent with their bursts of aggression. It is as if violent individuals are in the grip of a restlessness that they cannot control and the bursts of aggression are a sort of safety valve.

So if you have accidentally rammed into the back of another car and the driver steps out, jack in hand, with the intention of smashing your head open, don't try to placate him by giving him a book about comets or a season ticket to the film club, it won't be any use. In such cases it is far better, as Pietro Moroni would have put it, to scram.

The point of the foregoing explanation is to establish two facts.

1) Federico Pierini was the meanest boy in the whole area.
2) Federico Pierini was a duffer at school. The teachers said he didn't concentrate, thus implicitly supporting the theories of the American neurophysiologists.

He was tall, lean and well proportioned. He shaved his moustache and wore an earring. An aquiline nose separated two small eyes that were as black as coal and always half closed. A white quiff hung over his forehead along with his raven fringe.

He had all the essential qualities of a pack leader.

He was cunning.

Bold of manner, sure of gesture, he took all the decisions but led his sidekicks to believe that they shared in them. He had no doubts about anything. All events, even the most terrible ones, seemed barely to affect him, as if he were immune to suffering.

'I don't give a shit about anyone,' he used to say.

And that was pretty well true. He didn't give a shit about his father, who he said was a pathetic failure with no balls. He didn't give a shit about his grandmother, who was a senile old bag. He didn't give a shit about school and that bunch of jerks the teachers.

'They'd better not fuck me around,' was his favourite expression.

Stefano Ronca was small and dark, with curly hair and lips that were always moist. As lively as a flea on speed, unstable, ready to bare his throat as soon as anyone attacked him and to jump on them as soon as they turned their backs. He had the high-pitched voice of a castrated know-all, a petulant, hysterical whine that jarred the nerves, and the longest, sharpest tongue in the school.

Andrea Bacci, known as Snack because of his partiality for take-away pizza, had two problems:

1) He was the son of a cop. 'And all cops must die,' in Pierini's opinion.
2) He was as round as a caciocavallo. His face was covered with freckles. His fair hair shaven right off. Small, gappy teeth still anchored to a gigantic silvered brace. When he talked you couldn't understand a word he said. He spat out a mixture of words and phlegm, rolled his Rs in his throat and lisped his zeds.

The natural reaction, on seeing him so round and so white, was to take the piss out of him, but that was a bad mistake.

Once a rash individual had tried it, drawing his attention to the fact that he was a freckle-faced ball of lard, and had found himself flat on the ground with Bacci raining punches on his face. It had taken four people to drag him off and for a quarter of an hour the fat lump had gone on spitting and shouting incomprehensible insults, kicking at the door of the toilet cubicle they'd locked him in.

Only Pierini could get away with teasing him, because he would alternate the insult 'You know you eat like a sewer?' with the sweeter and more accurate compliment 'You're definitely the strongest boy in the school and I reckon that if you got really angry you could even beat Flame.' He kept him in a state of constant insecurity and dissatisfaction. Sometimes he told him he was his best friend and then he'd suddenly prefer Ronca.

Every day, according to mood and time, the ranking order of

his best friends changed. At other times he would disappear, abandoning them both, and go off with the grown-ups.

In short, Pierini was as changeable as a November day and as elusive as a buzzard, and Ronca and Bacci competed, like rival lovers, for their leader's affections.

Bacci drew closer to Pierini. 'What are we going to do now? What are we going to tell Miss Rovi tomorrow?'

The science teacher had assigned them a research project on ants and anthills. They'd decided to take some pictures of the large anthills in the Acquasparta woods, but had blown the money for the film on cigarettes and a pornographic comic. Then they had gone to break open a condom machine behind the chemist's in Borgo Carini.

They'd ripped it off the wall and laid it on the railway track. When the Intercity had passed, the machine had shot up into the air like a missile and come to earth fifty metres away.

The upshot was that now they possessed enough condoms to screw every schoolgirl in the area three times over. But the money box still lay there, as closed and impenetrable as a Swiss bank vault.

They'd gone behind a tree and tried them on.

Ronca had put his penis in the condom and started masturbating quickly, jumping about and shouting: 'Can I fuck the black girls with this thing on?'

The point of this remark was that Pierini claimed to have sex with the black girls on the Aurelia. He said he went to see the black whores with Riccardo (the waiter at the Old Wagon), Giacanelli and Flame. And that he'd done it on a sofa at the side of the road, and the girl had cried out in African.

And who knows, it might even be true.

'The black girls wouldn't even feel a lamp-post, they've had it so often. They'd die laughing if they saw that little thing,' Pierini had said, peering at his penis.

Ronca had begged Pierini on his knees to show him his.

And Pierini had lit a cigarette, narrowed his eyes and pulled out his piece.

Ronca and Bacci had been amazed. Now they understood why the black girls went with their leader.

When it had been Bacci's turn, he'd said he wasn't too keen. 'Poof! You're a poof!' shouted Ronca in ecstasy. And Pierini had added: 'Either you show it to us or you can fuck off.'

And poor Bacci had been forced to pull it out.

'It's minuscule . . . Look at it . . .' Ronca had jeered.

'It's because you're fat,' Pierini had explained to him. 'If you lose weight, it'll grow.'

'I've already started a diet,' said Bacci hopefully.

'Some diet. You ate five thousand lire's worth of pizza yesterday,' Ronca had retorted.

The condom game had degenerated when Ronca had pissed into one and walked round triumphantly with that yellow balloon attached to his pecker. Pierini had punctured it with his cigarette end and Ronca had wet his trousers and almost burst into tears.

Anyway, later they had gone to look for anthills in the wood but had only got as far as catching some cockroaches as big as soap bars, soaking them in petrol and tossing them, like shot-down bombers crashing in flames, into the anthills.

Well, they'd shown willing, at any rate.

'We could tell Miss Rovi . . . that we couldn't find any anthills. Or that the photos didn't come out,' panted Bacci.

Although they were pedalling slowly and it was bitterly cold, Bacci was actually sweating.

'She'll never swallow that . . .' Ronca objected. 'Maybe we could copy something. Cut out the photographs from the book.'

'No. We won't go to school tomorrow,' declared Pierini, after taking a drag from the cigarette that hung from his lips.

There was a moment's silence.

Ronca and Bacci were considering the idea.

It certainly was the simplest and neatest solution.

Except that: 'Nooo. I can't. My father's coming to fetch me from school tomorrow and if he doesn't find me there . . . Besides, that other time, when we went down to the sea front, I got a thrashing,' said Bacci timidly.

'Nor can I,' added Ronca, suddenly turning serious.

'Both chickenshit, as usual . . .' Pierini allowed a few seconds to pass so that they could assimilate this concept and then added: 'Anyway, you don't have to play truant. Tomorrow's a holiday, nobody's going to school. I've had an idea.'

It was an idea that had been going round and round in his head for some time, and now it was time to put it into practice. Pierini often had brilliant ideas. And they always involved smashing things up.

Here are a few of them: on New Year's Eve he had put a bomb in the local postbox, another time he had broken open the back door of the Station Bar and stolen the cigarettes and sweets. He had also punctured the tyres of Miss Palmieri's car.

'What? What do you mean?' Ronca didn't understand. The next day was a perfectly normal Wednesday. There was no strike. No public holiday. Nothing.

Pierini took his time, finished the stub and threw it far away, keeping his friends on tenterhooks.

'Well, listen carefully. We're going to the school, then we're going to take your chain and put it round the gate,' and he pointed to the chain that hung below the saddle of Bacci's bike. 'So tomorrow morning, nobody will be able to get in and they'll send us all home.'

'Great! Brilliant!' Ronca was full of admiration. How did Pierini get these brainwaves?

'See? Nobody's going . . .'

'Well, yeah. Except that . . .' Bacci didn't seem entirely satisfied with the idea. He was very fond of that chain. He had a Graziella, small and rickety and short of a front mudguard, when he pedalled his knees came up into his mouth, and that chain his father had given him was the only good thing about the bike. '. . . I don't want to waste it like that. It's worth a lot of money. Anyway, my bike might get stolen.'

'Don't be stupid. Your bike's a fucking thief repellent. Any thief who saw it would throw up. Well, I suppose the police might steal it and use it as a test for spotting thieves. They grab someone and show him your Graziella, if he throws up it means he's a thief,' Ronca jeered.

Bacci brandished his fist. 'Fuck off, Ronca! Why don't you use your own chain?'

'Listen, Andrea,' Pierini intervened, 'my chain and Stefano's aren't strong enough. Tomorrow morning the headmaster would call the locksmith, he'd cut through it in no time and we'd go into school straight away, but if he finds yours, there's no way he'll cut through it. Just imagine, us lounging happily in the bar while he doesn't know what to do and the teachers cursing and swearing. They'll have to call the fire brigade in from Orbano. And all thanks to your chain. Get it?'

'And we won't have to worry about looking for fucking ants,' added Ronca.

Bacci was torn.

Certainly, the thought that your chain was stymieing a school and the Orbano fire brigade was a pleasant one. 'All right. Let's use it. Who cares. I'll put the old chain on my bike again.'

'Great! Let's go.' Pierini was pleased.

They had work to do.

But Ronca started laughing and repeating: 'What fools! What fools you are! What idiots! It won't work . . .'

'What's the matter now? What the hell are you laughing about, you halfwit?' Pierini said. One of these days he was going to ram Ronca's teeth down his throat.

'You've forgotten something . . . ha, ha, ha.'

'What?'

'Something very nasty. Ha, ha, ha.'

'What?'

'Italo. He'll see us when we put the chain on the gate . . . He has a perfect view of it from his house. He'll get out his shotgun and start blazing away . . .'

'What are you laughing about? It's no fucking joke. That puts us in the shit. Don't you see, if we don't chain up the gate, we're going to have to take the project in tomorrow. Only a moron like you would laugh about a thing like that.' Pierini gave him a shove and Ronca nearly fell off his bike.

'Sorry . . .' he muttered, his eyes averted.

But Ronca was right.

It was a problem.

That arsehole of a caretaker could ruin the whole operation. He lived next to the gate. And ever since burglars had broken in he'd been guarding the school like a Neapolitan mastiff.

Pierini's heart sank.

This made things dangerous, Italo might see them and tell the head, and besides he was crazy, mad as a hatter. It was rumoured that he kept a loaded shotgun by his bed.

How can we possibly do it? We'll have to drop the idea . . . no, we're not doing that.

They couldn't abandon such a brilliant idea just because of that old fogey. Even if they had to burrow their way underground like grubs through a dunghill, they'd put the chain on that gate.

I can't do it, he mused. *I was suspended a month ago. Ronca will have to. The problem is, he's so stupid he's bound to give himself away.*

Why oh why had he teamed up with the thickest pair of wankers in the village?

But just at that moment a bicycle lamp appeared in the distance.

11

Calm.

Keep calm.

You must seem normal. Don't let them see you're scared. Or that you're in a hurry, Pietro kept repeating to himself like an Ave Maria.

He advanced slowly.

Although he had made up his mind not to think about it, he kept asking himself why those three picked on him.

He was their favourite toy. The mouse that you learn to use your claws on.

What have I done wrong?

He never bothered them. He kept to himself. Didn't talk to anyone. Let them get on with whatever they wanted to do.

You want to rule the roost, fine. You're the toughest guys in the school, no problem.

So why didn't they leave him alone?

And Gloria, who hated them even more than he did, had told him over and over again that he must keep out of their way, that sooner or later they would . . .

(*beat me to a pulp*)

. . . get him.

Keep calm.

They were in front of him. A few metres away.

It was too late now to avoid them, hide, do anything.

He slowed down. Now the dark forms behind the bicycle lamps were beginning to take shape. He moved over to the side, to let them by. His heart was beating fast, his saliva had disappeared and his tongue felt dry and swollen, like a piece of foam rubber.

Keep calm.

They were no longer talking. They had stopped in the middle of the road. They must have recognised him. And be getting ready.

He advanced again.

They were ten metres away, eight, five . . .

Keep calm.

He took a deep breath and forced himself not to lower his gaze but to look them in the eye.

He was ready.

If they tried to surround him, he must take them by surprise and dash through them. And if they didn't manage to grab him, they'd have to turn their bikes round, which would give him a bit of a start. It might be enough for him to reach home safe and sound.

But instead, what happened was something incredible.

Something surreal, more surreal than meeting a Martian riding on a cow singing *'O sole mio*. Something Pietro would never have expected.

And which completely threw him.

'Hi, Moroni. Is that you? Where are you off to?' he heard Pierini ask.

This was incredible for several reasons.

1) Pierini had not called him Dickhead.
2) Pierini was addressing him in a friendly tone. A tone which that bastard's vocal cords had never been heard to produce until that evening.
3) Bacci and Ronca were waving to him. Like two nice, polite little boys greeting their auntie.

Pietro was speechless.

Watch out. It's a trap.

He sat on his bike there, like a fool, in the middle of the road. Only a few metres separated him from the three of them.

'Hi!' Ronca and Bacci said in chorus.

'Hi . . . i' he heard himself replying.

This was possibly the first time Bacci had ever greeted him.

'Where are you off to?' Pierini repeated.

'. . . home.'

'Oh. Going home, are you?'

Pietro, foot on pedal, was ready to make a break for it. If this was a trap, sooner or later they'd go for him.

'Have you done your science project?'

'Yes . . .'

'What on?'

'Malaria.'

'Ah. Interesting subject, malaria.'

Despite the darkness, Pietro could see Bacci and Ronca, behind Pierini, nodding. As if they had suddenly been transformed into a trio of microbiologists expert in tropical diseases.

'Did you do it with Gloria?'

'Yes.'

'Ah, good. Clever girl, isn't she?' Pierini didn't wait for a reply and continued. 'We've done a project on ants. Not nearly as interesting as malaria. Listen, do you really have to go home?'

Do I really have to go home? What sort of question is that?

What should he say in reply?

The truth.

'Yes.'

'Oh, what a shame! We were thinking of doing something . . . something cool. You could come with us, after all it concerns you too. Pity, we'd have enjoyed it more if you'd been there.'

'Yeah, we'd have enjoyed it more,' underlined Ronca.

'Much more,' repeated Bacci.

What a routine. Three ham actors performing a third-rate script. Pietro understood this at once. And if they were trying to arouse his curiosity, they were failing. He couldn't care less about their cool idea.

'I'm sorry, but I have to go home.'

'Oh, I quite understand. It's just that we can't do it on our own, we need a fourth person and we thought that you . . . well, might help us . . .'

The darkness concealed Pierini's face. Pietro could only hear his fluty voice and the wind rustling between the trees.

'Oh, come on, it won't take long . . .'

'To do what?' Pietro finally blurted out, but in such a low voice that nobody understood. He was forced to repeat: 'To do what?' Pierini surprised him again. With one bound he dismounted his bike and grabbed his handlebars.

Brilliant. Well done. Now you've landed yourself in the shit.

But instead of hitting him, Pierini looked this way and that and put his arm round his neck. Something halfway between a wrestler's armlock and a brotherly hug.

Bacci and Ronca closed in too. Before Pietro even had time to react he found himself surrounded and he realised that if they wanted to they could make mincemeat of him.

'Listen. We're going to chain up the school gate,' Pierini whispered in his ear as if he were revealing the whereabouts of some hidden treasure.

Ronca nodded his head contentedly. 'A brainwave, isn't it?'

Bacci showed him the chain. 'With this. They'll never break it. It's mine.'

'But why?' asked Pietro.

'So there'll be no school tomorrow, you see? The four of us will chain it up and we'll all go happily off home. Everyone will wonder who it was. And it'll have been us. And we'll be heroes for a long time afterwards. Just think how furious the head and the deputy head and all the others will be.'

'Just think how furious the head and the deputy head and all the others will be,' parroted Ronca.

'So what do you say?' Pierini asked.

Pietro didn't know what to reply.

He didn't like the idea at all. He wanted to go to school. He was ready for the oral presentation and he wanted to show Miss Rovi the poster.

And imagine what'll happen if you're caught . . . If these guys want you to go along, there must be a catch somewhere.

'Well, will you come with us?' Pierini pulled out his packet of cigarettes and offered him one.

Pietro shook his head. 'I can't, I'm sorry.'

'Why not?'

'My father . . . he's . . . expecting me.' Then he plucked up courage and asked: 'But why do you want me to come with you?'

'No special reason. Since it's such a cool idea . . . I thought we could do it together. It'd be easier with four of us.'

It all sounded so fishy.

'I'm sorry, but I have to go home. I can't, really.'

'It won't take long. And think about tomorrow, think what the others will say about us.'

'Really . . . I can't.'

'What's up? Shitting yourself, as usual? Are you scared? Have you got to run home to Papa to eat your rusks and pee in your potty?' interposed Ronca with that voice as irritating as the drone of a blowfly.

Here we go, first they'll jeer at you and then they'll beat you up. That's how it always ends.

Pierini glared at Ronca. 'Shut your mouth! He's not scared! It's just that he's got to go home. I've got to be home early too.' And accommodatingly: 'Otherwise my grandmother will be furious.'

'But what can he have to do at home that's so important?' Ronca persisted obtusely.

'What business is that of yours? He's gotta do what he's gotta do.'

'Typical of you, Ronca, always sticking your nose into other people's affairs,' Bacci backed him up.

'Quiet. Let him decide in his own time . . .'

The situation was this: Pierini was offering him two possibilities.

1) To say no, in which case they, he would bet a million to one, would start to jostle him and then, when he fell down, kick him black and blue.
2) To go with them to the school and see what happened. There anything might happen: they might beat him up or he might manage to get away or . . .

Quite frankly, he much preferred all those 'ors' to being beaten up on the spot.

Pierini's affable persona was fading. 'Well?' he asked him more harshly.

'All right, let's go. As long as we're quick about it.'

'Quick as a flash,' the other replied.

12

Pierini was feeling pleased. Very pleased.

Dickhead had fallen for it. He was following them.

He swallowed it.

He must be a complete idiot to think they really needed a jerk like him.

It was easy. I had him eating out of my hand. Go on, come with us. We'll be heroes. Heroes my arse.

Silly little twat!

He'd kick him all the way to the gate and force him to put the chain on. He sniggered to himself. Hey, what if Italo spotted Dickhead while he was fiddling with the gate!

It would be worth a week's suspension, maybe even two.

Maybe he could let out a yell so loud the old fool would fall out of bed. Except that then the whole plan would go down the tubes.

That pea-brain Bacci had drawn up alongside him and was coughing at him knowingly.

Pierini glared at him to keep quiet.

What if he refuses to go and put it on?

He smirked.

I only hope he does. Please God, make him refuse. Then we'll really have some fun.

He moved closer to Dickhead. 'It'll be a piece of cake.'

And Dickhead nodded with that dick-like head of his.

How he despised him.

For the weedy way he bent his head.

It gave him strange, violent urges. He wanted to hurt him, grab his little head and smash it on something sharp.

Besides, the guy would put up with anything.

If you told him his mother was a whore and let truck-drivers bugger her day and night, he would just nod his head. *It's true. It's perfectly true. My mother peddles her arse.* Nothing made any difference to him. He didn't react. He was worse than those two clowns Pierini hung around with. At least that fat slob Bacci didn't let anyone push him around and Ronca, now and then, made him laugh (and Pierini was not renowned for his sense of humour).

It was the smug little bastard's faint air of superiority that gave him itchy hands.

Moroni's the kind of guy who never talks in class, never plays with the other kids during PE, walks around with his nose in the air but is in fact a total nonentity. You're nobody, you're trash, do you understand, pal?

Only a prick-teaser like Gloria Celani, little miss I'm-the-only-girl-who's-got-one, could have wanted that wimpish creature as her

(*boyfriend?*)

friend. Those two tried their best not to show it, but Pierini had twigged that they were lovers, or something of the sort, anyway that they spent a lot of time together and maybe were even screwing.

The story of little miss I'm-the-only-girl-who's-got-one had lodged like a thorn in his gullet.

Sometimes he awoke in the night and couldn't get back to sleep for thinking about the little bitch. It was an obsession that was slowly driving him mad and if he really went mad he might do something he'd regret.

A few months ago that skuzz Caterina Marrese, from 3A, had organised a birthday party at her house one Saturday afternoon. Neither Pierini nor Bacci had been invited, let alone Ronca (or even Pietro, come to that).

But our fine friends never let the lack of an invitation get in the way of their attending a party.

They'd been joined on that occasion by Flame, a sixteen-year-old airhead with the character and IQ of an inbred pitbull. A pathetic misfit who unloaded crates at the Co-op in Orbano and cackled like a lunatic when he fired his pistol at sheep or at any living organism that was unlucky enough to cross his path. One night he had entered the Moroni's farm and shot the donkey in the forehead because the day before he'd seen *Schindler's List* on TV and been much taken with the blond Nazi.

To excuse themselves for coming to the party uninvited they'd brought along a gift.

A dead cat. A big fat tabby they'd found squashed flat on the Aurelia.

'Pity, if it didn't smell so bad Caterina could make herself a fur coat out of it. It would suit her. Come to think of it, she can use it anyway – the smell of the cat will mingle with her smell to create a whole new stink,' Rocca had remarked, examining the carcass closely.

On entering, they had found an atmosphere that was to say the least dullsville. Dimmed lights. Chairs against the walls. Pansy music. And couples dancing and smooching.

First Flame had changed the music and put on a cassette of Vasco Rossi. Then he had started dancing on his own in the middle of the living room, which might have been acceptable if he hadn't started whirling the cat around like a mace, hitting anyone within range.

Not content with that, he had gone and cuffed all the boys round the head while Bacci and Ronca wolfed down crisps, mini-pizzas and soft drinks.

Pierini sat aloof in an armchair, smoking and watching with approval the entertainment his pals were laying on.

'Congratulations, you've brought the whole gang of louts.'

Pierini had turned. Sitting on the arm of the chair was Gloria. Dressed not in her usual jeans and T-shirt but in a short red dress which suited her incredibly well.

'Can't go anywhere on your own, can you?'

Pierini had gaped like an idiot. 'Of course I can . . .'

'Bollocks.' She looked at him with a tarty little smirk that set his guts churning. 'You feel lost if you don't have your goons tagging along.'

Pierini didn't know what to say.

'Can you dance, at least?'

'No. I don't like dancing,' he had said, taking a can of beer out of the pocket of his leather jacket. 'Want some?'

'Thanks,' she had said.

Pierini knew that Gloria was a tough one. She wasn't like all the other little bimbos who fled like a herd of deer as soon as he approached. She knew how to drink a beer. Looked you straight in the eye. But she was also the shittiest rich kid in the whole area. And he hated rich kids. He'd passed her the beer.

Gloria had made a face. 'Ugh, it's warm . . .' and then asked him: 'Do you want to dance?'

That was why he liked her.

She wasn't shy. A girl asking you to dance was unheard of in Ischiano Scalo. 'I told you I don't like it . . .' Actually he wouldn't at all have minded doing a slow dance with that little girl and smooching a bit. But he hadn't been lying, he was a lousy dancer and he didn't want to look stupid.

So it was out of the question. Period.

'What's the matter, are you scared?' she had persisted, remorselessly. 'Scared they'll take the piss out of you because you're dancing?'

Pierini had glanced around.

Flame was upstairs and Bacci and Ronca were in a corner laughing amongst themselves and it was dark and that beautiful song, *Clear Dawn*, was playing – just right for dancing cheek to cheek.

He had put the cigarette in his mouth, stood up and, as if it were something he had always done, slipped one hand round her waist and the other in his jeans pocket and started dancing, swaying his hips. He had held her close and smelled her sweet scent. A scent of cleanliness, of bath foam.

Shit, did he like dancing with Gloria.

'You see you can do it?' she had whispered in his ear, making the hairs on his neck bristle. He hadn't replied. His heart was thumping.

'Do you like this song?'

'Yeah.' He must go out with her, he had told himself. She was made for him.

'It's about a little girl who's always alone . . .'

'I know,' Pierini had mumbled and all at once she had started rubbing her nose on his neck and he had almost fainted. A painful erection had risen in his jeans and with it an irresistible desire to kiss her.

And he would have done so if the lights hadn't come on.

The police!

Flame had set about Caterina's father with the dead cat, so they'd had to run for it. He'd left her there and fled, without even saying goodbye, see you, nothing.

Afterwards, in the bar, he had fumed with rage. He could have killed that lunkhead Flame for ruining everything. He had gone home and shut himself in his room to turn the memory of that dance over and over in his mind like a precious stone.

Next day, outside school, he had walked decisively up to Gloria and asked her: 'Do you want to go out with me?'

And she had first looked at him as if she'd never seen him before, then burst out laughing. 'Are you crazy? I'd rather go out with Alatri (he was the priest who taught religion). Stick to your cronies.'

He had grabbed her roughly by the arm (*why did you want to dance with me then?*), but she had wriggled free. 'Don't you dare touch me, okay?'

And Pierini had stood there, unable even to slap her face.

That's why he couldn't stand Moroni, the bosom pal of little miss I'm-the-only-girl-who's-got-one.

What the hell did a girl who was so

so what?

. . . beautiful (how beautiful she was! He dreamed of her at night. He imagined taking off that little red dress, then her knickers, and at last being able to see her naked. And he would touch her all over as if she were a doll. He'd never tire of looking at her, of inspecting her all over because, he was certain, she was perfect. In every part of her body. *Those small tits and those nipples that you can glimpse behind her T-shirt and her navel and those few blond hairs underneath her armpits and her long legs and her sparsely haired pussy with untidy curls as fair and soft as rabbit's fur . . . Stop!*) see in a little nerd like that?

He couldn't stop thinking about her, and couldn't think about her without getting cramp in his stomach, without wanting to punch her in the face for the way she'd treated him: like shit.

And that little tart liked a boy who didn't say anything when you punched him, didn't complain, didn't ask for mercy and didn't cry, like all the others, but stood there motionless, and looked at you with those eyes . . . those poor-little-puppydog, Jesus-of-Nazareth eyes, odious eyes that reproached you.

One of those people who believe that crap the priests put around: if anybody hits you, turn the other cheek.

Try hitting me and I'll ram your nose back through your face.

The blood rose to his head when he saw him sitting good as gold at his desk drawing shitty little pictures while everyone else in the class was yelling and bombarding each other with the blackboard-rubber.

How he wished he could turn into a bloodhound so that he could pursue him across valleys, rivers and mountains and flush him out like a hare and watch him grovelling and floundering in the mud. Oh yeah, then he would kick him and break his ribs and see if he didn't ask for mercy and forgiveness and finally become like any other kid, not some kind of fucking extraterrestrial.

Once, in the summer, little Pierini had found a large tortoise in the vegetable patch. It was eating the lettuce and carrots quite calmly, as if it were in its own home. He'd picked it up and taken it into the garage, where his father's working table was. He'd clamped it in the vice. He'd waited patiently till the animal put out its legs and head and started waving them about and then, with the hammer, the big one that was used for breaking bricks, he had hit it right in the middle of its shell.

Stok.

It had been like breaking an Easter egg, but much, much harder. A long crack had opened between the plates of the carapace. And a damp reddish pulp had oozed out. But the tortoise didn't seem to have noticed, it kept wiggling its legs and head and hanging there mute between the jaws of the vice.

Pierini had moved closer and searched for something in its eyes. But he had found nothing. Nothing. Neither pain, nor astonishment, nor hatred.

Nothing whatsoever.

Two stupid little black balls.

He had struck it again and again until his arm was too sore to continue. The tortoise lay with its carapace turned into a jigsaw puzzle of bones dripping blood, but its eyes were the same. Staring. Stupid. With no secrets. He had removed it from the vice and put it on the ground, in the garage, and it had started walking off, leaving a trail of blood behind it, and he had started screaming.

Yes, that was it, Dickhead was just like that tortoise.

13

Graziano Biglia woke up at about seven o'clock in the evening, still feeling bloated after the enormous lunch. He took a couple of Alka-Seltzers and decided to spend the rest of the evening at home. Just lazing around.

His mother brought him tea and pastries in the sitting room.

Graziano picked up the remote control, but then told himself he could do something better, something he was going to have to start doing regularly, since country life had a lot of long pauses that had to be filled and he didn't want to become a couch potato. He could read a book.

The library of the Biglia household did not offer a wide choice.

The *Animal Encyclopaedia*. A biography of Mussolini by Mack Smith. A collection of essays by Enzo Biagi. Three cookery books. And Luciano De Crescenzo's *History of Greek Philosophy*.

He opted for De Crescenzo.

He sat down on the sofa and read a couple of pages, then it occurred to him that Erica hadn't called yet.

He consulted his watch.

Strange.

When he'd left Rome that morning, Erica, still half asleep, had said she would call him as soon as the audition was over.

And the audition had been at ten o'clock in the morning.

It should have finished a long time ago.

He tried her mobile.

The number was not available at present.

How come? She always keeps it on.

He tried ringing her at home, but there was no reply there either.

Where can she have got to?

He tried to concentrate on Greek philosophy.

14

They were fifty metres from the school.

Their bikes dumped in a ditch, the four of them were crouching behind a laurel hedge.

It was cold. The wind had got up and was shaking the black trees. Pietro huddled into his denim jacket and blew on his hands to warm them.

'Well, how shall we do it? Who's going to put the chain on?' asked Ronca in a low voice.

'We could draw lots,' suggested Bacci.

'No lots.' Pierini lit a cigarette and turned to Pietro. 'What did we bring Dickhead for?'

Dickhead . . .

'Right. It's Dickhead who's got to put the chain on. A shitty, puky little Dickhead who's got no guts and has to go home to his darling mama,' commented Ronca contentedly.

There it is.

There's the truth.

The reason they'd made him come.

All that song and dance because they were too scared to chain up the gate themselves.

In films the villains are usually exceptional people. They fight the hero, challenge him to duels and do incredible things like blowing up bridges, kidnapping the families of decent folk, robbing banks. Sylvester Stallone had never come up against villains who pussyfooted around like these three cowards.

This made Pietro feel better.

He'd show them. 'Give me the chain.'

'Watch out for Italo. He's crazy. He'll shoot you. He'll fill your bum so full of holes you'll have six arseholes all spurting out squit,' Ronca guffawed.

Pietro took no notice. He pushed his way through the hedge and made for the school.

They're scared of Italo. Always acting so tough and they don't even dare put a padlock on a gate. Well, I'm not scared.

He concentrated on what he had to do.

The sombre black silhouette of the school seemed to be floating in the mist. Via Righi was deserted at night, because there were no houses there. Only a neglected public garden, with some rusty swings and a fountain full of mud and reeds, the Segafredo Bar with graffiti on its shutters and a streetlamp that crackled, making an irritating buzz. No cars passed.

The only danger was that lunatic Italo. The cottage he lived in was right next to the gate.

Pietro stopped, with his back against the wall. He opened the padlock. Now he only had to crawl as far as the gate, shut it and go back again. It was easy, he knew, but his heart didn't agree, he felt as if he had a steam engine inside his chest.

A noise behind him.

He turned. The three bastards had moved closer and were watching from behind the hedge. Ronca was waving his arms, urging him to get on with it.

He dropped flat and crawled along on his hands and knees. He held the key between his teeth and the chain in his hand. The ground was covered with mud, rotting leaves and soggy paper. He was getting his jacket and trousers filthy.

From that position it wasn't easy to tell whether Italo was at the window. But he noticed that no light was visible through the cracks in the blinds, not even the bluish glare of the television. He held his breath.

There was total silence.

He steeled himself, stood up and with an agile leap caught hold of the gate and scaled it to the top. He looked past the house, to where Italo kept his car, the 131 Mirafiori, and . . .

It's not there. The 131's not there.

Italo's not there! He's not there!

He must be in Orbano, or more likely he'd gone to the farm, which was not far from Pietro's house.

He jumped down from the gate, coolly wound the chain round the lock and closed the padlock.

Done it!

He sauntered back more casually and coolly than Fonzie and feeling an almost irresistible desire to whistle. But instead he pushed his way through the branches and entered the garden to look for the chickenshits.

15

The panda has a fairly simple diet: bamboo leaves for breakfast, bamboo leaves for lunch, bamboo leaves for dinner. But if it doesn't get those leaves it's in the shit, in a month it'll die of hunger. Since bamboo is hard to come by, only the richest zoos can afford to keep the great black-and-white bear among their prison populations.

It's a classic example of a specialist species, a kind of animal that has been driven by evolution into a tiny ecological niche where its existence is precariously poised on a delicate relationship with the environment. You only have to remove one element (bamboo leaves for the panda, eucalyptus leaves for the koala, algae for the Galapagos marine iguana, and so on) and for these creatures extinction is certain.

The panda doesn't adapt, it dies.

Italo Miele, the father of Bruno Miele, Graziano's policeman friend, was, in a sense, a specialist species. The caretaker of the Michelangelo Buonarroti school was the classic kind of guy who, if you didn't give him a dish of bucatini with plenty of sauce and didn't let him go with prostitutes, would gutter out like a candle.

That evening, too, he was endeavouring to satisfy his vital needs.

He was sitting, napkin tucked into his collar, at a table in the Old Wagon and guzzling down the speciality of the house, sea-and-mountain pappardelle. A concoction of boar-gravy, peas, cream and mussels.

As happy as a pearl in its oyster. Or rather, as a meatball in its tomato sauce.

Miele, Italo. Weight: one hundred and twenty kilos.

Height: one metre sixty centimetres.

It must be said, however, in the interests of accuracy, that his fat was not flabby, it was as firm as a hard-boiled egg. He had chubby hands with short fingers. And that bald head, as large and round as a watermelon, drooped between his rounded shoulders and made him look like a monstrous Russian doll.

He was a diabetic, but refused to accept the fact. The doctor had told him he must follow a balanced diet, but he took no notice. He was also lame. His right calf was as round and hard as a bread roll and under the skin his veins twisted, swollen, one over the other, forming a tangle of blue worms.

There were days, and this was one of them, when the pain was so acute that his foot lost all feeling, a numbness rose up to his groin and Italo's only wish was to have that damned leg amputated.

But the Old Wagon's pappardelle put him at peace with the world again.

The Old Wagon was an enormous place, built in rustic Mexican style, fenced round with prickly pear and cattle-bones and situated on the Aurelia, a few kilometres beyond Antiano. It was also a motel, a disco, pub and sandwich bar, a billiard room, a service station, an electrical repair workshop and a supermarket. Whatever you were looking for, you would find it there, or something very like it.

Its main clientele was truck drivers and passing travellers. That was one of the reasons why it was Italo's favourite restaurant.

No one to bother you, no one you have to say hallo to. The food's good and the prices are reasonable.

Another reason was that it was a stone's throw from the Meat Market.

The Meat Market, as the locals called it, was a stretch of asphalted road about five hundred metres long which branched off the Aurelia and petered out in the middle of the fields. In the intentions of some megalomaniac engineer it was going to be the new sliproad for Orvieto. But for the moment it was just the Meat Market.

Open twenty-four hours a day, three hundred and sixty-five days a year, no holidays, no rest days. The prices were moderate and fixed. Credit cards and cheques not accepted.

The hookers, all Nigerian, waited at the roadside sitting on stools, and when it rained or the sun was too hot, they would get out their umbrellas.

A hundred metres away, on the main road, there was also a van that made the famous Bomber sandwich, filled with char-grilled chicken, cheese, pickled aubergines and peppers.

But Italo wasn't satisfied with the Bomber, and once a week he gave himself a treat, his evening de luxe.

First the Meat Market, then the Old Wagon. An unbeatable combination. Once he had tried inverting the order. First the Old Wagon and then the Meat Market.

A disaster. He had felt sick. While he was humping away the sea-and-mountain pappardelle had come up again and he had vomited all over the dashboard of his car.

About a year ago Italo had stopped switching prostitutes and become a regular client of Alima. He would arrive at seven on the dot and she would be waiting in her usual place. He'd let her into the 131 and they would park behind a billboard nearby. The whole thing lasted about ten minutes, so by eight o'clock they were already at their table.

Alima, it must be admitted, was no Miss Africa.

Rather plump, she had a bum the size of a mooring buoy, cellulite and two flat empty boobs. On her head she wore a stringy blond doll's wig. Italo had seen more attractive whores, but Alima was, to use his own words, *a human suction-pump*. When she gave head, she really applied herself. He couldn't swear to it, but he was pretty sure she enjoyed it.

Sometimes he had screwed her, but both of them being on the large side (and there was the problem of his lame leg too), they were a tight fit inside the 131 and it became more of an ordeal than a pleasure. Besides, she charged fifty thousand for that.

This way it was perfect.

Thirty thousand for the blow job and thirty thousand for dinner.

Two hundred and forty thousand lire a month well spent.

You've got to taste the high life once a week, otherwise what's the point of living?

Italo had also made a discovery. Alima was quite a gourmet. She loved Italian cooking. And she was really good company. He found her easier to talk to than his wife, whom he'd had nothing to say to for twenty years or more. So he took her to the Old Wagon, and to hell with the local gossip.

That evening, strangely, they were sitting at a different table than usual, by the window that overlooked the Aurelia. The headlights of the cars would flash for a moment in the restaurant and disappear, swallowed up by the darkness.

Italo had in front of him a dish piled high with pappardelle, Alima one of orecchiette with ragù.

'What I'd like to know is why your Allah won't let you eat pork and drink wine, but allows you to be a whore,' said Italo, continuing to chew. 'I think it's stupid, myself. I don't say you ought to stop being a whore but, since you don't exactly live a saintly life, at least you could treat yourself to a nice pork chop and a couple of sausages. Eh?'

Alima no longer even bothered to answer.

He had asked her that question a million times. At first she had tried to explain to him that Allah understood everything and that she didn't mind doing without wine and pork, but that she couldn't not be a prostitute, because she sent the money to her children, in Africa. But Italo would just nod and the next time ask her exactly the same question again. Alima had realised that he didn't really expect a reply and that the question had a purely ritual function, like saying enjoy your meal.

But that evening she was in for a shock.

'How's the ragù? Is it good?' asked Italo contentedly. He had already practically finished a bottle of Morellino di Scansano.

'Good, good!' said Alima. She had a nice broad smile, which opened over regular white teeth.

'Good, is it? You know that's not beef ragù but sausage meat?'

'I don't understand.'

'There's . . . po . . . pork in that.' Italo talked with his mouth full, pointing to Alima's plate with his fork.

'Pork?' Alima didn't understand.

'Pork. Pig.' Italo grunted to make his meaning clearer.

The penny dropped. 'You've made me eat pork?'

'That's right.'

Alima stood up. Her eyes were suddenly blazing. She started shouting. 'You shit. All shit. I never want to see you again. You're disgusting.'

The diners around them stopped eating and directed fish-like gazes at them.

'Keep your voice down. Everyone's looking at us. Sit down. It's a joke, come on.' Italo talked in a low voice, cowering low over the table.

Alima was shaking and stammering and fighting back tears. 'I knew you were all shit and that you . . . but I thought . . . FUCK YOU!' She spat in the plate, picked up her handbag and fur coat and waddled like an angry pachyderm towards the door.

Italo rushed after her and grabbed her by the arm. 'Come on now, come back. I'll give you thirty thousand lire.'

'Let me go. Shit.'

'It was a joke . . .'

'LET ME GO!' Alima broke free.

Now the whole restaurant had gone quiet.

'All right, I'm sorry. I'm sorry. Okay. You're right. I'll eat the sausage. You take my pappardelle. It's got mussels and wild boa . . . which is not a pi . . .'

'Fuck off.' Alima went out and Italo looked round and, seeing that everyone was looking at him, tried to regain his self-possession, puffed out his chest, stretched out his hand and yelled in the direction of the door. 'Well you know what I say to you, then? Fuck off yourself!' He turned round and went back to the table to finish his meal.

16

'Here you are.' Pietro held out the keys.

The three of them were sitting on swings.

'I've done it. Here you are.' But nobody got up.

'Didn't Italo see you?' asked Bacci.

'No. He's not there.' Pietro felt an intense, satisfying pleasure as he said it, like having a pee that you've been holding back for a long time.

What a bunch of cowards you are. All that fuss and he's not even at home. Aren't you great. How he would have loved to be able to say that to them.

'What do you mean he's not there? Bullshit!' Pierini accused him.

'He's not there, I swear he's not! The 131's not there. I looked . . . Now can I go ho . . . ?

He hadn't even finished the sentence when he flew backwards and crashed violently on the ground.

He couldn't breathe. He lay there in the mud and squirmed. The blow on his back. That was what had done it. He opened his mouth wide, eyes goggling, tried to breathe but it was useless. As if he were suddenly on Mars.

It had happened in a flash.

Pietro hadn't even had time to react when he'd seen him there in front of him.

Pierini had jumped off the swing and hurled his full weight against him, pushing him back like a door that had to be opened.

'Can you go where? Home? You're going nowhere.'

Pietro was dying, or at least that was what it felt like. If he didn't start breathing again in three seconds, he would die. He made a big effort. He sucked. Sucked. Wheezing faintly. And at last he began to breathe again. Just a little. Enough to stop him dying. His chest muscles had finally decided to collaborate and he took in and threw out air. Bacci and Ronca were laughing.

Pietro wondered if he too would one day be able to become like Pierini. Knock someone over with such malice.

He often dreamed that he was punching the waiter of the Station Bar. But although he put all his strength and rage into it and dealt him the most violent blows in the face, he didn't even hurt him.

Will I ever have the courage? Because it takes a lot of courage to knock someone down and punch them in the face.

'Are you sure, Dickhead?' Pierini was sitting on the swing again. He seemed not even to have noticed that Pietro had been on the point of choking.

'Are you sure?' repeated Pierini.

'What about?'

'Are you sure the 131's not there?'

'Yes. I swear it's not.'

Pietro tried to get up, but Bacci jumped on him. He sat on his stomach, all sixty kilos of him.

'Hey, it's really comfortable here . . .' Bacci pretended to be in an armchair. He crossed his legs, leant back, used Pietro's legs as the arms of the chair. And Ronca jumped around him happily. 'Fart on him! Go on, Bacci, fart on him!'

'I'm try-ing! I'm try-ing!' moaned Bacci. That fat, moonlike face went purple with the effort.

'Stink him out! Gas him!'

Pietro struggled to get free, but only succeeded in tiring himself. He couldn't move Bacci one millimetre, he could hardly breathe and the acrid smell of that barrel's sweat sickened him.

Keep calm. The more you struggle the worse it is. Keep calm.

What kind of situation had he got himself into?

He should have been home by now. In bed. Warm and snug. Reading the book about dinosaurs that Gloria had lent him.

'In that case, in we go.' Pierini got off the swing.

'In where?' asked Bacci.

'Into the school.'

'How?'

'Piece of cake. We climb over the gate and get in through the girls' toilets, by the volleyball court. The window doesn't close properly. You only have to push it,' explained Pierini.

'It's true,' confirmed Ronca. 'Once I looked through it and saw Alberti crapping. Pooh, what a stink . . . Yeah, let's go in. It'll be cool.'

'But what if we get caught? What if Italo comes back? I . . .' said Bacci worriedly.

'You nothing. He won't. Stop bleating.'

'And what are we going to do with Dickhead? Beat him up?'

'He's coming with us.' They pulled him to his feet.

His chest and ribs hurt and he was covered in mud.

He didn't try to escape. It would have been useless anyway.

Pierini had decided.

Better to follow them and keep quiet.

17

Graziano Biglia had abandoned De Crescenzo's history of philosophy and was trying to watch a video of the Italy–Brazil match from 1982. But he couldn't work up any enthusiasm, he kept wondering where Erica could have got to.

He tried calling her for the umpteenth time.

No luck.

Still that odious recorded voice.

A faint anxiety was tickling, like a goose-feather, the half-digested remains of the fettuccine in hare sauce, the triple helping of cold cuts and the crème caramel which were lying in his stomach and which, in response, had begun to churn around.

It's a nasty thing, anxiety.

Everyone, sooner or later, has experienced this disagreeable emotional state. Usually it's only transitory and is caused by external factors, but sometimes it generates itself spontaneously, for no apparent reason. In some individuals it even becomes chronic. There are people who live with it all their lives. Some manage to work, sleep, have social relationships, with this feeling of oppression inside them. Others are overwhelmed by it, can't even get out of bed and need drugs to alleviate it.

Anxiety depresses you, it drains and disturbs you, makes you feel as if an invisible pump were sucking out of you the air you are desperately trying to swallow. The word 'anxiety' derives from the Latin verb *angere*, 'to squeeze', and that is exactly what it does: it squeezes your bowels and paralyses your diaphragm, it's an unpleasant massage of your lower belly and is often accompanied by a sense of foreboding.

Graziano had a tough hide, impervious to many of the common anxieties of modern life, and he had an intestine capable of digesting a stone, but now, with every passing minute, his apprehension grew and turned into panic.

That silence seemed to him a very bad sign.

He tried watching a Lee Marvin film. It was even worse than the soccer match.

He rang her again. No reply.

He must calm down. What was that fear now?

She hasn't phoned you yet. So what? Are you afraid that . . .

He banished that odious little voice.

Erica's always got her head in the clouds. She's a scatterbrain. She's probably gone shopping with her mobile uncharged.

As soon as she got home she was bound to call him.

18

'"You bastard, you make me sick." How dare you speak to me like that? And what a fool you made me look. Everyone staring at me like that . . . What are you all gawping at? Why don't you mind your own business? People are so damn nosy around here. And anyway, come on, I only played a little practical joke on her. Where's the harm in that? Even if the priest put a bit of white nougat in my mouth instead of the Host, I wouldn't care. She's a real cow. And she's too sensitive. Okay, okay, I was wrong. I said, I WAS WRONG. I didn't mean it. I'm sorry, for Christ's sake!' Italo Miele was driving and talking to himself.

That bitch had ruined his dinner. After she'd gone he'd lost his appetite. He'd left his second course of sea bass all'acqua pazza unfinished. To make things worse, he'd downed another litre of Morellino and was now thoroughly pissed. He was driving along with his nose against the windscreen and had to keep wiping away the condensation with his hand.

Everything about him felt heavy: his head, his eyelids, his breath.

'Where can she have got to? The pigheaded bitch . . .'

He was looking for her, but he didn't know exactly what he wanted to tell her. On the one hand he wanted to apologise and on the other he wanted to put her in her place.

He had gone back to the Meat Market. He had asked the other whores, but none of them had seen her.

He turned onto the coast road, which ran along a ridge parallel to the railway line. With the darkness a cold north wind had risen. In the sky the clouds had shredded and were chasing each other with a rolling motion and the waves on the beach had white plumes of foam.

He turned on the heater.

'. . . Oh well, I give up. I've done my best. Now what? Back to school, or home to the farm?'

He suddenly remembered that he'd promised his wife that he'd change the lock on the door but hadn't done it. He had to replace it every six months, otherwise the old bat couldn't sleep.

'Now I'll never hear the end of it. She'll go on about it all night . . . Tomorrow. I'll change the lock tomorrow. I'm going back to school.'

For the past two years Ida Miele had lived in constant fear of burglars.

One night, when Italo was at the school, a van had stopped in front of the farmhouse. Three men had emerged, smashed the kitchen window and climbed into the house. They had started collecting all the electrical appliances and furniture and putting it in the van. Ida, who slept upstairs, had been awoken by the noise.

Who could it be?

There was nobody at home. Her son was in Brindisi doing his

military service, her daughter was at Forte dei Marmi working as a waitress. It must be Italo, he must have decided to come home for the night.

But what on earth was he doing?

Had he decided to rearrange the kitchen furniture at three o'clock in the morning? Was he out of his mind?

In nightdress and slippers, without her false teeth and trembling like a leaf, she had gone downstairs. 'Italo? Italo, is that you? What are you do . . . ?' She had entered the kitchen and . . .

All at once, a man with a balaclava on his head had popped out from behind the door like a jack-in-a-box and shouted in her ear: 'Wah!'

Poor Ida had collapsed with a heart attack. Italo had found her next morning still lying there, next to the door, more dead than alive and freezing cold.

Since that night she had never entirely recovered her wits.

The experience had aged her twenty years. She had lost her hair. She hated being alone in the house. She saw black men everywhere. And she refused to go out after sunset. But that was the least of it, the worst thing was that now she talked obsessively of ultrasonic and infrared burglar alarms, of the Beghelli Lifesaver, of telephonic devices that automatically called the carabinieri and of armoured doors ('For goodness' sake, why don't you go and ask Antonio Ritucci for a job, he'd hire you on the spot,' Italo had said to her once in exasperation. Antonio Ritucci was the burglar-alarm specialist in Orbano).

Italo knew perfectly well who they were, those three men who had addled his wife's brain and destroyed his peace of mind.

Them.

The Sardinians.

Only the Sardinians would break into your house like that, not giving a damn about who's inside, and steal everything. Not even the gipsies would have stolen a broken cooker. Yes, I'd bet my daughter's life it was them.

If the people of Ischiano Scalo now lived in fear, with bars on their windows, afraid to go out at night and terrified of being kidnapped or raped, in Italo Miele's modest opinion it was all down to the Sardinians.

'They came here without permission. They got their filthy hands on our land. Their sickly sheep graze our meadows and produce that foul pecorino cheese. Heathen savages. Robbers, bandits, drug dealers. They steal. They think this is their land. And they've filled the schools with their little brats. They've got to go.' How often he had said this to the people in the bar!

And those feeble old codgers who sat round the tables would agree with him, they'd let him talk and swell up like a turkey, they'd say that they ought to organise patrols and catch them but then, in the end, would do nothing. And he'd seen how as he was leaving they would nudge each other and laugh.

And he'd discussed it with his son, too.

The great policeman!

All he did was talk, polish his pistol and stroll round the village like Christ come down from heaven. He'd never caught a single Sardinian.

Italo didn't know who was worse: those gutless old fools, that idiot of a son of his, his wife or the Sardinians.

He couldn't take any more of Ida.

He hoped she would go completely off her head, so that he could bundle her into the car and take her off to the loony bin, then this whole business would be over and he'd be able to start living a normal life again. He felt no remorse for his extramarital activities. That old bag was only good for sausage meat now, and he, though well over sixty and lame in one leg, had more energy in his body than many a man half his age.

Italo stopped at the Ischiano Scalo level crossing.

Oh, to find the barrier up just once in my life!

He switched off the engine, lit a cigarette, laid his head back, closed his eyes and waited for the train.

'Damned Sardinians . . . How I hate you. How I hate you . . . God, am I drunk . . .' he murmured, and he would have fallen asleep had the pendolino, racing towards the North, not whooshed past him. The barrier lifted. Italo switched on the ignition again and drove into the village.

Four dark streets. Silence. Few lights in the low houses. Nobody about. The whole life of Ischiano was in the bar-cum-tobacconist's and the games arcade.

He didn't stop.

His packet of cigarettes was still half full. And he had no wish to play tressette and talk about Persichetti's hound or the next football coupon. No, he was tired and only wanted to climb into bed, with the boiler turned up to maximum, the Maurizio Costanzo Show on TV and a hot water bottle.

Those two little rooms beside the school were a godsend.

It was then that he saw her.

'Alima!'

She was walking southwards along the Aurelia.

'There you are. I've found you at last.'

19

It was true.

As usual Pierini was right. The toilet window didn't close properly. You only had to push it.

Pierini entered first, then Ronca and Pietro and lastly Bacci, who could barely squeeze through. It took two of them to pull him inside.

Inside the toilet you couldn't see a thing. It was cold and there was a pungent smell of ammonia-based disinfectant.

Pietro kept to one side, leaning against the damp tiles.

'Don't switch on the lights. We might be seen.' The trembling flame of the cigarette lighter drew a half moon on Pierini's face. In the darkness his eyes shone like a wolf's. 'Follow me. And keep quiet. For Pete's sake.'

Who's talking?

No one dared to ask him where they were going.

The Section B corridor was so dark it was as if someone had

painted it black. They walked in Indian file. Pietro trailed his hand along the wall.

The doors were all shut.

Pierini opened the door of their classroom.

The pale moonlight entered lazily through the large windows and tinged everything with yellow. The chairs, neatly placed on top of the desks. The crucifix. At the back, on a shelf, a cage containing some curled-up hamsters. A rubber plant. A poster of the human skeleton.

The four of them stood there by the door, spellbound. So empty and so silent, it didn't seem like their classroom.

They went on.

Silent and fearful, like profaners of holy places.

Pierini led the line, showing the way with his lighter.

The footsteps echoed hollowly, but if the four boys stopped and stood still without talking, beneath that apparent peace there were noises, hisses and creaks.

The flush in the boys' toilet dripping. Plip . . . plip . . . plip . . . The ticking of the clock at the end of the corridor. The wind thrusting at the windows. The wood of the cupboards creaking. The radiators muttering. The woodworm eating the teachers' desks. Sounds that didn't exist in daytime.

In Pietro's mind that place had always been inseparable from the people who were in it. One huge creature made up of pupils, teachers and walls. But no, when everyone went away and Italo locked the front door, the school continued to exist, to live. And things came to life and talked to each other.

Like in that fairy tale where the toys (the soldiers who advance in rows, the little cars that race across the carpet, the teddy bear that . . .) come to life as soon as the children leave the room.

They reached the stairs. Opposite, beyond the glass doors, were the headmaster's room, the secretary's office and the main entrance.

Pierini lit the basement stairs that plunged into the darkness. 'Down we go.'

20

'Alima! Where are you going?'

She was walking along the side of the road, not looking at him. 'Leave me alone.'

'Wait, stop for a moment.' Italo had drawn alongside her and stuck his head out of the window.

'Go away.'

'Just for a moment. Please.'

'What do you want?'

'Where are you going?'

'To Civitavecchia.'

'Are you crazy? What do you want to go there for in this weather?'

'I can go wherever I want.'

'Of course you can. But why Civitavecchia?'

She slowed down and looked at him. 'My friends live there, okay? I'm going to hitch a lift at the service station.'

'Stop. Let me get out of the car.'

Alima stopped walking and put her hands on her hips. 'Well? I've stopped.'

'Er . . . I . . . I . . . Oh, hell! What I did was wrong. Here. Look.' He held out a packet wrapped in tinfoil.

'What is it?'

'Some tiramisù. I bought some specially for you at the restaurant. You haven't eaten anything. You like tiramisù, don't you? There's no liqueur in it, either. It's really good.'

'I'm not hungry.' But she took it.

'Try some and you'll finish it, you'll see. Or you could have it tomorrow, for breakfast.'

Alima dipped in a finger and brought it to her mouth.

'What's it like?'

'Good.'

'Listen. Why don't you come and spend the night at my house? In the cottage. It's nice there. There's a comfortable sofa bed. It's warm. I've got some peaches in syrup, too.'

'At your house?'

'Yes. Come on, we can watch television, Maurizio Costanzo. Next to each . . .'

'I'm not fucking you. You make me sick.'

'Who wants to fuck? Not me. I swear. Seriously, that's not what I want. We'll sleep.'

'And what happens tomorrow morning?'

'I'll take you to Antiano. Early, though. If I get caught I'll be in trouble.'

'What time?'

'Five o'clock.'

'All right, then,' said Alima.

21

Pierini knew exactly where he was going.

To the technical education room. Where there was a big twenty-eight-inch Philips TV and a Sony VHS video recorder.

That had been his objective ever since he had known that Italo was out.

The video-didactic equipment (that's what they called it) was mostly used by the science mistress for showing her pupils documentaries.

The savannah. The wonders of the Great Barrier Reef. The secrets of water, and so on.

But every now and then the Italian teacher used it too.

Miss Palmieri had persuaded the school to buy a set of videos about the Middle Ages, and every year she showed them to the second form.

In October it had been 2B's turn.

She had sat the kids down in front of the screen and Italo had started the cassette.

Federico Pierini couldn't care two hoots about the Middle Ages, and so, as soon as the lights had gone out, he'd sneaked out and gone to play volleyball with the third form. At the end of the lesson he had returned, careful not to be seen, and had sat down, all hot and sweaty.

The next week the second episode was scheduled and Pierini had arranged another match. This time he had been caught.

'Please listen carefully, children, and take notes. And you, Pierini, will write a report at home – let's say five pages long – since you preferred to sneak off and play last time. And if you don't bring it to me tomorrow, you'll get a suspension,' Miss Palmieri had said.

'But Miss . . .' Pierini had tried to object.

'No buts. This time I mean it.'

'Please, Miss, I can't do it today. I have to go to hospital . . .'

'Oh, you poor little thing! Would you mind telling us what major health problem you are suffering from? What was your excuse last time? That you had to go to the oculist's? And then I saw you in the piazza playing football. Or what about the time you told me you hadn't done your homework because you'd had a renal cholic? When you don't even know what a renal cholic is. At least try to be a bit more imaginative when you tell lies.'

But Pierini, that day, was telling the truth.

In the afternoon he had to go to Civitavecchia hospital to see his mother, who was in bed with stomach cancer and who had telephoned him complaining that he never went to see her, and he had promised her he would go.

And now that redheaded bitch dared to call him a liar and make fun of him in front of the class. Being made fun of was something he couldn't stand.

'Well, why do you have to go to hospital?'

And Pierini with a mournful expression had replied: 'Well, Miss . . . you see, the trouble is, whenever I watch documentaries on the Middle Ages it gives me a bad case of the runs.'

The whole class had burst out laughing (Ronca had rolled on the floor clutching his stomach) and he had been sent to see the head. Then he'd had to stay at home all afternoon to write the summary.

And when his father had come home he had given him a thrashing for not going to the hospital.

He didn't care about the thrashing. Didn't even feel it. But he did care about not keeping his promise.

And then, in November, his mother had died and Miss Palmieri had told him she was sorry and that she hadn't known his mother was ill.

You can stuff your apologies.

From that day on Pierini had stopped studying Italian and doing his homework. Whenever Miss Palmieri was in the classroom, he would clap on his headphones and put his feet up on the desk.

She said nothing, pretended not to see him, never tested him on his homework. And when he stared at her, she'd lower her eyes.

Not content with that, Pierini had played a series of amusing little tricks on her. Punctured the tyres of her Y10. Burnt the register. Thrown a stone and smashed a window of her house.

And he was sure she knew he'd done it, but she didn't say anything. She was shit scared.

Pierini was constantly challenging her and came out the winner every time. Having a hold over her gave him a strange pleasure. An intense, sordid, physical elation. It excited him.

He'd get into the bathtub and masturbate, imagining that he was fucking the redhead. He'd tear her clothes off. Ram his cock in her mouth. Stick enormous dildos in her vagina. Punch her in the face and she'd enjoy it.

She acted so shy but she was a slut. He knew it.

He had never liked her, but after the video incident, some turbid sensual fantasies had taken root in Federico Pierini's mind which left him frustrated and dissatisfied.

Now he was going to raise the stakes.

And see how the redhead would react.

22

The 131 stopped outside the school gate.

'Here we are. This is the place.' Italo turned off the engine and pointed to his cottage. 'I know it looks like a dump from the outside. But inside it's very cosy.'

'Have you really got some fruit in syrup?' asked Alima, who was beginning to feel hungry.

'Yes. My wife made it with the peaches from my tree.'

Italo wrapped his scarf round his neck and got out of the car. He took the keys from his coat pocket and inserted them in the lock.

'Who put this here?'

There was a chain around the gate.

23

'One!'

On contact with the floor the TV screen exploded with a deafening bang. Millions of fragments scattered everywhere, under the desks, under the chairs, into the corners.

Pierini seized the video recorder, lifted it over his head and hurled it against the wall, reducing it to a mass of metal and printed circuits.

'Two!'

Pietro was stunned.

What on earth had got into him? Why was he smashing everything up?

Ronca and Bacci were standing to one side, watching that force of nature unleash itself.

'Now I'd . . . like to . . . see you . . . show us . . . another fucking video . . . about the . . . fucking Middle Ages,' panted Pierini, in between kicks at the machine.

He's out of his mind. He doesn't realise what he's doing. They'll make him repeat the year for this.

(*And if they find out that you were here with him . . .*)

Oh no, what's he doing now? I don't believe it . . .

He was smashing the hi-fi equipment too.

(*You must do something . . . quickly.*)

Agreed. But what?

(*STOP HIM.*)

If only he were . . .

(*Chuck Norris Bruce Lee Schwarzy Sylvester Stallone*)

. . . bigger and stronger . . . It would be easier.

He had never felt so helpless in his life. He saw his happy school-days coming to an end before his very eyes and couldn't do a thing about it. His mind seized up when he tried to imagine the consequences in terms of suspensions, repeated years, reports to the police. And he felt as if a bread roll was stuck in his gullet.

He went over to Bacci. 'Say something to him. Make him stop, please.'

'What can I say?' muttered Bacci disconsolately.

Meanwhile Pierini continued to vent his fury on what was left of the speakers. Then he turned round and saw something. A crafty smile curled his lip. He walked over to a large metal cupboard containing books, electrical appliances and other material.

What's he up to now?

'Come here, Ronca. Help me. Give me a leg-up.'

Ronca went over and linked his fingers, Pierini planted his right foot on them and hoisted himself up level with the top of the cupboard. With one hand he knocked off a cardboard box, which came open, and a dozen cans of spray paint rolled out.

'Now we'll have some fun!'

24

What silly fool had chained up the gate?

Some stupid little idiot who wants to repeat the year.

Italo fiddled with the chain, not knowing what to do. He was beginning to get tired of these stupid practical jokes.

What's the matter with these kids?

If you told them off, they swore at you and laughed in your face. They had no respect for the teachers, the school, anything. At thirteen years old they were already well on their way towards a future as delinquents and junkies.

It's the parents' fault.

Alima put her head out of the window. 'What's going on, Italo? Why don't you open the gate? It's cold.'

'Just a minute. I'm thinking.'

This time, I swear to God, I'm going to give them hell.

They must be caught and punished, or they'd burn the school down next time.

But how am I going to get in?

He was getting really furious. He felt a rising anger and an almost uncontrollable urge to start smashing the whole place up.

'Italo?'

'Shut up, will you? Can't you see I'm trying to think? Just wait . . .'

'Well, fuck you then! Take me ba . . .'

BANG.

An explosion.

Inside the school.

Muffled but loud.

'What the hell was that? Did you hear it?' stammered Italo.

'What?'

'What do you mean, what? That noise!'

Alima pointed at the school. 'Yes. It came from over there.'

Italo understood. He understood everything.

It was all absolutely, completely and unequivocally clear to him.

'THE SARDINIANS!' He started raving. 'THE BLOODY SARDINIANS!'

Then, realising that he was shouting like a madman, he put his finger to his lips, shambled like an orang utan over to Alima and went on in a low voice. 'Shit, it's the Sardinians. It wasn't the kids who chained up the gate. The Sardinians are in the school.'

Alima looked at him in bewilderment. 'Sardinians?'

'Keep your voice down! The Sardinians. It was them that chained up the gate, don't you see? So that they can loot the place without being disturbed.'

'I don't know . . .' Alima was sitting in the car, finishing the tiramisù. 'Italo, who are the Sardinians?'

'What kind of a stupid question's that? The Sardinians are the Sardinians. But they've made a big mistake. I'll show them this time. You wait here. Don't move.'

'Italo?'

'Quiet! I told you not to talk. Just wait.' Italo limped round the side of the building.

There wasn't a single light on in the school.

It wasn't just my imagination. Alima heard the explosion too.

He went on round.

The cold air slipped down through the neck of his shirt, making his teeth chatter.

Maybe something just fell down. There was a draught and a door slammed. But what about the chain?

But then he saw a dim glow on the back wall of the building. It came from some gratings over the technical education room.

'There they . . .' *are, the Sardinians.*

What should he do? Fetch the police?

He calculated that it would take him at least ten minutes to drive to the police station, another ten to explain to those halfwits that the school was being burgled and another ten to get back. Thirty minutes.

Too long. They'd be well away by then.

No!

He'd have to catch them himself. Catch them red-handed.

At last he would have something to show all those sons of bitches at the Station Bar who made fun of him.

Italo Miele isn't scared of anyone.

The problem was getting over the wall.

He ran to the car, wheezing like one of those air pumps they use for blowing up rubber dinghies. He grabbed Alima by the arm and pulled her out of the car. 'Come on, you've got to help me.'

'Leave me alone. Take me to the Aurelia.'

'Like hell I will. You're going to help me whether you like it or not.' Italo dragged her towards the gate. 'Now crouch down and I'll climb on your shoulders. Then stand up. So I can get over. Crouch down, quick.'

Alima shook her head and stayed put. It was a ridiculous idea. The effort would give her a hernia.

'Crouch down.' Italo had his hands on her shoulders and was pushing her downwards, trying to make her squat.

'No, no, no, I won't!' Alima stiffened up.

'Quiet! Quiet! Get down!' Italo would not give up and tried to climb on her shoulders and make her crouch down at the same time.

'Get down!' Since that didn't work, he started begging her. 'Please, Alima, please. You must help me. Or I'm finished. It's my job to look after the school. I'll be sacked. Thrown out on my ear. Please help me . . .'

Alima breathed out and relaxed her muscles for a moment. Italo was quick to seize the opportunity, he pushed her down and with a leap that belied his bulk mounted her shoulders.

The two of them, one on top of the other, had become a monstrous giant. With two crooked black legs. A body like a two-litre bottle of Coca-Cola. Four arms, and a little head as round as a bowling ball.

Alima, under those one hundred-plus kilos, couldn't control her movements. She staggered this way and that and Italo, on top, swayed backwards and forwards like a rodeo cowboy.

'Hey! Hey! Where are you going? Look out, we'll fall over. The gate's that way. Go forward. Turn round! Turn round!' Italo tried to give her directions.

'I can't . . . do it . . .'

'Be careful, we'll fall. GO! GO! GO FOR GOD'S SAKE!

'I ca . . . Get off. Ge . . .'

Alima caught her foot in a rut and the heel of her shoe snapped. She teetered for a moment, took two more steps, then lost her balance completely and bent double. Italo was thrown forward and to stop himself falling grabbed with both hands at Alima's hair, as if it were the mane of a bucking bronco.

This was not a wise move.

Italo fell flat on his face, open-mouthed, in the mud, both hands still clutching her wig.

Alima ran round the little piazza, screaming and feeling her scalp. He'd torn away quite a bit of her hair along with the wig. But then, seeing him lying there still, face down in the mud, she went over to him. 'Italo? Italo!' She pushed him, rolling him over. 'What's the matter? Are you dead?'

Italo had a mask of mud on his face. He opened his mouth, spluttered, opened his eyes and, jumping up from the ground like a spring, dashed to the 131.

'No, I'm not dead. The Sardinians are.'

He opened the door, freed the handbrake and pushed the car alongside the gate. He climbed the bonnet and up onto the roof. He grasped the points of the railing. And tried to clamber over.

It was no good. He couldn't do it. He didn't have enough strength in his arms to pull himself up.

He tried again, gritting his teeth.

Impossible.

He was puce with the effort and his pulse was throbbing in his ears.

Now you're going to have a heart attack and collapse on the ground and die like a fool for playing the hero.

Although the rational, prudent half of his brain told him to stop what he was doing, get in the car and drive to the police station, the other half, the bloody-minded part, told him not to give up, to try again.

This time, instead of pulling himself up with his hands, Italo stretched out his bad leg and rested it on the edge of the wall. Now it was easier. With an effort that he would never have thought himself capable of, he hoisted himself up, supporting himself on that wasted limb, and found himself spread out like a lion's skin on the roof of his cottage.

He lay there, filling and emptying his lungs, for a couple of minutes, waiting for his galloping heart to slow down.

Getting down was easier. The old wooden ladder he used for pruning the cherry tree was leaning against the wall.

Behind the gate Alima was sitting on the bonnet of the car with her arms folded, muttering angrily to herself.

'Get in the car. I'll be back a moment.' Italo entered the cottage without turning on the lights. He crossed the living room with his arms outstretched and didn't notice the trunk that he used as a table for snacks when he watched TV. He hit the corner of it hard with his good knee. He saw stars. He swallowed the pain, cursed between his teeth and headed, stoically, for the old wardrobe, opened it and rummaged frantically among the clean linen till he felt under his fingertips the reassuring coldness of steel.

The tempered steel of his double-barrelled Beretta.

'Now we'll see . . . You Sardinian bastards. Now we'll see. I'll blast you all the way back to your island, so help me God,' and he hobbled towards the school.

25

PALMIERI STIK YOUR VIDEOS UP YOUR ARSE

This scrawl, in huge red letters, covered the entire back wall of the technical education room. The letters were lopsided, they intertwined with each other like gnarled fingers and were one 'c' short, but the message was clear, unequivocal.

Pierini had written his sentence and now it was the others' turn to express themselves. 'Come on! What are you waiting for, daybreak?' You guys write something!' He gave Bacci a shove. 'What's up, fatso? You look like a bunch of morons, are you all scared?'

Bacci had the same look of despair as when his mother took him to the dentist's.

'Well, what's the matter with you all? Write something! Have you all turned into poofs?' Pierini slammed Bacci against the wall.

Bacci hesitated for a moment, perhaps he would have liked to say something, but then he drew a big swastika.

'Good! Perfect. Now you, Ronca, what are you waiting for?'

Ronca, without waiting for further encouragement, set to work with his spray can:

THE HEADMASTER SUCKS THE DEPUTY HEADMISTRESS'S COCK

Pierini approved. 'Great, Ronca. Now it's your turn.' He went over to Pietro.

Pietro kept his eyes on his shoes. The bread roll in his gullet had become a baguette. He kept shifting the can from one hand to the other as if it were red hot.

Pierini cuffed him on the back of the head.

'Well, Dickhead?'

Nothing.

Another cuff.

'Well?'

I don't want to.

'Well?'

A harder one.

'I don't . . . I don't want to,' he blurted out finally.

'Oh? How come?' Pierini didn't seem surprised.

'I don't . . .'

'Why not?'

'I just don't want to. I don't feel like it . . .'

What could Pierini do to him? At the worst break his leg or his nose or his hand. He wouldn't kill him.

Are you sure?

It couldn't be worse than when, as a child, he had fallen off the roof of the tractor and broken his ankle. Or when his father had beaten him for blunting his screwdriver. *Who gave you permission, eh? Who gave you permission? Will you tell me that? I'll teach you to take things that don't belong to you.* He'd spanked him with the carpet beater. And he hadn't been able to sit down for a week. But it had passed . . .

Go on, then, beat me up and let's get it over with.

He would curl up on the floor. Like a hedgehog. *I'm ready.*

They could hit him till he swelled up like a bagpipe, kick him as hard as they liked, but he wouldn't write anything on that wall.

Pierini walked away and sat on the teacher's chair. 'How much do you want to bet, Dickhead, old pal, that you're going to write something too . . . How much do you want to bet?'

'I'm . . . not . . . writing . . . anything. I told you. You can beat me up, if you want.'

Pierini held the spray can up to the wall. 'What if I put your signature, below this?' he pointed to his composition. 'If I write in great big letters Pietro Moroni. Eh? Eh? What are you going to do then?'

This is too much . . .

How could he be so evil? How? Who had taught him? A person like that will always get the better of you. You can try with all your might but he'll always win.

'Well? What do I do?' Pierini pressed him.

'Go ahead and sign my name then, who cares. I'm not writing anything.'

'Okay. You'll get all the blame. They'll say you wrote all the graffiti. They'll expel you. They'll say YOU smashed everything up.'

The atmosphere in the room had become unbreathable. As if there were a heater turned full on. Pietro's hands were ice cold and his cheeks were burning.

He looked around.

Pierini's malice seemed to drip from everything. From the paint-bedaubed walls. From the yellow neon lights. From the remains of the smashed television.

Pietro went over to the wall.

What can I write?

He tried to think of a drawing or a terrible phrase but it was no good, he just kept seeing a stupid image.

A fish.

A fish he'd seen at Orbano market.

It lay there on the stall, among the crates of calamari and sardines, still alive and gasping, a fish covered in spines and with a huge mouth and bright red gills. A lady had wanted to buy it and had asked the boy to clean it. Pietro had moved closer to the steel sinks. He wanted to see how it was done. The fishmonger's boy had laid down the fish, made a long cut down the middle of its swollen belly and gone away.

Pietro had stood there watching the fish die.

Out of the wound had emerged a pincer, then another and then the rest of a crab. A big, lively green crab which had scuttled away.

But it didn't end there. Another crab, just like the first, had climbed out the fish's belly, then another and another. Loads of them. They ran diagonally across the steel surface looking for somewhere to hide and fell down on the ground and Pietro wanted to tell the boy (*The fish is full of live crabs and they're escaping!*), but he was busy selling mussels at the stall so Pietro had reached out and closed the wound with his hand to stop them getting out. And the fish's swollen belly was teeming with life, full of movement, full of little green legs.

'If you haven't written something in ten seconds flat, I'll do it. Ten, ni . . .'

Pietro tried to banish the image.

'. . . seven, six . . .'

He took a deep breath, pointed the spray gun at the wall, pressed the top and wrote:

ITALO'S GOT FISHY FEET

His mind conceived this sentence.

And Pietro, without a moment's thought, transcribed it onto the wall.

26

If someone wearing infrared goggles had seen Italo Miele advancing in the dark, he might have mistaken him for the Terminator.

With that shotgun clutched in his hands, his blank gaze and his stiff leg, the caretaker moved like an android.

Italo passed the secretary's office and the teachers' common room.

His mind was clouded with rage and hatred.

Hatred for the Sardinians.

What was he going to do to them?

Kill them, drive them out, lock them in a classroom, what?

He wasn't quite sure.

But it didn't matter.

At that moment he had only one aim: to catch them red-handed.

The rest would come later.

Experienced hunters say that African buffaloes are terrifying beasts. You need real guts to face one when it's angry. It makes an easy target – even a child couldn't miss. It's huge and it just stands there, calmly chewing the cud on the savannah, but if you shoot at it and don't kill it outright you'd better have prepared yourself a den to hide in, a tree to climb up, a strongroom to lock yourself in, a grave in the cemetery to be buried in.

A wounded buffalo could rip apart a Range Rover with a couple of twists of its horns. It's blind and furious and has only one desire: to destroy you.

And Italo was as mad as an African buffalo.

In its rage, the caretaker's mind had regressed to a lower stage on the evolutionary scale (the bovine stage, in fact) and naturally tended to focus exclusively on the objective it wanted to attain. The rest – the details, the context – was filed away in a secondary drawer of his brain, so it was only natural that he should have forgotten that Graziella, the caretaker responsible for the second floor, was in the habit of shutting the glass door that separated the stairs from the corridor before she went home.

Italo hit it at top speed, bounced back like a rubber ball, fell to the ground and found himself flat on his back.

Anyone else, after a head-on crash like that, would have fainted, died, screamed with pain. Not Italo. Italo railed at the darkness. 'Where are you? Come on out! Come on out!'

Who was he talking to?

The impact against the door had been so violent he was convinced some Sardinian, lurking in the darkness, had hit him in the face with an iron bar.

Then he realised to his horror that he had collided with the door. He swore and scrambled to his feet, dazed. He didn't know what was going on. Where was the shotgun? His nose hurt badly. He touched it and felt it swelling between his fingers like a crispy pancake in boiling oil. His face was wet with blood.

'Shit, I've broken my nose . . .'

In the darkness he searched for the shotgun. It had slid into a corner. He retrieved it and set off again, even wilder than before.

What a bloody fool I am! he reproached himself. *They might have heard me.*

27

They'd heard him all right.

They'd jumped in the air, all four of them, like champagne corks.

'What happened?' said Ronca.

'Did you hear that? What was it?' said Bacci.

Pierini was disorientated too. 'What could it be?'

Ronca, who was the first to regain his composure, threw aside his spray-can. 'I don't know. Let's get out of here.'

Pushing and shoving, they piled out of the classroom.

In the dark corridor they stood in silence, listening.

Curses could be heard from the floor above.

'It's Italo. It's Italo. Didn't he go home?' whimpered Bacci, addressing Pierini.

No one bothered to answer him.

They must get away. Out of the school. At once. But how? By which route? In the technical education room there was only a small skylight on the ceiling. To the left was the gym. To the right the stairs and Italo.

The gym, Pietro said to himself.

But that was a dead end. The door onto the yard was locked and the windows had iron gratings.

28

Italo descended the stairs, holding his breath.

His nose was puffy and swollen. A trickle of blood ran down onto his lips and he licked it away with the tip of his tongue.

Like an old bear that has been wounded but not beaten, he moved warily and silently, flat against the wall. The shotgun was slippery in his sweating hands. From behind the corner at the bottom of the stairs a golden patch of light spread over the black floor.

The door was open.

The Sardinians were in the technical education room.

He must take them by surprise.

He flicked off the safety catch and took a deep breath.

Go! Now!

He made something resembling a bound and entered the room. He was dazzled by the neon lights.

Eyes closed, he pointed the shotgun at the middle of the room. 'Hands up!'

Slowly he opened them again.

The room was deserted.

There's nobody here . . .

He saw the walls bedaubed with paint. Graffiti. Obscene drawings. He tried to read. His eyes were getting used to the light.

The . . . headmaster su . . . su . . . sucks the deputy headmistress's sock.

He goggled in bewilderment for a moment.

What does it mean?

He didn't understand.

What sock did they mean? He took his glasses out of his jacket pocket and put them on. He read it again. *Oh, I see! The headmaster sucks the deputy headmistress's cock*. He moved on to the next scrawl. *Italo's got what? Feet! Fishy feet.*

'You sons of bitches, I bet your own feet smell a lot worse!' he roared.

Then he saw the other graffiti and on the floor, smashed to pieces, the television and the video recorder.

It couldn't have been the Sardinians.

They didn't give a damn about the headmaster or Miss Palmieri, let alone whether he had smelly feet.

All they cared about was stealing. It must have been some pupils who'd made all this mess.

So much for his dreams of glory.

He had already imagined the scene. The police arriving and finding the Sardinians bound hand and foot and ready for jail and he with his trusty smoking shotgun would have said that he had only been doing his duty. He would have received an official commendation from the headmaster, been patted on the back by his colleagues, stood glasses of wine at the Station Bar, awarded an increase in his pension for the courage and disregard for his own safety that he had shown in the field but now none of that was going to happen.

None of it at all.

This made him even more furious.

He had hurt his knee and broken his nose, and all because of a couple of little hooligans.

They were going to pay dearly for this little stunt. So dearly that they would describe it to their grandchildren as the most traumatic experience of their lives.

But where had they got to?

He turned round. He switched on the lights in the corridor.

The door of the gym was ajar.

An evil smile curled his mouth and he began to laugh, louder and louder. 'Oh well done! What a clever idea to hide in the gym. You want a game of hide-and-seek? All right then, let's play hide-and-seek!' he shouted with all the breath in his body.

29

The green high-jump mattresses were leaned one against the other and tied to the wall-bars.

Pietro had slipped in between them and was standing still with his eyes closed, trying not to breathe.

Italo hobbled round the gym.

Tm sssssssss tm ssssssssss tm ssssssssssssssss.

Footfall and drag, footfall and drag.

I wonder where the others are hiding.

When they had entered the gym, he had hidden in the first place he had found.

'Come on out! Come on! I won't hurt you. Don't worry.'

Never. Never trust Italo.

He was the biggest liar in the world.

He was a bastard. Once, when Pietro was in the first year, he had slipped out of school with Gloria and gone to the bar across the road to buy some croissants. It had taken them a minute, no more. When they came back with their little bag, Italo had caught them. He had confiscated the croissants and dragged the two of them into class, pulling them by the ear. And for two hours afterwards his ear had remained as hot as a radiator. And he was sure Italo had eaten the croissants in the porter's lodge.

'I swear I won't hurt you. Come out. If you come out of your own accord I won't tell the head. We'll wipe the slate clean.'

What if he found Pierini and the others?'

They would be bound to say Pietro was with them and would swear blind that he'd forced them to come in and that it had been him who had smashed the television and written the graffiti . . .

A host of distressing thoughts whirled around in his head and weighed him down, not least the thought of his father, who would flay him alive when he got home (*but will you ever get home?*) because he hadn't shut Zagor up in his kennel and hadn't taken the rubbish to the bin.

He was tired. He must relax.

(*Sleep . . .*)

No!

(*Just for a little while . . . a little while, that's all.*)

How wonderful it would be to go to sleep. He rested his head against the mattress. It was soft and a bit smelly, but that didn't matter. His legs sagged. He could sleep standing up, as horses do, he was sure, squeezed in between those two mattresses. His eyelids drooped. He let himself go. He was on the point of collapsing when he felt the mattresses shaking.

His heart leaped to his mouth.

'Come out! Come out! Come out of there!'

He bit on the filthy material and stifled a scream.

30

He couldn't understand it.

The gym was empty.

Where had they gone?

They must be there, hiding somewhere.

Italo shook the mattresses and used his shotgun as a carpet-beater. 'Come out of there!'

There was no escape for them. The door onto the volleyball court was locked and the door of the equipment room was also lo . . .

Wait a minute, let's see if it really is.

cked.

The wood by the lock was splintered. They had forced it.

He smiled.

He opened the door. Darkness. He stood in the doorway and put in his hand, groping for the light switch. It was just round the corner. He pressed it. Nothing. The lights weren't working.

He stood there for an instant, undecided, then walked through the doorway, plunging into the darkness. He heard fragments of the neon light crunch under his feet.

'I'm armed. Don't try any tri . . .'

He was struck on the back of the head by a medicine ball, one of those ten-kilo ones full of sawdust. Before he'd had time to recover from the surprise, another ball hit him on the right shoulder, and then another ball, a basketball this time, thrown with deadly force, hit him smack on his swollen nose.

He squealed like a pig in an abattoir. Sharp spirals of pain radiated all over his face, wrapped round his throat, strangling him, and bit his stomach. He fell to his knees, and brought up the sea-and-mountain pappardelle, the crème caramel and all the rest.

They ran past him, clambered over him, as black as shadows and as quick as arrows, and he tried, God did he try, while he was vomiting, to reach out and grab one of the little buggers, but all his fingers grasped was the useless consistency of some jeans.

He fell face down in the vomit and splinters of glass.

31

He heard them run, bang into the door and race out of the gym.

Pietro quickly slipped out of the mattresses and dashed after them towards the corridor.

He was almost safe when suddenly the big window by the door exploded.

Pieces of glass flew into the air and fell around him, disintegrating.

Pietro stopped short, and when he realised he'd been shot at, he pissed himself.

He parted his lips, his spine slackened, his limbs relaxed and a sudden warmth spread through his groin and thighs and ran down to his shoes.

I've been shot at.

The fragments that were still imprisoned behind the grating continued to fall.

He turned round very slowly.

On the other side of the gym he saw a figure lying on the ground, dragging itself out of the storeroom on its elbows. Its face was painted red. And it was pointing a gun at him.

'Stop. Stop or I'll shoot you. I swear on the head of my children I'll shoot you.'

Italo.

He recognised the caretaker's deep voice, though it sounded different. As if he had a heavy cold.

What had happened to him?

He realised that the red on Italo's face wasn't paint but blood.

'Stay there, boy. Don't move. Do you hear? Don't move.'

Pietro stood still and just moved his head.

The door was there. Five metres away. No, less than five metres.

You can do it. One jump and you're out. Run for it! He couldn't let himself be caught, that was out of the question, he must flee at all costs, even at the risk of being shot in the back.

Pietro wished he could do it but didn't think he could move. In fact, he was sure he couldn't. He could feel the soles of his shoes glued to the ground and his legs made of jelly. He looked down. A pool of urine had formed between his feet.

Run for it!

Italo was laboriously trying to get to his feet.

Run for it! It's now or never!

And he found himself in the corridor running for all he was worth and he slipped over and scrambled to his feet again and tripped on the stairs and got up again and ran towards the girls' toilets and freedom.

And meanwhile the caretaker was shouting. 'Hurry! Hurry! Hurry! It makes no difference . . . I recognised you . . . Don't kid yourself!'

32

Who could he ring to ask about Erica?

Of course, her agent!

Graziano Biglia picked up his address book and called Erica's agent, the son-of-a-bitch who had made her go through that pointless farce. Predictably he wasn't in, but he managed to speak to a secretary. 'Erica? Yes, we saw her this morning. She did the audition and left,' she said in a flat voice.

'Oh, she left . . .' breathed Graziano, and felt a sense of relief spread through him. The cannonball he had swallowed had suddenly disappeared.

'With Mantovani.'

'Mantovani?'

'That's right.'

'Mantovani? Andrea Mantovani?'

'That's right.'

'The presenter?'

'Who else?'

The cannonball in his stomach had been replaced by a gang of hooligans who were trying to break into his oesophagus. 'Where did they go?'

'To Riccione.'

'To Riccione?'

'To Channel Five's Grand Gala.'

'To Channel Five's Grand Gala?'

'That's right.'

'That's right?'

He could have gone on like that all night, repeating what the secretary said and adding a question mark.

'I'm sorry, I'm going to have to hang up . . . There's someone on the other line,' she said, trying to get rid of him.

'But why has she gone to Channel Five's Grand Gala?'

'I haven't the faintest idea . . . Now I'm sorry, but . . .'

'Okay, I'll hang up now. But first, could you give me the number of Mantovani's mobile?'

'I'm sorry. I'm not allowed to. Now, if you'll excuse me, I really must answer . . .'

'Wait a minute, pl . . .'

She had hung up.

Graziano stood there holding the receiver.

For the first twenty seconds, strangely enough, he heard nothing. Only the vast, unfathomable void of sidereal space. Then his ears were assailed by a loud buzzing noise.

33

The others had gone.

He leaped on his bike and sped away.

He went out onto the road.

And away towards home, riding through the deserted village and taking the short cut behind the church, a mud track that ran across the fields.

It was pouring with rain. And you couldn't see a thing. The wheels skidded and slipped in the mud. *Slow down, you'll fall off.* The wind chilled his wet trousers and underpants. He felt as if his willy had hidden away between his legs like a tortoise's head.

Hurry! It's late.

He looked at his watch.

Nine twenty. Oh, my God, it's late. Hurry! Hurry! Hurry! (It makes no difference . . . I recognised you. Don't kid yourself.)

Hurry! Hurry!

He couldn't have recognised him. It was impossible. He had been too far away. How could he? He wasn't even wearing his glasses.

He had lost all feeling in his fingertips and his ears, and his calves were as hard as stones, but he had no intention of slowing down. Mud splashed on his face and clothes, but Pietro didn't ease up.

Run! Ru . . . recognised you.

He'd been bluffing, trying to scare him. To make him stop so that he could take him to the headmaster. But he hadn't fallen for it. He wasn't stupid.

The wind ballooned his jacket. His eyes watered.

Nearly home.

34

Graziano felt as if he had stepped into a horror film, one of those films where a poltergeist lifts objects up in the air and whirls them round. Except that nothing was whirling round in his living room, except for his head.

'Mantovani . . . Mantovani . . . Mantovani . . .' he kept gurgling as he sat there on the sofa.

Why?

He mustn't think about it. Mustn't think about what all this meant. He was like a climber hanging over a precipice.

He lifted the receiver and dialled the number again.

With all the telepathic force at his command he willed Erica to answer that bloody mobile. He had never wanted anything so badly in his life. And . . .

Toooo. Toooo. Toooo.

Huh? Line free! It works!

Toooo. Toooo. Toooo.

Answer! Damn you! Answer!

'This is Erica Trettel's voicemail. Leave a secret.'

Graziano was dumbfounded.

Her voicemail?

Then, trying to sound calm and not succeeding, he spoke. 'Erica? It's Graziano. I'm in Ischiano. Can you call me? Please. On my mobile. Immediately.' He hung up.

He took a deep breath.

Had he said the right things? Should he have told her he knew about Mantovani? Should he call again and leave a more forthright message?

No. He should not. Definitely not.

He grabbed the receiver and called back.

'Telecom Italia Mobile, the number you have dialled is unobtainable at present.'

Why wasn't the voicemail working now? Was she playing games with him?

In his rage he started kicking the Flemish-style chest of drawers, then collapsed exhausted into the armchair, his head in his hands.

At that moment Mrs Biglia entered the living room pushing a trolley laden with a soup tureen full of tortellini in broth, a serving dish containing ten different kinds of cheese, chicory dressed with lemon juice, boiled potatoes, sautéed kidneys with garlic and parsley and a Saint Honoré bulging with cream.

At the sight of it Graziano nearly threw up.

'Uuuuunch. Bwooooooth,' howled Mrs Biglia and turned on the television. Graziano ignored her.

'Uuuuuuunch,' she persisted.

'I'm not hungry! And didn't you take a vow of silence? If you've taken a vow of silence you have to keep quiet, for Christ's sake. That's breaking the rules. If you moan like a mongoloid you'll go to hell,' exploded Graziano, and slumped back on the armchair. His hair over his face.

The bitch has gone off with Mantovani.

Then another voice, the voice of reason, made itself heard. *Wait. Don't be hasty. Maybe she just asked him for a lift. Or perhaps it was a work assignment. Don't worry, she'll call you and you'll see that it's all a misunderstanding. Relax.*

He began to hyperventilate, trying to calm himself.

'Good evening everybody, from the Vigevani theatre in Riccione. Welcome to the eighth edition of Channel Five's Grand Gala! This is the evening of the stars, the evening when the final awards are given . . .'

Graziano looked up.

On the TV they were showing the Grand Gala.

'It's going to be a long evening, during which we will award the TV Oscars,' said the female presenter. A buxom blonde with a smile of twenty-four thousand teeth, every one of them gleaming. Beside her stood a portly tuxedoed man who was also smiling contentedly.

The camera panned along the front rows of the theatre. Men in tuxedos. Women revealing acres of thigh. And scores of major and minor celebrities. Even a couple of Hollywood actors and the odd foreign singer.

'First of all,' continued the blonde presenter, 'a word about our generous sponsor, who has made all this possible.' Applause. 'Synthesis! The watch for people who know the value of time.'

The camera panned up over the blonde and the little fat man and glided in a perfect parabola over the heads of the VIPs to zoom in on a wrist wearing a magnificent gleaming Synthesis sports watch. The wrist was attached to a hand, and the hand was clamped round a black self-supporting stocking, and the stocking, in turn, veiled a woman's thigh. Then the camera drew back to reveal who all this belonged to.

'Erica! Mantovani!' Graziano spluttered.

Erica wore a blue satin dress with a plunging neckline. She had taken her hair up casually, allowing a few locks to dangle, emphasising her long neck. Beside her sat Andrea Mantovani, wearing a tuxedo. A fair-haired man, with a large nose, small round spectacles and the smile of a contented pig. He continued to keep the clamp on Erica's thigh. As if to say, this is my property. His was the classic attitude of a guy who has just copulated and is now using his paw to mark out his territory.

'And now a commercial!' announced the female presenter.

A commercial for Pampers.

'I'll ram that hand up your arse, you bastard,' roared Graziano, baring his teeth.

'Eeeeeeiaa?' asked Mrs Biglia.

Graziano didn't bother to answer. He picked up the telephone and retired to his bedroom.

He dialled the number of her mobile at the speed of light. He intended to leave her a clear and simple message: 'I'm going to kill you, you bitch.'

'Hallo, Mariapia! Did you see me? Well, how do you like my dress?' Erica's voice.

Graziano was speechless.

'Hallo? Hallo? Mariapia, is that you?'

Graziano recovered his composure. 'No, it's not Mariapia. It's Graziano. I've just . . .' Then he decided it was better to feign ignorance. 'Where are you?' he said, trying to sound nonchalant.

'Graziano . . . ?' Erica was surprised, but then seemed delighted. 'Graziano! It's so nice to speak to you!'

'Where are you?' he repeated coldly.

'I've got some wonderful news. Can I ring you back later?'

'No, you can't, I'm not at home and my mobile's running down.'

'Tomorrow morning?'

'No, tell me now.'

'Okay. But I can't talk for long.' Her tone had suddenly changed, from radiant to irritated, very irritated, then immediately became radiant again. 'I got the job! I still can't believe it. They chose me at the audition. I'd already done the audition and I was getting ready to go home when along came Andrea . . .'

'Andrea who?'

'Andrea Mantovani! He sees me and says: 'We must try this girl, I like the look of her.' Those were his very words. So they gave me a second audition. I read a script and danced a bit and they gave me the job. Oh, Graziano, I'm so thrilled! I GOT THE JOB! CAN YOU BELIEVE IT? I'M GOING TO BE THE SHOWGIRL ON *YOU REAP WHAT YOU SOW*!'

'Oh.' Graziano was as stiff as a frozen hake.

'Aren't you pleased?'

'Yes, of course. And when are you coming here?'

'I don't know . . . We're starting rehearsals tomorrow . . . Soon . . . I hope.'

'I've got everything organised. We're expecting you. My mother's cooking and I've told my friends the news . . .'

'What news? . . .'

'That we're getting married.'

'Listen, can we discuss this tomorrow? The commercial break's just ending. I must hang up.'

'Don't you want to marry me any more?' He had just stabbed himself in the side.

'Can we discuss it tomorrow?'

Now, at last, Graziano's anger had reached its limit, saturation point. It could have filled an Olympic swimming pool. He was wilder than a stallion in a rodeo, than a Formula One driver who is just about to win the world championship when his engine breaks down on the final bend, than a student whose girlfriend accidentally deletes his Ph.D. thesis from his computer, than a patient who's just had the wrong kidney taken out by mistake.

He was beside himself with fury.

'You bitch! You whore! Who are you trying to kid? I saw you on TV! With that poof Mantovani in the middle of a crowd of jerks. You said you were coming to join me here. But instead you preferred to let that poof screw you. You bitch! That's the only reason he gave you the job, you fool! You must be really thick if you don't realise that. You can't even stand in front of a TV camera, the only thing you're any good at is sucking cocks.'

There was a moment's silence.

Graziano allowed himself a smile. He had crushed her.

But the reply came, as violent as a hurricane across the Caribbean. 'You bastard. I don't know why I ever went out with you. I must have been out of my mind. I'd throw myself under a train rather than marry you. You want to know something? You bring bad luck. As soon as you went away I got a job. You're a jinx. You just wanted to drag me down, you wanted me to come to that lousy dump. Never. I despise you, and everything you represent. The way you dress. The bullshit you talk in that know-all tone of yours. You don't know anything. You're just an ageing, failed drug dealer. Get out of my life. If you dare call me again, if you dare come and see me, I swear to God I'll pay someone to smash your face in. The show's starting again. Goodbye. Oh, and one last thing, that poof Mantovani has got a bigger one than you.'

And she hung up.

35

At first sight Fig-Tree Cottage might have been mistaken for a junk yard. What created this impression was all the scrap metal piled up around the farmhouse.

An old tractor, a blue Giulietta, a Philco fridge and a doorless Seicento lay rusting among the thistles, chicory and wild fennel on either side of the gate made of two double-bedsprings.

Behind all this was a muddy yard strewn with pot-holes and puddles. To the right was a heap of gravel which Mr Moroni had been given by a neighbour and which no one had ever bothered to spread. To the left, a long shed, supported by tall metal posts, which served as a shelter for the new tractor, the Panda and Mimmo's motocross bike. In late summer, when it was filled with bales of hay, Pietro would climb up and search for pigeons' nests among the rafters.

The house was a two-storey cottage, with a red-tiled roof and the wooden beams stripped of their paint by the cold and heat. In many places the plaster had fallen away revealing the bricks, which were green with moss.

The northern side was hidden by a cascade of ivy.

The Moronis lived on the first floor and had converted the loft to make two bedrooms and a bathroom. One bedroom for them, the other for Pietro and his brother Mimmo. On the first floor there was a large kitchen with a fireplace, which also served as a dining room. Behind the kitchen, a pantry. On the ground floor, the storeroom. Here were the tools, the carpentry workshop and a few barrels and casks which were full of oil, when the few olive trees they possessed were not afflicted by some disease.

Everyone called it Fig-Tree Cottage because of the enormous tree that spread its twisted branches over the roof. Hidden behind two cork oaks were the chicken run, the sheep fold and the dog's enclosure. A long asymmetrical pen made of wood, wire netting, old tyres and corrugated iron.

Among the weeds you could just make out a neglected orchard and a long concrete trough full of stagnant water, reeds, mosquito larvae and tadpoles. Pietro had put some minnows in it that he had caught in the lagoon.

In summer they had a lot of young and he would give them to Gloria, who would put them in her fishpond.

* * *

Pietro left his bicycle beside his brother's motorbike, ran to the dog's enclosure and heaved his first sigh of relief that evening.

Zagor was lying on the ground in a corner in the rain. When he saw Pietro, he raised his head listlessly, wagged his tail and then let it fall back again limply between his legs.

He was a big dog, with a large square head, mournful black eyes and somewhat rickety hind legs. According to Mimmo, he was a cross between an Abruzzese sheepdog and a German shepherd. But who could say for sure? Certainly he was as tall as an Abruzzese and had the typical black-and-tan coat of the German shepherd. At any rate, he stank to high heaven and was covered in ticks. And he was absolutely crazy. There was something amiss in the brain of that hairy beast. Maybe it was all the beatings and kicks he had received, maybe it was the chain, maybe it was some hereditary defect. He had been beaten so often that Pietro wondered how he could still stand up and move his tail.

What have you got to wag your tail about?

And he never learned. Not a thing. If you locked him up in his pen at night, he would escape and come crawling back next morning with his tail between his legs, his coat caked in blood and tufts of fur between his teeth.

He loved killing. The smell of blood made him wild and happy. At night he would roam the hills howling and attacking any suitably sized animal: sheep, hens, rabbits, calves, cats, even wild boars.

Pietro had seen the film of Dr Jekyll and Mr Hyde on television and had been taken aback. He was just like Zagor. They had the same disease. Angelic in the daytime and monsters by night.

'Animals like that have got to be put down. Once they've tasted blood they become like drug addicts, you can hit them as hard as you like but as soon as they get the chance they'll escape and do it again, see? Don't let his eyes fool you, he's a faker, he seems friendly enough now, but later . . . And he can't even keep guard. He's got to be put down. He's just too much trouble. I won't make him suffer,' Mr Moroni had said, pointing his shotgun at the dog as he lay in a corner, worn out by a night of madness. 'Look what you've done . . .'

Scattered round the yard were pieces of sheep. Zagor had killed it, dragged it all the way home and then torn it apart. Its head, neck and two front legs were by the barn. Its stomach, guts and other innards were out in the middle, in a pool of clotted blood. With a cloud of flies buzzing around them. And the worst of it was that the sheep was pregnant. The tiny fetus wrapped in its placenta had been hurled to one side. The hind quarters, with half the backbone still attached, protruded from Zagor's kennel.

'I've already had to pay that bastard Contarello for two sheep. I've had enough. Money doesn't come out of my arse. I've got to do it.'

Pietro had started crying, clung to his father's trousers, pleaded with him desperately not to kill him, saying that he loved Zagor and that he was a good dog, just a little crazy, and that all you had to do was keep him in his enclosure and he would make sure it was locked every night.

Mario Moroni had looked at his son imploring him, clinging round his ankle like an octopus, and something, something weak and soft in his character that he didn't understand, had made him hesitate.

He had pulled Pietro to his feet and stared at him with those eyes which when they were on you seemed to be peering into your soul. 'All right. You're taking on a responsibility. I won't shoot him. But Zagor's life depends on you . . .'

Pietro nodded.

'Whether he lives or dies depends on you, do you understand?'

'Yes.'

'The first time you forget to put him in his kennel, and he gets out, and he kills so much as a sparrow, he dies.'

'All right.'

'But you'll have to do it. I'll teach you to shoot and you'll kill him. Do you accept those terms?'

'Yes.' And as Pietro was saying that decisive, grown-up yes, there had passed through his mind a chilling scene which would plant itself there like a stake. Shotgun in hand he approaches Zagor, who wags his tail and barks, urging him to throw a stone for him, and he . . .

Pietro had always kept his side of the bargain, returning home early, before darkness fell, when Zagor was out.

Or at least he had until that evening.

So when he saw him in his pen, he felt much better.

It must have been Mimmo who put him in.

He went up the steps, opened the front door and entered the little cloakroom that separated the entrance from the kitchen.

He looked at himself in the mirror that hung on the door.

He was a mess.

His hair ruffled and encrusted with mud. His trousers soiled with earth and pee. His shoes ruined. And he had torn his jacket pocket climbing out of the toilet window.

If Papa finds out I've torn my new jacket . . . It didn't bear thinking about.

He hung his jacket on the coat rack, put his shoes on the shelf and donned his slippers.

He would have to dash up to his room and take off his trousers straight away. He would wash them himself, in the sink in the garage.

He entered cautiously, not making a sound.

It was pleasantly warm.

The kitchen was in semi-darkness, lit only by the glow of the television and the embers dying in the fire. A smell of tomato sauce, fried meat and, beneath it, something vaguer, less easy to pinpoint: the damp of the walls and the aroma of the salamis hanging by the fridge.

His mother was dozing on the sofa, wrapped in a blanket. Her head resting on the thigh of her husband who, deep in a heavy alcoholic sleep, was sitting beside her with the remote control in his hand. His head lolling over the back of the sofa, his mouth open. His balding brow reflected the blue of the screen.

He was snoring. In spasms, alternating pauses with breathing and grunts.

Mario Moroni was fifty-three, small and thin. Although he was practically an alcoholic and ate like a docker, he never put on an ounce of fat. He had a lean, wiry physique and so much strength in his arms that he could lift the share of the big plough on his own. There was something disturbing about his face. Perhaps it was the extraordinarily blue eyes (which Pietro hadn't inherited), or the colour of his sunbaked skin, or perhaps it was the fact that few emotions appeared on that stony visage. His hair was fine and black, almost blue, and he slicked it back with brilliantine. Strangely, he didn't have a single grey hair on his head, whereas his beard, which he shaved twice a week, was completely white.

Pietro stood in a corner to warm himself.

His mother hadn't noticed that he had come home.

Maybe she's asleep.

Should he wake them up?

No, better not. I'll go to bed . . .

Tell them about the terrible thing that had happened to him?

He reflected for a moment and decided against it.

Maybe tomorrow.

He was about to go upstairs to his bedroom, when something he hadn't noticed before made him stop.

They were sleeping beside one another.

Strange. Those two never came very close together. Like electric wires of opposite valencies which cause a short circuit if they touch. In their room the beds were separated by a bedside cabinet and by day, during the little time his father spent in the house, they were like creatures from two different planets forced by some inscrutable necessity to share life, children and home.

To see them like that made him feel uneasy. It was embarrassing.

Gloria's parents touched, but that didn't bother him at all, let alone embarrass him. When her father came home from work, he would put his arms round her mother's waist and kiss her on the neck and she would smile. Once Pietro had gone into the living room to look for his schoolbag and had found them by the fireside kissing. Their eyes were closed, luckily. He had turned and fled into the kitchen like a mouse.

His mother suddenly sat up and saw him. 'Oh, you're back. Thank goodness. Where have you been all this time?' Then she rubbed her eyes.

'At Gloria's. It took longer than I thought.'

'Your father was cross. He says you must come home earlier. You know that.' She spoke in a flat tone.

'It took longer than I thought . . .

(*shall I tell her?*)

. . . we had to finish the project.'

'Have you had supper?'

'Yes.'

'Come here.'

Pietro went towards her, the water dripping off him.

'Look what a mess you're in. Go and have a wash and get into bed.'

'Yes, Mama.'

'Give me a kiss.'

Pietro drew near and his mother hugged him. He would have liked to tell her what had happened, but instead he squeezed her tightly and felt like crying and rained kisses on her neck.

'What's the matter? Why all these kisses?'

'No reason . . .'

'You're soaking wet. Run upstairs or you'll catch your death of cold.'

'Okay.'

'Off you go, then.' She patted him on the cheek.

'Good night, Mama.'

'Good night. Sleep tight.'

After he had washed, Pietro tiptoed into the bedroom in his underpants without switching on the light.

Mimmo was asleep.

The room was quite small. Beside the bunk beds was a small table where Pietro did his homework, a wardrobe made out of hard-board which he shared with Mimmo, a small metal bookcase where he kept, besides his school books, his collection of fossils, sea urchin shells, sun-dried starfish, a mole's skull, a praying mantis in a jar of formalin, a stuffed owl which Uncle Franco had given him for his birthday and a lot of other nice things that he had found on his walks through the woods. In Mimmo's bookcase there were a radio-cassette recorder, some cassettes, a pile of *Diabolik* comics, a few issues of *Motorcycling* and an electric guitar with its amplifier. On the walls, two posters: one of a motocross bike in mid-air and the other of Iron Maiden, which showed a kind of demon emerging from a grave brandishing a bloody sickle.

Pietro climbed the bunk ladder, holding his breath and trying not to make it creak. He put on his pyjamas and slipped under the blankets.

How good it felt.

Under the blankets the terrible adventure he had just been through seemed far away. Now that he had before him a whole night to sleep on it, that business seemed smaller, less important, not so serious.

If the caretaker had recognised him, then it would.

But he hadn't.

He had got away and Italo couldn't have seen who he was. In the first place, he wasn't wearing his glasses. And secondly he was too far away.

No one would ever find out.

And a grown-up thought, the thought of a person who has experience, not of a child, passed through his brain.

This thing, he said to himself, would pass because in life things always do pass, as in a river. Even the most difficult things which you think you'll never get over you do get over, and in a trice you find they're behind you and you have to go on.

New things await you.

He curled up under the blankets. He was worn out, his eyelids felt leaden and he was about to drift off into sleep when his brother's voice called him back. 'Pietro, I've got something to tell you.'

'I thought you were asleep.'

'No, I was thinking.'

'Oh . . .'

'I've got some good news about Alaska.'

36

At this point we had better break off for a moment and talk about Domenico Moroni, known to all as Mimmo.

Mimmo, at the time of this story, was aged twenty (he was eight years older than Pietro) and worked as a shepherd. He tended the small family flock. Thirty-two sheep in all. In his spare time, to earn a few extra lire, he worked for an upholsterer in Casale del Bra. He preferred sheep to sofas and described himself as the only metalhead shepherd in Ischiano Scalo. As indeed he was.

He would stomp across the fields wearing a leather jacket, skin-tight jeans, a belt studded with silver knobs, huge army boots and a long chain that hung down between his legs. Headphones on his ears and crook in hand.

Physically, Mimmo in many ways resembled his father. He was skinny, like him, though taller, he had the same blue eyes, though without their fixed, sullen expression, and the same raven-black hair, though he wore it long, almost half-way down his back. He had his mother's mouth, wide and with prominent lips, and a small chin. He was no beauty, and in his metalhead gear he looked even less prepossessing, but it was no use telling him, that was of one his fixations.

Yes, Mimmo had fixations.

They attached themselves to his neurons as limescale does to pipes, making him monomaniacal and, in the long run, boring. So he didn't have many friends. After a while he wearied even the most patient of people.

His first fixation was Heavy Metal.

'Only the classic stuff, though.'

For him it was a religion, a philosophy of life, everything. His hero was Ozzy Osbourne, a weirdo with long hair and the brain of a psychopathic teenager. Mimmo worshipped him because at his shows the fans threw him the carcasses of dead animals and he would eat them and once he had swallowed a dead bat and caught rabies and had to have an injection in his stomach. 'And you know what old Ozzy said? Those injections were worse than having twenty golf balls shoved up your arse . . .' Mimmo was fond of repeating.

What he found so great about all this is not clear. But there's no doubt that he worshipped old Ozzy. He also worshipped Iron Maiden and Black Sabbath, and bought as many of their T-shirts as he could find. He didn't have many of their albums, though. Seven or eight at most, and he seldom listened to them.

Sometimes, when his father was out, he would put on an AC/DC record and jump round the room like a madman with Pietro. 'Metal! Metal! Mosh! Mosh! Smash things up!' they would shout at the tops of their voices, and push and shove each other about till they both fell exhausted on the bed.

To tell the truth, Mimmo couldn't stand that music.

It was too loud (he didn't mind Richard Clayderman). What he liked about the Heavy Metal singers was the way they looked, the way they lived and the fact that 'they're outsiders, they don't give a fuck about anything, they can't even play the guitar and yet they have loads of women, motorbikes, make pots of money and smash things up. Man, they're cool . . .'

His second fixation was motocross bikes.

He knew the motorbike yearbook by heart. The makes, the models, the engine capacities, the prices. With an enormous effort and with savings that had made him a virtual ascetic for two years, he had bought a secondhand KTM 300. An old two-stroke that guzzled petrol and broke down every day. With all the money he had spent on spare parts he could have bought three brand new motorbikes. He had even entered a couple of races. A disaster. The first time he had broken the fork, the second his tibia.

His third fixation was Patrizia Loria. Patti. His girlfriend. 'Definitely the most beautiful girl in Ischiano Scalo.' In some ways it was hard to disagree with him. Patti had a fantastic figure. Tall, curvy and in particular 'a bum that doesn't just talk, it sings'. All perfectly true.

The only problem was her face, which was horrible. Her forehead was covered with a thick layer of spots. With all those craters, her skin was like a photograph of the surface of the moon. Patrizia would smother it with Topexan, homoeopathic remedies, herbal creams, anything she could find, but it was no good, her acne just seemed to lap it up. After the treatment she would be even more seborrhoeic and pimply than before. Her eyes were small and horribly close together and her nose was dotted with blackheads.

But Mimmo didn't seem to notice. He was besotted with her. To him she was beautiful and that was the main thing. He swore that the day she was finally cured of her acne she'd 'kick even Kim Basinger's ass'.

Patrizia was twenty-two, she worked as a shop assistant but dreamed of becoming a primary school teacher. Her character was strong and decisive. She made poor Mimmo toe the line.

And then we come to his last fixation, the worst. Alaska.

A certain Fabio Lo Turco, a hippy type who claimed to have sailed single-handed round the world but had really set out from Porto Ercole and only got as far as Stromboli, where he had set up a market stall selling Indian wares and Jim Morrison T-shirts, had gone up to Mimmo one evening in the Lighthouse pub in Orbano, cadged a drink and cigarettes and talked to him about Alaska.

'You see, Alaska's the turning point. You sail up there, in that freezing cold, and you turn. You embark on a big Findus trawler at Anchorage and head for the North Pole to fish. You stay there for seven or eight months, at twenty degrees below zero, you never come back down. It's mainly cod fishing up there. There are Japanese masters on the ship who are expert at cutting up live fish. They teach you how to make fish fingers, because Findus fish fingers are all hand-sliced. Then you put them in boxes and stack them in the refrigerators . . .'

'When do they put the breadcrumbs on?' Mimmo had interrupted him.

'Later, on dry land. What the hell has that got to do with it?' the hipster had bristled, but had then gone rambling on in his guru-like manner. 'There are people from all over the world working on the ships. Eskimos, Finns, Russians, quite a few Koreans. The pay's good. You can make big money. A couple of years up there and you could buy yourself a hut on Easter Island.'

Naively, Mimmo had asked why they paid so well.

'Why? Because the work's exhausting. You've got to be as tough as old boots to work at minus thirty. Your eyeballs freeze at that temperature. There can't be more than thirty or forty thousand people in the whole world, apart from the Eskimos and Japanese of course, who are capable of working in those terrible conditions. The owners of the trawlers know that. In the contract they make you sign it says that if you don't last the full six months they won't pay you a lira. Do you know how many people have embarked and then had themselves flown out by helicopter after only three days? Hundreds. People go out of their minds up there. You have to be strong, and have a skin as thick as a walrus's hide . . . If you stick it out, though, it's great. There are colours that don't exist in any other part of the world . . .'

Mimmo had taken the story very seriously. It was no laughing matter.

Lo Turco was right, this could really be the turning point of his life. And Mimmo had no doubt that his own skin was as tough as a walrus's hide, he had seen the evidence on some icy mornings out with the sheep.

All he had to do was prove it.

Yes, he felt he was made for deep-sea fishing, Arctic seas, sunlit nights.

And he'd had all he could take of living with his parents, he felt as if he was going mad every time he entered the house. He would barricade himself in his room so as not to be near his father, but continued to feel that bastard's presence oozing through the walls like a deadly poison.

How he hated him! Even he didn't really know how much. It was a painful hatred, a rancour which poisoned his body at every moment and never left him, which he had learned to live with but which he hoped might end the day he went away.

Away.

Yes, away. Far away.

He would have to put at least one ocean between him and his father before he could feel absolutely free.

He was always ordering him about, telling him he was a layabout, a spineless idiot, incapable even of looking after a few sheep, that he dressed like a fool, that he could go away if he wanted, no one was trying to keep him.

Never a kind word, never a smile.

So why did he stay, ruining his life alongside the man he hated?

Because he was waiting for his big opportunity.

And the big opportunity was Alaska.

How often, while out on the pastures, he had dreamed of telling his father, 'I'm leaving for Alaska. I don't like it here any more. I'm sorry if I'm not the son you wanted, but you're not the father I wanted either. Goodbye.' What bliss! Yes, those would be his very words. He would kiss his mother and brother and off he would go.

The only problem was the ticket. It was very expensive. When he had gone in to ask at the travel agency, the girl at the counter had looked at him as you might look at a madman and, after tapping away at her computer for a quarter of an hour, told him the price.

Three million two hundred thousand lire.

An astronomical sum!

And that was what he was thinking about when he heard his brother enter the bedroom.

'Pietro, I've got something to tell you.'

'I thought you were asleep.'

'No, I was thinking.'

'Oh . . .'

'I've got some good news about Alaska. I've thought of a way of raising the money.'

'What is it?'

'Listen. I could ask your friend Gloria's parents. Her father's a bank manager and her mother inherited all that land. They'd have no problem lending me the money, so I could go. Then as soon as I got my first pay packet I could repay them, in one go. See?'

'Yes.' Pietro had curled up, the bed was cold. His hands tucked between his thighs.

'It would be a short-term loan. The only thing is, I don't know them well enough, you'd have to ask Mr Celani . . . You know them really well. The Celanis love you like a son. What do you think?'

37

He wasn't convinced.

In the first place he would be embarrassed.

I wanted to ask you a favour. My brother . . .

No.

It wasn't nice to ask for a loan like that, it was like begging. Anyway, his father had already had a loan from Mr Celani's bank. And he wasn't sure (though he wouldn't have told them this even if they'd killed him) that Mimmo really would repay them. It didn't seem right, either, that his brother always tried to use others to solve his problems. It was too easy, as if the Count of Monte Cristo, instead of making all that effort to dig the hole with a teaspoon to escape from his cell, had found the prison key under his bed and all the guards asleep. He ought to earn his money, and then it really would be great and, as Mimmo always said, he'd *have fucked Papa*.

Besides, he wasn't too keen on the idea of Mimmo leaving for Alaska.

He would be left all alone.

'Well, what do you think?'

'I don't know,' Pietro hesitated. 'Maybe I could tell Gloria . . .'

Mimmo, underneath him, fell silent but not for long. 'Okay, never mind. I'll find some other way. I could sell my motorbike. Though I wouldn't get much for it . . .'

Pietro was no longer listening.

He was wondering if he should tell Mimmo what had happened at school.

Yes, perhaps he should, but he was worn out. The story was too long. And besides, it hurt him to drag up the fact that those three bastards had tricked him and forced him to . . . His brother would say he was a wuss, a snotty-nosed kid, that he'd let himself be pushed around, and right now that it was the last thing he wanted to hear.

I know that already.

'. . . a plane and you can join me. We could live in Alaska in the winter and with all the money I'll have earned, in the summer we could go to an island in the Caribbean. Patti would come too. Beaches with palm trees, just imagine it, the coral reef, all the fish . . . It would be gr . . .'

Yes, it would be really great. Pietro let his thoughts drift off.

To live in Alaska, to have a dog sled, a heated shack made of corrugated iron. He would look after the dogs. And go for long walks on the ice, muffled up in his parka and with snowshoes on his feet. And then in the summer, deep-sea diving among the coral with Gloria (Gloria would join them along with Patti).

How often he and Mimmo had talked about it, sitting on the hillside near the sheep. Making up incredible stories, adding a new detail every time. The helicopter (Mimmo would get a pilot's licence as soon as possible) that landed on an iceberg, the whales, the little hut with hammocks, the fridge full of cool drinks, the beach in front, the turtles laying their eggs in the sand.

That evening, for the first time in his life, Pietro really hoped for it, with all his might, desperately.

'Mimmo, can I really come too? Tell me the truth, please.' He said it in a broken voice and with such intensity that Mimmo didn't reply at once.

In the darkness he heard a suppressed sigh.

'Yes, of course. If I can get away . . . You know how things are, it's difficult . . .'

'Goodnight, Mimmo.'

'Goodnight, Pietro.'

Beretta Force

On the Aurelia, about twenty kilometres south of Ischiano Scalo, there's a long two-lane descent that ends in a wide, sweeping curve. All around is open countryside. There are no dangerous crossings. On that stretch of road even ageing Pandas and diesel Ritmos find a new lease of life and elicit unsuspected power from their clapped-out engines.

Even the most careful drivers, on their first trip along the Aurelia, are tempted by that wonderful incline to step on the gas a bit and feel the thrill of speed. Those who know the road well, however, restrain themselves, because they know that there will almost certainly be a police car lying in wait just around the bend, ready to cool their automotive ardour with fines and licence confiscations.

The police are not as lenient here as they are in town, they're more like the traffic cops who populate the American freeways. Tough guys who stick to the rules and with whom it's impossible to argue, let alone bargain.

They throw the book at you.

Driving without a seat belt? Three hundred thousand lire. Brake light out of order? Two hundred thousand. Missed your annual check-up? They impound your car.

Max (Massimiliano) Franzini knew all this perfectly well, he drove down that road with his parents at least ten times a year to reach the seaside resort of San Folco (the Franzinis owned a villa in a complex called 'The Agaves' directly opposite Red Island) and his father, Professor Mariano Franzini, a consultant orthopaedist at the Gemelli hospital in Rome and the owner of two private clinics on the Rome orbital, had more than once been stopped and heavily fined for speeding.

But that rainy night Max Franzini was two weeks past his twentieth birthday, had only had his driving licence for three months and was at the wheel of a Mercedes that went from zero to two hundred and twenty kilometres an hour in the space of one kilometre and on the seat beside him was Martina Trevisan, a girl he really fancied, and he had smoked three joints and . . .

When it's raining as hard as this the police never bother to stop you. Everybody knows that.

. . . the road was deserted, it was not a weekend, the Romans weren't leaving for their holidays, there was no reason not to drive fast and Max wanted to get to the villa as soon as possible and his father's car certainly didn't impede the fulfilment of that wish.

He was wondering how to organise the night with Martina.

I'll take my parents' room, then I'll ask her if she prefers to sleep alone in the guest room or with me in the double bed. If she says she'll join me, I'm home and dry. It means she's game. In practice I don't have to do anything. We get into bed and . . . But if she says she prefers to sleep in the guest room, it's more complicated. Though it won't necessarily mean she's not game, she might just be shy. Or I could ask her if she'd like to watch a video in the living room and we could sit on the sofa with the blanket and I could play it by ear . . .

Max had problems making out with girls.

With the first approaches, the chatting up, the larking about, the cinema, the phone calls and all the other stuff he was fine, but when it came to the crucial moment of making a move, the kiss test, as we might call it, all his bravado would evaporate, he would be seized by a fear of rejection and freeze like a gawky teenager on his first date. (Something similar happened to him at tennis. He could go on returning the ball for hours with powerful forehands and backhands, but when he had to make the killer shot and win the point he would panic and hit it into the net or out of court. In order to win he had to count on his opponent's errors.)

For Max, making sexual advances was like diving off a high cliff. You step up to the edge, look down, turn back muttering never in a million years am I going to do that, you try again, hesitate, shake your head and, when everyone else has already dived and got fed up with waiting for you, you cross yourself, shut your eyes and jump off, screaming as you go.

What a disaster.

And all those joints certainly didn't make it any easier to sort his ideas out.

And Martina was rolling another.

She's a real pothead, this one.

Max realised that they hadn't said a word to each other since Civitavecchia. All that smoke had somewhat clouded his mind. *And that's not a good thing*. Martina might think he didn't have anything to say, which wasn't true. *There is the music, though*. They were listening to REM's latest CD.

Okay, now I'll ask her a question.

He concentrated, turned down the stereo and spoke in a slurred voice. 'Do you prefer Russian literature or French?'

Martina took a drag and held in the smoke. 'How do you mean?' she croaked.

She was so thin as to be bordering on the anorexic, with close-cut hair dyed electric blue, piercings in her lip and in one eyebrow, and black varnish on her fingernails. She was wearing a little Benetton dress with blue and orange stripes, a black cardigan, open at the front, a buckskin jacket and boots which had been spray-painted green and which she was resting on the dashboard.

'Which do you prefer? Russian writers or French ones?'

Martina snorted. 'That, if you don't mind my saying so, is a pretty stupid question. It's too general. If you asked me which book is better, this one or that one, I could answer you. If you asked me who is better, Schwarzenegger or Stallone, I could answer you. But if you ask me whether I prefer French or Russian literature, I don't know . . . It's too general.'

'So who is better?'

'Eh?'

'Schwarzenegger or Stallone?'

'Stallone. Far better, in my opinion. Schwarzenegger has never made a film like *Rambo* or *Rocky*.'

Max pondered for a moment. 'That's true. But Schwarzenegger made *Predator*, which is a masterpiece.'

'That's true, too.'

'You're right. I asked you the classic stupid question. Like when people ask you whether you prefer to take your holidays at the seaside or in the mountains. It depends. If by seaside you mean Ladispoli and by mountains you mean Nepal, I prefer the mountains, but if by seaside you mean Greece and by mountains you mean Abetone, I prefer the seaside. Right?'

'Right.'

Max turned up the stereo.

Max and Martina had met for the first time that morning at the university, in front of the Modern History noticeboard. They had got talking about the imminent exam and the enormous tomes they had to study and about how if they didn't get down to some hard work neither of them would be ready to take the exam this time round. Max had been rather surprised by Martina's openness. So far in a whole year of university he hadn't succeeded in talking to a single girl. Besides, all the girls on his course were plain, greasy-skinned and bookish. But this one was really pretty and seemed to be a nice person too.

'Oh no . . . I'm never going to make it in time,' Max had exclaimed, exaggeratedly anxious. In fact he had already made up his mind weeks ago that he was going to skip this session of exams.

'Nor am I . . . I suppose I'll have to give it a miss and try again in three months' time.'

'I think what I'm going to have to do is go to the seaside and study there. Hide away in some quiet place.' After a carefully measured pause he had gone on. 'Christ, it's boring at the seaside on your own, though. It's enough to drive you out of your mind.'

This was complete and utter bullshit.

Rather than go to the seaside on his own he would have cut off his own little finger, and his ring finger too. But he'd tossed out the remark rather as a fisherman trying his luck throws a piece of bread-and-cheese bait to the tuna.

You never know your luck.

And sure enough the tuna had taken the bait. 'Can I come too? Would you mind? I've quarrelled with my parents, I'm fed up with them . . .' Martina had asked, straight out.

Max had been speechless with amazement but then, struggling to suppress his enthusiasm, had applied the finishing touch. 'Sure, that'd be fine. We'll leave this evening, if that's all right with you.'

'Okay. We will study, though.'

'Of course we will.'

They agreed to meet at seven o'clock at Rebibbia underground station, near Martina's home.

Max was as nervous as if he were on his first date. And in a sense he was. Martina was nothing like the girls he usually went around with. Two different breeds. The girls he knew wouldn't have gone to the seaside with a stranger if you'd paid them two million dollars. Their lives revolved around the Parioli, the city centre and the Fleming, and they didn't even know what Rebibbia was. Even Max, though he had a pony tail and five earrings in his left ear, wore trousers three sizes too big for him and hung around the communal squats, had had to look Rebibbia up in *Rome A to Z*.

Map 12, C2. A real suburban slum. Wow!

Max was convinced he could make a go of it with Martina. Even though he was rich and lived in the Parioli and had picked her up in a Mercedes worth a couple of hundred million lire and was taking her to a two-storey villa complete with sauna, gym and a fridge as big as a Swiss bank vault, he didn't give a damn about any of that crap. His ambition was to be a drummer and he wasn't going to slave his life away doing some crappy job like his boring old fart of a father.

He and Martina were on the same wavelength, he dressed scruffily as she did and they were similar even though they came from two different worlds, this was proved by the fact that they both liked XTC, the Jesus & Mary Chain and Husker Du.

It wasn't his fault if he'd been born in the Parioli.

So here they were, Max and Martina, racing down the slope at a hundred and eighty kilometres an hour in the Mercedes of Professor Mariano Franzini who at that moment was sleeping beside his wife at the Hilton Hotel in Istanbul where he had gone to attend an international conference on hip replacements, convinced that his new car was in its garage in Via Monte Parioli and not in the hands of that good-for-nothing son of his.

The lamps of the fishing-boats shining in the night. The warm air. The fishermen grilling your supper on the boat. Calamari at midnight. Walks in the tropical forest. The four-star hotel. The swimming pool. The two-day stopover in Colombo, the most colourful city of the East. The sun. The suntan . . .

All these images spooled like a film through the mind of police officer Antonio Bacci as he stood numb with cold in the icy rain at the roadside, in a soaking wet uniform, clutching his signal stick and fuming with rage and frustration.

He looked at his watch.

By this time he should already have been two hours into his holiday on the Maldives.

He could still hardly believe it. He stood in the rain, incredulous that his trip to the Tropics had gone up in smoke because of those layabouts.

I'd succeeded in organising everything.

He'd requested holiday leave. Antonella, his wife, had also taken ten days off work. Andrea, his son, would go and stay with his grandmother. He had even bought a silicone underwater mask, flippers and a snorkel. A hundred and eighty thousand lire down the drain.

If he couldn't come to terms with this he would go mad. The holiday he had dreamed of for five years had vanished in five minutes, the duration of a single phone call.

'Good morning, Mr Bacci, this is Cristiana Piccino from

Francorosso. I'm calling to say that we're awfully sorry but your trip to the Maldives has been cancelled owing to circumstances beyond our control.'

Circumstances beyond our control?

He'd had to get her to repeat it three times before it sunk in that the holiday was off.

Circumstances beyond our control = strike by pilots and cabin crew.

'You bastards, I hate you!' he howled despairingly into the night.

They were the human category he hated most of all. More than the Arab integralists. More than the Northern League. More than the anti-prohibitionists. He had hated them with tenacity and determination ever since his childhood, when he had first begun to watch the TV news and to understand that in the world the worst are always the ones who come out on top.

A strike every week. What have you got to strike about?

They had everything life could offer. A salary he would give his eye teeth for, plus the chance to travel, screw air hostesses and pilot a plane. They had it all and they went on strike.

What kind of protest should I make, then?

What kind of protest should officer Antonio Bacci make, he who spent one half of his life in a layby on the state highway freezing his balls off and fining truck drivers, and the other half quarrelling with his wife? Should he go on hunger strike? Let himself die of starvation? No, better shoot himself in the mouth and have done with it.

'Fuck it!'

Besides, it wasn't himself he was worried about. He would survive somehow even without the bloody Maldives. With a broken heart, but he would keep going. Not his wife. Antonella wouldn't let the matter rest. With that brooding nature of hers, she would take it out on him for the next millennium. She was already making his life hell, as if it were his fault the pilots had gone on strike. She wouldn't speak to him, treated him worse than a stranger, she'd slam his plate down on the table and sit in front of the TV all evening.

Why was he so unlucky? What had he done to deserve this?

Stop it. Drop the subject. Don't think about it.

He was torturing himself pointlessly.

He huddled his raincoat round him and moved closer to the road. Two headlights appeared round the bend, Antonio Bacci raised his baton and prayed that this Mercedes contained a pilot or a member of the cabin crew, or better still, both.

'In case you hadn't noticed, you've just been flagged down by the police,' Martina announced, taking a drag on her joint.

'Where?' Max slammed his foot on the brake.

The car skidded and swerved along the wet road. Max tried in vain to control it. Finally he pulled the handbrake (never pull the handbrake in a moving car!) and the Mercedes did two pirouettes and finally came to rest with its nose half a metre away from the roadside ditch.

'Phew, that was close . . .' Max gasped, with what little breath he had left. 'We nearly went over the edge.' He was as white as a sheet.

'Didn't you see them?' Martina was perfectly calm. As if they had just spun round in a fairground dodgem and not at a hundred and sixty kilometres per hour on a state highway where they could easily have broken their necks.

'Yes . . . Well, no, actually.' He had seen a blue glow, but had taken it for a pizzeria sign. 'What shall I do?' Through the rain-streaked rear window the police car's flasher looked like a lighthouse in the storm. 'Go back?' He couldn't speak. His throat had gone dry.

'I don't know . . . if you don't.'

'I reckon we should drive on. They can't have read the number plate in this rain. I reckon we should go on. What do you think?'

'I think that's a fucking stupid idea. They'll chase you and beat the shit out of you.'

'Shall I go back, then?' he turned off the stereo and put the car into reverse. 'Yeah, why not, all our papers are in order. Fasten your seat belt. And throw away that joint.'

* * *

He didn't even slow down.

He had come round the bend at a hundred and sixty at least and gone roaring on by.

Officer Antonio Bacci hadn't even had time to write down the number.

CRF 3 . . . then what? He couldn't remember.

Giving chase wasn't an option. It was the last thing he felt like doing at that moment.

It would mean getting into the car, persuading that idiot Miele to shift his arse out of the driving seat, you'd have to quarrel with him because he wouldn't want to, finally you'd get going, you'd set off hell for leather in pursuit, but by the time you caught up with them you'd have gone at least as far as Orbano, and at the risk of ending up wrapped around a tree. And for why? All because some stupid idiot didn't see a roadblock.

'No. Not tonight, thank you.'

In an hour's time I'll knock off, go home, have a nice shower, make myself some packet soup and go to bed and if my damned wife won't speak to me, so much the better. If she doesn't talk at least she won't be moaning.

He glanced at his watch. It was Miele's turn to stand outside. He approached the police car, dried the window with his hand and peered in to see what his colleague was doing.

He's asleep. Fast asleep!

He had been standing in the rain for half an hour and that piece of shit had been snoring away happily. According to regulations, the man in the car had to listen to the radio. If there was an emergency and he didn't reply, there would be hell to pay. And because of that damn fool, he would be for it too. The guy was irresponsible. He'd only been in the force for a year and he thought he could have a snooze while Bacci did all the work.

It wasn't the first stupid thing he'd done. And he was such a bastard. Bacci couldn't stand him. When he had told him he had missed his holiday because of the pilots' strike and that his wife was livid, the guy hadn't had one kind word for him, one friendly gesture, he'd said that he would never have let the travel agencies mess him around and that he always went on holiday by car. *Smart arse!* And what a moronic face he had! With that squashed nose and those bulging eyes. With that blondish hair plastered down with gel. And he smirked in his sleep.

I stand in the rain like an idiot and he sleeps . . .

The anger he had repressed with such difficulty till that moment began to press like a toxic gas on the walls of his oesophagus. He tried counting, to calm himself down. 'One, two, three, four . . . Oh, to hell with it!'

A crazed grin distorted his face. He started hammering on the windscreen with his fists.

Bruno Miele, the officer inside the car, wasn't really asleep.

Head back, eyes closed, he was musing that although Graziano Biglia couldn't be blamed for bedding Marina Delia, he'd have done much better to go for a showgirl.

You can keep your actresses, I'd take a showgirl any day.

And what turned him on, if possible, even more than showgirls was showgirls who presented sports programmes. It was an odd thing, but when those tarts talked about soccer and made predictions about the league table (invariably wrong) and gave analyses of team tactics (invariably ludicrous), it gave him a hard-on.

He'd figured out what those shows were really for. They were for getting those girls into bed with footballers. It was all set up for that purpose, the rest was just a sham. You only had to look at how many of them intermarried.

The club chairmen organised the shows so that the players would get laid, and consequently feel indebted to them and go and play in their teams.

If he hadn't chosen a police career, that's what he would have liked to be, a footballer. He shouldn't have stopped playing so early. Who knows, if he'd worked harder at it . . .

Yeah, I'd love to be a footballer.

Not just any old footballer, mind you, if you're a run-of-the-mill player the showgirls don't give you a second glance, no, he'd have to be a top striker like Del Franco. Then he'd be invited to appear on the shows and would get to screw them all: Simona Reggi, Antonella Cavalieri, Miriana . . . ? Miriana whatshername, Luisa Somaini when she still worked for Telemontecarlo, and Michela Guadagni. Yes, every one of them, the more the merrier.

He was beginning to get horny.

Michela Guadagni. Man, does she turn me on. Underneath that peaches-and-cream exterior there's a slut just waiting to get out. Only you have to be a fucking sports star to get anywhere near her.

He began to imagine himself engaged in an orgy with Michela, Simona and Andrea Mantovani, the presenter.

He smiled. With his eyes closed. As happy as a little child.

Bam bam bam bam.

A violent burst of knocking made him jump in the air.

'What's going on?' He opened his eyes and screamed. 'Ahhhh!'

Behind the glass a monstrous face was leering in at him.

Then he recognised it.

That son of a bitch Bacci!

He lowered the window a couple of centimetres and roared. 'Are you out of your mind? You nearly gave me a heart attack! What do you want?'

'Get out!'

'Why?'

'Because I say so. You were asleep.'

'No I wasn't.'

'Get out!'

Miele looked at his watch. 'It's not my turn yet.'

'Get out of the car.'

'It's not my turn yet. Half an hour each.'

'I've been out here for well over half an hour.'

Miele checked his watch and shook his head. 'No you haven't, there are still four minutes to go. I'll get out in four minutes.'

'Fuck you, I've done over forty minutes. Get out.'

Bacci made a dive for the door handle but Miele was quicker, he pushed down the safety catch before that lunatic could open the door.

'You son of a bitch, get out,' yelled Bacci and started pummelling on the window again.

'What's the matter? What's got into you, are you crazy? Relax. Calm down. Okay, so you didn't get your holiday in the Tropics, relax. It's only a holiday, it's not the end of the world.' Miele tried not to laugh, but the guy was such a loser, he had bored the pants off him for two months with his talk of tropical atolls, Napoleon wrasse and palm trees, and after all that, he hadn't even got on the plane. It was such a hoot.

'What are you laughing about, you bastard? Open the door! Or I'll smash the window and ram your teeth down your fucking throat, so help me!'

Miele was tempted to rub it in and tell him he shouldn't get so angry, it didn't matter if he hadn't gone to Mauritius, he was getting plenty of water anyway, but he restrained himself. Something told him the guy really might smash the window.

'Open up!'

'No, I won't. I'm not opening up until you calm down.'

'I am calm. Now open up.'

'No you're not, I can see you're not.'

'I am calm, I swear. Completely calm. Open the door now, come on.' Bacci drew back from the car and held up his hands. By now he was soaked to the skin.

'I don't believe you.' Miele glanced at his watch again. 'Anyway, there are still two minutes to go.'

'So you don't believe me, eh? Well, take a look at this.' Bacci drew his pistol and pointed it at him. 'Do you see how calm I am? Do you see?'

Miele couldn't believe this, how could he believe the fool was pointing his Beretta at him? He must have gone off his head, like those guys who get sacked and murder their bosses. But Miele wasn't prepared to get killed by a psychopath. He drew his own gun. 'I'm calm too,' he said with a mocking leer. 'We're both calm. High on camomile.'

'Look what the cop's doing,' said Martina.

Her tone contained a hint of surprise.

'What is he doing? I can't see.' Max was leaning over towards her but he couldn't see a thing, the seat belt restricted his movements and it was dark outside.

The blue light illuminated a human form.

'He's holding a gun.'

Max nearly choked. 'A gun?'

'He's pointing it at the car.'

'The car?' Max put his hands up and started shouting. 'We're innocent! We're innocent! I didn't see the road block, I swear I didn't!'

'Shut up, you idiot, not our car.' Martina opened her mini-rucksack, took out a packet of Camel Lights and lit one.

'Well, what car, then?'

'Be quiet a minute. Let me see.' She lowered the window. 'The police car.'

'Ah!' Max sighed with relief. 'But why?' he asked.

'I don't know. Maybe there's a thief inside.' Martina blew out a cloud of smoke.

'You think so?'

'Could be. He might have slipped in while he was stopping cars. Police cars are always getting stolen like that. I read about it somewhere. But the cop must have caught him.' She seemed very pleased with this theory.

'Well, what shall we do, then? Drive on?'

'Wait. Wait a minute . . . Let me handle this.' Martina put her head out of the window. 'Officer! Officer, do you need any help? Can we do anything for you?'

Now I know why she came with me even though she'd never met me before, thought Max in a panic, *she's completely stupid. The girls I know have nothing on this, she's completely stupid.*

'Officer! Officer, do you need any help? Can we do anything for you?' A distant voice.

Bacci looked up and saw it, at the side of the road, the blue Mercedes that hadn't stopped. A female voice was calling to him.

'What's that?' he shouted. 'I can't hear you.'

'Do you need any help?' shouted the girl.

Do I need any help? 'No!'

What kind of a dumb question was that? Then he remembered his gun and quickly put it back in its holster. 'Are you the guys who didn't stop earlier?'

'Yes. We are.'

'Why have you come back?'

The girl waited for a moment before replying. 'Didn't you flag us down with your stick?'

'Yes, but that was earlier . . .'

'Can we go, then?' asked the girl hopefully.

'Yes,' said Bacci, but then had second thoughts. 'Just a minute, what's your job?'

'We haven't got jobs. We're students.'

'What do you study?'

'Italian literature.'

'You're not an air hostess, by any chance?'

'No. I swear I'm not.'

'Why didn't you stop, before?'

'My boyfriend didn't see the road block. It was raining too hard.'

'It's hardly surprising your boyfriend didn't see me, he was driving like a maniac. One kilometre back down the road there's a great big sign that says 80. That is the speed limit on this stretch of road.'

'My boyfriend didn't see it. We're sorry. We really are. My boyfriend's extremely sorry.'

'Okay, I'll let you off this time. Don't drive so fast, though. Especially when it's raining.'

'Thanks, officer. We'll drive really slowly.'

Inside the car Max was jubilant, for three reasons.

1) Because Martina had said 'my boyfriend'. This probably didn't mean anything, but it might do. People don't just say 'my boyfriend' for the hell of it. There must be an intention, a remote one, perhaps, but it must be there.

2) Martina wasn't stupid after all. Far from it. She was a genius. She had sweet-talked the policeman brilliantly. The way things were going, the cops would end up escorting them home.
3) He hadn't been fined. His father would have made him pay back every last lira, not to mention the fact that he'd taken his new car . . .

But Max was wrong to be jubilant, for at that very moment Bruno Miele's half hour began.

When he had seen that peach of a car pull in, officer Miele had shot out of the police car as if there had been a swarm of wasps inside it.

A 650 TX. The finest car in the world, according to the American magazine Motors & Cars.

He switched on his torch and shone it on the car.

Cobalt blue. Yes, the only colour for a 650 TX.

'You in the Mercedes, pull right in,' he said to the two of them and turned to Bacci. 'Leave this to me. I'll deal with it.'

The powerful beam of the torch made the drops of rain glitter as they fell, dense and regular. Behind them was the face of a squinting, dazzled girl.

Miele peered at her.

She had blue hair, a ring in her lip and another in her eyebrow.

A punk? What the hell's a punk doing in a 650 TX?

Miele couldn't stand the idea of punks in a Panda, let alone in the flagship of the German firm.

He hated their dyed hair, their tattoos, their rings, their sweaty armpits and all their other anarcho-communist crap.

Once Lorena Santini, his girlfriend, had told him she fancied putting a ring in her navel like Naomi Campbell and Pietro Mura. 'You do that and we're through,' he had snapped. And the whim, as quickly as it had appeared, had vanished from Lorena's mind. If she'd had a boyfriend with less balls, she'd probably have rings in her pussy by now.

A worrying thought struck him. *What if Michela Guadagni has rings in her pussy?*

They'd suit her. Michela Guadagni isn't like Lorena. She can do that kind of thing.

'Your partner told us we could go,' said the punk girl, shielding her eyes with her arm, in a hoarse Roman croak.

'Well, I say you've got to stay. Pull in.'

The car parked in the lay-by.

'It's true. I told them they could go,' protested Bacci in an undertone.

Miele didn't lower his volume by one decibel. 'I heard. And you were wrong. They failed to stop at a road block. That's a serious offence . . .'

'Let them go,' Bacci interrupted him.

'No. No way.' Miele stepped towards the Mercedes, but Bacci grabbed him by the arm.

'What the hell are you doing? I stopped them. It's none of your business.'

'Let go of my arm.' Miele shook him off.

Bacci started jumping up and down with rage and breathing in and out through the corners of his mouth. His cheeks swelled and deflated like a pair of bagpipes.

Miele looked at him, shaking his head. *Poor guy. What a pathetic sight. He's gone completely off his head. I'll have to report that he's in a serious mental state. He's not responsible for his own actions any more. He's dangerous. He doesn't realise how sick he is.*

If those two were students, he was a merengue dancer. And that imbecile wanted to let them go . . .

They were car thieves.

How did a punk bitch come to be in a car like that? It was obvious. They were taking the Mercedes to a fence. But if they thought they could pull the wool over Bruno Miele's eyes, they were making a big mistake.

'Listen, get into the car. Dry yourself, you're soaked through. I'll deal with this. It's my turn now. Half an hour each. Go on,

Antonio, get in, please.' He tried to make his tone as conciliatory as possible.

'They came back. I'd flagged them down and they came back. Why? Do you reckon they would have come back if they'd been thieves?' Bacci now seemed exhausted. As if he'd just given three litres of blood.

'So what? Get into the car, go on.' Miele opened the door of the police car. 'You've had a hard day. I'll check their papers and let them go.' He pushed him in.

'Hurry up, and let's go home,' said Bacci, completely drained.

Miele closed the door and released the safety catch on his pistol.

Now then.

He straightened his cap and strode towards the stolen Merc.

Bruno Miele's role models were early Clint Eastwood – Dirty Harry – and Steve McQueen in *Bullitt*. Tough guys. Cool customers who'd shoot you in the mouth without turning a hair. Short on chat, long on action.

Miele intended to become like them. But he had realised that in order to achieve this you had to have a mission, and he had found one. Reclaiming the area from urban blight and crime. And if he had to use force, so much the better.

The trouble was, he hated the uniform he wore. It made him sick. It was awful, pathetic. Lousy cut. Shoddy cloth. Like something made for the Polish police force. He would look at himself in the mirror and feel like throwing up. With that uniform on he would never be able to give of his best. Even Dirty Harry, in an Italian police uniform, would have been a nonentity, not for nothing did he wear tweed jackets and hip-hugging trousers. One more year and he'd be able to request a transfer to the special branch. If he was accepted he'd wear plain clothes and then he would feel at ease. A P38 in his shoulder holster. And that smooth white trenchcoat he'd bought at Orbano in the summer sales.

Miele knocked on the driver's window with his torch.

The window came down.

At the wheel was a boy.

He sized him up without showing any emotion (another distinctive feature of early Clint).

He was very ugly.

About twenty years old.

In five, maybe six years at the most, he would be bald. Miele could spot a baldy a mile off. Although this guy's hair was long and tied in a pony tail, above his forehead it was as sparse as the trees in a burnt-out forest. And his ears were as big as doughnuts, the left one sticking out more than the right. As if the deformity weren't obvious enough, five silver rings dangled from the lobe. The punk probably thought he looked like Bob Marley or some other fucking junkie rock star, but he looked more like Stan Laurel dressed up as the Wizard Zurlì.

The little turquoise-haired tart looked straight ahead with her jaw set. She had headphones over her ears. She wasn't that bad looking. Without that hardware on her face and that dye in her hair she would have been passable. Nothing to write home about even then, but okay for a blow job or a quickie with the lights turned off.

Miele leaned into the window. 'Good evening, sir. Can I see your papers, please?'

A strong aroma, as distinctive as that of cow dung, stimulated his receptors, creating a flow of ions which rose through his cranial nerves into his encephalon, where it discharged neuromediators onto the synapses of his memory centre. And Bruno Miele remembered.

He was sixteen and sitting on the beach at Castrone singing *Blowing in the Wind* with some kids from the Albano Laziale branch of Communion and Liberation who were camping nearby. Suddenly some hipsters had come along and started rolling cigarettes. They had offered him one and he, to impress a Catholic brunette, had accepted. One inhale and he had started coughing and spluttering and when he had asked what the hell it was, the hipsters had burst out laughing. Then someone had explained to him that the cigarette was filled with marijuana. He'd felt terrible for the rest of the week, because he thought this had made him a junkie.

In this Mercedes there was the same smell.

Hashish.

Smoke.

Drugs.

Stan Laurel and Pretty Hair had smoked a lot of joints. He aimed his torch at the ashtray.

Bingo. And that fool Bacci wanted to let them go . . .

Not just a lot, heaps of the damn things. The stubs were overflowing from the ashtray. They hadn't even bothered to get rid of them. Either they were two mental retards or they were too high to carry out even such a simple operation.

Stan Laurel opened the drawer in the dashboard and gave him his road tax booklet and insurance form.

'And your licence?'

Stan Laurel's real name was Massimiliano Franzini. He had been born on 25 July 1975 and his residence was in Rome, in Via Monti Parioli, 128.

His licence was in order.

'Who does the car belong to?'

'My father.'

He checked the registration documents. The car was registered in the name of Mariano Franzini, resident in Via Monti Parioli, 128.

'And your father can afford a car like this?'

'Yes.'

Miele reached out and with the tip of the torch touched the girl's thigh. 'Take off those headphones. Let's see your papers.'

Pretty Hair shifted one earphone, made a face as if she'd swallowed a dead rat, took her identity card out of her bag and handed it to him with a truculent gesture.

Her name was Martina Trevisan. She, too, was Roman and her address was Via Palenco, 34. Miele wasn't very expert in the place names of the capital, but he seemed to remember that Via Palenco was near Piazza Euclide. Parioli.

He handed back the documents and looked the two of them over.

Two snotty little Parioli kids playing at being punks.

Worse than car thieves. Much worse. At least thieves risked their own arses. These didn't. These were spoiled brats dressed up as tearaways. Born with silver spoons in their mouths and brought up on hundred-thousand-lire handouts and with parents who told them that they were the lords of the universe, that life is a bowl of cherries and that if they wanted to smoke pot it was fine and if they wanted to dress like bums it was no problem.

A broad grin spread across Miele's face, revealing a full set of yellow teeth.

That 'A' for anarchy written with marker pens on their jeans was an affront to someone who slaves away in the icy cold rain to uphold the rule of law, those joints chucked in the ashtray were a slap in the face to someone who once inadvertently took a drag from a joint and spent a whole week of his life in mortal dread of being a drug addict, those Coca-Cola cans contemptuously thrown under the seats of a car that no normal human being could afford even if he scrimped and saved all his life were an insult to someone who owns an Alfa 33 Twin Spark and washes it on Sundays at the drinking fountain and scratches around for second-hand spare parts. Everything those two represented, in short, was a raised middle finger to him and the entire police force.

Those sons of bitches were taking the piss out of him.

'Does your father know you've taken his car?'

'Yes.'

Making a show of checking the insurance form, Miele went on in a casual tone: 'Do you like smoking?' He glanced up and saw Stan Laurel nearly have a fit.

This galvanised him.

The cold had vanished. The rain no longer made him wet. He felt good. At peace with the world.

It's a thousand times better being a cop than a footballer.

He had them in the palm of his hand.

'Do you like smoking?' he repeated in the same casual tone.

'Sorry, officer, I didn't quite catch that,' stammered Stan Laurel.

'Do you like smoking?'

'Yes.'

'What?'

'What do you mean, what?'

'What do you like smoking?'

'Chesterfields.'

'Not joints?'

'No.' Stan's voice, however, quivered like a violin string.

'No? Why are you trembling, then?'

'I'm not trembling.'

'Oh, I see. You're not trembling, I do apologise.' He smiled contentedly and shone the light in Pretty Hair's face.

'The young man says you don't like hash. Is that so?'

Martina, shielding her eyes with her hand, shook her head.

'What's up, are you too strung out to talk?'

'We smoked a couple of joints, so what?' replied Pretty Hair in a voice as shrill and grating as a fingernail on a blackboard.

Ah . . . so you're a tough one! Not a little wimp like Flappy-Ears.

'So what? You may not be aware of the fact, but in Italy that constitutes an offence.'

'It's for personal use,' retorted the little bitch in a schoolmistressy tone.

'Oh, for personal use, is it? Well, just watch. Watch this.'

Max found himself in the water.

Flat on his face, arms outstretched, like a lion skin.

He hadn't had time to react, defend himself, do anything.

The door had opened and that bastard had grabbed his ponytail with both hands and yanked him out. For a moment he had feared he meant to tear his hair out by the roots, but the son of a bitch had swung him out into the middle of the lay-by as if he were a weight tied to a rope. And Max had flown forward, head down, and fallen nose down in a puddle.

He couldn't breathe.

He pulled himself up to his knees. The impact on the asphalt had compressed his sternum, making his lungs collapse. He opened his mouth and emitted some guttural sounds. Nothing. He tried to breathe, but couldn't suck air. He gasped, bending forward in the rain, and around him everything evaporated and became darkness. Black and yellow. Yellow flowers blossomed in their hundreds before his eyes. In his ears he heard a low throbbing buzz like the distant engine of an oil tanker.

I'm dying. I'm dying. I'm dying. Shit, I'm dying.

Then, when he was sure he was a goner, something opened in his chest, a valve perhaps, something relaxed, anyway, and a thin stream of air was sucked voraciously into his thirsty lungs. Max breathed. And breathed and breathed again. His face turned from puce to scarlet. Then he started coughing and spluttering and was again aware of the rainwater running down his neck and drenching his hair.

'Get up. Come on.'

A hand seized him by the collar. He found himself on his feet.

'Are you all right?'

Max shook his head.

'Of course you are. I've cleared away that haze that had descended over you. Now I bet you understand me better.'

Max looked up.

That piece of shit was standing in the middle of the lay-by, soaking wet, and opening his arms like a crazed preacher or something. His face concealed in the darkness.

Martina was there, too. Standing. Legs spread apart. Hands against the door of the Mercedes.

'Even though what you people have consumed was, as the young lady quite rightly informs us, for personal use, we must now make quite certain that there aren't any drugs hidden somewhere, because then it would be more serious, much more serious, do you want to know why? Because then it would be illegal possession of drugs for the purpose of dealing.'

'Max, is everything all right? Are you okay?' Martina, without turning, called to him anxiously.

'Yes. How about you?'

'I'm okay . . .' Her voice was broken. She was on the point of tears.

'Wonderful. I'm okay too. That makes three of us who are all okay. So now we can devote our attention to more serious problems,' said the policeman in the middle of the lay-by.

He's mad. Raving mad, Max said to himself.

Maybe he wasn't even a policeman. Maybe he was a dangerous psychopath disguised as a policeman. Like in *Maniac Cop*. What had happened to the other one, the officer they'd seen before, the one with the gun? Had he killed him? The light inside the police car was on, but the rain on the windows made it impossible to see in.

He was dazzled by the policeman's torch.

'Where's the stuff?'

'What stuff? There isn't a . . . ny . . . stuff.' *Oh shit, I'm starting to cry too*. He felt the emotion wrapping its merciless coils round his Adam's apple and windpipe. And an uncontrollable tremor shook him from head to foot.

'Strip!'

'What do you mean, strip?'

'Strip! I've got to search you.'

'I haven't got anything on me.'

'Prove it.' The policeman had raised his voice. And he was losing his temper.

'But . . .'

'No buts. You have to obey. I represent the established order and you represent anarchy, and you have been caught in the act of violating the law, so if I order you to strip you strip, do you understand? Do I have to draw my gun and insert it between your tonsils? Is that what you want me to do?' He had regained that calm tone, that tone which presaged disasters and violence.

Max took off his checked shirt and laid it on the ground. Then he took off his fleece and his T-shirt. The policeman watched him with folded arms. He nodded to him to continue. He undid his belt and his three-sizes-too-big trousers, which slipped down like a torn curtain, leaving him in his underpants. His legs were hairless, white and twig-thin.

'Take everything off. You might have hid . . .'

'Here! Here it is! He hasn't got it, I have,' shouted Martina, who was still standing with her hands against the car. Max couldn't see her face.

'What have you got?' The policeman went over to her.

'Here! Look.' Martina opened her bag and took out some pot. A tiny amount. A couple of grams at most. 'Here it is.'

It was all they had.

Only half an hour earlier, on a planet light-years away from there, a planet with adjustable heating, the music of REM and leather seats, Martina was talking. 'I tried to buy some more. I rang Pinocchio' (and Max had thought to himself, pushers always have the same corny nicknames) 'but he wasn't in. It's not much, but never mind. We'll make do. Besides, if we get smashed we won't be able to study . . .'

'Give it here.' The policeman took the piece of hashish and held it to his nose. 'Don't make me laugh. These are the crumbs, where's the main stash? In the car? Or has one of you got it on you?'

'I swear, I swear to God it's all we've got. There isn't any more. It's the truth. Fuck you. You son of a bitch. It's the tru . . .' Martina stopped talking and began to cry.

She seemed smaller now that she was finally crying. The snot ran down from her nose and the eye-shadow had dissolved under her eyes and the blue brush she wore on her head had wilted, sticking to her forehead. A little teenager sobbing her heart out.

'Is it in the car? Tell me, have you hidden it in the car?'

'Go and see for yourself, you bastard. There isn't a fucking thing in there,' Martina screamed and then flew at him with clenched fists and the policeman grabbed her wrists and Martina growled and cried and the policeman shouted. 'What are you trying to do? What are you trying to do? You're only making things worse for yourself' and he twisted her arm behind her back, making her shriek with pain. Then he handcuffed her wrist to the window frame.

Max, with his trousers down, watched his fellow student and future girlfriend being manhandled, without lifting a finger.

It was the policeman's tone that prevented him from reacting. It was too calm. As if to him it were the most normal thing in the world to grab a guy by the hair and hurl him on the ground and then beat up a girl.

He's completely nuts. This thought, instead of throwing him into an absolute panic, calmed him down.

He was crazy. That was why Max must not do anything.

Some people have had the experience of dying and being brought back to life. A matter of a few seconds, during which the lungs are immobile, the electrocardiogram is flat and there is no sign of life. They are clinically dead. Then the efforts of the doctors, the adrenaline, the electric shocks and the cardiac massages revive the heart, which gradually starts beating again and these lucky people revive.

On reawakening, if we may call it that, some have reported having the impression, while they were dead, of seeing themselves on the operating table surrounded by doctors and nurses. They had watched the scene from above, as if a TV camera (the soul, others say) which had been ballasted down in their mortal remains, had broken free and tracked away backwards and upwards.

A feeling similar to that which Max was experiencing at that moment.

He saw the scene from afar. As in a film, or rather on a set where a film was being made. A violent film. The blue light of the police car. The headlights of the Mercedes glaring in the puddles. The darkness lashed by the rain. The cars racing by on the road. The distant chimes of a bell.

I hadn't noticed that bell, till now.

And that phoney policeman and, on her knees, a thin girl

who I only met this morning

who was sobbing, handcuffed to the door of the car. And then there was him, in his underpants, shivering, teeth chattering, helpless.

It was perfect. Just like a film script.

And the most absurd thing was that it was true and that it was happening to him, the great action-film fan, who had seen *Duel* dozens of times, *Deliverance* four times and *The Hitcher* at least twice, and who, if he'd been sitting in the second row of the Embassy with a packet of popcorn in his hand, would have revelled in such a hardhitting scene. He would have delighted in its realism. In the unusual violence that the director had succeeded in putting into it. How strange that he, who would have applauded so enthusiastically, should now be on the receiving end . . .

Does not try hard enough and does not join in.

How often had they written that crap on his school report?

'LEAVE HER ALONE!' he shouted at the top of his voice. At vocal-chord-breaking pitch. 'LEAVE HER ALONE!'

He charged like a wounded animal at that bastard motherfuckingsonofabitch but fell flat on his face after barely taking a step.

He had tripped over his trousers.

And he lay there in the cold night, crying.

Maybe I'm being a trifle heavy-handed.

It was the sight of Stan Laurel tripping over his trousers and falling in a puddle squealing like a stuck pig that caused this moral doubt to form in the mind of officer Bruno Miele.

It might have been hilariously funny, like something out of Mr Bean, that poor bastard with his trousers round his ankles trying to attack him and falling over, but instead the scene had frozen the smile on his face. Suddenly he felt rather sorry for the guy. A twenty-year-old who starts blubbing like a kid and can't face up to his own responsibilities. When he had seen the film *The Bear*, at the moment where the hunters kill mama bear and the cub understands that the Earth is an awful place populated by sons of bitches and that he is going to have to fend for himself, he had felt something similar. A lump in his throat and an involuntary contraction of the facial muscles.

(*What the hell's the matter with you?*)

The matter? Nothing!

He didn't feel at all sorry for the girl.

Quite the opposite. He felt like giving her a good slap across the face. He found her so repulsive, with that hysterical little voice like the whine of an electric saw, that he wouldn't even have screwed her. Yes, he really felt like slapping her face. But that bastard had better stop crying, or he would start crying himself soon.

He squatted down beside Stan . . . What was his name? Massimiliano Franzini. He addressed him in a tone as sweet as a Sicilian cassata. 'Get up. Don't cry. Come on now, you'll catch cold, lying on the ground like that.'

No response.

It seemed as if he hadn't heard him, but at least he'd stopped crying. He took him by the arm and tried to pull him up, but without success. 'Come on, don't cry. I'll check the car and if I don't find anything I'll let you go. How about that?'

He had said this to induce him to stand up. He wasn't so sure that he was going to let them go so easily. There were still the matter of all those joints they had smoked. And he would have to ask the station to check their names. The report to write. A whole lot of things to do.

'Get up or I'm going to lose my temper.'

Flappy Ears finally raised his head. His face was smeared with grime and a second mouth in his forehead was spewing blood. His eyes were tearful and tired, but gleamed with a strange determination. He showed his teeth. 'Why should I?'

'Because I say so. You can't stay on the ground.'

'Why not?'

'Because you'll catch cold.'

'Why? Why do you do this?'

'Do what?'

'Why do you behave like this?'

Miele took two steps backwards.

As if suddenly it was no longer Stan Laurel on the ground but a venomous cobra swelling its neck.

'Get up. I'll ask the questions. Ge . . .'

(*Explain to him why you behave like this.*)

'. . . t up,' he stammered.

(*Tell him.*)

What?

(Tell him the truth. Explain it to him, go on. Don't give him any crap. That way you'll explain it to us, too. Because we don't really understand either. Tell him, go on, what are you waiting for?)

Miele backed away. He looked like a tailor's dummy. The trousers of his uniform were soaked up to the knees, his jacket had a dark patch on the shoulders and back. 'You want me to tell you, do you? Okay then, I'll tell you, if that's what you want.' He went up to Flappy Ears, grabbed his head and turned it in the direction of the Mercedes. 'Do you see that car there? That car comes on the road, without optionals, at a hundred and seventy-nine million lire including VAT, but if you add the folding roof, the wide wheels, the computerised air conditioning, the hi-fi unit with the boot-mounted CD changer and the active subwoofer, the leather interiors, the lateral airbag and all the rest, we easily get up to two hundred and ten, two hundred and twenty million. That car has a braking system controlled by a sixteen-bit processor identical to the one used by McLaren in Formula One, it has a sealed box containing a chip produced by Motorola which controls the set-up of the vehicle, regulates the tyre pressure and the height of the shock-absorbers, even though all these things, actually, are things you could find – not quite the same, a bit worse – on a top-of-the-range BMW or Saab. The exceptional thing about that car, the thing that gets enthusiasts literally masturbating, is the engine. It has a capacity of six thousand three hundred and twenty-five cc distributed over twelve pistons made of a special alloy whose exact composition is known only to Mercedes. It was designed by Hans Peter Fleming, the Swedish engineer who created the propulsion system of the Space Shuttle and of the American atomic submarine *Alabama*. Have you ever tried starting in fifth? Probably not, but if you did you'd find that this car will do it. It has an engine so flexible you can change gear without using the clutch. It has an acceleration that will leave all those crappy coupés that are so fashionable nowadays trailing in its wake and can hold its own with a Lamborghini or a Corvette, if you get the picture. And what about its shape? Elegant. Sober. Nothing flashy. No Martian headlamps. No plastics. Sophisticated. The classic three-litre Mercedes. This car is the preferred drive of Gianmaria Davoli, the Grand Prix presenter, who could use a Ferrari 306 or a Testarossa like I use a pair of sandals. And you know what our prime minister said at the Turin Motor Show? He said that this car is a target to aim at and that when we in Italy succeed in making a car like it we'll be able to say we're a democratic country. But I don't think we ever will, we don't have the right mentality to make a car like that. Now, I don't know who your father is, or how he earns his money. He may be a mafioso or a corrupt politician or a pimp, I don't give a shit. I respect your father, he's a person who deserves respect because he owns a 650 TX. Your father is a man who appreciates things of value, he's bought this car, he's spent a lot of money and I bet my life he doesn't know that you, you son of a bitch, have stolen it from him to chauffeur around a little tart with blue hair and rings on her face and to smoke joints in it and throw half-eaten sandwiches on the floor. You know what I think? I think you two are the first people in the world who have ever smoked pot in a 650 TX. Maybe some rock star has sniffed a few lines of coke in one, but nobody, and I mean nobody, has ever smoked pot in one. You two have committed an act of sacrilege, of blasphemy. Getting high in a 650 TX is like shitting in St Peter's. Now do you understand why I behave like this?'

If officer Antonio Bacci hadn't fallen asleep as soon as he set foot in the police vehicle, perhaps the Bruno Miele Magic Show, live from the hundred-and-twelfth kilometre of the Via Aurelia, would not have gone off so well and Max Franzini and Martina Trevisan would not have kept telling the story of that terrible nocturnal experience for years to come (Max, in corroboration, would point to the scar on his balding forehead).

But Antonio Bacci, as soon as he entered the warmth of the car, had loosened his bootlaces, folded his arms and, without realising it, fallen into a heavy sleep peopled by coconuts, puffer fish, silicone masks and bikini-clad air hostesses.

When the radio crackled into life, Bacci woke up. 'Patrol car 12! Patrol car 12! This is an emergency. Go at once to the junior high school in Ischiano Scalo, there's been a break-in. Patrol c . . .'

Shit, I fell asleep, he realised, seizing the microphone and looking at his watch. *Jesus, I've been asleep for over half an hour! What's Miele doing out there?*

It was a few seconds before headquarters' instructions sank in, but at last he managed to reply. 'Message received. We'll get going straight away. Should be there in ten minutes at the outside.'

Burglars. In his son's school.

He got out of the car. It was raining as hard as ever and on top of that there was a blustery wind which blew you off track. He hurried forward two steps, but immediately slowed down.

The Mercedes was still there. Handcuffed to the door was the girl with blue hair. She was sitting on the ground, hugging her legs with her arm. Miele was crouching in the middle of the lay-by talking to the boy, who was lying in his underclothes in a puddle.

He approached his partner and in an incredulous voice asked him what was going on.

'Oh, there you are.' Miele looked up and beamed contentedly. He was completely drenched. 'Nothing. I was just explaining something to him.'

'And why is he in his underclothes?'

The boy was shaking like a leaf and had a gash on his head.

'I searched him. I caught them smoking hashish. They handed some over, but I have reason to believe that they have more, hidden in the car. We must check . . .'

Bacci took him by the arm and pulled him away, where those two couldn't hear. 'Have you gone out of your mind? Did you hit him? If they report you you're going to be in real trouble.'

Miele shook himself free. 'How many times have I told you not to touch me! I didn't hit him. He fell down. Everything's under control.'

'Why did you handcuff the girl?'

'She's hysterical. She tried to attack me. Calm down. Nothing's happened.'

'Listen. We've got to go to the junior high school in Ischiano right away. There's an emergency. Apparently there's been a break-in and shots have been heard . . .'

'Shots?' Miele had begun to get agitated. His hands twitched frenetically. 'Shots have been heard in the school?'

'Yes.'

'In the school?'

'I said yes.'

'Ohmygodohmygodohmygodohmygod . . .' Now those fingers as agitated as a grasshopper's legs had clutched Miele's face and were pinching his lips, his nose, ruffling his hair.

'What's the matter?'

'My father's in there, you fool. The Sardinians! Papa was right. Let's go, quick, there's no time to lose . . .' said Miele in a panicky voice and went towards the two youngsters.

Oh yes. It had slipped Bacci's mind. *Miele's father is the school caretaker* . . .

Miele ran over to the boy, who was now on his feet, picked up from the ground his clothes, now reduced to soaking wet rags, and thrust them into his hand, then went over to the girl and released her, started back but then stopped. 'Listen, you two, this time you've got away with it, but you won't next time. Quit smoking pot. It rots your brain. And quit dressing like that. I'm telling you this for your own good. We've got to go. Dry yourselves or you'll catch flu.' Then he addressed the boy alone. 'Oh, and tell your father from me he's got a beautiful car.' He rejoined Bacci and the two policemen got into the patrol car and drove off, siren blaring.

Max saw them disappear along the Aurelia. He threw aside the clothes, pulled up his trousers, ran over to Martina and embraced her.

They stood clinging together, like Siamese twins, for a good while. And silently they cried. They ran their fingers through each other's hair while the icy, indifferent rain continued to lash them.

They kissed each other. First on the neck, then on the cheeks and finally on the lips.

'Let's get into the car,' said Martina, pulling him inside. They shut the doors and turned on the computerised air conditioning which in a few seconds turned the car into a furnace. They undressed, dried themselves, put on the warmest things they had and kissed again.

And that is how Max Franzini passed the daunting kiss test.

And those kisses were the first of many. Max and Martina started going out, lived together for three years (in the second year a baby girl was born whom they called Stella), then got married in Seattle, where they opened an Italian restaurant.

During the next few days, in the villa at San Folco, they thought long and hard about reporting that bastard, but in the end they decided to drop the matter. You never knew how it would end and then there was the problem of the hashish and the car he had taken without his father's permission. Better just forget about it.

But that night remained for ever etched on their memories. The terrible night when they experienced the misfortune of bumping into officer Miele and the great joy of emerging unscathed and becoming lovers.

Max turned on the ignition, slotted the REM album into the CD player and drove off out of this story.

10th December

38

Dring dring dring.

When the phone started ringing, Miss Flora Palmieri was dreaming that she was in the beautician's studio. She was lying peacefully on the couch when the door opened and in came a dozen silver-coated koalas. She knew, without knowing why, that those marsupials were bent on trimming her toenails.

They had nail clippers in their hands and they danced around her, singing merrily.

'*Trik trik trik*. We're dear little bears, as everyone knows, we're going to trim the nails on your toes. *Trik trik trik dring dring dring.*'

With their clippers in their hands.

Dring dring dring.

And the phone kept ringing.

Flora Palmieri opened her eyes.

Darkness.

Dring dring dring.

She fumbled for the switch and turned on the lamp.

She looked at the digital alarm clock on the bedside table.

Five forty.

And the phone kept ringing.

Who on earth can it be?

She got up, put on her slippers and hurried into the sitting room.

'Hallo?'

'Hallo, is that you, Miss Palmieri? I'm sorry to disturb you at this hour . . . It's Giovanni Cosenza.'

The headmaster!

'Did I wake you up?' he asked hesitantly.

'Well, it is five forty in the morning.'

'I'm sorry. I wouldn't have rung you, but something very serious has happened . . .'

Flora tried to imagine what could have been so serious as to justify the headmaster's calling her at this ungodly hour, but she couldn't think of anything.

'What is it?'

'There's been a break-in at the school during the night. They've smashed the whole place up . . .'

'Who?'

'Vandals.'

'Really?'

'Yes, they got in and smashed the television and the video recorder, sprayed paint all over the walls, and chained up the school gate. Italo tried to stop them but he's in hospital and the police are here . . .'

'What's happened to Italo?'

'I think he's got a broken nose and he hurt his arms.'

'But who was it?'

'We don't know. There are some things written on the wall which seem to suggest they might have been pupils from the school, but I'm not sure . . . Anyway, the police are here, there are a lot of things to do, decisions to take, and these scrawls . . .'

'What kind of scrawls?'

The headmaster hesitated. 'Nasty ones . . .'

'How do you mean, nasty?'

'Nasty. Nasty. Very nasty, Miss Palmieri.'

'Nasty? What does it say?'

'Er . . . Could you come here?'

'When?'

'Now.'

'Yes, of course, I'll come right away . . . I'll get dressed and I'll be there . . . shall we say in half an hour?'

'All right. I'll be expecting you.'

She put down the phone, very agitated. 'Oh my goodness, what can have happened?' She wandered round the house for a couple of minutes, not knowing what to do. She was a methodical woman. And emergencies threw her into a panic. 'Oh yes, I must go to the bathroom.'

39

Ra ta ta ta ta ta . . .

There was a helicopter in Graziano Biglia's brain.

An Apache, one of those huge combat machines.

And if he lifted his head off the pillow it was even worse, because the helicopter started napalming his poor aching brain.

What was that again? You weren't going to let anyone take you for a ride? Everything would be fine? I can get along perfectly well without her? . . . Bah!

And to think that everything had been going smoothly till he'd gone into that crummy Western Bar-Tobacconist's.

His recall of the night was like a black, moth-eaten cloth. Every now and then you found a little hole through which a bit of light shone.

He'd gone down to the seashore. That he did remember. It was bitterly cold and he'd slipped and fallen among the beach huts. He'd wandered about in the rain singing.

Wave on wave, the ship, cast adrift, the bananas, the raspberries . . .

Ra ta ta ta ta . . .

He must take something, quickly.

A magic pill that would shoot down the helicopter caged inside his head. Its rotor was whisking up his brain like a vanilla Danette.

Graziano reached out and turned on the light. He opened his eyes. He shut them again. He opened them slowly and saw John Travolta.

At least I'm at home.

40

Every morning Flora Palmieri had a long ritual to go through.

First of all a bath, in foam scented with Irish lily of the valley. Then listening to the first part of *Good Morning Italy* with Elisabetta Baffigi and Paolo d'Andreis on the radio. And breakfast with cereal.

This morning all that would have to go by the board.

Those nasty things written on the wall. She was sure they were about her.

What on earth could they say?

Actually, in a way she was pleased. At least now the headmaster and the deputy headmistress, faced with this crisis, would be forced to act.

For several months someone had been playing practical jokes on her. At first they had been harmless pranks. The blackboard rubber glued to her desk. A toad in her handbag. A caricature on the blackboard. Drawing-pins on her chair. Then they had stolen the register. Not content with that, they had raised the stakes by puncturing the tyres of her Y10 and jamming a potato in her exhaust pipe. And to cap it all, one evening while she was watching television a stone had smashed the sitting-room window. She'd nearly had a heart attack.

At that point she had gone to see the deputy headmistress and told her the whole story. 'I'm sorry, but there's nothing I can do about it,' the old dragon had said. 'We don't know who's responsible. And we're powerless to act because it happened outside school. Anyway, in my opinion, if you don't mind my saying so, Miss Palmieri, it's partly your own fault that things have come to such a pass. You just don't seem to be able to establish a constructive dialogue with your students.'

Flora had reported the matter to the police, but they hadn't done anything.

Maybe now . . .

Finally she collected her thoughts and entered the bathroom, adjusted the flow of the shower and took off her clothes.

41

He was dressed.

Timberlands on his feet. A rancid, pungent smell of . . .

'Damn I've puked on myself.'

Another little hole.

Graziano had been in the car and driving. Suddenly a sour stream of Jack Daniel's had risen up through his gullet and he'd turned his head and vomited out of the window. Only the window had been closed.

Ugh, what a mess . . .

He opened the drawer and began fishing out bottles at random.

Alka-Seltzer. Panadol. Aspirin. Anadin. Senokot. Nurofen.

He hadn't made it. He hadn't managed to hold out, to resist the enormous wave of shit that had hit him.

And to think that for a couple of hours after the phone call he'd lived in a strange, euphoric Zen-like detachment.

42

That Miss Palmieri had a beautiful body there wasn't a shadow of doubt.

She was tall and slim, with long shapely legs. Maybe she didn't have much in the way of hips, but nature had endowed her with a full bosom which was set off by her slender body. Her skin was white, pure white, the white of the dead. Completely hairless except for a little carrot-coloured tuft on her pubes.

Her faced seemed carved out of wood. All hard edges and pointed cheekbones. A wide mouth with thin bloodless lips. Strong, yellowish teeth. A long wafer-thin nose divided two eyes that were as round and grey as river pebbles.

She had a prodigious mass of red hair, a curly mane that reached halfway down her back. Out of doors she always wore it in a bun.

When she emerged from the shower, despite her haste she glanced in the mirror.

This was something she had seldom done in the past, but lately she had been doing it more and more often.

She was ageing. Not that this bothered her, quite the contrary, in fact. She was intrigued by the way that with every passing day her skin became less fresh, her hair less glossy, her eyes duller. She was thirty-two and might have looked younger if it hadn't been for that cobweb of thin lines around her mouth and for the slightly loose skin on her neck.

She looked, and didn't like what she saw.

She hated her breasts. They were too big. She wore a five, but when she had her period it could hardly contain them.

She took them in her hands. She felt an urge to squeeze them till they burst like ripe melons. Why had nature played this obscene trick on her? Those two monstrous, hypertrophic glands were out of all proportion to her slight figure. Her mother had never had two things like that. They made her look like a loose woman and, if she didn't crush them into elasticated bras, if she didn't disguise them under prim-looking clothes, she felt men's eyes on her. She would have paid to have them surgically reduced, if she'd had the courage.

She put on her bathrobe, went into the little kitchen and pulled up the shutters.

Another rainy day.

She went to the fridge and took out some cooked chicken livers, courgettes and boiled carrots. She put them all in the blender.

'I've got to go out, Mama,' she said aloud. 'I'm going to give you your breakfast a little earlier than usual this morning, I'm sorry but I must rush to school . . .' She switched on the blender. In an instant the ingredients turned into a pink mush. She switched it off.

'That was the headmaster on the phone. I've got to hurry to school.' She took the lid off the blender and poured in some water and soy sauce. She stirred it. 'There's been a break-in at the school. I'm rather worried.' She put the mixture into a large feeding bottle. She warmed the bottle in the microwave. 'They've written some nasty things . . . Probably about me.'

She walked across the kitchen with the bottle and entered a dark bedroom. She turned on the switch. The neon crackled and lit up a small room. Not much bigger than the kitchen. Four white walls, a small window with the shutters down, grey linoleum on the floor, a crucifix, an aluminium-framed bed, a chair, a bedside table and a drip stand. That was all.

Lying on the bed was Lucia Palmieri.

43

Graziano had taken a long shower and gone out at nine thirty the previous evening.

Destination? The Mignon Cinema in Orbano.

Title of film? *Knock Off.*

Actor? Jean-Claude Van Damme. One of the greats.

When your heart has been ripped out of your body and mashed to a pulp the best cure's a trip to the cinema, he had said to himself.

After the film a pizza, and then to bed, like a wise old man.

Everything would probably have gone according to plan had he not stopped at the Western to get some cigarettes. He had bought them and was about to leave when it had occurred to him that after all one little whisky couldn't do him any harm, in fact it might cheer him up.

And indeed it might have, had it been only been one.

Graziano had sat at the bar and downed a series of harmless whiskies and the pain, hitherto stifled in the depths of his being, had begun to writhe and howl like a tortured mongrel.

Ditched me, have you? Fine. Who cares? No problem. Graziano Biglia is better off without you, you slut. To hell with you. Go ahead and screw Mantovani. I don't give a shit.

He had started talking out loud. 'I'm fine. Couldn't be better. What did you think I was going to do, burst into tears? Well you were wrong, baby. Sorry to disappoint you. Do you know how many women there are in the world who are sexier than you?

Millions. You'll never hear of me again. You'll miss me, you'll come looking for me, but I'll be gone.'

A group of children, sitting at a table, were looking at him. 'What are you lot staring at? Come over here and tell me to my face if there's anything you object to,' he'd barked and then, taking the bottle from the counter, he'd sat down wounded and forlorn at the darkest table in the bar and had taken out his mobile.

44

Before her illness, Lucia had been as tall as her daughter. Now she was about one metre fifty-two and weighed thirty-five kilos. As if some alien parasite had sucked out all her flesh and innards. She was reduced to a skeleton covered with loose, bluish skin.

She was seventy and suffered from a rare and irreversible form of degeneration of the central and peripheral nervous systems.

She lived, if it could be called living, confined to that bed. More insensate than a bivalve mollusc, she didn't speak, didn't feel, didn't move a muscle, didn't do a thing.

Well, there was one thing she did.

She looked at you.

With two huge grey eyes, the same colour as her daughter's. Eyes that seemed to have seen something so immense that they'd burnt out, short-circuiting her whole body. Having been immobile for so long, her muscles had turned to jelly and her bones had shrunk and twisted like the branches of a fig tree. When her daughter had to make her bed she would pick her up and cradle her in her arms like a baby.

45

Graziano had dialled the first number memorised in the phone book of his mobile.

'Hallo, this is Graziano, who's that?'

'Tony.'

'Hi, Tony.'

Tony Dawson, deejay of the Anthrax disco and Erica's ex.

(Of course Graziano didn't know about that last detail.)

'Graziano? Where are you?'

'At home. In Ischiano. How are things?'

'Not bad. Too much work. How about you?'

'Fine. Great.' Then he'd swallowed the tennis ball in his throat. 'I've split up with Erica,' he had added.

'No!'

'Yes.' And I'm glad about it, he had intended to add, but hadn't managed to.

'How come? You seemed so well suited to each other . . .'

There it was. There was the bloody question that would haunt him in the coming years.

How come he'd been such a fool as to leave an incredible piece of ass like that?

'The usual reasons. We hadn't been getting on so well lately.'

'Ah! Did you dump her or . . . or did she dump you?'

'Well, let's say I dumped her.'

'Why?'

'Oh, I don't know. You might say we split up because of incompatibility of character . . . We're such different people, our outlooks on life are light-years apart.'

'Ah . . .'

Despite the whisky that was marinating his stomach, Graziano had noticed that that 'Ah . . .' contained a good deal of scepticism, disbelief, pity and other things he didn't like at all. It was as if that bastard had said, 'Yeah, sure, pull the other one.'

'Yes, I dumped her because, to be quite honest, she's a bit unhinged. I'm sorry, I know she's a friend of yours, but Erica's got water where her brain should be. She's that kind of girl. Untrustworthy. I don't know how you can still be her friend. Especially as she says some pretty nasty things about you behind your back. Says you're the kind of guy who'll screw you as soon as he gets half a chance. If I were you – and I'm not saying this just because I'm angry you know – I'd steer clear of her. She's just a sl . . . ah, forget it.' At this point Graziano had had a vague perception which warned him to terminate that phone call. Tony Dawson wasn't the most, shall we say, appropriate person to confide in, being one of the Slut's closest friends.

As if that weren't enough, the deejay, as treacherous as an asp, had given him the final push. 'Erica's a bit of a gold-digger. That's the way she is. I know, I know.'

Graziano had swallowed a tot of whisky and taken new heart. 'So you'd noticed? Thank God for that. Yes, she's a real slut. One of those girls who'd walk over your dead body for a bit of success. You've no idea what she's capable of.'

'What, for example?'

'Anything. You know why she dumped me? Because they took her on as an assistant on *You Reap What You Sow*, the show presented by that poof Andrea Mantovani. And naturally she didn't want any deadweight preventing her from expressing herself as her nature impels her to, in other words like the slut she is. She dumped me because . . . how did she put it?' Graziano attempted a whining imitation of Erica's Trento accent. 'Because I despise you, and everything you represent. The way you dress. The bullshit you talk . . . You slut.'

There was a deathly hush at the other end, but Graziano didn't care, he was unloading the wagonful of shit he had accumulated in six months of torture and frustration and even if it had been Michael Jackson on the phone, or Eta Beta or Sai Baba in person, he didn't give a damn. He had to get it off his chest.

'Despise me and everything I represent! Can you believe that? What the hell do I represent, eh? The fool who showered gifts on you, put up with you, loved you as no other man ever has, who did everything, everything, ev . . . Shit! I must be going. Bye.'

He had cut short the conversation because a pain as sharp as a bee sting had shot through his carotid artery, and the fragile Zen superstructure had by now completely collapsed.

Graziano had picked up the bottle of whisky and staggered out of the Western Bar-Tobacconist's.

The cruel night had opened its jaws and swallowed him.

46

'Here you are. It's delicious, you'll see. I've put some chicken livers in it . . .' Flora Palmieri lifted her mother's head and put the bottle in her mouth. The old woman began to suck. With those bulging eyeballs and her head reduced to a skull, she looked like a newly hatched chick.

Flora was a perfect nurse, she poured homogenised soup down her throat three times a day and washed her every morning and in the evening helped her do her exercises and emptied the faeces and urine bags and twice a week changed her sheets and gave her a revitalising drip and always talked to her and told her lots of things and gave her enormous quantities of medicines and . . .

. . . she had been in this state for twelve years.

And she seemed to have no intention of leaving. That organism clung to life like a sea anemone to a rock. She had a pump inside her that beat as regularly as a Swiss clock. 'Congratulations! Your mother has the heart of an athlete, you can't imagine how many people wish they had such a good one,' the cardiologist had told her once.

Flora propped her mother up a bit higher. 'Tasty, isn't it? Did you hear what I said? There's been a break-in at the school. They've smashed everything up. Gently, gently or you'll choke . . .' She wiped away a little stream of pulp that was trickling down from the corner of her mouth. 'Now they'll see for themselves what some of the pupils are like. Hooligans. They talk of dialogue. And the pupils break into school during the night . . .'

Lucia Palmieri went on sucking voraciously and staring at a corner of the room.

'Poor Mama, having to have breakfast at this time of night . . .' Flora brushed her mother's white hair into place. 'I'll try to be back early. But now I really must go. Be good.' She detached the catheter and picked up the urine bag from the floor, kissed her on the forehead and went out of the room. 'This evening we'll have a bath. You'll like that, won't you?'

47

The fear which he had succeeded in banishing the previous evening tugged him roughly out of his sleep.

Pietro Moroni opened one eye and brought into focus the large Mickey Mouse clock ticking away merrily on the bedside cabinet.

Ten to six.

No way am I going to school today.

He felt his forehead, hoping he had a temperature.

It was as cold as that of a corpse.

A bit of light entered through the small window next to the bed, brightening one corner of the room. His brother was asleep. His pillow over his head. One foot, as long and white as a hake, stuck out of the blankets.

Pietro got up, put on his slippers and went to have a pee.

In the bathroom it was freezing. Steam came out of his mouth. While he was peeing, he rubbed his hand over the wet window and looked out.

What foul weather.

The sky was covered with a uniform mass of clouds which loured over the sodden countryside.

Whenever it rained hard, Pietro would catch the yellow school bus. The stop was about a kilometre away (it didn't come to the house, because the road was too badly rutted). Sometimes his father gave him a lift, but usually he walked, sheltering under his umbrella. If the rain wasn't hard, he would put on his yellow cape and galoshes and go by bike.

His mother was already in the kitchen.

There was a clanking of pans and a smell of fried onions.

Zagor was barking.

He looked out of the window.

His father, hidden under his rainproof cape, was in the dog's enclosure, fetching the bags of cement heaped up near the kennel. Zagor, on his chain, was whining and flattening down in the mud and trying to attract his attention.

Shall I tell him?

His father ignored the animal, as if it didn't exist. He would pick up a bag, hoist it on his shoulder and then, head down, throw it on the trailer of the tractor and start all over again.

Should he tell him? Tell him everything, tell him they'd forced him to break into the school?

(*Excuse me, Papa, I've got something to tell you, last night . . .*)

No.

He had a feeling his father wouldn't understand and would be angry. Furious, in fact.

(*Won't it be even worse if he finds out later?*)

But it wasn't my fault.

He gave his willy a vigorous shake and hurried back to his room.

He must stop thinking it wasn't his fault. It didn't change anything, in fact it only made things more difficult. He must stop thinking about school. He must sleep.

'Oh God, what a mess,' he whispered, and leaped back up into his warm bed.

The Washing Machine

It was a strange business, guilt.

Pietro still hadn't figured out how it worked.

Everywhere – at school, in Italy, all over the world – if you make a mistake, if you do something you shouldn't do, something naughty, then you're guilty and you get punished.

Justice should mean that everyone pays for his own misdeeds. But that wasn't how it worked in his family.

Pietro had learned this at a very early age.

Guilt, in his home, crashed down from the sky like a meteorite.

Sometimes – often, in fact – it fell on you. At other times, by sheer luck, you managed to avoid it.

It was a lottery, in other words.

And it all depended on what mood Papa was in.

If he was in a good mood, you might have done something really terrible, yet nothing would happen to you, but if he was in a bad mood (and this was becoming more and more common) even an air crash in Barbados or a successful coup in the Congo was your fault.

In the spring Mimmo had broken the washing machine.

'Stonewashed', he had read on the label of Patti's jeans. He liked those trousers very much. His girlfriend had explained to him that the reason they were so nice was that they were literally washed with stones. Stones could make jeans white and soft. Mimmo hadn't wasted much time thinking about it, he'd filled a bucket with stones and emptied it into the washing machine along with his jeans and half a litre of bleach.

Result: both the jeans and the drum of the washing machine were a write-off.

When Mr Moroni had found out, he'd nearly had a fit. 'How is it possible that I have such a boneheaded son? It's difficult to be so unlucky,' he had roared, thumping his chest, and then he had blamed his wife's genetic inheritance for flooding her children with idiocy.

He had called customer service and the day the technician was to come coincided with the one when he had to take his wife to a doctor's appointment in Civitavecchia, so he had said to Pietro: 'Now, I want you to stay at home. Show the technician where the washing machine is. He'll take it away. Your mother and I will be back this evening. Whatever you do, don't go out.'

And Pietro had stayed quietly at home, done all his homework and at five thirty on the dot had sat down in front of the television to watch *Star Trek*.

Then his brother had arrived with Patti and they too had sat down to watch *Star Trek*.

But Mimmo had no intention of following the adventures of Captain Kirk and co. It was rare for his mother to leave the house and he meant to seize his chance. He squeezed and groped his girlfriend like an octopus on heat.

But Patrizia wriggled away and slapped his hands and snorted. 'Leave me alone, don't touch me. Stop it, will you?'

'What's the matter? Why don't you want to? Have you got your period?' Mimmo had whispered in her ear and then tried to explore it with the tip of his tongue.

Patrizia had jumped to her feet and pointed at Pietro. 'You know perfectly well why. Your brother's here. It's as simple as that. He's always hanging around . . . He's a pest, he gawps at us . . . He spies on us. Get rid of him.'

This wasn't true.

The only thing Pietro was interested in was what had happened to Mr Spock, nothing was further from his mind than watching those two necking and pawing at each other.

The truth was different. Patti was angry with Pietro. She was jealous. The two brothers stuck together and joked too much for her liking and Patrizia, on principle, was jealous of anyone who had too close a relationship with her boyfriend.

'Can't you see? He's watching TV . . .' Mimmo had replied.

'Get rid of him. Otherwise, forget it.'

Mimmo had gone over to Pietro. 'Why don't you go and play outside? Go for a ride on your bike.' And then he had tried a little ruse. 'I've already seen this episode, it's rubbish.'

'I like it . . .' Pietro had retorted.

Mimmo had wandered dispiritedly round the room searching for a solution and at last had found one. Simple. Put his parents' two beds together to make a double.

Brilliant.

'What time are Mama and Papa coming back?' he'd asked Pietro.

'They've gone to the doctor's. About eight thirty, nine. Late. I don't know.'

'Great. Come on, let's go.' Mimmo had grabbed Patti by the

hand and tried to yank her away. But it was no good. She wouldn't budge.

'No way. I'm not coming. Not with that pest in the house.'

Mimmo had then played his last ace. With a show of generosity, he had taken ten thousand lire from his wallet and had told Pietro to go and buy him some cigarettes. ' . . . and you can keep the change. Buy yourself a nice ice cream and have a couple of games in the arcade.'

'I can't. Papa said I've got to stay at home. I've got to wait for the washing machine man,' Pietro had answered solemnly. 'He'll be cross if I go out.'

'Don't worry about that. I'll see to it. I'll show him the washing machine. You go and get the cigarettes.'

'But . . . but . . . Papa'll be cross. I don't . . .'

'Get out. Vamoose.' Mimmo had put the money in his trouser pocket and shoved him out of the house.

Naturally everything goes as badly as it possibly could go.

Pietro dashes off to the village, and on the way there meets Gloria who is on her way to a riding lesson and implores him to go with her and he, as usual, lets himself be talked into it. Meanwhile the Rex repair man arrives. He finds the cottage door shut and rings the bell but Mimmo can't hear, he is fighting a ferocious battle with Patti's elasticated trousers (she, perfidious girl, does hear but keeps quiet). The repair man goes away. At seven thirty, an hour earlier than expected, Mr Moroni and wife park the Panda in the yard.

Mario Moroni gets out of the car in a filthy mood because he has spent three hundred and ninety thousand five hundred lire on neuro-crap for his wife and, shouting 'it won't do you a blind bit of good, all it'll do is fuck you up completely and put more money into the pockets of a bunch of conmen,' goes into the storeroom and discovers that the washing machine is still there. He goes upstairs. No sign of Pietro. He feels his hands grow suddenly warm and itchy as if he had nettle rash and his bladder is exploding, so he rushes upstairs (he's been dying for a pee ever since he left

Civitavecchia), pulls out his pecker in the corridor, opens the toilet door and gapes.

Sitting on the toilet is . . .

. . . *that little tart Patrizia!*

Her hair is wet and she is wearing his blue bathrobe and painting her toenails with red varnish, but when she sees him with his penis sticking out of his fly she starts screaming and yelling as if he were trying to rape her. Mr Moroni puts his penis back in his trousers and slams the toilet door so hard that a large piece of plaster is dislodged from the wall and falls on the floor. As wild as a warthog, he brings down his fist on the mahogany sideboard like a hammer on an anvil, splitting it in two. He breaks a couple of bones in his hand. He stifles a howl of agony and goes to seek out Mimmo in his room.

Mimmo isn't there.

He opens the door of HIS room and finds him sprawling on HIS bed, snoring away contentedly, stark naked, looking serene and satisfied, like a little angel who has just been the recipient of a blow job.

They've been scr . . . screwing on on my bed you you fucking little bastard respect no respect fucking little whore I'll teach you some respect I'll kill you I swear it respect a lesson you'll remember for the rest of your life I'll teach you some manners.

A primitive, brutal fury, hidden in the most ancient sites of his DNA, reawakens with a roar, a blind rage that demands immediate release.

I'll kill him I swear it I'll kill him I'll go to jail I'll go to jail I don't give a fuck I'll stay there for the rest of my life better much better I don't give a damn I'm tired shit shit shit I can't stand any moooooore.

Fortunately he manages to control himself and grabs his son by the ear. Mimmo wakes up and starts wailing like a banshee. He tries to free himself from the vice-like grip that is clamped on his ear. To no avail. His father drags him out into the corridor shouting obscenities and gives him a kick with the sole of his foot and Mimmo goes careering down the stairs and succeeds, he doesn't know how, a miracle perhaps, in remaining on his feet all the way down but on the last step he trips, cruelly bad luck, and twists his ankle and collapses on the ground, gets up again and dragging his leg, rushes out of the house, naked and aching all over, into the countryside. Mr Moroni runs after him, goes out onto the front steps and roars. 'Don't you ever show your face here again. If you come back I'll break every bone in your body. I swear I will, so help me Mary Madonna. Don't ever show your face here again. Don't ever show your face or . . .' He goes back into the house and his hands are still itching and he hears behind him a stifled moan, a whimper. He turns.

His wife.

She is sitting there by the fire, hands over her face, crying. That stupid woman is sitting there by the fire, snivelling and sniffing. That's all she does. Cries and sniffs.

Oh yes well done that's the only thing you can do isn't it cry your fucking eyes out that's how you've brought your kids up isn't it that's what you are a pathetic little fool and I have to do everything and pay because you do nothing but cry and cry . . . pathetic little doped-up fool.

'Why? What's he done?' sobs Mrs Moroni, her face hidden in her hands.

'What's he done? You want to know what he's done? He's been screwing in our bedroom! In our bedroom, for God's sake! Now I'm going upstairs and I'm going to throw that little slut out . . .' He heads for the staircase but Mrs Moroni runs after him, clutches his arm.

'Mario, wait, wai . . .'

'Let go of my arm!'

And he hits her across the mouth with the back of his hand.

How can I convey to you the sensation of being on the receiving end of a backhander from Mr Moroni? Well, it's a bit like getting a smack in the teeth from Mats Wilander's racket.

His wife crumples like an inflatable doll that has been sliced in two and lies there.

And just at that moment who should enter the house?

Pietro.

Pietro, happy because he has just ridden Princess all round the paddock on his own and then helped Gloria to wash her down with soap and a brush. Pietro, who has run to buy the MS Lights for his brother. Pietro, who hasn't had an ice cream but has put aside five thousand lire towards a catfish he's seen in the petshop in Orbano.

'The ciga . . .' The sentence remains unfinished.

'Ah, there you are at last, young man. Have we had a good time? Have we been enjoying ourselves? Been for a nice walk, have we?' his father sneers.

Pietro takes in the scene. His father with his shirt untucked. Hair unkempt, face flushed, eyes glistening, the clown picture on the floor, the chair overturned and, behind, a kind of bundle. A bundle with his mother's legs and his mother's outdoor shoes.

'Mama! Mama!' Pietro runs towards her, but his father grabs him by the scruff of the neck, lifts him in the air and whirls him round and it seems as if he is going to hurl him against a wall and Pietro screams, kicks, wriggles like an electric toy that has short-circuited, trying to get free, but his father's grip is firm, secure, holds him fast like a lamb that is about to be slaughtered.

Mr Moroni kicks open the front door and goes down the steps while Pietro struggles in vain to free himself, carries him into the storeroom and stands him on the floor.

In front of the washing machine.

Pietro is in floods of tears, his features distorted and his mouth open as wide as an oven door.

'What's that there?' asks his father, but the boy can't answer, he is crying too much.

'What's that there?' His father seizes him by the arm and shakes him.

Pietro is red in the face. He can't breathe, he gasps desperately for air.

'What's that there?' he smacks him hard on the back of the head, then seeing how he wheezes he sits down on the stool, closes his eyes and starts to massage his temples slowly.

He'll get over it, no one has ever died of crying.

Again. 'What's this thing here?'

Pietro sobs and doesn't answer. His father smacks him again, less hard this time.

'Well? Are you going to answer me? What's this thing here?'

And at last Pietro manages to blurt out, between his sobs: 'Hhha wahh sh shing mma sh sh shine Hha wahh sshing mma . . .'

'Correct. And what's it doing here?'

'It isn't it isn't my my fault. I didn't wa wa want to go out. Mimmo Mimmo . . . told me . . . It isn't isn't my fault.' Pietro bursts into tears again.

'Now listen to me. You're wrong. It is your fault, do you hear?' says Mr Moroni, suddenly calm and didactic.' It is your fault. What did I tell you to do? Stay at home. And you went out . . .'

'But . . .'

'No buts. Any sentence beginning with but is wrong from the outset. If you hadn't listened to your brother and you'd stayed at home as I told you to, none of this would have happened. The repair man would have taken away the washing machine, you brother wouldn't have done what he did, and nothing would have happened to your mother. Whose fault is it, then?'

Pietro is silent for a moment, then turns his big hazel eyes, now bloodshot and glistening, into his father's icy gaze and sighs:

'Mine.'

'Say it again.'

'Mine.'

'Good. Now run along and see how your mama is. I'm going to the club.'

Mr Moroni tucks his shirt into his trousers, smooths down his hair, puts on his old working jacket and is on the point of leaving when he turns round. 'Pietro, remember one thing, the first rule in life is to accept your own responsibilities. Do you understand?'

'Yes, I understand.'

Five hours later, at midnight, the cyclone of violence that had descended on Fig-Tree Cottage has blown over.

Everyone is asleep.

Mrs Moroni is curled up in a corner of her bed, with a swollen lip. Mr Moroni is lying on the other bed, deep in a dreamless alcoholic sleep. He is snoring like a pig with his bandaged right hand resting on the bedside table. Mimmo is asleep downstairs in the garage, hidden among the tractor tyres, in an old moth-eaten sleeping bag. Patti, a few kilometres away, is asleep with her long legs covered in sticking plaster. She scratched them in making her escape through the toilet window. She grabbed hold of the drainpipe but slipped and fell into a mass of rambling roses.

The only person who is not yet asleep, but is on the point of dropping off, is Pietro. His eyes are closed.

How he cried!

His mother had to cuddle him and rock him in her arms as she used to when he was a baby, and repeat to him, despite the blood trickling down onto her chin: 'There, there, it's all over, it's all over, it's all right now. Don't cry now, there's a good boy. You know what your father's like . . .'

But now Pietro feels good.

As if he's had a long walk which has drained all his strength. Limbs relaxed. Feet clasping the hot water bottle. He keeps murmuring as if it were a lullaby, 'It wasn't my fault it wasn't my fault it wasn't . . .'

The Moroni family was rather like those South Sea islanders who live in a state of perpetual apprehension, ready to abandon the village as soon as they recognise in the sky the premonitory signs of a hurricane. Then they run away to shelter in caves and let the forces of nature unleash themselves. They know the storm will be violent but brief. When it's over, they return to their huts and patiently, philosophically, put back together again the few planks of wood that serve to cover their heads.

48

At six o'clock in the morning a scarecrow disguised as Graziano Biglia was sitting in a corner of the Station Bar. Slumped forward, forehead propped on his fist. In front of him, a cold cappuccino which he had no intention of drinking.

Luckily there was no one around to bug him.

He needed to think. Though any thought he formulated was a nail driven into his head.

First of all he had a serious problem to solve. How was he going to square things with the villagers and his friends?

Everyone, for twenty kilometres around, knew he was getting married.

What a fool I was to talk about it. Why did I tell everyone?

The question was a rhetorical one and didn't expect an answer. Rather like a beaver asking itself, 'Why the hell do I keep building dams?' If it could, the rodent would probably reply: 'I don't know, it just comes naturally. It's in my blood.'

When they discovered that he wasn't getting married after all, they'd go on taking the piss out of him until 2020.

And imagine what they'll say if they find out she's got something going with the Poof . . .

Gastritis churned his stomach.

He'd even told them the Slut's name. And they'd have seen her on TV. Or in those trashy magazines they read.

Lovers in the Limelight: Mantovani with his new squeeze Erica Trettel . . . I can see it now.

And what about Saturnia, too?

Of all the idiotic ideas, he had chosen the most idiotic of all. He'd always loathed bathing in the thermal baths at Saturnia ever since he was a child. The stench of the sulphurous water disgusted him. A smell of rotten eggs that impregnates your hair, your clothes, the seats of your car and never goes away. Not to mention the Arctic cold that hits you when you emerge from that lukewarm swill. And all this to show those meatheads the Slut's body.

Only he could have dreamed up such a stupid idea.

If he thought about it he felt like vomiting. Though the only thing he had left to throw up by now was his soul.

And what about his mother and her vow?

'Oh, my poor stomach . . . Oh God, it hurts,' moaned Graziano.

Such an utterly bird-brained mother would be hard to find. *How could anyone make such a stupid vow . . . ?* There was nothing for it but to tell her the truth. She must have been wondering after last night's phone call. And then he would have to go to his friends and say: 'Sorry about Saturnia, boys, it's all off. You see, I'm not getting married after all.'

Too difficult. Impossible, in fact. It would have been like kicking your own ego to pieces. And Graziano wasn't born to suffer. The only thing to do was get in his car and get the hell out of there.

No!

That was no good either. It wasn't his style. Graziano Biglia didn't run away.

He must go to Saturnia anyway.

With another woman.

Right. He must find another woman. A real sex-bomb. The Marina Delia type. But who?

He could call the Venetian, Petra Biagioni. She was really tasty. But he hadn't been in touch with her for a long time and their last encounter hadn't been exactly amicable. He could phone her and say: 'Hey, how about driving four hundred kilometres down here for a bathe at Saturnia?' No.

He must find something around there. Something new. Something that would set tongues wagging and banish the wedding from his friends' minds.

But who?

The problem was that Graziano Biglia had sucked, like a greedy mosquito, everything this barren land had to offer. All the females who were worth the trouble (and, to be honest, a good many who weren't) had already passed through his hands. He was famous for it. There was a saying among the village girls that if you hadn't had your baptism with Biglia you were a skank and would never get a man. Some had even offered themselves to him just to keep up with their friends.

And Graziano had been generous to them all.

But those glory days had gone. Now he had returned to the quiet of the village to rest, like a Roman centurion tired of campaigning in foreign fields, and he didn't know any new girls.

Ivana Zampetti?

No . . . That monster wouldn't fit into the pools at Saturnia. And what kind of novelty would she be, anyway? All the best-looking women were married by now and while one or two might still be prepared to spend an afternoon with him in a motel in Civitavecchia, none of them would be prepared to go to the baths.

Better just to forget about it.

It was sad, the only solution, cowardly but necessary, was to do a runner. He would go home and tell his mother to break off her culinary Le Mans and revoke her vow, then he would make her swear on the Madonna of Civitavecchia not to divulge the truth and would confess to her: 'Mama, the wedding's off. Erica has dump . . .' Well, he would tell her and ask her to cover for him with a little white lie, such as: 'Graziano had to leave unexpectedly for a tour in Latin America.' Or better: 'Paco de Lucia called this morning. He begged him to go to Spain to help him finish his new album.' Something along those lines, anyway. And lastly he would ask her for a loan so that he could buy a ticket to Jamaica.

That was what he must do.

He would heal his wounds in Port Edward getting as high as a kite and screwing coloured girls left, right and centre. The very idea of the jeans shop suddenly seemed ridiculous. He was a musician, for God's sake. *Can you imagine me as a shopkeeper? I must have been out of my mind. I'm an albatross borne on positive currents which I control with a gentle flap of my wings. To hell with it.*

He already felt better. Much better.

He picked up his cappuccino and finished it in one draught.

49

Miss Palmieri didn't like the Station Bar.

The girl behind the bar was rude and the place was a den of perverts. They mentally undressed you. Talked behind your back. You could hear them squeaking away like mice. No, she didn't feel at ease there. So she never entered.

But that morning she decided to stop by, for two reasons.

1) It was very early, so there wouldn't be many people.
2) She'd left home in such a hurry that she hadn't had breakfast. And without breakfast she just couldn't function.

She stopped the Y10, got out and entered the bar.

50

Graziano was paying when he saw her.

Who's that?

It took him a moment or two to place her.

I know who she is. She's the . . . the teacher from the junior high. La . . . Pal . . . Palmiri. Something like that.

He'd seen her a few times. Shopping in the supermarket. But he'd never spoken to her.

Some men touched their testicles when she went by. Said she was a jinx. And he himself had sometimes made the two-horn sign behind her back when he used to live in Ischiano. People said she was unfriendly, weird, a kind of witch.

He knew very little about her. She came from outside, of that he was sure, she had suddenly appeared a few years before and she lived in one of those clusters of little houses on the Castrone road. Someone had told him she lived alone and had a sick mother.

Graziano studied her carefully.

Sexy.

No, not sexy, beautiful. A cold, strange, Anglo-Saxon kind of beauty.

He'd seen them, the men who lounged around the tables of the Station Bar. Seen how they'd stop leafing through the *Gazzetta*, playing tressette, joking with each other, when the schoolmarm walked across the piazza.

They called her a jinx, but you could bet they wanked away in private . . .

He sized her up.

How old must she be?

Thirty. Give or take a year or two.

Under her raincoat she wore a knee-length grey skirt which revealed tapering calves and slender ankles. Nice legs, no doubt about it. On her feet she had low-heeled dark shoes. She was tall. Slim. Aristocratic neck. He had always seen her with her hair up, but he guessed it was long and soft. And she must have beautiful boobs. Her black round-necked jumper formed two mountains on her chest. Her face was very odd. Those high, protruding cheekbones. The pointed chin. The wide mouth. The blue eyes. Those small schoolmistressy glasses . . .

Yes, she's really strange. And she's got a really beautiful arse, he concluded.

How come such an attractive woman lived alone and no one had tried to approach her?

Maybe it was true that she was stand-offish, as they said. But Graziano wasn't so sure. She was just an incomer who minded her own business. The quiet type.

And in this village if you keep yourself to yourself, they say you're a bitch, you're jinxed, you're a witch. What open-minded bastards we are.

Maybe someone had made a pass at her, as men do in villages, coarsely, and she'd told him to get lost. So the guy had put it about that Miss Palmieri was a jinx. And that was it. Her fate was sealed. The males of Ischiano were used to a diet of small rodents, frogs and lizards, they didn't have the wit to catch this swallow which flew too high for their teeth. And they had excluded her.

She had become withdrawn, frightened and unapproachable.

But while that might go for other men, it didn't for Graziano Biglia. Where women were concerned, unapproachable was a word that didn't exist in his vocabulary. Graziano had succeeded in making the Slut his girlfriend, he was damned if he couldn't win the affections of an Italian teacher from Ischiano Scalo.

The first rule of the ladykiller is that every woman has her weak point, all you have to do is find it. Even the strongest building in the world has its breaking point, you only have to hit it there to bring the whole thing crashing down. And Graziano was an expert at breaking points.

She could be the one.

He felt a deep affinity with this woman whom he didn't know. He, too, had been told by a Slut that he was a jinx. And he knew how bad you feel when someone says such a hurtful thing to you. It's the best way of wounding you, excluding you and breaking your heart.

Yes, he would help her. And he would prove that there was no such thing as a jinx. That it was a primitive and cruel notion. He would free her from her segregation. He felt charged with a great mission, a mission worthy of Bob Geldof or Nelson Mandela.

Yes, she's the one.

That night he would take her to Saturnia, to the pools.

He would screw her.

And Roscio, Miele and the Franceschini brothers would have to bow their heads, acknowledge once again his superiority, his bold ingenuity, his defiance of village obscurantism.

Yes, this could be the last performance of a Latin lover. Like a great boxer's farewell to the ring. Then he would hang up his condom and head for Jamaica.

He smoothed back his hair and walked over to the schoolmistress.

51

Flora Palmieri had been wrong, the perverts were there even at this hour.

She couldn't drink her cappuccino. One man was staring at her. She felt his gaze run down her like a scanner. And when men did that she got clumsy. She'd already dropped the sugar and nearly spilled her cappuccino over herself. She hadn't turned to look at him. But she'd seen him out of the corner of her eye.

He was a guy who always used to hang around the bar until some time ago, then had disappeared. She hadn't seen him for a couple of years at least. A handsome, swaggering lout. He used to ride around on a motorbike and show off, with some poor girl behind him. In those days his hair had been black, short on top and long at the sides. Now, with those long blond locks and that deep suntan, he looked like Tarzan.

He was one of the guys who made the two-horn sign when she walked by. That alone was enough to place him on the lowest rung of humanity, along with a lot of other men who frequented that bar.

She heard him come over and stand beside her. She moved away.

'Excuse me, are you Miss Palmiri?'

What does he want now? Flora began to get flustered.

'Palmieri,' she murmured, looking into her cappuccino.

'Palmieri. Sorry. Miss Palmieri. Sorry. I wanted to ask you something, if I'm not disturbing you . . .'

For the first time she looked him in the face. He looked like the corsair of mystery island, a character out of one of those low-budget pirate films that were made in Italy in the Sixties. A cross between Fabio Testi and Kabir Bedi. With that bleached hair . . . and those gold earrings . . . He didn't seem in great form either, he looked as if he'd been up all night. His eyes were ringed and his beard stubbly.

'What is it?'

'I've got a problem. You see . . .' The dandy suddenly stopped as if his brain had seized up, but then got a grip on himself. 'I'm sorry, I haven't introduced myself, my name's Graziano Biglia. We haven't met. I'm the son of the lady who runs the haberdasher's shop. I've been away for a while . . . Abroad, on business . . .' He held out his hand.

Flora shook it delicately.

He seemed at a loss how to go on.

Flora wanted to tell him that she was in a hurry. That she had to go to school.

'You see, I wanted to ask you a favour. In a few months I'm going to work in a tourist village on the Red Sea. Have you ever been to the Red Sea?'

'No.' *Oh my goodness, what on earth does he want?* She plucked up courage and whispered: 'I'm in a bit of a hurry . . .'

'Oh, I'm sorry. I'll try to be quick. The Red Sea's an incredible place, with white beaches. It's the bits of coral that make them white. Then there's the reef . . . Well, it's beautiful. I'm going to play at the village, I play the guitar, you know, and I'll have to be an entertainer too, organise games for the guests. Anyway, to cut a long story short, they've asked me to send them a CV. And I'd like to make it a good one, not the usual list-type resumé, something fresh. Something that'll really make them sit up. You see, I'm really keen on this job . . .'

What does he mean by something fresh?

'If you would help me to write it, I'd be eternally grateful to you. I have to send it off tomorrow without fail. It's the last day. It wouldn't take us long and if they give me the job, I swear I'll invite you to the village.'

Thank goodness, at last he'd come clean. He wasn't capable of writing his own CV.

'I'd have been glad to help you any other day. But today I'm very busy . . . I really can't.'

'Please. I don't want to be a nuisance, but it would be so wonderful if you'd help me, it'd make me so happy . . .' Graziano said this with such childlike candour that Flora couldn't help smiling.

'Ah, at last, a smile. How nice, I thought you didn't know how to. It'll only take us ten minutes . . .'

Flora was lost for words. What was she to do? How could she refuse him? He had to send it tomorrow, and if he was left to his own devices she was sure he'd make a complete hash of it.

You mustn't help him. He's one of the guys who gave you the two-horn sign, a voice in her head told her.

Yes, she replied, *but that was years ago, maybe he's changed. He's been abroad . . . It's no trouble, really . . . And actually he's very polite.*

'All right, I'll help you. But I don't know if I'll be any good.'

'Thank you. I'm sure you will. What time could we meet?'

'I don't know, would six-thirtyish suit you?'

'Fine. Shall I come round to your house?'

'My house?' Flora gasped.

No one (except doctors and nurses) had ever been to her house. Once the parish priest had come to give his Christmas blessing and on the pretext of sprinkling incense had poked his nose into all the rooms and Flora had been very upset. 'Don't you want me to say a prayer for your mother?' he had asked.

'Leave my mother alone,' she'd snapped, with a violence that had surprised even her. She didn't believe in prayers. And she didn't like having strangers in the house. It put her on edge.

Graziano moved closer. 'It would be better. You see, my mother's always around at my house. She's such a chatterbox. She wouldn't let us work.'

'All right, then.'

'Great.'

Flora looked at her watch.

It was very late. She'd have to rush to school. 'But now I must be going, I'm sorry.' She took the money from her coat pocket and stretched out her hand towards the cashier but he grasped it. Flora jumped back and snatched her hand away as if he had bitten it.

'Oh, I'm sorry. Did I startle you? I just didn't want you to pay. Breakfast is on me.'

'Thank you . . .' Flora stammered and made for the door.

'See you this evening, then,' said Graziano, but the teacher had already gone.

52

It's in the bag.

The CV idea had worked.

The teacher was very shy and scared of men. A complete beginner. When he'd touched her hand, she'd jumped two metres in the air.

She would be a difficult prey, but a stimulating one. Graziano didn't foresee any great difficulty in carrying out his mission.

He paid and went out.

It had started raining. Lousy weather today, yet again. He would go home, have a siesta and prepare for their meeting.

He did up his jacket and started walking.

Uncle Armando

Who was this strange creature called Flora Palmieri, and what was she doing in Ischiano Scalo?

She'd been born in Naples thirty-two years earlier. The only child of an elderly couple who'd struggled to have a baby but whose efforts had finally been rewarded by nature with the birth of a little girl who weighed three and a half kilos, was as white as an albino salamander and had an incredible quiff of red hair.

The Palmieris were unassuming people who lived in a flat at the Vomero. Lucia taught in an infants' school and Mario worked in an insurance office down by the harbour.

Little Flora had grown older, gone to nursery school and then to infants' school, in her mother's class.

Mario had died suddenly, when Flora was ten, of fulminant lung cancer, leaving mother and daughter grief-stricken and very short of money.

Life had immediately become hard. Lucia's salary and Mario's meagre pension were barely enough for them to make ends meet. They had cut down their expenses, sold the car and stopped taking holidays at Procida but still they were in dire financial straits.

Little Flora liked reading and studying and when she had finished junior high her mother had sent her to high school despite the enormous efforts it would entail. She was a shy, introverted child. But she did well at school.

One evening – Flora was fourteen – she was sitting at the dinner table finishing her homework when she heard a shriek in the kitchen. She rushed in.

Her mother was standing in the middle of the room. The knife on the floor. One hand clutching the other, which was contracted like a claw. 'It's nothing. It's nothing, dear. It'll pass. Don't worry.'

For some time Lucia had been complaining of pains in her joints, sometimes at night her legs would be paralysed for a few moments.

The doctor was called. He said it was arthritis. The hand had indeed begun to function again after a few days, though it hurt when she clenched it. Now Lucia found it difficult to teach, but she was a strong woman, used to dealing with pain, and she didn't make a fuss. Flora saw to the shopping, the cooking and the cleaning and still found time to study.

One day Lucia had woken up with one arm completely paralysed.

This time they consulted a specialist, who admitted her to the Cardarelli hospital. They did dozens of analyses, called in famous neurophysiologists and concluded that Mrs Palmieri was suffering from a rare form of degeneration of the cells of the nervous system.

The medical literature had little to say about it. Few cases were known and at present there was no treatment. Maybe in America, but that would have been very expensive.

Lucia spent a month in hospital and returned home paralysed down her right side.

At this point Uncle Armando, Lucia's younger brother, made his appearance.

A gruff man, covered with black hairs, which stuck out of his collar, his nose and his ears. As ugly as sin. He owned a shoe shop at the Rettifilo. A guy interested only in money and with a fat, surly wife.

Uncle Armando salved his conscience by giving them a paltry sum of money each month.

The only reason Flora could still go to school was that the concierge's wife, a kindly woman, looked after her mother during lesson hours.

With the passing months the situation did not improve. Quite the opposite, in fact. By now Lucia could only move her left hand, her right foot and half her mouth. She had difficulty in speaking and was no longer self-sufficient. She had to be washed, fed, cleaned.

Uncle Armando came to see them once a month, sat beside his sister for an hour or so, holding her hand, and then, after giving Flora the monthly payment and a packet of pastries, would leave.

One morning – Flora was sixteen – she woke up, made breakfast and went in to see her mother. She found her curled up in a corner of her bed. As if her limbs, during the night, had suddenly snapped free of the springs that kept them taut and shrivelled like the legs of a dried-up spider.

Her face against the wall.

'Mama . . . ?' Flora stood beside the bed. 'Mama . . . ?' Her voice trembled. Her legs trembled.

No response.

'Mama . . . ? Can you hear me, Mama?'

She stood there for a long time like that, biting her knuckle. And crying silently. Then she ran downstairs screaming, 'She's dead. She's dead. My mother's dead. Help me.'

The concierge arrived. Uncle Armando arrived. Aunt Giovanna arrived. The doctors arrived.

Her mother wasn't dead.

She was no longer there.

Her mind had left, moved to a distant world, a world perhaps inhabited by darkness and silence, and had left nothing behind but a living body. The hopes of its returning, they explained to her, were very slim.

Uncle Armando assumed command, sold the house at the Vomero and took Flora and her mother in to live with him. He put them in a little room. A bed for her and one for her mother. A little table to do her homework on.

'I promised your mother you'd finish high school. And so you will. Afterwards you'll come to work in the shop.'

And so began the long period in Uncle Armando's house.

They didn't treat her badly. But nor did they treat her well. They ignored her. Aunt Giovanna hardly spoke to her. The house was big and dark and living there wasn't much fun.

Flora went to school, looked after her mother, studied, did the cleaning in the house and meanwhile grew. She was seventeen. She was tall, her bosom had swelled and was a cumbersome thing that embarrassed her.

One day when Aunt Giovanna had gone to visit some relatives in Avellino, Flora was having a shower.

Suddenly the bathroom door opened and . . .

And voilà, Uncle Armando.

Usually Flora locked the door, but that day he'd said he was going to the races at Agnano, yet here he was.

He was wearing a dressing gown (*a red and blue striped silk one I'd never seen him in before*) and slippers.

'Flora, dear, do you mind if I join you?' he asked her, as non-chalantly as if he were asking someone to pass the bread at table.

Flora was dumbstruck.

She would have liked to scream, push him away. But the sight of that man there, where she was naked, had paralysed her.

How she would have loved to kick him, punch him, shove him out of the window so that he plunged three floors down and landed in the middle of the road a split second before the number 38B bus passed. Instead there she was, as immobile as a stuffed animal, and she couldn't scream or even walk two metres to reach her towel.

All she could do was look at him.

'May I help you soap yourself?' Without waiting for an answer, Uncle Armando came towards her, picked up the soap, which had fallen into the bottom of the bath, rubbed it over his hands, working up a good lather, and began to soap her. Flora, standing there, breathed through her nose, holding her arms over her breasts, her legs tight together.

'You're so beautiful, Flora . . . You're so beautiful . . . You've got a lovely figure and you're all red, even here . . . Let me soap you. Take away those hands. Don't be frightened,' he said in a hoarse, strangled voice.

Flora obeyed.

And he started to soap her breasts. 'Isn't that nice? What big boobs you've got . . .'

All the better to eat you, she felt like replying.

That monster was squeezing her nipples and the only thing she could think of was Little Red Riding Hood.

And anyway, no, it's not nice. It's the most disgusting thing in the world. The most disgusting thing in the world. Nothing's more disgusting than this.

Flora stood there, petrified, incapable of reacting to the horror of that monster touching her.

Suddenly, incredibly, she saw something that made her smile. A long thick dark thing had emerged from Uncle Armando's dressing gown. It looked like one of those wooden soldiers standing to attention, arms against their sides. Uncle Armando's (*enormous!*) penis had peeped out from behind the curtain. *He wanted to have a look too, you see?*

Uncle Armando noticed and a satisfied smile spread along those moist, fleshy lips. 'May I shower with you?'

His dressing gown fell to the ground, revealing in all their splendour that squat, hairy body, those short legs with calves as thick as a ship's fenders, those long arms and those big hands and that dick there, as upright as a ship's mast.

Uncle Armando took his weapon in his hand and stepped into the bath.

On contact with the ogre, something inside Flora finally snapped and the awful glass ball that imprisoned her shattered into a thousand pieces and she woke up and pushed him, and Uncle Armando, all ninety kilos of him, slipped back and as he slipped clutched like a falling orang-utan at the waterproof curtain and the rings began to break off and *stak* one after another and *stak* flew all over the bathroom and *stak* Flora leapt out of the bath but one foot caught against the edge and so she tripped and fell on the floor and clinging on to the basin she got to her feet, even though her knee hurt and Uncle Armando was shouting and she was screaming and she got to her feet and slipped on Uncle Armando's red-and-blue-striped dressing gown and found herself on the floor again and struggled to her feet and grabbed the handle and turned it and the door opened and she was in the hall.

In the hall.

She fled and locked herself in her bedroom. She cuddled up to her mother and burst into tears.

Her uncle called her from the bathroom. 'Flora? Where are you? Come here. Are you cross with me?'

'Mama, please. Help me. Help me. Do something. Please.'

But her mother stared at the ceiling.

The dirty old man didn't try it again.

Why can that have been?

Maybe he'd drunk too much at the races that day and his inhibitory brakes had been loosened. Maybe Aunt Giovanna noticed something, the shower curtain, the bruise on her husband's arm, maybe he had only yielded to an uncontrollable fit of lust of which he later repented (an unlikely hypothesis). The fact remains that from that day onwards he never molested her again and he became sweeter than marzipan.

Flora never spoke to him again, and even when she finished high school and started working in the shop she ignored him. At night she studied like mad, there in the little room with her mother. She'd enrolled for a degree course in Italian literature. In four years flat she graduated.

She took the exam to become a teacher. She passed and accepted the first posting she was offered.

It was Ischiano Scalo.

She left Naples with her mother in an ambulance, never to return.

53

But what had happened at the school after Pietro and the others had made their escape?

Alima, who was waiting in the car, had seen three boys emerge like black devils from a window of the school, climb over the gate and disappear into the gardens opposite.

For a moment she had been uncertain what to do. Enter, go away?

A gunshot had interrupted her deliberations.

A couple of minutes later, another boy had emerged from the same window, he too had climbed over the gate and run off.

That maniac Italo must have shot somebody. Or had somebody shot him?

Alima had stuffed her wig in her coat pocket, clambered out of the 131 and hurried away.

She wasn't stupid. She had no residence permit and if she was caught mixed up in a business like that she'd find herself back in Nigeria in three days.

She'd walked three hundred metres in the rain, cursing Italo, this shitty country and the dirty job she was compelled to do, but had turned back.

What if Italo was dead or badly hurt?

She'd climbed over the gate and entered Italo's cottage and performed a heinous deed, which offends against the ethical code of any prostitute.

She'd called the police.

'Go to the school. The Sardinians have shot Italo. Hurry.'

A quarter of an hour later, officers Bacci and Miele had been driving at high speed towards the school when they'd seen a black woman hiding behind a bush.

Bruno Miele had leaped out, she'd run away but he'd pointed his gun at her. He'd grabbed her, handcuffed her and put her in the police car.

'I called the police. Let me go,' Alima wept.

'Sit down and shut up, you whore,' Miele had replied and they'd raced off with sirens blaring towards the school.

They'd emerged from the car, guns at the ready.

Starsky and Hutch.

From outside everything seemed normal.

Miele had seen his father's cottage in darkness, but there were lights on in the school.

'Let's go in,' he'd said. A sixth sense told him something nasty had happened in there.

They'd climbed the gate, glancing behind them. And then, with pistols raised and legs wide apart, they'd hopped their way into the school.

They'd searched the whole building without finding anything and then, one after the other, flat against the wall, they'd sidled down the stairs into the basement. At the end of the corridor a door was open. The light was on.

They'd taken up positions on either side, holding their guns two-handed.

'Ready?' Bacci had asked.

'Ready!' Miele had replied, and did a clumsy somersault into the gym and got to his feet again swinging his gun right and left.

At first he hadn't seen anyone.

Then he'd looked at the floor. There was a body.

A corpse?

A corpse that reminded him of his . . .

'Papa! Papa!' Bruno Miele had wailed and had run over to his father (and as he ran he couldn't help thinking of that marvellous film where the cop Kevin Costner finds the corpse of Sean Connery, who had been like a father to him and, distraught with grief, wreaks his private revenge, hunting down the mobsters. What the hell was the title?). 'Have they killed you, Papa? Answer me! Answer me! Have the Sardinians killed you?' He'd knelt down beside his father's corpse as if there were a movie camera somewhere around. 'Don't worry, I'll avenge you.' And he'd realised that the corpse was alive and was moaning. 'Are you hurt?' He saw the shotgun. 'Did they shoot you?'

The caretaker murmured some incomprehensible words. A walrus after a collision with a steamer.

'Who hurt you? Was it the Sardinians? Tell me!' Bruno had put his ear to his mouth.

'Naaa . . .' Italo had managed to say.

'Did you chase them off?'

'Yeee . . .'

'Well done, Papa.' He'd stroked his forehead, barely able to hold back his tears.

What a hero! What a hero! Now no one would be able to tell him his father was a coward. And all the people who said that when there'd been a break-in two years ago his father had hidden away would have to eat their words. He was proud of his pappy.

'Did you shoot at them?'

Italo, with his eyes closed, had nodded.

'But who was it you shot at?' Antonio Bacci had asked.

'Who? Who? The Sardinians, of course!' Bruno had snapped. What stupid questions that idiot asked!

But Italo with an effort had shaken his head.

'It wasn't the Sardinians, Papa? Who did you shoot at, then?'

Italo had taken a deep breath and gurgled: 'The . . . the . . . pu . . . pils.'

'The pupils?' the two policemen chorused.

The ambulance and fire brigade had arrived an hour later.

With one snip of his cutters the fireman had severed the indestructible chain. Officer Bacci hadn't noticed that the chain was the same one he'd given his son a few months earlier. The two ambulance men had gone into the school with a stretcher and put the caretaker on it.

Then they'd called the headmaster.

54

At seven o'clock Flora Palmieri parked her Y10 in the school yard.

Already there were the headmaster's Ritmo, the deputy head's Uno and . . .

A police car? Good heavens!

She went in.

Miss Gatta, the deputy headmistress, and Mr Cosenza, the headmaster, were standing in a corner of the entrance hall, muttering conspiratorially.

When she saw her, Miss Gatta came to meet her. 'Ah, there you are at last.'

'I came as quickly as I could . . .' said Flora apologetically. 'But what's happened?'

'Come and see what they've done . . .' said Miss Gatta.

'Who was it?'

'We don't know.' Then she turned to the head. 'Giovanni, let's go downstairs and show Miss Palmieri what a fine job our pupils have done.'

She set off and Flora and the headmaster followed her.

55

To see them together, Mr Cosenza and Miss Gatta, you might think you'd suddenly been transported into the Upper Jurassic.

Mariuccia Gatta, sixty years old and unmarried, with that big shoebox-like head, those deep-set eyes as round as marbles and that blunt nose, was a dead ringer for a Tyrannosaurus Rex, the most notorious and feared of dinosaurs.

Giovanni Cosenza, aged fifty-three, married and a father of two, was like a Docodon. This apparently insignificant mouse-like little creature, with its pointed nose and protruding incisors, is thought by some palaeontologists to have been the first mammal to appear on the planet when the reptiles still ruled the roost.

Small, unseen, these progenitors of ours (we're mammals too!)

raised their young in underground burrows, ate berries and seeds and crept out after dark when the dinosaurs slept, their metabolisms slowing, and snaffled their eggs. When the great cataclysm came (meteor, ice ages, shift in the earth's axis, and all the rest of it) those great scaly monsters dropped like flies and the Docodons suddenly found themselves lords of all creation.

Life's often like that, the people you wouldn't give a penny for end up rubbing your face in the dirt.

And sure enough the Docodon had become headmaster and the T. Rex, deputy headmistress. But this didn't mean a thing, because it was Miss Gatta who held power in the school and fixed the timetables, the shifts, the make-up of the classes and everything else. She took all the decisions, and without hesitation. She was the bossy type and she ordered the head, the teaching staff and the pupils about like a troop of soldiers.

The first thing you noticed about the headmaster, Giovanni Cosenza, when you talked to him, was his protruding teeth, his moustache and those eyes that looked everywhere except at you.

The first time Flora had met him she'd been very disconcerted, while he was talking he stared up at a point on the ceiling, as if there were, I don't know, a bat or a huge crack up there. He moved jerkily, as if every movement were produced by a single muscular contraction. For the rest he was dull and ordinary. Skinny. With a greying fringe that fell over his tiny face. As timid as a weasel. As ceremonious as a Japanese.

He had two suits. A summer one and a winter one. The intermediate seasons might just as well not have existed as far as he was concerned. When it was cold, as it was that day, he would put on his dark-brown flannel suit, when it was warm, his pale-blue cotton one. In both suits the trousers were far too short and the shoulders too thickly padded.

56

She knew who'd done it as soon as she saw the scrawl (PALMIERI STIK YOUR VIDEOS UP YOUR ARSE) and the wrecked television and video recorder.

Federico Pierini.

It was a message to her.

You made me to watch that video on the Middle Ages and this is what you get.

It was obvious.

Since the day she had punished him she had sensed a fierce resentment of her growing in that boy. He'd stopped doing his homework and he put on headphones during her lessons.

He hates me.

She'd realised this from the way he looked at her. With evil, frightening eyes that accused her, full of all the hatred in the world.

Flora had understood and she had stopped giving him oral tests in class and at the end of the year she would award him a pass.

She didn't know exactly how, but she had a feeling that this hatred was connected with the death of Pierini's mother. Maybe because she had died on the day she had forced him to stay at school.

Who knows?

At any rate Pierini was really furious with her.

I did wrong, it's true. But I didn't know. He'd driven me to distraction, he wouldn't let me work, he was disruptive, he told all those lies and I didn't know, I swear I didn't, about his mother. I went out of my way to apologise to him.

And he had looked at her as if she were the scum of the earth.

And then the practical jokes: the smashed window, the punctured tyres, and all the rest.

It had been him. Now she was certain.

That boy scared her. Scared her a lot. If he'd been older he would have tried to kill her. To do horrible things to her.

Whenever she saw him, Flora felt an impulse to say: 'I'm sorry, I apologise for whatever it is I've done, please forgive me. I was wrong, but I'll never bother you again, if only you'll stop hating me.' But she knew that this would only have intensified his hostility.

He hadn't broken into the school on his own.

That was clear. The different kinds of handwriting on the wall proved that. He must have taken some of his cronies along. But she would bet her life it had been him who had smashed the TV.

'Look at the mess,' groaned the head, bringing her back down to earth.

In the technical education room, as well as Flora, the head and the deputy head, there were two police officers writing a report. One was Andrea Bacci's father. Flora knew him because he had come to school a couple of times to talk about him. The other was the son of Italo, the caretaker.

She read the other graffiti.

The headmaster sucks the deputy headmistress's cock.

Italo's got fishy feet.

Flora couldn't help smiling. It was certainly a comic image. The headmaster on his knees and the deputy headmistress with her skirt lifted up and . . . *Maybe it's true, the deputy headmistress is a man.*

(*Stop it, Flora . . .*)

She saw Miss Gatta's malicious eyes scrutinising her, trying to read her thoughts. 'You see what they wrote?'

'Yes . . .' murmured Flora.

The deputy head clenched her fists and raised them to the sky. 'Vandals. Wretches. How dare they? We must punish them. We must apply an immediate remedy to this running sore which is afflicting our poor school.'

If Miss Gatta had been a normal woman, a scrawl like that might have set her thinking seriously about the way her sexual identity and her relationship with the head were viewed by some of the pupils.

But Miss Gatta was a superior being and didn't have such thoughts. Nothing shifted her from her perfect obtuseness. Not a trace of embarrassment, not a hint of unease. The ruffians who had broken into her school had merely reawoken her fighting spirit and now the Prussian general was ready for the fray.

Mr Cosenza, however, was red in the face, proof that the words on the wall had struck home.

'Do you have any suspicions?' asked Flora.

'No, but we'll find out who did it, Miss Palmieri, you can bet your salary on that,' snapped Miss Gatta. She had never seen her so furious in all the time she'd known her. One corner of her mouth was quivering with rage. 'Have you read the one about you?'

'Yes.'

'It sounds like a message to you,' she said in Hercule Poirot-like tones.

Flora said nothing.

'Who can it have been? Why a video, precisely, and not a . . .' Miss Gatta realised she was about to say something unseemly and broke off.

'I don't know . . . I've no idea,' said Flora, shaking her head. Why, now that she had the chance to report Pierini, hadn't she done so? *I'd get him into trouble.*

You could see a mile off that the law was going to twine like a climbing plant round that boy's life and she didn't want to be the one who initiated this symbiosis.

There was also a simpler and more utilitarian reason. She was afraid that when Pierini found out that it had been her who had reported him, he would make her pay dearly for it, very dearly.

'Miss Palmieri, I asked Giovanni to summon you here before the other teachers because some time ago you came to me to complain that certain pupils were playing you up. They might have been the same children who did this. Do you see what I mean? I'm wondering if this might have been a way of getting back at you. You said you couldn't communicate with your pupils, and sometimes such failures in mutual understanding manifest themselves in this way.' She turned to the head for confirmation. 'Isn't that so, Giovanni?'

'Yes . . .' he concurred, bending down to pick up a piece of broken glass.

'Please, Giovanni! Don't touch that! You'll cut yourself!' shouted the deputy head, and the headmaster immediately stood to attention. 'Miss Palmieri, might that not be the case?'

Then why did they write what they did about the headmaster doing that to you? How she would have loved to answer the harpy like that. But instead she stammered: 'Well . . . I don't think so . . . Otherwise why would they have written the other . . . graffiti?' She said it in fits and starts but she said it.

Miss Gatta's eyes disappeared into their bags. 'What's that got to do with it?' she growled. 'Remember that the head and I are the highest authorities here. It's only natural that they should feel resentful towards us, but it's not at all natural that they should feel resentful towards you. You were singled out above all the other teachers. Why didn't they write about Miss Rovi? She uses the video recorder too. Let's not be silly about this, Miss Palmieri. The person who wrote those words has a grudge against you. And I'm not surprised you have no idea who it could have been, you don't observe your pupils as carefully as you ought to.'

Flora lowered her eyes.

'What shall we do now?' interjected the head, trying to calm the T. Rex down.

'Do? Tidy up. We can discuss this young lady's teaching methods on some other occasion,' said the deputy head, rubbing her hands together.

'The children will be here soon. Perhaps it would be better if they didn't come in . . . if we sent them home and called a staff meeting to decide on an effective response to this outrage . . .' suggested the head.

'No. I don't think that's the best course. We must let the children in. And we'll hold lessons as usual. The technical education room must be locked. One of the science teachers has booked it for this morning, but he can teach upstairs. The pupils mustn't know anything. Even the teachers must be told as little as possible. We'll call Margherita and have her clean up and then, this afternoon, we'll call in the painter to redecorate the walls, and the two of us . . .' Miss Gatta glared at Flora. ' . . . no, the three of us – you, Miss Palmieri, will come along to help us in our inquiries – will go to Orbano to see how Italo is and try to find out who the culprits are.'

The head trembled all over. Like those skinny little dogs that quiver at the sight of their masters. 'Quite right, quite right. Good, good.' He glanced at his watch. 'The children are due any time now. Shall I give the order to unlock the doors?'

Miss Gatta gave him a leer of assent.

The head left the room.

The deputy head now turned her attention to the two policemen. 'Well, what are you two dithering about? If you're going to take photographs, get on with it. We're going to have to lock up. There's no time to lose.'

57

The noise the cartilage of a broken nose makes when you put it back into place is not unlike the sound of teeth sinking into a Magnum.

Scrooooskt.

What makes your nerves explode, your heart race, your flesh creep, is not so much the pain as that noise.

Italo Miele had already suffered this unpleasant experience once before, at the age of twenty-three, when a hunter had stolen a pheasant he had shot. They had started fighting in the middle of a sunflower field, and the other man (a boxer, no doubt) had quite without warning hit him full in the face. On that occasion his father had straightened his nose.

That was why now, in the outpatients' department of the Sandro Pertini hospital in Orbano, he was shouting and swearing that he wasn't going to let anyone touch his nose, least of all some young upstart of a houseman.

'Look, it can't stay as it is. It's your decision, of course . . . but you'll be left with a crooked nose,' muttered the young doctor, in an aggrieved tone.

Italo struggled up from the litter on which they had laid him. A plump nurse tried to stop him, but he batted her aside like a midge and approached the mirror.

'Mamma mia . . .' he muttered.

What a mess!

A baboon.

His nose, as purple and fat as an aubergine, hung to the right. It felt as hot as a steam iron. His eyes were hidden under two swollen ring doughnuts which started out magenta and shaded into cobalt blue. A deep wound sutured with nine stitches and dabbed with tincture of iodine split his forehead in half.

'I'll put it back into place myself.'

Grasping his jaw with his left hand and his nose with his right, he took a gulp of air and . . .

Scrooooskt . . .

. . . he wrenched it back into line.

He stifled a wild scream. His stomach churned and filled with gastric juices. He almost retched with the pain. His legs gave way for an instant and he had to lean against the basin to stop himself collapsing on the floor.

The doctor and the two nurses stared in amazement.

'That's done, then.' He limped back to the litter. 'Now take me back to bed. I'm worn out. I want to sleep.'

He closed his eyes.

'We'll have to staunch the blood and give you some medication.' The querulous voice of the doctor.

'All right . . .'

God, he was tired . . .

More exhausted, drained, battered and bruised than any human being on earth. He was going to have to sleep for two days at least. That way he wouldn't feel the pain, wouldn't feel anything, and when he woke up he'd go home and have three weeks of convalescence being cared for and pampered and pitied by the old woman. He'd eat endless dishes of fettuccine with ragù and watch TV and plan how to make them pay for what they'd done to him that terrible night.

Oh yes, they were going to pay.

The state. The school. The families of those hooligans. Never mind who. Someone was going to pay, down to the last goddamn lira.

A lawyer. I need a lawyer. A good one. Someone with balls, who'll take them for every penny.

As the doctor and the nurses inserted cotton-wool tampons into his nostrils, he reflected that this was the chance he'd been waiting for all these years. And it had come just at the right moment, with perfect timing, on the eve of his retirement.

Those little bastards had done him a favour.

Now he was a hero, he had done his duty, he had driven them out of the school, and he was going to clean up on it.

A complex fracture of the nose with severe respiratory complications. Permanent scars, grazes and a lot of other things that would come out in due time.

All that must be worth a cool . . . what? twenty million. No, that's too low. If it turns out that I can't breathe through my nose any more, it'll be at least fifty million, maybe more.

He was quoting figures off the top of his head, but it was in his impulsive nature to start making wild guesses at the amount of the compensation without having the slightest knowledge of the facts.

He would buy himself a new car, complete with air conditioning and radio, get a larger television and change all the kitchen appliances and the windows and shutters on the upper floor of the farmhouse.

And he'd be getting all these things for a broken nose and a few piddling little injuries.

Although those three incompetents were hurting him like mad, he felt a surge of spontaneous, sincere affection and gratitude to the little thugs who had done this to him.

58

Behind the black hills the sky was covered with big clouds that twisted and rolled over each other to the accompaniment of thunder and lightning like something out of Noah's flood. The wind brought over sand and the smell of brine and seaweed. The white oxen, on the meadows, didn't give a damn about the rain. They grazed slowly and methodically and now and again raised their heads and looked without interest at the raging storm.

Pietro was dashing to school. Although it was raining hard he had gone by bike.

He hadn't been able to bring himself to stay at home. Curiosity, the desire to know what had happened, had prevailed over his plan to feign illness.

He had held the thermometer under the hot tap, but when the moment had come to tell his mother that he had a temperature of thirty-seven point five he had said nothing.

How could he stay in bed all day, not knowing if they had managed to open the gate, not hearing the reactions of his schoolmates and the teachers?

When he had taken the decision to move it had already been late, so he had dressed hurriedly, gulped down his caffè latte, swallowed a couple of biscuits, donned his cape and galoshes and to get there more quickly had taken his bike.

Now that he was less than a kilometre from the school, every turn of the pedals was another twist at his guts.

59

On entering the ward Miss Palmieri had the impression that she wasn't in an Italian hospital but in a veterinary centre in southern Florida. In the middle of the large room, under the white lights, stretched out on a bed, was a manatee.

Flora, though no expert in zoology, knew what a manatee was, having seen a *National Geographic* documentary on television a few weeks earlier.

The manatee is a sirenian, a kind of gigantic, flabby albino seal that lives in Lake Chad and in the estuaries of the great rivers of South America. Being naturally lazy, slow animals, they often get caught by boats' propellers.

The caretaker, lying flat on his back in his underpants, looked just like one of those creatures.

He was monstrous. As round and white as a snowman. His taut, swollen belly was like an Easter egg about to explode. On the summit was a thick tuft of white hairs which joined up with those on his chest. His short stumpy legs were hairless and covered with thick blue veins. The calf of the lame leg was purple in colour and as round as a cottage loaf. His arms, stretched out on the bed, seemed like fins. His fingers were as thick as cigars. Cruel mother nature had not seen fit to supply him with a neck, and that big round head slotted directly between his shoulder blades.

He was in a pretty bad way.

His forearms and his knees were covered with scratches and grazes. His forehead stitched up and his nose bandaged.

Flora didn't like him. He was a layabout. Aggressive with the pupils. And a pervert. When she passed the porter's lodge, she felt herself being mentally undressed. And Miss Cirillo had told her he was also a notorious frequenter of prostitutes. He went every night with those poor coloured girls who hustled on the Aurelia.

It gave her no pleasure at all to be there playing detective with those two. She wished she were in school. Teaching.

'Come along . . . hurry up,' Miss Gatta said to her.

The three of them sat down by the caretaker's bed.

The deputy head nodded in greeting and then spoke in the most worried voice in the world. 'Well, Italo, how are you?'

Despite the scratches and bruises that he had on his battered face, a disgusting, sly expression appeared in the caretaker's piglike eyes.

60

'Terrible. How am I? Terrible!'

Italo reminded himself of the part he had to play. He must cut a pathetic figure, seem like a poor cripple in need of care who had sacrificed himself for the good of the school and the teachers in combating juvenile delinquency.

'Now, Italo, if you can, I'd like you to explain exactly what happened last night in the school,' said the head.

Italo looked around and began to tell a story of which about sixty per cent was the truth, thirty per cent was complete fabrication and the remaining ten per cent was padded out with exaggeration, pathos, drama and pathetic tear-jerking details (. . . you've no idea how cold it can get in winter in that little room where I live, alone, far away from home, my wife and my darling children . . .).

He omitted a number of minor details, which would only have encumbered the narrative and complicated the plot. (My nose? How did I break it? One of those boys must have hit me in the face with an iron bar while I was walking in the dark.)

And he concluded. 'Now I'm here. You see me. In this hospital. A broken man. I can't move my leg and I think I've got a couple of broken ribs but it doesn't matter, I saved the school from the vandals. And that's the most important thing. Isn't it? All I ask of you is one thing: help me, you educated people. I'm just a poor ignorant old man. Help me get what I deserve after all these years of work and after this terrible accident which has robbed me of what little health I still had. In the meantime a whip-round among the teachers and parents wouldn't go amiss. Thank you, thank you very much indeed.'

Having finished his speech, he checked its effect on his listeners.

The headmaster was bent forward on his chair, his hands over his mouth and his gaze directed downwards. Italo judged that posture to be an expression of deep sympathy for his sad, unfortunate situation.

Good.

Then he moved on to inspect Miss Palmieri.

The redhead was staring at him blankly. But what could you expect from a woman like that?

And, finally, he explored the face of the deputy headmistress.

Miss Gatta had a face of marble which didn't seem to bode well. A derisive smile curled her lips.

What did it mean? Why was she giving him that nasty little leer? Didn't the sour old spinster believe him?

Italo screwed up his eyes and contracted his facial muscles, trying to express all the pain that he felt. And he lay there waiting for comfort, a friendly word, a handshake, anything.

The deputy headmistress coughed and took a notebook and her spectacles out of her little chamois handbag. 'Italo, I don't understand some of the things you said. They don't seem to correspond to the evidence we found at the school with the police. If you feel up to it, I'd like to ask you a few questions.'

'All right. But make it quick because I don't feel too well.'

'First of all, you said you spent the night on your own. Who is this Alima Guabré, then? It appears that it was this Nigerian girl – who, by the way, has no residence permit – who called the police.'

A sharp pain formed in the caretaker's bowels, shooting up to inflame his tonsils. Italo tried to hold back this flow of acidic gas that had risen from his oesophagus, but failed and gave a loud burp.

The three teachers pretended they hadn't heard.

Italo put his hand over his mouth. 'What did you say, deputy headmistress? Alima who? I don't know the woman, never heard of her . . .'

'How odd. The young lady, who apparently works as a prostitute, says she knows you very well, that you took her to the school and invited her to spend the night with you . . .'

Italo snorted. His nose was now pulsing like a broken radiator.

Wait, wait a minute . . . That old bitch was interrogating him. Him? The man who had saved the school, and nearly got killed in the process? What the hell was hap . . . . This was a stab in the back. And there was him expecting a hug, a box of Ferrero Rocher, a bunch of flowers.

'She must be mad. She's made it all up. Who is she? What does she want from me? I don't know her . . .' he said, waving his arms about as if trying to ward off a swarm of wasps.

'She says you dine together every week at the Old Wagon and she mentioned a practical joke . . .' the teacher grimaced and held the notebook away from her as if to read it more clearly. 'I didn't quite understand . . . The police say she was very angry with you . . . A trick you played on her during dinner . . .'

'How dare that fucking tar . . . ?' Italo only just managed to break off the sentence in time.

The deputy head gave him a glare as lethal as Mazinger Z's rotating mallet.

'I agree the whole story does sound extremely odd. One detail appears to confirm Miss Guabré's story. This morning your 131 was outside the chained-up gate. And then there's the testimony of the waiters of the Old Wagon . . .'

The caretaker started trembling like a leaf and looked at this heartless monster who was delighting in torturing him. He felt like leaping on her and wringing that scrawny neck and pulling out all her teeth and making them into a necklace. That wasn't a woman . . . it was a demon with no feelings and no pity. With a ball of lead where her heart should be and a freezer instead of a cunt.

'This leads me to believe that when the vandals entered the school you were not present . . . As was probably the case two years ago, when the burglars broke in.'

'Nooo! I was there that time, I was asleep! I swear to God. It's not my fault if I'm a sound sleeper!' Italo turned to the headmaster. 'Please, sir, surely you believe me. What does this woman want? I feel so bad. I can't bear to hear these scandalous accusations. Me going with prostitutes, not doing my duty. Me, with thirty years' honourable service behind me. Headmaster, please, say something.'

The little man looked at him as one might look at the last specimen of a now extinct species. 'What can I say? Try to be more honest, try to tell the truth. It's always best to tell the truth . . .'

Then Italo looked at Miss Palmieri, seeking sympathy, but didn't find any.

'Go away, the lot of you . . . go away . . .' he murmured with eyes closed, like a man on his deathbed who wishes to die in peace.

But Miss Gatta was not to be melted. 'You should be grateful to that poor unfortunate girl. If Miss Guabré hadn't been there, you would probably still be lying there unconscious in a pool of blood. You're an ungrateful wretch. And now let us move on to the subject which is of more concern to me. The shotgun.'

Italo felt faint. Luckily he had a vision which for a moment alleviated the pain in his nose and the constriction in his chest. That old spinster being impaled – yes, him ramming a lamp-post covered with chilli powder and sand up her arse, and her screaming in agony.

'You used a shotgun on school premises.'

'It's not true!'

'How can you deny it? They found it beside you . . . The gun doesn't seem to be licensed, nor, apparently, do you have a hunting licence or a firearms permit . . .'

'It's not true!'

'That is a very serious offence, punishable . . .'

'It's not true!'

Italo had adopted the last and most desperate strategy of defence. Denying everything. Anything. The sun is hot? It's not true! Swallows fly? It's not true!

Saying always and only no.

'You fired a shot. You tried to hit them. And you broke one of the gym windo . . .'

'It's not true!'

'Stop staying it's not true!' deputy headmistress Gatta shouted, shattering the calm she had maintained till that moment, and becoming a Chinese dragon with two vicious little eyes.

Italo deflated and rolled up in a ball like a beach flea.

'Mariuccia, please, calm down, calm down . . .' The head, paralysed on his chair, implored her. All the patients in the ward had turned round and the nurse was glaring at them.

The deputy head lowered her voice and, between her teeth, continued.

'My dear Italo, you are in a very serious predicament. And you don't seem to be aware of the fact. You risk a multiple charge of illegal possession of firearms, attempted murder, living off immoral earnings, being drunk and disorderly . . .'

'No no no no nooooo,' repeated Italo in despair, shaking his big head.

'You're a complete imbecile. What is it you want? Did I hear you correctly? Compensation? You even have the nerve to ask for a whip-round. Now listen to me very carefully.' Mariuccia Gatta rose to her feet and those cold eyes suddenly lit up as if they had thousand-watt light-bulbs inside them. Her cheeks flushed. She grabbed the caretaker by his pyjama lapels and almost lifted him off the bed. 'The headmaster and I are doing our best to help you and only because your son, a policeman, begged us to do so and said his mother would die of shame if she found out. That is the only reason why we haven't reported you. We are doing all we can to save your ar . . . to save you, to prevent you from spending a couple of years in prison, to stop you losing your job, your pension, everything, but now I absolutely must know who those vandals were.'

Italo gaped, like a large tench caught on the hook, then breathed out through his nose. Blood was beginning to trickle down from the tampons in his nostrils.

'I don't know. I don't know, I swear on the heads of my children,' he whimpered, writhing on his bed. 'I didn't see them. When I entered the storeroom it was dark. They threw medicine balls at me. I fell down. They trampled over me. There were two or three of them. I tried to catch them. I couldn't. Little bastards.'

'Is that all?'

'Well, there was another one. One who came out of the high-jump mattresses. And . . .'

'And?'

'Well, I'm not sure, I was some way away, I didn't have my glasses on, but he was so small and thin it might have been . . . yes, it looked like the shepherd's son, the one from Serra . . . I can't remember his name . . . But I'm not sure. The one in 2B.'

'Moroni?'

Italo nodded. 'Only it's strange . . .'

'Strange?'

'Yes, it's strange that a boy like that, such a well-behaved kid, could do something like that. But it might have been him.'

'Right. We'll check.' The deputy head released the caretaker's pyjamas and seemed satisfied. 'Now you take care of yourself. Afterwards we'll see what we can do for you.' Then she turned to her companions. 'Let's go, it's late. They're expecting us at school.'

Giovanni Cosenza and Flora Palmieri jumped to their feet as if they had springs under their backsides.

'Thank you, thank you . . . I'll do anything you want. Come and see me again.'

The three went out and left the caretaker trembling in his bed, terrified of spending the last years of his life in jail, without a lira to his name nor even a pension.

61

A war was going on inside him.

Curiosity was battling with the desire to go home again.

Pietro's mouth was as dry as if he'd eaten a handful of salt, the wind slipped under his hood and swelled his cape and the rain lashed his face, which had become as cold and unfeeling as a block of ice.

He shot through Ischiano practically in apnoea, through the middle of the puddles, and was about to turn into the school street when he screeched to a halt.

What would he find round that corner?

Dogs. Growling German shepherds. Muzzles. Studded collars. His schoolmates lined up, naked, shivering in the downpour. Their hands flat against the walls of the school. Men in blue tracksuits, with black masks on their faces and boots on their feet, walking in the puddles. If you don't tell us who did it, we'll execute one of you every ten minutes.

Who was it?

Me.

Pietro steps forward between his schoolmates.

It was me.

He would certainly find a lot of people with umbrellas, the bar crowded and the firemen sawing away at the chain. And in the midst of them would be Pierini, Bacci and Ronca enjoying the show. He had no wish to meet those three. Much less to share with them the secret that was burning his soul.

How he would have loved to be someone else, one of those who stood outside the bar enjoying the show, and who would go home without that great burden that weighed on his mind.

Another thing he was terribly anxious about was meeting Gloria. He could already imagine her. She would start making a fuss, jumping around all excited, trying to discover who the great genius was who had chained up the gate.

And what do I do, tell her? Describe to her exactly what happened?

(*Get moving, for Christ's sake. Are you going to cower behind this wall all day?*)

He turned the corner.

There was nobody outside the school. Or outside the bar.

He rode on. The gate was open as usual. No sign of firemen. In the car park were the teachers' cars. Italo's 131. The classroom windows were lit up.

There is school, then.

He pedalled slowly, as if he were seeing the building for the first time in his life.

He entered the gate. He checked to see if there were any remnants of the chain on the ground. There weren't. He leant the bike against the low wall. He glanced at his watch.

Nearly twenty minutes late.

He was in danger of getting a black mark but he walked up the steps slowly, spellbound, like a soul ascending the long stairway to heaven.

'What are you doing? Get a move on! It's late!'

Graziella, the caretaker.

She had opened the door and was beckoning him in.

Pietro ran inside.

'Are you crazy, coming by bike like that? Do you want to catch pneumonia?' she scolded him.

'Eh? Yes . . . No!' Pietro wasn't listening.

'What's the matter with you?'

'Nothing. Nothing.'

He trudged off towards his classroom.

'Where do you think you're going? Can't you see you're dripping all over the floor? Take that thing off and hang it on the rack!'

Pietro turned back and took off his cape. It dawned on him that she was the caretaker from Section A and that Italo should have been there, in the porter's lodge.

Where was he?

He didn't want to know.

Things were fine as they were. Italo wasn't there and that was that.

His trouserlegs were wet, but it was nice and warm and they would soon dry out. He rested his frozen hands on the radiator for a moment. The caretaker had sat down and was leafing through a magazine. Otherwise the school was deserted. The only sounds were the rain beating on the windows and the water gushing down the drainpipes.

Lessons had started and everyone was in class. He headed for his own classroom. The door of the secretary's office was open and the secretary was on the phone. The door of the headmaster's office was closed. As usual. The staffroom empty.

Everything's normal.

Before going into class he simply must go down and see the technical education room. If everything was normal there, too, and there was no writing on the wall, and the TV was undamaged, one of two things might have happened. Either he had dreamed the whole thing, which was equivalent to saying that he was completely mad, or the good extraterrestrials had come and cleared everything up. *Pow!* One ray from a photon gun and the TV and the video recorder were as good as new (like when you see a film running backwards). *Pow!* And the graffiti had gone from the walls. *Pow!* And Italo was disintegrated.

He descended the stairs. He turned the handle, but it was locked. So was the gym.

Maybe they've decided to clear everything up and pretend nothing happened.

(*Why?*)

Because they don't know who did it so it's best to play possum. Right?

This conclusion reassured him.

He hurried to his classroom. As soon as he put his hand on the door handle, his heart began to race wildly. Fearfully he pushed it down and entered.

62

Flora Palmieri was sitting on the back seat of the headmaster's Ritmo.

The car was struggling up Orbano hill. The rain was teeming down. All around was a grey thundering mass, with the occasional flash of lightning in the distance, out at sea. The raindrops drummed frenziedly on the roof. The wiper was having trouble keeping the windscreen clear. The road was like a torrent in full flood and the lorries sped past the car, as dark and menacing as whales, churning up spray like speedboats.

Mr Cosenza was hunched over the wheel. 'I can't see a thing. And these truckers are utterly reckless.'

Miss Gatta was navigating. 'Overtake him, what are you waiting for? Can't you see he's making room for you? Step on it, Giovanni.'

Flora was pondering what the caretaker had said and the more she pondered, the more ludicrous it seemed.

Pietro Moroni break into school and smash the place up?

No. The story didn't convince her.

It wasn't like Moroni to behave like that. To get a word out of the little lad you almost had to go down on your knees and beg him. He was so quiet and good that Flora often forgot that he even existed.

It had been Pierini who had written that sentence, she was sure of it.

But what had Moroni been doing there with Pierini?

A few weeks earlier, Flora had set class 2B as homework the hoary old essay: 'What do you want to do when you grow up?'

And Moroni had written:

> I would love to study animals. When I grow up I would like to be a biologist and go to Africa and make animal documentaries. I would work very hard and make a documentary about the Sahara frogs. Nobody knows it but there are frogs in the Sahara. They live under the sand and hibernate for eleven months and three weeks (one year minus a week) and wake up in the exact week when the rain falls on the desert and floods it. They have very little time and have to do many things, such as eating (especially insects), having babies (tadpoles), and digging themselves another hole. That is their life. I would like to go to high school but my father says I have to be a shepherd and look after the fields like my brother Mimmo. Mimmo doesn't want to be a shepherd either. He wants to go to the North Pole to fish for cod but I don't think he will. I would love to go to high school, and university too, to study animals but my father says I can study sheep. I have studied sheep and I don't like them.

That was Pietro Moroni.

A little dreamer, a searcher for frogs in the desert, as timid and inoffensive as a sparrow.

And now what had happened to him?

Had he suddenly turned into a hooligan and teamed up with Pierini?

No.

63

In the classroom everyone was present.

Pierini, Bacci and Ronca threw him some anxious looks. Gloria in the front row smiled at him.

They were all very quiet, a sign that Miss Rovi was doing an oral test. You could cut the tension with a knife.

'Moroni, are you aware that you're late? Hurry up, what are you waiting for? Come in and go to your place,' Miss Rovi rapped, peering at him through her lenses, as thick as bottle-ends.

Diana Rovi was a dumpy old woman with a round face. Hunched up at her desk she looked faintly like a raccoon.

Pietro went to his desk, in the third row, by the window and started taking his books out of his backpack.

The teacher resumed her questioning of Giannini and Puddu, who were standing on either side of her desk, expounding their project: butterflies and their life cycle.

Pietro sat down and nudged Tuna, his neighbour, who was revising his project on grasshoppers.

Antonio Irace, known to all as Tuna, was a tall lanky boy with a small oval head, a studious boy with whom Pietro had never really made friends but who left him in peace.

'Tuna, has anything unusual happened today?' he whispered, with his hands in front of his mouth.

'What do you mean?'

'I don't know, anything . . . Have you seen the deputy head or the head around?'

Antonio didn't look up from his book. 'No, I haven't seen them. Let me revise, please, she's going to pick me soon.'

Gloria meanwhile was waving her arms trying to catch his attention. 'I was afraid you wouldn't come,' she called out in a low voice, leaning right over. 'It'll be our turn soon. Are you ready?'

Pietro nodded.

At that moment the class test was the least of his worries.

If it had been any other day, he would probably have been shitting himself, but today his mind was on other things.

Pierini threw him a ball of paper.

He opened it. It said:

DICKHEAD WHAT THE HELL HAPPENED DID YOU CLOSE THE PADLOCK PROPERLY? WHEN WE ARRIVED EVERYTHING WAS NORMAL. WHAT THE FUCK AVE YOU DONE?

Sure he'd closed it properly. He'd even tugged at the chain to check. He tore a page out of his exercise book and wrote:

I CLOSED IT TIGHT

He screwed it up and threw it to Pierini. His aim was awry and it landed on the desk of Gianna Loria, the tobacconist's daughter, the nastiest and most spiteful girl in the class, who grabbed it and with a malicious smirk put it in her mouth and would have swallowed it had Pierini not made a timely intervention by giving her a well-placed slap on the back of the neck. Gianna spat the note out on the table and Pierini, quick as a ferret, whipped it away and shot back into his place.

None of the three had noticed that old Rovi, behind her bulletproof lenses, had seen it all.

'Moroni! Has all that rainwater rotted your brain? What's the matter with you? You arrive late, you talk in class, you throw balls of paper, what the devil's got into you?' Miss Rovi said all this without any anger, she seemed merely curious to understand the extraordinary behaviour of that little boy who was usually neither seen nor heard. 'Have you done your project, Moroni?'

'Yes, Miss . . .'

'Who did you do it with?'

'Celani.'

'Good. Well, come here, both of you, and entertain me.' Then she addressed the two pupils standing beside her. 'You may go. Make room for Moroni and Celani. Let's hope they do better than you did and at least merit a pass.'

Miss Rovi was like a huge, slow petrol tanker which ploughs

through the sea of life, come fair weather or foul. A thirty-year career had made her proof against the billows. She could get the children to work while retaining their respect, with very little effort.

Pietro and Gloria stood on either side of the teacher's desk. Gloria began, describing the life habits of mosquitoes and the acquatic larval phase. As she talked, she sought out Pietro's eyes. *See? I learned it well in the end.*

Science was Pietro's favourite subject and he had to force Gloria to study it. With infinite patience, while her attention was constantly wandering, he would repeat the lesson to her.

But now she's going really well.

And she was breathtakingly beautiful.

There's nothing better than having a beautiful girl as your best friend. It means you can look at her whenever you like without her thinking you're trying to get off with her.

When it was his turn, he began without hesitation. Perfectly calm. He talked about the draining of the marshes and DDT and, as he talked, he felt euphoric and happy. As if he were drunk.

The danger had passed and there WAS school and they could talk about mosquitoes.

He made a long digression on the best methods for keeping mosquitoes out of the home. He explained the advantages and disadvantages of mosquito coils, electronic repellents, ultraviolet lamps and Autan. Then he talked about a cream he himself had made out of basil and wild fennel, which you spread over yourself and which was so effective that when mosquitoes smelled it they didn't just go away, they fled for their lives and became vegetarians.

'All right, Moroni. That's enough. You've both done very well. What more can I say?' Miss Rovi interrupted him approvingly. 'Now I just have to decide what mark to give y . . .'

The door opened.

The caretaker.

'What is it, Rosaria?'

'Moroni is to go to the headmaster's office.'

The teacher turned to Pietro.

'Pietro . . . ?'

He had turned pale and was breathing through his nose and kept his lips tightly shut. As if he had been told that the electric chair was ready. With bloodless hands he gripped the edge of her desk as if he wanted to snap it off.

'What's the matter, Moroni? Are you all right?'

Pietro nodded. He turned and without looking at anybody walked towards the door.

Pierini got up from his desk and grabbed Pietro by the neck and before he could leave whispered something in his ear.

'Pierini! Who told you to get up? Go back to your place at once!' shouted Miss Rovi, slamming the register on the table.

Pierini turned towards her and smirked impudently. 'Sorry, Miss. I'll go back to my place straight away.'

The teacher looked round for Pietro again.

He had vanished behind the door with Rosaria.

Italo recognised me.

When the caretaker had announced that he had to go and see the headmaster, Pietro had seriously contemplated jumping out of the window.

But there were two problems. First, the window was shut (*I could always smash my way through it head first*) and second, even if he had managed to open it, his classroom was on the first floor and if he landed on the volleyball court he would be paralysed, at worst break a leg.

He wouldn't die, in other words.

And what he needed was to be killed outright.

If there had been a just God, his classroom would have been on the top floor of a skyscraper so high they would have found him down there, smashed to a pulp like a rotten tomato, and the police would have investigated and discovered that he was innocent.

And at his funeral the priest would have said that he was innocent and that it wasn't his fault.

He walked towards the headmaster's office and felt physically sick.

'If you split on us, if you mention any names, I'll cut your throat, I swear on my mother's head,' that's what Pierini had whispered in his ear. And Pierini's mother had only recently died.

He felt a desperate urge to pee. To crap. To vomit.

He looked at that pitiless jailer who was about to hand him over to the executioner.

Can I ask her for permission to go to the bathroom?

(*No. Out of the question.*)

When the head's expecting you, you can't go anywhere, and besides she would certainly think he intended to slip out through the window.

(*You shouldn't have come to school. Why didn't you stay at home?*)

Because I was born stupid. He was disconsolate. *I was born stupid because they made me that way. A perfect idiot.*

Italo had recognised him. And had told the headmaster.

He recognised me.

He had never been summoned to the head's office before. Gloria had, twice. Once when she had hidden Loria's bag in the toilet cistern, and the other time when she had fought with Ronca in the gym. She had been given two black marks.

I've never even had one. Why did he only recognise me?

(*You hid between the mattresses. Why did you hide between the mattresses? If you'd hidden with them . . . He saw you.*)

But he didn't have his glasses on, he was too far away . . .

(*Now calm down. You're scared shitless. They'll notice at once. Don't say anything. You don't know anything. You were at home. You don't know anything.*)

'In you go . . .' The caretaker pointed to the closed door.

Oh God, how terrible he felt, his ears . . . his ears had caught fire and he felt streams of sweat trickling down his sides.

He opened the door slowly.

The headmaster's office was a stark room.

Two long neon lights bathed it in a wan, morgue-like yellow. To the left was a paper-strewn wooden desk and a metal bookcase containing some green files, to the right a small leatherette sofa, two shabby armchairs, a glass coffee-table, a wooden ash-tray and a rubber plant which leaned precariously to one side. On the wall, between the windows, a lithograph of three men on horse-back driving a herd of cattle.

All three were there.

The head was sitting in one of the armchairs. In the other was the deputy head (the nastiest woman in the world). Miss Palmieri was sitting slightly further back, on an upright chair.

'Come in. Sit here,' said the headmaster.

Pietro shuffled across the room and sat on the sofa.

It was nine forty.

64

Disturbed children.

That was the teachers' jargon for kids like Moroni.

Kids with problems integrating into the class group. Kids with difficulties in establishing relationships with their classmates and communicating with teachers. Aggressive kids. Introverted kids. Kids with personality disorders. Kids with serious family problems. With fathers with problems with the law. With fathers with drinking problems. With mothers with mental problems. With brothers with learning problems.

Disturbed children.

As soon as Flora saw him enter the headmaster's office, she realised that Pietro Moroni was about to go through a very nasty experience.

His face was as white as a sheet and he was . . .

(*guilty*)

. . . terrified.

(*as guilty as Judas.*)

He oozed guilt through every pore.

Italo was right. He broke into the school.

65

By nine fifty-seven Pietro had confessed to breaking into the school and was crying.

He cried as he sat up straight on the leatherette sofa in the headmaster's office. Silently. Now and then he would sniff and dry his eyes with the palm of his hand.

Miss Gatta had succeeded in making him talk.

But now he wasn't going to say anything else, even if they killed him. They had tricked him.

The head was the good cop. Miss Gatta the bad cop.

Together they broke you down.

First the head had put him at his ease, then Miss Gatta had confronted him with the truth. 'Moroni, Italo saw you in the school last night.'

Pietro had tried to deny it but his words didn't sound convincing even to him, let alone to them. The deputy headmistress had asked him: 'Where were you at nine o'clock yesterday evening?' And Pietro had said at home, but then he had made a mistake and said at Gloria Celani's house and Miss Gatta had smiled. 'Right, we'll just call Mrs Celani and ask her to confirm that.' And she had picked up the desk diary with the phone numbers and Pietro didn't want Gloria's mother to talk to Miss Gatta because Miss Gatta would tell Gloria's mother that he broke into schools and was a vandal and that would be terrible, so he had confessed.

'Yes, it's true, I broke into the school.' Then he had started crying.

Miss Gatta was unmoved by his tears. 'Was anyone else with you?'

(*If you split on us, if you mention any names, I'll cut your throat, I swear on my mother's head.*)

Pietro had shaken his head.

'You mean to say you chained up the gate and broke in and smashed the television and then wrote the graffiti and hit Italo all on your own? Moroni! You must tell the truth. If you don't, you can forget about passing the end-of-year assessment. Do you understand? Do you want to be expelled from all the schools in Italy? Do you want to go to jail? Who was with you? Italo says there were others. Tell us, or there'll be serious trouble!'

66

That's enough.

The whole situation was becoming unbearable.

What was this, the Spanish Inquisition? Who did that harridan think she was, Torquemada?

First Italo. Now Moroni.

Flora was upset, she felt terribly sorry for that little boy.

The cunning Miss Gatta was terrorising him and Pietro by now was in floods of tears.

So far she had sat there in silence.

But enough is enough!

She stood up, sat down, stood up again. She went over to Miss Gatta, who was pacing from one side of the room to the other, puffing at a cigarette.

'Can I speak to him?' Flora asked in an undertone.

The deputy headmistress blew out a cloud of smoke. 'Why?'

'Because I know him. And I'm sure that this isn't the best way of asking him things.'

'Oh, you know a better way, do you? Well, show me, then . . . Go ahead, let's see you in action . . .'

'Could I speak to him alone?'

'Let Miss Palmieri try, Mariuccia. Let's leave them alone. We'll go to the bar . . .' the head intervened in a conciliatory tone.

Miss Gatta irritably stubbed out her cigarette in the ashtray and went out with the headmaster, slamming the door.

At last they were alone.

Flora knelt down in front of Pietro, who was still crying and covering his face with his hands. For a few seconds she did nothing, then she stretched out her hand and stroked his head.

'Pietro, please. Don't cry. Nothing irreparable has happened. Don't worry. Now listen, you must tell them who was with you. The deputy headmistress wants to know, she won't let the matter rest. She'll get it out of you.' She sat down beside him. 'I think I know why you won't say. You don't want to tell tales, do you?'

Pietro took his hands away from his face. He had stopped crying but his breath still came in gasps.

'No. It was me . . .' he stammered, drying away the snot with the cuff of his pullover.

Flora squeezed his hands. They were warm and sweaty. 'It was Pierini, wasn't it?'

'I can't, I can't . . .' He was begging her.

'You must say. Then everything will be easier.'

'He said he'd cut my throat if I sneaked.' And he burst into tears again.

'No, he's just a loudmouth. He won't hurt you.'

'It wasn't my fault . . . I didn't want to break in . . .'

Flora hugged him. 'There, there, stop crying now. Tell me what happened. You can trust me.'

'I can't . . .' But then, with his face buried in his teacher's cardigan, Pietro, in between sobs, told her about the chain and about how Pierini, Bacci and Ronca had forced him to go into the school and write that Italo had smelly feet and how he had hidden between the mattresses in the gym and how Italo had shot at him.

And as Pietro talked Flora thought about how unjust this world they lived in was.

Why do mafiosi who turn state evidence and talk get offered a new identity, a lot of guarantees and a reduced sentence, when a defenceless child gets nothing but terror and threats?

The situation Pietro found himself in was no better than that of the mafia informers and a threat from Pierini was no less dangerous than one from a Cosa Nostra boss.

When Pietro finished his tale, he raised his head and looked at her with bloodshot eyes. 'I didn't want to break in. They made me. Now I've told the truth. I don't want to fail the year. If I do my father will never send me to high school.'

Flora felt a surge of affection for Pietro which took her breath away. She hugged him tightly.

She wished she could take him away with her, adopt him. She would have given anything for him to be her son, so that she could have looked after him and sent him to high school, somewhere miles away from that village of brutes and make him happy. 'Don't worry. You won't fail. I swear to you. Nobody will hurt you. Look at me, Pietro.'

And Pietro directed those red-rimmed eyes at hers.

'I'll say it was me who put to you the names of Pierini and the other two. You just said yes. It's not your fault. You didn't do all that damage. Miss Gatta will give you a few days' suspension, and so much the better. Pierini won't think you sneaked on him. There's nothing to worry about. You're a clever boy, you're doing well at school and you won't fail the year. Do you understand? I promise.'

Pietro nodded.

'Now go to the bathroom, wash your face and return to your class. I'll sort it out.'

67

Five days' suspension.

For Pierini. For Bacci. For Ronca. And for Moroni.

And the parents must accompany the children on their return to school and speak to the headmaster and the teachers.

So decreed Miss Gatta (and Mr Cosenza).

The technical education room was hastily repainted. The remains of the television and video recorder were thrown away. Permission was requested from the board of governors to use school funds to buy new video-didactic equipment.

Moroni had confessed. Bacci had confessed. Ronca had confessed. Pierini had confessed.

One after another they had been summoned to the headmaster's office and had confessed.

A whole morning of confessions.

Miss Gatta had a right to feel pleased with herself.

68

Now there was another problem.

Telling Papa.

Gloria had given him some advice. 'Tell your mother. Send her to talk to the teachers. And tell her not to mention it to your father. During these five days you can pretend to go to school, but in fact you'll come over to my house. You can stay in my room and read comics. If you're hungry you have a sandwich and if you feel like watching a film you put on a video. Easy.'

That was the great difference between the two of them.

For Gloria everything was easy.

For Pietro nothing was.

If something like this had happened to Gloria, she would have gone to her mother and her mother would have given her a cuddle and taken her shopping in Orbano to console her.

His mother wouldn't do anything of the sort. She would burst into tears and keep asking him why.

Why did you do it? Why are you always getting into trouble?

And she wouldn't listen to his answers. She wouldn't be interested in whether or not it was Pietro's fault. The only thing she would be worried about would be the fact that she had to go and talk to the teachers (it's too much, you know I'm not well, you can't ask that of me, Pietro) and that her son was suspended and everything else. The actual reasons would go in one ear and out the other. She wouldn't take them in.

And finally she would whimper, 'You know your father's the one you must talk to about this sort of thing. There's nothing I can do about it.'

* * *

His father's tractor was outside the farmers' club.

Pietro dismounted from his bike, took a deep breath and went in.

There was hardly anyone there.

Good.

Only Gabriele, the barman, who with screwdriver and hammer in hand was taking the coffee machine apart.

His father was sitting at a table reading the paper. His black hair gleamed under the neon light. The brilliantine. Spectacles on the tip of his nose. A scowl on his face, he was following the lines of newsprint with his forefinger and muttering to himself. The news always got him riled.

He approached him in silence and when he was a metre away called out. 'Papa . . .'

Mr Moroni turned. He saw him. He smiled. 'Pietro! What are you doing here?'

'I came . . .'

'Sit down.'

Pietro obeyed.

'Do you want an ice cream?'

'No thanks.'

'Crisps? What would you like?'

'I won't have anything, thanks.'

'I've nearly finished. We'll go home in a minute.' He went on reading the paper.

He was in a good mood. That was promising.

Maybe . . .

'Papa, I've got something to tell you . . .' He opened his backpack, took out a letter and handed it to him.

Mr Moroni read it. 'What is it?' His voice had dropped an octave.

'I've been suspended . . . You've got to go and speak to the deputy head.'

'What have you been up to?'

'Nothing much. There was a bit of trouble last night . . .' And in thirty seconds he told him the story. He was fairly truthful. He omitted the part about the graffiti, but told him about the TV and the video recorder and how the other three had forced him to go in.

When he had finished, he looked at his father.

He gave no sign of anger, but continued to stare at the letter as if it were an Egyptian hieroglyphic.

Pietro said nothing and nervously clasped his hands as he waited for an answer.

Then at last his father spoke. 'And what do you want from me?'

'You have to go to the school. It's important. The deputy headmistress wants you to . . .' Pietro tried to say this as if it were a formality, a matter that could be settled in a minute.

'And what does she want from me?'

'Nothing really . . . She'll have to tell you . . . I don't know. That what I did was wrong. That I did something I mustn't do. Things like that.'

'What's that got to do with me?'

What do you mean, what's it got to do with you? 'Well . . . you are my father.'

'Yes, but it wasn't me who broke into the school. It wasn't me who let a bunch of idiots push me around. What I did last night was do my work and go to bed.' He went on reading.

The subject was closed.

Pietro tried again. 'So you won't go?'

Mr Moroni looked up from his paper. 'No. I certainly will not. I'm not going to apologise for the stupid things you do. Sort it out for yourself. You're old enough. You do stupid things and then you expect me to solve all your problems?'

'But Papa, it's not me who wants you to go and talk to her. It's the deputy headmistress who wants to talk to you. If you don't go, she'll think . . .'

'What will she think?' snapped Mr Moroni.

The apparent calm was beginning to crumble.

That I've got a father who doesn't care a shit about me, that's what she'll think. That he's crazy, someone who has problems with the law, a drunk. (That's what that bitch Gianna Loria had said to him once, when they had quarrelled over a seat on the bus. Your father's a stupid crazy drunk.) *That I'm not a normal child like all the others who have parents who go and speak to the teachers.*

'I don't know. But if you don't go they'll fail me. When you're suspended your parents have to go to the school. It's compulsory. That's the way it works. You've got to go and tell them . . .' *That I'm a good boy.*

'I haven't got to go anywhere. If they fail you, it'll be no more than you deserve. You'll repeat the year. Like that idiot brother of yours. And then we'll have no more of this talk about studying and wanting to go to high school. Now be quiet. I'm tired of talking. Go away. I want to read the paper.'

'You won't go?' Pietro asked again.

'No.'

'Are you sure?'

'Leave me alone.'

Mr Moroni's Catapult

But why did all the villagers say Mario Moroni was crazy, and what were these problems he'd had with the law?

It should be explained that when Mr Moroni was not working in the fields or going to the farmers' club in Serra to rot his liver with Fernet Branca, he had a hobby.

Woodwork.

Usually he made cupboards, picture frames, little bookcases. Once he had built a small trailer incorporating the wheels of a Vespa, to hook onto the back of Mimmo's motorbike. They used it for carrying hay to the sheep. In the storeroom he had a little workshop complete with circular saw, plane, chisels and all the other tools of the trade.

One evening Mr Moroni had seen a film about the ancient Romans on television. There was a big scene with thousands of extras. The legions were besieging a fortress with war machines.

Rams, testudos and catapults with which they hurled boulders and fireballs at the enemy ramparts.

This had made a deep impression on Mario Moroni.

Next day he had gone to the public library in Ischiano and, with the librarian's help, found some pictures of catapults in the illustrated encyclopaedia *Knowledge*. He had had some photocopies made and taken them home. He had studied them carefully. Then he had called his sons and told them he intended to build a catapult.

Neither of them dared to ask why. Such questions were better not asked of Mr Moroni. You just did what he said and never mind the reasons.

A sound principle of the Moroni household.

Pietro had taken to the idea at once. Nobody he knew had a catapult in their garden. They would be able to throw rocks, knock down a wall or two. Mimmo, however, was strongly opposed to the plan. It would mean them spending the next few Sundays slogging their guts out to build something that was no use to man or beast.

The following Sunday work had begun.

And after a few hours they had all begun to enjoy it. There was something grand and new about this labour to build a completely useless contraption. Although you worked and sweated just as hard, it was nothing like as much effort as building that new fence for the sheep.

Four of them worked on it.

Mr Moroni, Pietro, Mimmo and Poppi.

Augusto, nicknamed Poppi, was an old donkey with a coat that was patchy and white with age, who had laboured hard for many years until Mr Moroni had bought the tractor. Now he was in retirement, spending the twilight of his life browsing in the meadow behind the house. He was very bad-tempered and would let no one touch him except Mr Moroni. Other people he bit. And when a donkey bites it really hurts, so the rest of the family kept well away from him.

The first thing they did was to chop down a tall pine tree which grew at the edge of the woods. With Poppi's help they dragged it home and there, with chainsaw, hatchets and planes, they made it into a long pole.

Around this pole, over the next few weekends, they built the catapult. Sometimes Mr Moroni would get furious with his sons because they botched their work or were clumsy and then he would kick them in the backside. At other times, when he saw that they had done things properly, he would say, 'Well done, good work.' And a fleeting smile, as rare as a sunny day in February, would appear on his lips.

Then Mrs Moroni would arrive bringing ham and caciotta rolls and they would eat their lunch sitting beside the catapult discussing the next stage of the work.

Mimmo and Pietro were happy. Their father's good humour was infectious.

A couple of months later the completed catapult towered behind Fig-Tree Cottage. It was a strange machine, and rather ungainly to look at. It bore some resemblance to the Roman catapults but not a very close one. Essentially it was a huge lever. The fulcrum was fixed, with the help of a steel hinge (specially made by the blacksmith), to two upside-down Vs nailed to a four-wheeled trolley. Attached to the short end of the arm was a sort of basket full of sandbags (weighing six hundred kilos!). The long end terminated in a kind of spoon in which you put the rock you wanted to throw.

When it was wound up, the sandbag-filled basket rose and the spoon came down and was tied to the ground by a thick rope. To achieve this, Mr Moroni had designed a system of pulleys and ropes which were pulled round a winch which in turn was pulled round by poor old Poppi. Whenever the donkey stopped short and started braying, Mr Moroni would go over, stroke him and whisper in his ear and he would start turning again.

For the inauguration of the catapult there was a party. The only party ever held at Fig-Tree Cottage.

Mrs Biglia cooked three immense trayfulls of lasagne. Pietro put on his smart jacket. Mimmo invited Patti. And Mr Moroni shaved.

Uncle Giovanni arrived with his pregnant wife and his children.

Some friends from the farmers' club came, a fire was lit and some sausages and steaks barbecued. When everyone had had their fill of food and wine, it was launch time. Uncle Giovanni smashed a bottle of wine against one of the catapult's wheels and Mr Moroni, who was rolling drunk, drove up on his tractor whistling a military march and towing a trailer loaded with some more or less spherical rocks he had found along the road to Gazzina. It took four people to lift one and place it on the ready-primed catapult.

Pietro was really excited and even Mimmo, though he tried not to show it, was following proceedings closely.

Everyone stood back and with a clean blow of his hatchet Mr Moroni cut the rope. There was a loud crack, the drum full of sand dropped and the rock shot up, curved through the air and landed two hundred metres away in the woods. There was a sound of snapping branches and flocks of birds flew up from the treetops.

The audience clapped and cheered.

Mr Moroni was delighted. He went over to Mimmo and put his arm round his neck. 'Did you hear the noise it made? That's the sound I wanted to hear. Great work, Mimmo.' Then he picked up Pietro in his arms and kissed him. 'Run along now, go and see where it's landed.'

Pietro and his cousins dashed into the woods. They found the rock embedded in the earth beside a great oak. And some broken branches.

Then, at last, came Poppi's moment. They had decked him out in a new harness and coloured ribbons. He looked like a Sicilian ceremonial ass. With great effort the donkey started walking round the winch. Everyone laughed and said it would be the death of the poor beast.

But Mr Moroni didn't care about those sceptics, he knew Poppi could do it. He was as stubborn and unyielding as the finest of his species. When he was younger, Mr Moroni had loaded on that back the bricks and bags of cement he needed to build the upper floor of the house.

And now he was winding the catapult up, never stopping, never digging his heels in, never braying as he usually did. *He knows this is his moment*, Mr Moroni said to himself, deeply moved.

He was so proud of his animal.

When Poppi had finished, Mr Moroni started clapping and everyone else followed suit.

A second boulder was thrown and there was more applause, though more muted this time. Then everyone descended on the pastries.

It's understandable. Watching a catapult throw rocks into the woods isn't exactly the most enthralling pastime in the world.

It was Mr Moroni who found him.

The murderer had shot him in the head.

Poppi had dropped dead on the ground.

He lay there, stiff-legged, stiff-eared and stiff-tailed, by the fence that marked off Contarello's land.

'Contarello, you son of a bitch, I'm going to kill you, this time I'm really going to kill you,' gurgled Mr Moroni, kneeling by Poppi's corpse.

If his tear ducts hadn't been drier than the Kalahari desert, Mr Moroni would have wept.

The war with Contarello had been going on since time immemorial. It was a private feud, incomprehensible to the rest of the world, which had begun over a few square metres of pastureland which each of them considered his own. And it had been waged through insults, death threats, provocations and acts of spite.

It had never occurred to either man to check the documents in the land registry.

Mr Moroni kicked the mud, punched the trees.

'Contarello, you shouldn't have done this . . . You shouldn't.' Then he gave a wild roar at the sky. He grabbed Poppi's legs and with a strength born of fury hoisted the carcass onto his back. Poor Poppi weighed nearly a hundred and fifty kilos, but that little man who weighed sixty and drank like a fish walked forward across the grass, legs apart, swaying from side to side. His face, with the effort, was a mass of humps and furrows. 'Contarello, now you'll see,' he said, grinding his teeth.

He staggered as far as the farmhouse and threw Poppi on the ground. Then he tied a rope to the tractor and wound up the catapult.

He knew the exact position of Contarello's house.

Village legend has it that Contarello and family were in the sitting room watching *Carramba, What a Surprise!* when it arrived.

Raffaella Carrà had succeeded in reuniting two twins from Macerata who had been separated at birth and the two of them were hugging each other and crying and the Contarellos were sniffling, deeply touched. It was a tear-jerking scene.

But suddenly everything seemed to explode over their heads. Something had fallen on the house and shaken it to its foundations.

The television went off, so did all the lights.

'Good grief, what's happened?' screamed grandmother Ottavia, clutching her daughter.

'A meteorite!' shouted Contarello. 'We've been hit by a fucking meteorite. There was a report about them on *Quark Science*. It happens sometimes.'

The lights came back on. They peered around in terror, then looked upwards. One beam of the ceiling had split and some pieces of plaster had fallen down.

The family climbed the stairs, full of trepidation.

Everything seemed normal up there.

Contarello opened the bedroom door and fell on his knees. Hands over his mouth.

The roof had gone.

The walls were red. The floor was red. The eiderdown that grandmother Ottavia had made with her own hands was red. The windowpanes were red. Everything was red.

Bits of Poppi (guts and bones and shit and hairs) were scattered all over the room together with debris and roof tiles.

* * *

Nobody was around when Mr Moroni catapulted the corpse, but if anyone had been, they would have seen a donkey shoot up into the air, describe a perfect parabola, sail over the cork woods, the stream and the vineyard, and land like a Scud missile on the Contarellos' roof.

That little prank cost Mr Moroni dear.

He was reported to the police, charged and condemned to pay damages, and it was only because he had no previous convictions that he wasn't jailed for attempted murder. He now had a criminal record.

Oh, and he was ordered to dismantle the catapult.

69

Not thinking about anything is very difficult.

And it's the first thing you have to learn to do when you start yoga.

You try, you concentrate like mad and start thinking that you mustn't think about anything and you've already blown it because that's a thought.

No, it's not easy.

But to Graziano Biglia it came naturally.

He had assumed the lotus position in the middle of his room and kept his mind blank for half an hour. Then he'd taken a nice hot bath, got dressed and rung Roscio to tell him the Saturnia trip was still on but that he wouldn't be able to join them for dinner. He would go straight to the baths and meet them there at about half past ten or eleven.

All in all, his first day as a single hadn't gone too badly. He had spent the whole day indoors. He'd watched tennis on TV and had his lunch in bed. Depression had buzzed around him like a horsefly, ready to plunge its sting into his heart, but Graziano had organised things well, he had slept, eaten and watched sport in a kind of bovine apathy that was proof against the emotions.

Now he was ready for the schoolmistress.

He took one last look at himself in the mirror. He had decided to drop the country gentleman look. It didn't suit him, and anyway his shirt and jacket were spattered with vomit. He had opted for a blend of the casual with the elegant. Early Spandau Ballet, if you get the picture.

Black satin shirt with pointed collar. Red waistcoat. Black cord jacket with three buttons. Jeans. Python boots. Yellow ochre scarf. Black headband.

Oh yes, and under his jeans, a pair of purple Speedo bathing trunks.

He was putting on his overcoat when his mother emerged from the kitchen, mumbling. Without even trying to understand what she wanted, he replied: 'No, Mama, I won't be home for dinner. I'll be back late.'

He opened the door and went out.

70

Bath time was always a complicated affair.

And Flora Palmieri sensed that her mother didn't like it at all. She could see it in her eyes. (Flora, dear, why the bath? I don't feel like it . . .)

'I know it's a nuisance, Mama, but you must have one occasionally.'

It was a delicate operation.

If she wasn't careful, there was a risk of her mother's head going under the water and her drowning. And the heater had to be switched on at least an hour beforehand, otherwise she might catch cold, and that would be serious. With a blocked nose she couldn't breathe.

'Nearly done . . .' Flora, on her knees, finished soaping her and began rinsing with the shower that white, shrunken little body huddled in the corner of the bath. 'One more minute . . . and I'll pop you back into bed . . .'

The neurologist had said that her mother's brain was like a computer on standby. One tap on the keyboard and the screen lights up and the hard disk comes back to life. The trouble was her mother wasn't connected up to any keyboard, and there was no way of reactivating her.

'She can't hear you. It's out of the question. Your mother is not there. Don't delude yourself. She's electroencephically flat,' the neurologist had said with the sensitivity that is the hallmark of his profession.

In Flora's view the neurologist was talking through his hat. Her mother was there all right. A barrier separated her from the world, but Flora's words could pass beyond that barrier. She could see this from many signs, which would have been impossible to recognise for a stranger or for a doctor who relied solely on electroencephalograms, CAT scans, ultrasound and other scientific gadgets, but which were crystal clear to her. A twitch of an eyebrow, a tightening of the lips, a gaze less opaque than usual, a vibration.

This was her imperceptible way of expressing herself.

And Flora was sure it was her words that kept her alive.

There had been a time when her mother's health had deteriorated and she had required constant care, day and night. Eventually Flora hadn't been able to cope any longer and on the doctor's advice had taken a nurse who treated her mother like a mannequin. Never talked to her, never caressed her, and instead of improving, her mother's health had got even worse. Flora had dismissed the nurse and gone back to taking care of her herself and immediately her mother's health had improved.

And another thing, Flora had the clear perception that her mother could communicate with her mentally. Now and again she heard her voice break in upon her thoughts. She wasn't mad or schizophrenic, it was just that, being her daughter, she knew exactly what her mother would have said about this or that, knew what she liked, what she disliked, what she would have advised her to do when there was a decision to be taken.

* * *

'There we are, all done.' She lifted her out of the bathtub and carried her dripping wet into the bedroom, where she had prepared the towel.

She rubbed her down vigorously and was sprinkling her with talc when the house phone buzzed.

'Who can that be? Oh, my goodness . . . !'

The appointment!

The appointment she had made that morning at the Station Bar with the haberdasher's son.

'Oh my goodness, Mama, I'd completely forgotten. How could I be so stupid? There was a man who asked me to help him write a CV.'

She saw her mother's lips tighten.

'Don't worry, I'll get rid of him in an hour or so. I know, it's an awful nuisance. But he's here now.' She put her under the bedclothes.

The house phone buzzed again.

'All right! I'm coming. Just a minute.' She emerged from the bedroom, took off the apron she used when she was washing her mother and glanced at herself in the mirror . . .

Why are you looking at yourself?

. . . and picked up the receiver.

71

The schoolmistress was waiting for him in the doorway.

And she hadn't changed her clothes.

Does that mean meeting me isn't important to her? Graziano wondered, and then held out a bottle of whisky. 'I brought you a little something.'

Flora turned it over in her hands. 'Thank you, you shouldn't have.'

'That's all right. Don't mention it.'

'Come in.'

She led the way into the sitting room.

'Would you mind waiting for a minute . . . ? I'll be right back. Make yourself at home,' Flora said awkwardly and vanished into the dark corridor.

Graziano was left alone.

He checked his appearance, using the window as a mirror. He straightened his shirt collar. And with slow, measured paces, hands behind his back, he strolled round the room, inspecting it.

It was a square room, with two windows which looked onto the hills. Through one you could glimpse a segment of sea. There was a fireplace where some embers were smouldering. A little sofa covered in blue material patterned with little pink flowers. An old leather armchair. A stool. A bookcase, small but crammed full of books. A Persian carpet. A round table on which papers and books were tidily arranged. A small television on a stand. Two water-colours on the walls. One was a storm at sea. The other was a view of a beach on which a large tree trunk had been washed up by the tide. It looked like Castrone beach. They were simple and not particularly successful, but the colours were pale and subdued and conveyed a sense of nostalgia. Some photographs were neatly arrayed on the mantelpiece. Black and white. A woman who resembled Flora sitting on a low wall, behind her the bay of Mergellina. And one of a newly wed couple at a church door. And other family memories.

This is her den. It's here that she spends her lonely evenings . . .

That sitting room had a special atmosphere.

Maybe it's the low, warm lights. She's certainly a woman with great taste . . .

72

The woman with great taste was in her mother's bedroom talking in a low voice.

'Mama, you'd never imagine the get-up he's come in. With that shirt . . . And those tight-fitting trousers . . . How stupid I am, I shouldn't have let him come.' She pulled up her mother's blankets.

'All right. That's enough dithering. I'll go now. And get it over with.'

She fetched some blank sheets of paper from the cupboard in the hall, took a deep breath and went back into the sitting room. 'We'll write a rough draft and you can make a fair copy afterwards. Let's sit here.' She cleared the papers off the table and pulled up two chairs, opposite each other.

'Did you do those?' Graziano pointed at the watercolours.

'Yes . . .' Flora murmured.

'They're beautiful. Really . . . You're very talented.'

'Thank you,' she replied, blushing.

73

She wasn't beautiful.

Or at least, that morning she had seemed more beautiful.

If you took each part of her face separately, the aquiline nose, the wide mouth, the receding chin, the expressionless eyes, she was a disaster, but if you put them all back together, there emerged something strangely magnetic, with a disharmonious beauty all of its own.

Yes, he liked Miss Palmieri.

'Mr Biglia, are you listening to me?'

'Oh, yes . . .' His attention had wandered.

'I was telling you that I've never written a CV in my life, but I've seen some, and I think the best thing to do is to begin at the beginning, with your date of birth, and then go on from there, selecting any information that might interest the owners of that place you want to go to . . .'

'Right, let's get started, then . . . I was born in Ischiano on . . .'

And off he went.

He immediately lied about his date of birth. He knocked four years off his age.

It was a brilliant idea, the CV.

He would be able to tell her about the adventurous life he

had led, fascinate her with his innumerable interesting encounters all over the world, explain his passion for music and everything else.

74

Flora glanced at her watch.

More than half an hour had passed since he had started talking and she still hadn't managed to write a word. He had stunned her with such a flood of words that her head was spinning.

The man was a windbag. Sure of certainties based on nothing. So full of himself you'd think he would burst, so convinced of the importance of what he'd done you'd think he was the first man to set foot on the moon, or Reinhold Messner.

And the most unbearable thing was that he seasoned his adventures – as a DJ in a New York night club, as a supporting act for a Peruvian band on tour in Argentina, as a co-driver in a rally in Mauritania, as a cabin-boy on a yacht on which he had crossed the Atlantic in force-nine gales, as a volunteer in an isolation hospital for patients with infectious diseases, as a guest in a Tibetan monastery – with a phoney, second-hand philosophy. A jumble of New Age concepts, watered-down Buddhist principles, banal Kerouackian *On the Road* ideas, echoes of the Beat Generation, picture postcard images and teenage disco culture. In actual fact, if you eliminated the heroic deeds, the only thing this man seemed to be interested in was lying on a tropical beach playing that wretched Spanish music in the moonlight.

None of which was of the slightest use for a CV.

If I don't interrupt him he might go on all night. Flora was anxious to finish the job and send him away.

His presence in the house made her nervous. He looked at her in a way that made her blood run cold. There was something sensual about him that disturbed her.

She was tired. Miss Gatta had given her a hellish day and she sensed that her mother needed her.

'Now then, I'd forget about the reintroduction of red deer into Sardinia and try to concentrate on something more concrete. You were talking about that man Paco de Lucia. We could mention that you've played with him. Is he an important musician?'

Graziano sat up with a jolt. 'Is Paco de Lucia important? He's fundamental! Paco's a genius. He's made flamenco known to the whole world. He's like Ravi Shankar was for Indian music . . . Let's be serious now.'

'Good. In that case, Mr Biglia, we could add him . . .' She tried to write, but he touched her arm.

She stiffened.

'Miss Palmieri, would you do me a favour?'

'What?'

'Don't call me Mr Biglia. I'm Graziano to you.'

Flora gave him a look of exasperation. 'Very well, Graziano. Now then, Paco . . .'

'And what's your first name? May I know?'

'Flora,' she whispered, after a brief hesitation.

'Flora . . .' Graziano closed his eyes like a man inspired. 'What a lovely name . . . If I had a daughter, that's what I'd like to call her . . .'

75

She was a really tough nut to crack.

Graziano hadn't realised he was up against General Patton in person.

The stories he'd told her had cut no ice with her. And yet he'd pulled out all the stops, he'd been creative, imaginative, charming, the sort of thing that would have had them falling at his feet in droves at Riccione. And when he'd seen that his usual repertoire wasn't doing the trick, he had reeled off such a string of unlikely tales that if he'd done half the things he claimed to have done he would have been happy for the rest of his days.

But it was no good.

The schoolmistress was a grade-six ascent.

He glanced at his watch.

Time was passing and the possibility of taking her to Saturnia seemed suddenly remote, unattainable. He hadn't succeeded in creating the right atmosphere. Flora had taken the CV too seriously.

If I ask her to come for a bathe at Saturnia now, no prizes for guessing where she'll tell me to go . . .

What could he do?

Should he adopt the Zonin–Lenci (two of his Riccione friends) technique, and just leap on her? Suddenly, brutally, dispensing with all preliminaries?

You close in and then, quick as a cobra, before she knows what's happening, stick your tongue in her mouth. It was a possible method, but the Zonin–Lenci technique had a number of contraindications. In order for it to work the prey must be tame, that is to say, already used to approaches of a certain level, otherwise you might end up being charged with attempted rape, and anyway the technique is very much of the all or nothing variety.

And here it would be nothing, damn it. No, the only thing is to be more explicit but without alarming her.

'Flora, how about trying that whisky I brought? It's a special one. It was sent to me from Scotland.' And he began a slow, almost invisible but inexorable shifting of his chair towards the region of General Patton.

76

That's what Flora's problem was. She could never assert herself. Express her opinion. Get what she wanted. If she'd had a little more nerve, like the rest of the human race, she would have said, 'Graziano (and what an effort it was to use his first name), I'm sorry, it's late, you must go.'

But instead, here she was, bringing him a drink. She returned from the kitchen with the bottle and two glasses on a tray.

Graziano, in her absence, had got up and moved over to the sofa.

'Here we are. Excuse me, I'll be back in a moment. Only a tiny drop for me. I'm not too keen on alcohol. I drink limoncino now and then.' She put the tray on the coffee table in front of the sofa and rushed next door to have a time-out with Mama.

77

Eight forty-five!

There was no more time for delicate approaches.

It's going to have to be the Mullet technique, Graziano said to himself, shaking his head unhappily. He didn't like it, but he could see no other way.

Mullet was another pal of his, a junkie from Città di Castello, so called because of his resemblance to the bewhiskered fish.

Both had eyes as round and red as cherries.

Once, in a sudden fit of loquacity, Mullet had explained to him: 'It's quite simple. Suppose there's a girl you want to pull at a party, she's drinking her gin and tonic or some other alcoholic drink. You stand next to her and the moment she leaves her glass unguarded or turns away you drop in a particular kind of pill, and bingo. In half an hour she's as high as a kite, there for the taking.'

Mullet's technique wasn't very sporting, there was no question about that. Graziano had rarely used it and then only in very serious cases. In competitions it was prohibited, and if you were caught it meant instant disqualification.

But, as they say, needs must when the Devil drives.

Graziano took his wallet out of his inside pocket.

Let's see what we've got here, then . . .

He opened it and extracted from an inner compartment three blue pills.

'Spiderman . . .' he purred contentedly, like an old alchemist who finds himself holding the philosopher's stone.

* * *

Spiderman is a nondescript-looking pill. With that light-blue colour and that groove down the middle it could easily be mistaken for a headache or indigestion tablet, but it's not. It is most definitely not.

In those sixty milligrams there are more psychotropically active molecules than in an entire pharmacy. It was synthesised in Goa in the early Nineties by a group of young Californian neurobiologists who had been expelled from MIT for bioethically incorrect behaviour, in collaboration with a bunch of shamans from the Yukatan peninsula and a team of German behavioural psychiatrists.

After a quarter of an hour the mice on which they tested the drug were doing handstands, balancing upside down on one leg and twirling round like breakdancers.

The reason it's called Spiderman is that one of its many effects is to make you feel as if you were walking up walls. Another is that, if after you've taken it someone leads you to the registry office and puts you at the end of a long queue and tells you, 'Go and collect Carleo's birth certificate' and you haven't the faintest idea who Carleo is, you do so, as happy as a sandboy, and when you think back in later years you still remember it as the most hilarious experience of your life.

That is what Graziano Biglia dissolved in Miss Palmieri's whisky. And then, to be on the safe side, he added another. His own pill he popped in his mouth and washed down with a swig of whisky.

'And now let's see if she doesn't capitulate.' He undid a couple of shirt buttons, smoothed back his hair and waited for his prey to arrive.

78

Flora took the glass that Graziano offered her, closed her eyes and swallowed. She didn't notice the unpleasant bitter aftertaste – she never drank whisky, she didn't like it.

'Very nice. Thank you.' She gritted her teeth and sat down at the table again. She put on her spectacles and examined what she had written.

She spent the next ten minutes sorting out all that hot air, those rambling stories, trying to extract the essential information: languages spoken, education, computer skills, work experience, etc etc.

'I should say there's plenty of material here. The things we've jotted down should be sufficient. I'm sure you'll get the job, Mr Bigl . . . Graziano.'

Graziano was still on the sofa. 'I think I will. But there are a couple of other things that might impress the people who run the village. You see, they try to give everyone a good time . . . Put the guests at their ease . . . Create relationships between people . . .'

'How do you mean?' asked Flora, removing her spectacles.

'Well, I . . .' He seemed embarrassed.

She saw him shift on the sofa as if thorns had suddenly sprung out of the cushions. He got up and sat down at the table. 'You see, I won a cup . . .'

Now what's he going to tell me? That he won the Tour de France? Flora's heart sank.

'At Riccione. The Casanova Cup.'

'What's that?'

'Let's say I made the highest number of scores in one summer. An all-time record, in fact.'

'The highest number of what?'

'Scores! Pulls!' To Graziano it seemed the most obvious thing in the world.

But Flora didn't understand. What was he talking about? Pulls? Did he work in a bar or something?'

'Pulls?' she repeated, bemused.

'Women pulled.' Graziano contrived to sound both guilty and self-satisfied at the same time.

At last it dawned on her.

I don't believe it! This man's a monster.

They had competitions to see who could sleep with the most females. There was actually a place in this world where men competed to see who could bed the most women.

It's really true, you shouldn't be surprised at anything in life.

'You mean there's a contest, a sort of championship? Like in football?' she asked, and she noticed that her tone was strangely airy.

'Yes, it's an official event now, people come from all over the world to take part. At first there were only a few of us. A small group of friends who met at the Aurora beach club. Then gradually it became more important. Now there are points, a federation, judges, and at the end of the season there's a prize-giving ceremony in a disco. It's a very nice evening,' explained Graziano very earnestly.

'And how many women did you . . . pull? Is that the word?' She couldn't believe it. This man, in the summer, competed in pulling contests.

'Three hundred. Three hundred and three, to be precise. But those bastards of judges didn't confirm three of them. Because they were in Cattolica,' replied Graziano with a sly smile.

'Three hundred?' Flora jumped. 'It can't be true! Three hundred! Swear it!'

Graziano nodded. 'I swear to God. I've got the cup at home.'

Flora burst out laughing. And she couldn't stop.

What on earth has got into me?

She went on shrieking with laughter. One little glass of whisky and she was already drunk? She knew she couldn't take alcohol, but she had only drunk two fingers. In her whole life she had got drunk a couple of times. Once on a jar of cherries pickled in alcohol which she had been given by the mother of one of her pupils, and another time when she had gone out for a pizza with her class and had one beer too many. She had returned home decidedly merry. But she had never been as drunk as this.

Certainly, though, this pulling business was very amusing. She felt an urge to ask him a question, a rather vulgar one, *I shouldn't, but what the hell*, she said to herself, *here goes*. 'And how do you score a point?'

Graziano smiled. 'Well, you have to have complete intercourse.'

'Do everything?'

'That's right.'

'Absolutely everything?'

'Absolutely everything.'

(*Are you out of your mind?*)

A voice echoed in her head.

She was sure it was her mother's.

(*What are you laughing about? Look at you, you're completely drunk.*)

I can't look at me. What am I doing?

(*Behaving like a slut. That's what you're doing.*)

Please be quiet. Please be quiet. Don't call me that. I don't like you calling me that and now, please, I must do a calculation. Let me see, now . . . This man scored three hundred points, didn't he? That means he inserted his male sexual organ into three hundred female sexual organs. If with each of them he moved it, back and forth, let's say, an average of, how many times must it be? two hundred times each, more or less, give or take a thrust he made an average of six hundred, no, not six hundred, three hundred. Three hundred times two hundred makes six hundred. No, it doesn't, wait a minute. It's more than that.

She was totally confused.

A wind of images, lights, mangled thoughts, meaningless numbers and words was swirling in her head, yet she felt strangely elated and joyful.

'Damn your whisky,' she exclaimed, thumping her fist on the table.

She eyed him squarely for a moment.

Suddenly she felt an absurd desire.

(*Are you crazy? You can't say that to him! Nooo, you can't . . .*)

Oh yes I can.

She wanted to confess something to him, something secret, very secret, something she had never told anyone and had no intention of telling anyone for the next ten thousand years. In an instant

Flora felt all the weight of that uranium secret and wanted to be rid of it, to vomit it out to him of all people, this fellow, this stranger, this Mr Three Hundred Points who had won the Casanova Cup for his prowess as a seaside stud.

I wonder how he'll react?

How would he take it? Would he laugh? Would he say he didn't believe it?

It's true, though, I assure you. Would you like to know something, my dear Seducer, would you like to know how many points I've scored in my whole life?

Nul!

Zilch!

Not one teensy weensy little point. Once, a long time ago, my uncle tried to score a point with me but he didn't succeed, the dirty old man.

How many points have you scored in your life? Ten thousand? And I haven't even scored half – at the ripe old age of thirty-two I haven't even scored half a point.

Impossible, you think? It's true.

Who knows, had Flora made this revelation to Graziano our story might have taken a different turn. Perhaps Graziano, despite the Spiderman and that primitive, monitor-lizard-like determination which held him in thrall and made his life a mere series of aims to be achieved, would have desisted and in gentlemanly fashion stood up, taken his CV and withdrawn from the scene. Who can tell? But Flora, who possessed a natural reserve, which had been strengthened by sufferings and sorrow, held out like some infantryman in the trenches under the bombardment of those insidious molecules that could alter your psyche and loosen your tongue and make you confess the unmentionable.

She had another fit of giggles and admitted: 'Oh dear, I'm so drunk.'

She noticed that Graziano had moved closer. 'What's this, are you moving in for the kill?' She took off her spectacles and eyed him for a moment, swaying on her chair. 'Can I tell you something? But if I do, you must swear you won't be offended.'

'I won't be offended, I swear.' Graziano put his hand on his heart and then kissed his forefingers.

'Your hair doesn't suit you like that. Do you mind my telling you? It's looks terrible. Not that the way you had it before was much better. How was it? Black? Short on top and long at the sides? No, that didn't suit you much better. If I were you, do you know what I'd do?' She paused for a moment, then added: 'I'd have it normal. It would suit you.'

'How do you mean, normal?' Graziano was very interested. He was always interested when people discussed his appearance.

'Normal. I'd have it cut and not dye it, just let it grow, normally.'

'You know the problem, Flora? I'm beginning to get a few grey hairs,' Graziano explained, in the tone of one who confides a great secret.

Flora spread her arms. 'Well? What does that matter?'

'You mean I shouldn't worry about it?'

'I wouldn't.'

'Go for the George Clooney look, straw and hay?'

Flora couldn't contain herself. She bent over the table and shrieked with laughter.

'Wouldn't suit me, eh?' Graziano smiled, but he was slightly offended.

'It's not straw and hay! That's fettuccine! Pepper and salt, you mean.' Flora had laid her forehead on the table and was drying her tears with her fingers.

'Oh, yes. You're right. Pepper and salt.'

79

Wow, that Spiderman packed a punch.

Graziano was ripped.

He hadn't realised the pill was so strong.

Damn Mullet, damn him.

(*Think how that poor girl must be feeling.*)

I gave her two. Maybe I overdid it.

Indeed the schoolmistress had her head on the table and was giggling away.

It was time to go.

He glanced at his watch.

Nine thirty!

'It's very late.' He stood up and took a good deep breath, hoping to clear his head.

'Are you leaving?' asked Flora, barely raising her head. 'Good idea. I can't even stand up. I'm worried because I can't stop laughing. I think about something serious and I feel like laughing. You'd better go. If I were you, I'd rewrite the CV and add the story about the reintroduction of red deer into Sardinia.' And she collapsed in another fit of giggles.

At least it's had a positive effect on her, thought Graziano.

'Flora, why don't we go and get something to eat? I'll take you to a restaurant near here. What do you say?'

Flora shook her head. 'No thank you. I can't.'

'Why not?'

'I can't even stand up. And anyway I can't.'

'Why not?'

'I never go out in the evening.'

'Come on, I'll bring you home early.'

80

'Nooo, you go to the restaurant. I'm not hungry, I'd better go to bed.' Flora was trying to be serious, but she burst out laughing.

'Come on, shall we go?' Graziano pleaded.

It was a bit tempting, the idea of going out.

She felt a strange urge. To run, to dance.

It would be nice to go out. But this guy was dangerous, don't forget he had won that contest. And you could bet your life he'd try and notch up a point with her too.

No, it's out of the question.

But if she went to the restaurant, what could happen? Besides, a bit of fresh air would do her good. It would clear her head.

Mama has bathed and eaten, she's all right. I don't have to go to school tomorrow. I never go out, where's the harm in going out just for one evening? Here's Tarzan asking me out to dinner, I'd be Jane for one evening riding in a pumpkin drawn by horses – no, deer, Sardinian deer – and I'd lose my slippers and the seven dwarves would have to go looking for them.

She was expecting a negative response from her mother, but it didn't come.

'We'll be home early?'

'Very early.'

'Swear it.'

'I swear. Trust me.'

Go on, Flora, one little outing. He'll take you to the restaurant and you'll be home again.

'All right, then, let's go.' Flora leaped to her feet and almost collapsed on the floor.

Graziano grabbed her by the arm. 'Are you okay?'

'Not very . . .'

'Let me help you.'

'Thank you.'

81

She was in the car. With her seat-belt fastened. And she was holding on to the safety handle. There was a nice flow of hot air warming her feet. And this Spanish music wasn't at all bad, she had to admit.

Now and then she tried shutting her eyes, but always had to open them again at once, otherwise everything started spinning round and she felt as if she were sinking into the seat, between the springs and the foam rubber.

It was raining hard.

The sound of the rain drumming on the roof blended wonderfully with the music. The windscreen wipers went back and forth at an incredible speed. The nose of the car insatiably devoured the dark, winding road. The headlights made the rain-lashed asphalt glitter. The trees on either side, with those long black branches, seemed to reach out to grab them as they passed.

Occasionally the road opened out and they drove through ink, then the trees began again.

It was absurd, but Flora felt safe.

Nothing could stop them and if a cow should suddenly appear in front of them they would simply drive straight through it, leaving it unscathed.

Usually she was frightened when other people drove, but Graziano seemed an excellent driver.

I can see how he came to be competing in a rally in . . . where was it?

He didn't drive slowly, it was true. He forced the gears and the engine screamed but the car, as if by magic, remained perfectly glued to the middle of the road.

Goodness knows where he's taking me.

How long had they been in the car? She couldn't work it out. Maybe ten minutes, maybe an hour.

'Everything okay?' Graziano asked her suddenly.

Flora turned towards him. 'Yes. When will we get there?'

'Soon. Do you like this music?'

'Yes, I do.'

'It's the Gipsy Kings. This is their best album. Do you want one?' Graziano took out a packet of Camels.

'No, thanks.'

'Do you mind if I smoke?'

'No . . .' Flora found it hard to keep up a conversation. It wasn't polite to sit there in silence, but what the hell. If she kept quiet, with her eyes on the road, she felt incredibly good. She could sit there like that for ever, in that little box, with the elements raging outside. She should have been anxious, with a stranger driving her to goodness knows where, but she wasn't at all. And her drunkenness seemed to be wearing off too, she felt clearer in the head.

She looked at Graziano. With that cigarette in his mouth, intent on driving, he was handsome. He had a decisive, Greek profile. His nose was large but perfectly in harmony with the rest of his face. If only he would cut his hair and dress normally he could be attractive, a good-looking man. Sexy.

Sexy? What a word . . . Sexy. But if you can sleep with three hundred women in one summer . . . You must have something, mustn't you? What can it be? What has he got? What does he do?

(*Stop it, you idiot.*)

Suddenly she heard the *tick tack* of the indicator, the car slowed down and stopped on a Trough parking lot in front of a small house in the middle of the blackness. Above the door was a large sign. Bar and Restaurant.

'Are we there?'

He looked at her. His eyes shone like mica. 'Are you hungry?'

No. Not in the least. The very thought of eating made her feel sick. 'No, to be honest, I'm not really.'

'Nor am I. We could have a drink.'

'I'm too tired to get out. You go, I'll wait in the car.'

Never leave the magic box. The idea of entering that place, where there was light, noise, people, filled her with a terrible anxiety.

'Are you sure?'

'Yes.' While he was in the bar she would have a nap. Then she would feel better.

'Okay. I won't be a minute.' He opened the door and got out.

Flora watched his departing figure.

She liked the way he walked.

82

Graziano entered the bar, took out his mobile and tried to call Erica.

He got her voicemail.

He ended the call.

During the journey he'd begun to feel depressed, it must have been the effect of that bloody Spiderman. He hated synthetic drugs. He'd started thinking about Erica, their last night together, the blow-job, and his head had begun to spin around, tormenting him. He had felt a desperate longing to talk to her, it was utterly stupid, he knew, but he couldn't help it, he so needed to talk to her.

To understand.

It would be enough if he could understand why she'd said she wanted to marry him, why the hell she'd said she wanted to marry him and then gone off with Mantovani. If she would give him a simple, rational explanation, he'd understand and accept it.

Only the damned voicemail.

And there was the woman in the car, too.

It wasn't that he didn't like her or didn't find the situation exciting, it was just that with that slut in his head it all seemed more squalid and mundane.

And the truth was that he'd had to slip her a Spiderman to get her to come along.

And that wasn't his style.

And it was pouring with rain.

And it was bitterly cold.

He ordered a whisky from the teenage barman who was watching television. The boy reluctantly got up from the table where he was sitting. The place was sad and empty and as cold as a refrigerator store.

'I'll take a whole bottle, please.' Graziano took it and was about to pay, but then he had an afterthought. 'Have you got any limoncino?'

The teenager, without saying a word, pulled up a chair, stood on it, scanned the row of drinks above the fridge and pulled out a long, tapering, phosphorescent yellow bottle, gave it a token wipe and handed it to him.

Graziano paid and opened it.

'Enough of these thoughts!' He went out, took a swig of limoncino and grimaced in disgust. 'Ugh, it's revolting!'

Yes, the bottle was going to come in useful.

83

The silver-haired koalas were cutting her toenails with their clippers. Only they weren't very accurate with those big paws of theirs, so they were getting flustered. Flora, sitting on the couch, was trying to calm them. 'Slow down, boys. Slow down or you'll hurt . . . Be careful! Look what you've done!' A koala had sliced off her little toe. Flora saw the red blood spurting out of the stump, but amazingly, it didn't hur . . .

'Flora! Flora! Wake up.'

She opened her eyes.

The world started lurching this way and that. Everything was swaying and Flora felt dizzy and the sound of the rain on the roof and it was cold and where was she?

She saw Graziano. He was sitting beside her.

'I dozed off . . . Have you had your drink? Are we going home?'

'Look what I've bought.' Graziano showed her the bottle of limoncino, took a swig and passed it to her. 'I got it specially for you. You said you liked it.'

Flora looked at the bottle. Ought she to drink? She was already in such a state!

'Are you cold?'

'A little.' She was shivering.

'Have a drink, then, it'll warm you up.'

Flora took a swig.

How sweet it is. Too sweet.

'Feel better?'

'Yes.' The limoncino had spread over the walls of her stomach, restoring a bit of warmth to her body.

'Just a minute.' Graziano turned the heater full on, took his coat from the back seat and handed it to her.

Flora was about to say no, she didn't need it, when he moved closer and began to tuck it round her like a blanket and she held her breath and he moved even closer and she retreated sideways and pressed against the door hoping it would open and he stretched out his hand and clasped the back of her head and she was being pulled forward and smelled that smell of limoncino, cigarettes, perfume, mint and closed her eyes and all at once . . .

Her lips were attached to Graziano's.

Oh my goodness, he's kissing me . . .

He was kissing her. He was kissing her. He was kissing her. He was . . .

She opened her eyes. And he was there with his eyes closed, an inch away, that huge tanned face.

She tried to push him away. But it was no good, he was an octopus clinging to her mouth.

She breathed through her nose.

He's kissing you! You've fallen for it.

She closed her eyes. Graziano's lips on hers. They were soft, incredibly soft, and that nice smell of limoncino and cigarettes and mint was now a taste in Graziano's mouth and in hers. Graziano's tongue was trying to enter her mouth so Flora opened it a little further, just enough to let that slippery thing enter and then she felt it touch her own and a shiver ran down her spine and it was nice, so nice, so she opened her mouth wide and the long tongue began to explore it and play with her own tongue. Flora took a deep breath and he pulled her violently towards him and she let him squeeze her, and her hands, without her telling them to, began to run through Graziano's hair, to ruffle it.

This . . . This . . . This . . . is the thing . . . to do . . . This is . . . how . . . to live . . . life . . . Kiss . . . ing . . . It's the easiest . . . thing . . . in the world. Because kiss . . . ing is right . . . Because in life you . . . need to . . . kiss . . . And I . . . like kissing . . . And . . . it's not true . . . that it's wrong . . . to do it . . . It's right . . . to do it because it's . . . nice . . . It's the most . . . beautiful thing in the world . . . And . . . it's right to do it.

Suddenly Flora was overwhelmed by it all, she felt her legs melt and her feet boil and her hands tingle and her breathing catch as if she had been punched in the stomach. She felt she was dying and gently flopped down, like a puppet, with her face on Graziano's chest and in his smell.

84

Even a few kilometres short of the baths of Saturnia the atmosphere changes.

Any traveller who drove along that road and didn't know that there were hot springs in the neighbourhood would find it, at the very least, disconcerting.

Suddenly the downward slope and the bends come to an end, the oak wood vanishes, the road levels out and as far as the eye can see there are green fields, as green as the green of Ireland with all its shades and variations – perhaps it is that beneficent warmth, the water and the mixture of chemical elements from the depths of the earth that make the grass so luxuriant. And if all this were not enough to surprise the inattentive traveller, the mist that rises from the irrigation ditches that run parallel to the road certainly ought to arouse his curiosity. Now and again these gases drift up from the ditches, forming frayed banks barely half a metre high which cross the carriageway and spread like a sea of cream over the fields, making them resemble clouds seen from above. In the whiteness you catch glimpses of a fruit tree, a fence, half a sheep. It is almost as if someone had passed this way with one of those machines for creating mist on film sets.

And if even that were not enough, there would still be the smell. The inattentive traveller would certainly notice that. He could hardly help it. 'What's that terrible stink?' He would tighten his nostrils and look accusingly at his wife. 'I told you not to have that leek soup, you can never digest it,' but she would look at him equally accusingly and the inattentive traveller would say, 'Hey, it wasn't me.' Then both would turn towards Zeus, the boxer dog curled up on the back seat. 'Zeus, you're disgusting! What have you been eating?' Had Zeus been able to speak he would certainly have defended himself and said it was nothing to do with him, but the Lord in his inscrutable wisdom has decreed that animals (except parrots and mynah birds, which repeat words without understanding their meaning) should not possess this faculty, so all poor Zeus could do would be to wag his tail, pleased with the unexpected attention that his owners were giving him.

But suddenly the mist at the side of the road would lift, thicken and invade the surrounding woods, as if the source of the mist were there, and among the gases they would glimpse the corner of an old stone farmhouse.

Then the wife might say: 'There must be a fertiliser factory there, or maybe they're burning something chemical.' And they would still be in the dark. But when at last they came to the road sign which says in big letters, WELCOME TO THE SPA OF SATURNIA, they would finally understand and proceed more serenely on their journey.

85

At night the sulphurous fumes give the place an eerie atmosphere, and if in addition, as that night, the wind is whistling, the wolves howling, the rain beating down on the countryside and lightning is striking to right and left, you really feel as if you've reached the threshold of hell.

Graziano slowed down, switched off the stereo and turned onto the rough track that cuts through the woods and leads down towards the valley and the waterfall.

Flora was asleep, huddled up on her seat.

The track had turned into a quagmire full of puddles and stones. Graziano drove carefully. There's nothing worse for the suspension and sump. He braked, but the car continued its slow, inexorable descent through the mud. The headlights made the mist shine like the gas of a neon. One more tricky bend, but beyond it lay the car park and the waterfall. Graziano changed down and steered, but his car kept slithering straight on (*I don't even want to think about how we get out of here*) and finally came to a stop, right on the edge of the road.

He reversed a little way and found himself, without knowing how, with the bonnet pointing at the clearing.

The mist beyond was tinged with red, green and blue, and dark silhouettes could be seen moving in the haze.

It was as if a discotheque had taken root in the woods.

It's full of people.

He drove on down in first gear. The car park, which was on a slope, was full of vehicles parked untidily one next to the other.

Car horns. Music. Voices.

On one side there were two big tourist coaches.

What the hell's happened? Is somebody having a party?

Graziano, who hadn't been here for a long time, didn't know that the spa was always this crowded nowadays, like most of the places of any charm or interest in our beautiful peninsula.

He parked as best he could behind a coach with a Siena number-plate. He stripped down to his bathing trunks.

All that remained was to wake Flora.

He called her name without eliciting any response. She was dead to the world. He shook her and finally managed to get her to mumble a few words.

'Flora, I've brought you to a nice place. It's a surprise. Look,' said Graziano, in the most enthusiastic tone that he could manage.

Flora struggled to raise her head, looked for a moment at that colourful glare and slumped back. 'Lovely . . . Where . . . are we?'

'At Saturnia. For a bathe.'

'No . . . No . . . I'm cold.'

'The water's warm . . .'

'I haven't got a swimsuit. You go. I'll stay in the car.' She seized his hand, pulled him towards her, gave him a rather clumsy kiss and fell back again, senseless.

'Come on, you'll like it, you'll see. You'll feel better if you get out.'

No reaction.

Okay, if that's the way it's got to be.

He switched on the overhead light and began to undress her. He took off her coat. Pulled off her shoes. It was like dealing with a child who is sleeping too soundly to be able to help when its mother puts on its pyjamas. He sat her up and, after a moment's hesitation, slipped off her skirt and tights. Underneath she was wearing plain white cotton knickers.

Her legs were long and shapely. Really beautiful. Legs that would be perfect for high heels and suspenders.

Graziano was beginning to enjoy himself and his breathing grew fitful.

He took off her jumper. Underneath she had a pearl-coloured silk blouse buttoned right up to the collar.

Go on, then . . .

He began to undo them one by one, starting from the bottom. Flora muttered something, seemingly annoyed, but then her head lolled over. Her stomach was flat, without a trace of flab, and as white as milk. By the time he reached her bosom, his pulse had quickened and he could hear the blood throbbing in his ears. He took a deep breath and undid the last button, opening her blouse.

He was amazed.

Her breasts were incredibly big, straining at the bra. Two round, enticing mozzarellas. For a moment he was tempted to pull them out to view them in all their splendour, to squeeze them, lick their nipples. But he forbade himself to do so. It was strange, but inside him, hidden away somewhere, was a moral man (with a peculiar morality of his own) who every now and then came up to the surface.

Finally, he loosened her hair, which, as he had guessed, was a red cascade.

He looked at her.

She sat there, in bra and knickers, asleep, looking incredibly beautiful.

Perhaps she's even more beautiful than Erica.

Like a dog rose that had seeded itself among the rocks of a

quarry and grown without anyone tending it, without any gardener to water it, fertilise it or spray it with pesticides.

Flora herself was not aware of the worth of her body, or, if she was, punished it for sins never committed.

Erica's body, by contrast, seemed to have adapted perfectly to the aesthetic parameters that were currently in fashion (narrow waist, round breasts, mandoline-shaped bottom), a body which, if she had lived at the beginning of the century, would have been plump and voluptuous, in accordance with the taste of that time, a body which was nourished by training in the gym, by creams and massages, which was constantly monitored, compared with the bodies of other women, a flag to be on every possible occasion.

Whereas Flora was beautiful and real, and Graziano was happy.

86

It was cold.

Very cold.

Too cold.

And walking was agony. Sharp stones jabbed the soles of her feet.

And it was raining. The freezing water streamed down her body and Flora was shivering, her teeth chattering.

And there was an awful smell.

It was a good thing Graziano was holding her hand.

That made her feel very safe.

Where were they going? Into hell?

All right, then. Hell it is. What's the phrase, now? . . . I'll follow you even to the gates of hell.

Hell or not, she was past caring by now.

She was aware of being naked (*you're not naked, you've still got your bra and knickers on*). No, she wasn't naked, but if she had been she wouldn't have cared.

She walked along with her eyes closed and sought in her mouth for the taste of kisses.

We kissed in the car, that I do remember.

She half opened her eyes and looked around her.

Where was she?

In a mist.

And there was this horrible smell of rotten eggs, just like the smell in class when some idiot let off a stink bomb. And there were lots of cars. Some with their lights off. Others with their lights on but with their windows misted over and you couldn't see inside. And there was a stereo blaring out music with a thumping bass. Suddenly she saw some kids in bathing costumes running, shouting and jostling each other among the cars.

Graziano was pulling her along.

Flora did her best to keep up with him, but her legs were stiff with cold. A figure loomed up in front of her, a man in a bathing robe, who watched her pass. To the left, on a hillock of bare earth, was an old abandoned farmhouse whose roof had fallen in. Its walls were bedaubed with spray-painted graffiti. Through the glassless windows she glimpsed the flicker of a fire with some black figures sitting round it. More music. Italian, this time. And the crying of a baby. And a cluster of people sheltering under beach umbrellas.

A clap of thunder echoed in the night.

Flora started.

Graziano moved closer to her and put his arm round her waist. 'We're almost there.'

She would have liked to ask him where, but her teeth were chattering so much she couldn't talk.

They threaded their way between dripping wet tents, rubbish bags and picnic leftovers pulped by the rain.

And suddenly she felt something nice, and gasped. The water! The water under her feet was no longer icy but lukewarm, and the further they went the warmer it grew and that beneficent warmth rose up her legs.

'How lovely!' she murmured.

Now the sound of the waterfall was loud and there were lots of people, some in capes, others naked and she and Graziano had to push their way through the bodies. She saw them look at her but didn't mind, felt them brush against her but didn't care.

The only thing that mattered was keeping close to Graziano.

As long as I do that I won't get lost . . .

Now the water flowing under her feet was very warm, as warm as that of her bath. They passed through another wall of people. Germans, by the sound of it.

And they found themselves in front of a small waterfall, and below it a series of pools, some larger, some smaller, which descended like terraces towards the bottom and further down broadened out into a dark lake. A powerful floodlight fixed to the walls of the farmhouse tinged the steam with yellow. At first Flora thought there was nobody in the pools, but that wasn't the case, if you looked closely you could see a mass of black heads sticking out of the water.

'Careful, it's slippery.'

The rock was covered with a soft carpet of algae.

'This is where it starts to get really nice . . .' Graziano shouted to make himself heard above the noise of the waterfall.

Flora put one foot into the first pool. Then the other. It was marvellous. She tried to crouch down in that little natural basin, but Graziano pulled her away. 'Come on. There are deeper ones, away from all this noise.'

Flora would have liked to say that this one was fine, but she followed him. They entered a larger pool, but it was full of people laughing raucously and smothering their faces and hair with mud and couples embracing. She felt legs, bellies, hands brush against her. They entered another pool, which was deep enough to swim in, but this one too was full of people (men) and they were singing: 'No stockfish, landlord, it's too bristly, give us veal or chicken any day.'

'A bunch of poofs . . .' said Graziano in disgust.

Oh, the poofs are here too . . .

In the air, besides the sulphur and steam, there was a strange euphoria, a lewd, carnal sensuality, and Flora felt it and was on the one hand frightened, on the other almost excited, like a lapdog surrounded by a pack of hounds.

In one pool she at last saw some blonde women, German perhaps, who climbed out of the water and jumped in again stark naked, each time to wild cheering and a round of applause. It was a group of youngsters wearing bathing costumes on their heads like hats.

'Come on, keep going. This way.'

They began a slow arduous climb beside the the waterfall. There was a succession of huge slippery boulders and Flora had to use her hands and feet to clamber up. The noise of the water was deafening. She was still feeling dizzy and every step she took terrified her. She found herself in front of a smooth rockface with water cascading down it.

She'd never make it.

Why?

Why does Graziano want to go up there?

(*You know why.*)

One part of her brain which had lain low until now but which was lucid, active and able to solve the mysteries of the universe and her life, explained to her.

Because he wants to fuck you.

The CV had been just an excuse.

And she had understood without being aware of it, right at the beginning, when she had seen him arrive with that bottle of whisky in his hand.

Well let's fuck, then . . . She suppressed a giggle.

Not even in her wildest fantasies had she imagined that it would happen like this, in such a squalid setting and with a guy like Graziano.

She had always known it was a step she was going to have to take. As soon as possible. Before her virginity became chronic and trapped her in a paralysing, embittered spinsterhood. Before her head started playing tricks with her. Before she began to feel scared.

But she had dreamed of a very different kind of lover. And a romantic affair, with a sensitive man (à la Harrison Ford) who would charm her, whisper sweet nothings in her ear and swear his undying love in rhyming couplets.

And look what she had got, the seaside sex symbol, Mr Casanova, with his bleached hair and his earrings, the Valtour holiday village entertainer.

And she knew she meant nothing to Graziano. She was just another name on his endless list. A plastic container of food to be consumed and then discarded empty at the roadside.

But it didn't matter.

No, it didn't matter at all.

I'll always be grateful to him for what he has done.

He had put her on his list. Like so many others (beautiful, ugly, stupid, intelligent) who had spent the night with him, who had allowed this man's member to enter their bodies. Women to whom sex was as natural as eating lunch or brushing their teeth. Women who really lived.

Normal women.

Because sex is normality.

(*And aren't you frightened?*)

Yes. Of course I am. I'm terrified. My legs are trembling so much I can't even climb.

But she was convinced that taking that step would transform her.

Into what?

Into something else. At any rate, into something different from what she was now,

(*And what are you now?*)

Something abnormal.

something more like other women.

And if there was no romance, no love, well, what the hell. That was okay too.

Yes, she must climb.

She steeled herself, placed one foot on a jutting rock and pulled herself up, but a jet of warm water hit her full in the face and for a moment she lost her hold and was about to slip (and if she had slipped, what a nasty fall it would have been) when, as if by magic,

Graziano grabbed her by the wrist and hoisted her up, like a doll, over the waterfall.

She found herself in a kind of boiling pond. The trees above it formed a leafy vault through which the glare of the floodlight filtered here and there.

It was deserted.

The water was quite deep and the current was strong, but at the sides there were some protruding boulders which she clung onto.

'I knew it would be quiet here . . .' said Graziano, contentedly, and taking her hand he led her into little bay where the water was calm. 'Do you like it?'

'It's lovely.' The cries of the bathers had vanished, drowned by the rush of the waterfall.

At last Flora could immerse herself wholly in the water and get warm. Graziano drew closer, put his arms round her waist and began to kiss her neck. Thrills of pleasure curled on the back of her head. She grasped his arms and noticed that his right biceps was encircled by a tattoo. A geometric pattern. He was muscular and strong. And with that long wet hair clinging to his head and the mud smeared over him he looked like a savage from New Guinea.

He's so handsome . . .

She pulled him, tugged him, punched him, dug her fingernails into his skin and avidly sought his mouth and sank her teeth into his lips, with her tongue she found his tongue, his palate, took it out and licked him and lay back ready on the beach.

87

And Graziano?

Graziano was ready too. You bet he was.

He had looked for Roscio and the others down by the pools, but there was such confusion that he hadn't been able to see them. Perhaps they hadn't even come.

I don't really care. In fact, it's better this way. They would have spoiled it.

He could have kicked himself for giving her the Spiderman. If he hadn't, it would all have been better, more real. Even without that pill he would have got her to Saturnia. Flora had followed him through the pools without speaking, without resisting, without protesting, like a little dog following its master.

He held her tight, put his mouth close to her ear and sang softly: 'O minha macona, o minha torcida, o minha flamenga, o minha capoeira, o minha maloka, o minha belezza, o minha vagabunda, o . . .' He slipped off her bra and took her breasts in his hands. '. . . minha galera, o minha capoeira, o minha cahueira, o minha menina.'

He began to lick them and bite her nipples, he sank his face between them, smelling the odour of sulphurous mud.

He took off his trunks and led her where the water was deeper. They lay down on some submerged boulders.

He took her hand and put it on his cock.

88

She had it in her hand.

It was hard and big and soft-skinned.

She enjoyed the sensation of touching it. It was like holding an eel in her hand. She stroked it and the skin drew back, baring the tip.

What am I doing . . . ? But she stopped herself thinking about it.

She touched his testicles, played with them a little, then decided that this was it, the time had come, she was longing to do it, she must do it.

She slipped off her knickers and threw them onto a rock. She hugged him hard, feeling his erection press against her stomach, and whispered in his ear. 'Graziano, please be gentle. I've never done it before.'

89

It was obvious.

Why hadn't he realised?

What a fool he was! She was a virgin and he hadn't realised. He, who'd had more women than he'd had Margherita pizzas, hadn't realised. Those passionate yet clumsy kisses . . . He had put it down to the effect of the Spiderman but it was because she had never kissed anyone before.

He screwed up his face like a baboon.

He threaded his arm under her breast and pulled her onto the beach.

He lay her down.

It was a delicate operation, deflowering her. It required skill.

He looked into her eyes and saw in them an expectation and a fear that he had never seen in eyes of the old slappers he usually fucked on the Romagna riviera.

This is really fucking . . . 'Don't worry, don't wo . . .' he said in a strangled voice, tossed back his hair and kneeled down in front of her. 'I won't hurt you.'

He opened her legs (she was trembling), took his cock in his right hand and found her vagina with his left, opened the lips (they were wet) and with a swift, precise movement slipped it a quarter of the way in.

90

It had slipped inside her.

Flora held her breath.

She dug her hands in the mud.

But the pain, the terrible, legendary, agonising pain she had so dreaded didn't come.

No. It didn't hurt. Flora, expectant, open-mouthed, held her breath.

The intruder inside her continued to advance.

'I'm going to go on . . . Tell me if it hurts.'

Flora gasped and her breast rose and fell like a bellows. She panted, expecting the pain that didn't come. She felt filled, certainly, and that pole of flesh now pressed inside her but without hurting her.

She was so busy searching for the pain that pleasure had been completely set aside.

She saw it in Graziano's eyes.

He seemed possessed by the devil and was sighing and moving backwards and forwards faster and faster and more and more forcefully and he seized her by the hips and he was on top of her and Flora was underneath with that thing inside her. She closed her eyes. She clung to his back with her legs like a baby monkey and raised them to make it easier for him to enter.

Gasping breath in her ear.

He plunged into her. Right in.

Flora felt a stab of pleasure that blocked her carotid artery and made the back of her head tingle. And then another. And yet another. And if she let herself go, if she abandoned herself, she felt that now it was continuous, like a radioactive element pulsing pleasure in her bowels and her legs and running up her spine and into her throat.

'Do you . . . like it?' Graziano asked her, running his fingers through her hair, squeezing her throat.

'Yes . . . Yes . . .'

'It doesn't hurt?'

'Noooh . . .'

He rolled over onto his side and with that pole inside her she was lifted up and found herself on top of him. It was her turn to move now. But she didn't know if she could. It was too big and it was right inside her. She felt it in her belly. Graziano put his hands on her breasts, but couldn't restrain himself and squeezed them hard.

Another stab of pain that took her breath away.

He wanted her to stay like that, on top, in that embarrassing position, but she threw herself over and embraced him and kissed him on the neck and nibbled his ear.

She heard Graziano's gasps getting faster and faster and faster and

and he can't. He can't do it inside. I haven't got anything.

She must tell him. But she didn't want that wild madman to stop. She didn't want him to take it out. 'Graziano . . . you must be careful . . . I . . .'

He turned over again. And as he sought a new position, Flora tried to go along with him, but didn't quite know how to move, what to do.

'Gra . . .'

He had put her on her knees. Her hands in the mud. Her face in the mud. Her tits in her mouth. The rain on her back.

Like a bitch . . .

And him digging the fingernails of one hand into her buttock and with the other trying to grasp one of her breasts which slipped away from him and he drove into her as if he could penetrate up to her throat. And . . .

He can't take it out now.

He had taken it out and perhaps was about to come and Flora thought she would die of disappointment. She sighed. But an explosive blast of heat surrounded her neck, continued up into her jaws and spread onto her temples and nostrils and ears.

'Oh my God!'

He was touching her there, at the top of her vagina, and she realised that everything she had felt up to then had been chicken-feed. Child's play. Nothing. That finger, on that spot, was capable of making her lose her senses and driving her crazy.

Then he opened her legs and she opened them wider and perhaps, *let's hope*, he was going to put it back in.

91

And here Graziano made a mistake.

As he'd made a mistake in asking Erica to marry him, as he'd made a mistake in telling all his friends about it, as he'd made a mistake in giving Flora the Spiderman, as he'd been making mistakes practically every day for forty-four years, and it's not true what they say, that we learn from our mistakes, it's not true at all, there are some people who never learn anything from their mistakes, they just keep on making them, convinced that they're doing the right thing (or unaware of what they're really doing), and to this kind of person life is usually cruel, but even that doesn't mean anything, because these people survive their mistakes and live and grow and love and bring other human beings into the world and grow old and keep making mistakes.

That is their wretched destiny.

And that was the destiny of our sad stallion.

Who knows what went through his mind, who knows what he thought and how he organised it in his brain, that disastrous idea.

Graziano wanted more. He wanted to close the circle, he wanted to have his cake and eat it, he wanted to fish the moon from the well, he wanted to cut and thrust, he wanted his steer lassooed and branded, who knows what the hell he wanted, he wanted to deflower her fore and aft.

He wanted Flora Palmieri's arse.

He parted her buttocks, spat on them and pushed his cock into that contracted star.

92

It was like a roof tile landing on your head.

Without warning.

The pain was as sudden as an electric shock and as sharp as a piece of broken glass. And it wasn't where it should have been, it was . . .

Nooo! He's . . . .

She twisted to the right and kicked out her left leg, catching Graziano on the Adam's apple with her heel.

93

Graziano was flying backwards. Open-armed. Open-mouthed. Face up.

For an infinite length of time.

Then he plunged into that warm liquid. Hit his head against a rock. And came back to the surface.

Paralysed.

He was enveloped in a black cloud shot through with intermittent flashes of coloured light.

Why did she kick me?

The current pulled him towards the middle of the bend. He slid over algae-covered rocks like a drifting raft. His heels brushed along the slimy river-bed.

She must have hit him on one of those special points, one of those points that reduce a man to a mannequin, one of those points that only Japanese masters of martial arts ought to know.

How strange . . .

He could think, but he couldn't move. For example, he felt the cold rain on his face and realised that the warm current was carrying him towards the waterfall.

94

Flora cowered against a boulder.

Uncle Armando was floating in the middle of the river. It couldn't be him. Uncle Armando lived in Naples. It was Graziano. But she kept seeing Uncle Armando's belly appear like a little island among the sulphurous fumes and his nose cutting through the water like a shark's fin.

And now the river was going to sweep Uncle Armando or whoever it was away.

Uncle Armando/Graziano struggled to raise his arm. 'Flora . . . Flora . . . Help me . . .'

No, I won't . . . No, I won't . . .'

(*Flora, that is not Uncle Armando.*) There, at last, was her mother speaking to her again.

He's a pervert. He tried to . . .

'Flora, I can't mo . . .'

(*He's heading for the waterfall . . .*)

'Help. Help.'

(*Hurry up. Get moving. Stop all this nonsense. Hurry.*)

Flora crawled into the water. She held on to the branches of the trees to stop herself being swept away. But a branch snapped off in her hand and she thrashed about and spluttered as she was borne along by the current. She tried to get back to the bank, but couldn't. She turned and saw Graziano's body drifting a couple of metres from the brink of the waterfall. He had got snagged on a boulder, but sooner or later the current would catch him again and carry him on, down into the abyss.

'Flora? Flora? Where are you?' Graziano spoke like a blind man who has lost his way. Mildly concerned but not terrified. 'Flora?'

'I'm comi . . .' She swallowed two litres of that revolting water. She spluttered and struck out towards the middle again, flailing about with her arms, passed between two jutting crags and grabbed hold of a rock.

A metre away from Graziano. Three metres away from the waterfall.

Flora held out her arm, stretched and there was, oh God, there was, there were those cursed ten centimetres that prevented her from grabbing Graziano's big toe which stuck out of the water.

I can't lose him . . .

'Graziano! Graziano, stretch your foot out. I can't reach it,' she screamed, trying to make herself heard above the roar of the waterfall.

He was no longer answering (*He's dead! He can't be dead*) but then: 'Flora?'

'Yes! I'm here! How are you?'

'Not too bad. I must have hit my head.'

'I'm sorry. I'm sorry. I didn't mean to kick you! I'm terribly sorry.'

'No, it's me who should apologise. I was wrong . . .'

There they were, the two of them, on the brink of a waterfall with a relentless current, apologising to each other like two old ladies who'd forgotten to send each other Christmas cards.

'Graziano, stretch out your foot.'

'I'll try.'

Flora reached out her arm. And Graziano reached out his foot. 'I've got you! I've got you! Graziano, I've got you!' Flora shouted, and she felt like laughing and shrieking with joy. She had caught his big toe and she was not going to let go. She took a firmer hold on the boulder and began to pull, and drew him towards her, wresting him away from the current and, when at last she held him, she hugged him and he hugged her.

And there were kisses.

11th December

95

In the early hours of 11th December the weather improved.

The Siberian front that had settled over the Mediterranean basin, bringing cold, wind and rain to the whole peninsula, including Ischiano Scalo, was driven away by a ridge of high pressure from Africa, which left the sky clear and ready to welcome back the fugitive sun.

96

At a quarter past eight in the morning Italo Miele was released from hospital.

With that bandaged nose and those two purple medallions round his eyes he looked like an old boxer who has taken a lot of hard punches before hitting the canvas.

His son and his wife came to fetch him. They put him in the 131 and drove him home.

97

At about the same time, Alima was sitting in a large room at Fiumicino airport along with a hundred or so other Nigerians. She was sitting on a bench with her arms folded, trying to get some sleep.

She had no idea when she would leave. No one bothers to

inform illegal immigrants about the details of their repatriation. But it was certain that sooner or later she would be put on a plane.

She would have liked a drink of hot milk. But there was a long queue at the drinks machine.

She was going to return to her village and see her three children again, that was the meagre consolation.

But what then?

She preferred not to think about it.

98

Lucia Palmieri was in her bed. Safe and sound.

Flora heaved a sigh of relief. 'Mama, how are you?'

That night she'd dreamed about the silver-haired koalas again. They were carrying her mother's body on their backs along a completely deserted Aurelia. On either side were rocks, cactuses, coyotes and rattlesnakes.

Flora had woken up certain that her mother was dead. She had jumped out of bed in a panic, dashed into the little bedroom, switched on the light but in fact . . .

'Mama . . . I'm sorry. Yes, I know, it's late . . . I expect you're hungry, aren't you? I'll get you something to eat straight away . . .'

She had abandoned her. For one night her mother had not been at the centre of her thoughts.

She prepared the feeding bottle. Put it in her mouth. Emptied the bags. Combed her hair. And gave her a kiss.

Then she went to have a shower.

Her skin and hair were steeped in sulphur. She had to rinse herself several times to get rid of that unpleasant smell. When she had finished showering, she dried herself and looked at her reflection in the mirror.

Her face was pale. There were rings round her eyes. But the eyes themselves were shining and alive as never before. She didn't feel tired despite only having had a couple of hours' sleep. And her drunkenness had worn off without leaving a hangover. She spread moisturising cream over her body and discovered that she had painful scratches and bruises on her legs and back. It must have happened when the current had buffeted her about among the rocks above the waterfall. Her nipples were reddened, too. And the fleshy pads of her fingertips were numb.

She sat down on the stool.

She opened her legs and examined herself. Everything was normal there too, though a bit sore.

She sat there in the steam-filled bathroom, gazing at herself in the misted mirror.

Her mind kept showing the same pornographic film: Sex at the Spa.

The pools. The warmth. Graziano. The pond. The cold. The people. The music. The sex. The smell. The sex. The river. The sex. The kick. The fear. The waterfall. The sex. The warmth. The kisses.

A tangle of memories and emotions twined within her and when her mind got caught up in certain scenes, the embarrassment gave her goose pimples on her arms.

Whatever got into me?

Her body had reacted well, though. It hadn't disintegrated. Hadn't fallen to pieces. Hadn't been transformed into an insect cocoon.

She touched her breasts, her legs, her stomach. Despite the bruises and scratches, her body seemed firmer, fuller, and those aches in her muscles showed that it was alive and responded well to such stimuli.

It was a body suited to sex.

In recent years she had wondered a million times whether, at the fateful moment, she would be able to have sexual intercourse, whether it wasn't too late and whether her body and mind would be able to accept that intrusion or would reject it, whether her hands would be able to cling to a back, her lips to kiss strange lips.

She had succeeded.

She was pleased with herself.

In a parallel universe, Flora Palmieri, with that body and with a different brain, might have been a different person. She might have made love for the first time at the age of thirteen, might have been given to the pleasures of the flesh and had a promiscuous sex life, might have attracted men in their thousands, might have used her body to make money, displayed her tits on the covers of magazines, been a famous porno star.

She would have given anything to own the video of the sex she'd had with Graziano and to be able to see it over and over again. To view herself in those positions. To observe the expressions on her face . . .

That's enough. Stop it.

She banished the images.

She cleaned her teeth, dried her hair and dressed. She put on a pair of black jeans (the ones she used for walking on the beach), her tennis shoes, a white cotton T-shirt and a black cardigan. She began to put hairgrips in her hair but then had second thoughts. She removed them and let it hang loose.

She went into the kitchen. She wound up the shutters, and a shaft of sun entered the room, warming her neck and shoulders. It was a fine, cold day. The sky was bluer than ever and a light breeze stirred the branches of the eucalyptus in the yard. A group of seagulls were standing like hens in the middle of the red earth of the ploughed field across the road. Finches and sparrows were twittering in the trees.

She made the coffee, warmed the milk and tiptoed into the dimly lit sitting room carrying breakfast on a tray.

Graziano was curled up on the sofa fast asleep. The blanket with the black-and-white lozenge pattern enwrapped him like a bag. Strewn untidily on the floor were his boots and clothes.

Flora sat down in the armchair.

99

Fausto Coppi was the best cyclist in the world. The fastest. But above all the toughest. He never tired. He was a great rider. And he never gave in. Never let up.

Never.

And you're Fausto Coppi.

Pietro pedalled, pedalled, pedalled. Mouth wide open. Face distorted with the effort. Heart pumping blood into his arteries. Midges in his eyes. Fire in his lungs.

They're coming.

The excruciating noise of the broken silencer.

Were they gaining ground?

Yes. Definitely.

They were nearer.

He wanted to turn and look. But he couldn't. If he had he would have lost his balance, and balance for a cyclist is everything, if you're well balanced and keep the right position you never tire, and if he'd turned round he would have lost his balance and slowed down and that would have been the end. So he pedalled, hoping they'd never catch him.

(*Don't think about them. Just go. You're trying to beat the world record. You're not racing them. You're racing the wind. You're the hare being chased by the greyhounds. All those two guys behind you are doing is making you go faster. You're the fastest little boy in the world.*) That's what the great Coppi was telling him.

100

'Is this the best your crappy little scooter can do? Speed up! Speed up, for Christ's sake!' yelled Federico Pierini, hunched up behind Flame.

'I am!' shouted Flame, hunched up in turn over the handlebars of the Ciao. 'Now we'll get him. As soon as he slows down he's had it.'

Flame was right, as soon as Dickhead started to flag they'd catch him. Where could he go? The road ran straight across the fields for more than five kilometres.

'If only I'd known, I'd have brought my cousin's souped-up Vespa. Then we'd really have had some fun,' said Flame ruefully.

'What about your gun? Did you bring your gun?'

'No, I didn't.'

'You stupid fool. We could have shot him from this range. Bam!' Pierini guffawed.

101

They were getting closer.

And Pietro was beginning to tire.

He tried to keep his breathing regular, maintain his concentration and push rhythmically on the pedals, so as to turn into a human motor, fuse with the bike to create a perfect being made of flesh and heart and muscles and tubes and spokes and wheels. He tried not to think about anything. To keep his mind blank. To be pure coordination and will, but . . .

His cursed legs were beginning to stiffen and his mind to fill with ugly images.

You're Fausto Coppi. You can't slow down.

He quickened his rhythm a little and the sound of the scooter grew fainter.

It was a futile race. On a never-ending road. Across cultivated fields. Against a scooter. When they finally caught up with him, he wouldn't even have the strength to stand up.

(*I might as well stop . . .*)

Cyclists lose because they think victory has a meaning. Victory doesn't have a meaning. The aim is not victory. The aim is to pedal. Fausto Coppi was talking to him. *Pedal till you drop.*

The noise behind him increased again.

They were getting closer.

102

On the return journey from Saturnia Flora had driven.

Graziano hadn't felt up to it. The bump on his head was large and painful. He had put his hand on her thigh and fallen asleep.

And Flora, with wet hair and wet clothes, had got behind the wheel, slithered her way up that muddy track and headed for Ischiano Scalo.

In silence.

A long trip, crowded with thoughts.

What's going to happen after all this?

That was the sixty-four thousand dollar question that was being debated in her mind as she changed gear, accelerated, steered and braked, driving over hills, through woods and sleeping villages.

What's going to happen after all this?

The answers were legion. There was a long succession of them, each popping up spontaneously, dangerous and not to be contemplated (travel, distant islands, country cottages, churches, childr . . .).

To answer the question rationally, Flora had told herself, she must think about who Graziano was and who she was.

Lucidly.

And Flora, at three o'clock in the morning, after what had happened to her, felt lucid and logical.

She had looked at Graziano asleep against the window and shaken her head.

No.

They were too different to have a future together. Graziano would soon leave for the Valtour village and then go to some exotic country and have another thousand love affairs and forget about her. She would continue to live the life she had always lived and go to school and look after her mother and watch TV in the evening and go to bed early.

That was the situation and

(*Don't kid yourself this man's going to change just for your sake . . .*)

so it was clear that the relationship couldn't work.

It's one of those what do you call them . . . One-night stands. Try to see it that way. A sex thing.

A sex thing. She couldn't help smiling.

It was painful to admit, but that was the truth of it. And when she had climbed up those rocks, though she'd been dazed and bewildered, she had kept saying it over and over to herself (*you're just another one on the list . . . and you've got to accept it*), so now she mustn't start fantasising like some inexperienced young girl.

But I am inexperienced.

It was dangerous to indulge in fantasies. Flora had hardened herself so as to resist the blows of life, but she suspected that she was still vulnerable to some knocks.

Graziano had served to make a woman of her.

And that was all.

I must be strong. As I've always been.

(*You mustn't see him again.*)

I know, I mustn't see him again.

(*Never again.*)

And yet when they had reached Ischiano Scalo and the sky was growing lighter, Flora had parked the car in front of the haberdasher's and was about to wake Graziano and tell him she would walk home, but she hadn't been able to bring herself to do it.

She had sat in the car for a quarter of an hour stretching out her hand towards Graziano and then withdrawing it and finally she had started up the engine and taken him home with her.

She had put him on the sofa.

That way, if he was still in pain, she could attend to him.

That's what I'm best at.

No, it couldn't end like this.

That would be dreadful. She must speak to him one last time and explain to him how important that night had been to her, then she would part with him for good.

Like in the movies.

103

It's a strange thing, suspension.

It's the most serious punishment of all, but instead of locking you up in school day and night on bread and water they give you a week's holiday.

Though of course it's not much of a holiday, especially when your father has just told you he has no intention of going to speak to the teachers.

Pietro had racked his brains all night to find a solution. Asking his mother was pointless. He would get more response out of Zagor. But what if in the end nobody went?

The deputy headmistress would ring his home and if Papa answered on one of his bad days . . . it didn't bear thinking about, and if Mama answered she would mutter a few long-drawn-out yeses and nos, swear on the heads of her children that she would go next day and then not go.

And those two would come back.

In a green Peugeot 205 with a Rome number plate.

The social assistants (a name which meant nothing but which scared him far more than drug dealer or wicked witch).

Those two.

He, a great beanpole of a man, dressed in loden and Clarks, with a grey goatee beard and tufts of hair plastered down over his forehead and those thin lips that looked as if he had just smeared them with lip balm.

She, a dumpy little woman, with embroidered stockings and lace-up shoes and those inch-thick glasses and that gossamer-thin hair pulled back so hard from the temples that it seemed as if the skin of her forehead would sooner or later split like the covering of a worn-out armchair.

Those two who had appeared after the trouble with the catapult, Poppi, the Contarellos' roof and the court.

Those smiling two who had called him into the staff room while his classmates were having their break and had sat him down on a chair and offered him liquorice sweets which he loathed and some stupid Mickey Mouse comics.

Those two who asked a lot of questions.

Are you happy in your class? Do you like school? Do you enjoy yourself? Do you have any friends? What do you do after school? Do you play with your father? Do you play with your mother? Is your mother sad? How do you get on with your brother? Does your father get cross with you? Does he quarrel with your mother? Does he love her? Does he kiss you at night before you go to bed? Does he like drinking wine? Does he help you undress? Does he do anything strange? Does your brother sleep in the same room as you? Do you have fun together?

Those two.

Those two who wanted to take him away. To an institution.

Pietro knew. Mimmo had explained it to him. '*Watch out, or they'll take you away and put you in an institution with the spastics and the junkies' kids*.' And Pietro had said that his was the best family in the world and that in the evenings they all played cards together and watched films on TV and on Sundays they went for walks in the woods and there was Zagor too and Mama was kind and Papa was kind and didn't drink and his brother took him for rides on his motorbike and that he was old enough to dress and wash on his own (*why the hell do they want to know about those things?*).

It had been easy to answer. While he was talking he had thought about the little house on the prairie.

They had gone away.

Those two.

Gloria had called at eight o'clock in the morning and told Pietro that if he wasn't going to school she wouldn't either. Out of solidarity.

Gloria's parents were away. They would spend the morning together and think up some way of persuading Mr Moroni to go to the school.

Pietro had got out his bike and set off for the Celanis' villa. Zagor had escorted him for a kilometre and then gone back home.

Pietro had turned onto the Ischiano road and the sun was out and the air was warm and after all that rain it was a real pleasure to pedal slowly along with the rays warming your back.

But suddenly, without any warning, a red Ciao had materialised behind him.

And Pietro had started to pedal for all he was worth.

104

Sitting in the armchair in the living room, Flora watched Graziano as he slept.

His lips were apart. A dribble of saliva ran down from the corner of his mouth. He was snoring softly. The cushion had stamped red lines on his forehead.

How strange. In less than twenty-four hours her attitude towards Graziano had been turned on its head. The day before, when she had met him at the Station Bar and he had come over to speak to her, she had found him insignificant and vulgar. Now, the more she looked at him the handsomer he seemed, more attractive than any man she had ever met before.

Graziano opened his eyes and smiled.

Flora smiled back. 'How are you feeling?'

'All right, I think. I'm not quite sure.' Graziano felt the back of his head. 'I've got a nice big bump. What are you doing there in the dark?'

'I made you some breakfast. But it'll be cold by now.'

Graziano stretched out his hand towards her. 'Come here.'

Flora laid the tray on the floor and approached him shyly.

'Sit down.' He made room for her on the sofa. Flora sat down primly. He took her hand. 'Well?'

Flora smiled faintly. (*Tell him.*)

'Well?' Graziano repeated.

'Well what?' Flora murmured, squeezing his hand.

'Are you happy?'

'Yes . . .' (*Tell him.*)

'I like you with your hair down . . . It suits you much better. Why don't you always wear it like that?'

Graziano, I've got to talk to you . . . 'I don't know.'

'What's the matter? You seem strange . . .'

'Nothing . . .' *Graziano, we can't see each other any more. I'm sorry*. 'Are you hungry?'

'A bit. We didn't have much to eat last night in the end. I could do with something . . .'

Flora got up, took the tray and went towards the kitchen.

'Where are you going?'

'To warm your coffee.'

'No. I'll drink it as it is.' Graziano pulled himself up into a sitting position and stretched.

Flora poured out the coffee and milk and watched him drink and dunk the biscuits and realised that she loved him.

That night, unknown to her, a dam inside her had burst. And the affection that been compressed for so long in some obscure part of her being had gushed out and flooded her heart, her mind, everything.

She felt breathless and a lump was rising slowly but surely up her throat.

He finished eating. 'Thank you.' He glanced at the clock. 'Oh God, I must be going. My mother will be worried sick,' he said anxiously, and he hurriedly dressed and pulled on his boots.

Flora, on the sofa, watched him in silence.

Graziano checked his appearance in the mirror and shook his head disapprovingly. 'I look a mess, I must have a shower straight away.' He put on his coat.

He's going.

All the things Flora had thought in the car were true, then, and there was nothing more to say, nothing more to explain, because now he was leaving, and it was normal and right that he should, he had got what he had wanted and there was nothing to discuss, nothing to add and thank you and goodbye and it was terrible, no, it was better, much better this way.

Go. It's better if you just go.

105

He was flying along, was that Dickhead.

He had stamina, no doubt about it. But it was wasted effort. Sooner or later he would have to stop.

Where do you think you can run to?

Dickhead had sneaked and must be punished. Pierini had warned him, but he hadn't listened, he'd gone ahead and squealed and now he must suffer the dire consequences.

Simple.

Actually Pierini wasn't so sure it had been Moroni who had sneaked. It might well have been that cow Palmieri. But it didn't make any difference. Moroni needed to be helped to behave properly in future. It must be impressed upon him that Federico Pierini's words were to be taken seriously, very seriously.

He would deal with Miss Palmieri later. At his leisure.

I'm afraid the future looks bleak for your nice shiny Y10, Miss.

'He's slowing down . . . He can't go on. He's burnt out,' shouted Flame excitedly.

'Move alongside. I'll give him a kick and bring him down.'

106

Flora was so cold. Like a different person. She must have swallowed a block of ice for breakfast. Graziano had the distinct impression that she didn't want him around. That the affair was over.

I made too much of a mess of things last night.

So he would have to leave.

But he continued to wander round the living room.

Hell, I'm going to ask her. The worst she can do is say no. I've got nothing to lose.

He sat down next to Flora, leaving a little space between them, looked at her and brushed her lips with a kiss. 'Okay, I'm off, then.'

'Okay.'

'Bye, then.'

'Bye.'

But instead of going to the door and leaving, he nervously lit another cigarette and started pacing up and down like an expectant father. Suddenly he stopped, in the middle of the room, plucked up courage and said: 'I don't suppose I could see you this evening?'

107

I can't go on.

Pietro saw them coming out of the corner of his eye. They were ten metres away.

Now I'm going to stop, turn round and set off again.

It was a daft idea. But he couldn't think of a better one.

Shreds of heart kept contracting in his chest. The fire in his lungs had spread to his throat and was tearing at his pharynx.

I can't go on, I can't go on.

'Dickhead, pull over!' Pierini shouted.

Here they come.

On the left. Three metres behind.

What if I cut across the fields?

Wrong again.

There was a deep ditch on either side of the road and even if he'd had ET's bike he couldn't have jumped over them. He would have crashed down into the ditch.

Pietro saw Fausto Coppi pedalling along beside him and shaking his head disapprovingly.

What's the matter?

(*You're not thinking right. It works like this: you're faster than that clapped-out Ciao. They can only catch up with you if you slow down. But if you accelerate, if you gain ten metres and don't slow down again, they'll never catch you.*)

'Dickhead, I only want to talk to you. I won't hurt you, I swear to God I won't. I want to explain something to you.'

(*But if you accelerate, if you gain ten metres and don't slow down again, they'll never catch you.*)

He saw Flame's face. A horrible sight. He was twisting his mouth into a smirk that was meant to be a smile.

I'm going to brake.

(*If you brake, you've had it.*)

Flame stuck out a long leg which terminated in an army boot.

They want to knock me off my bike.

Coppi continued to shake his head in exasperation. (*You're thinking like a loser. If I'd thought the way you do I'd never have become the greatest and I'd probably have been killed. When I was your age I was the butcher's boy and all the villagers used to make fun of me and call me a hunchback and say I looked ridiculous on that bike which was so big my feet didn't touch the ground, but one day, it was wartime and I was taking some steaks to the hungry partisans who were hiding in a farmhouse in the country . . .*)

Pietro was knocked violently to the left by a kick from Flame. He threw all his weight to the right and managed to straighten up again. He started pedalling again as fast as he could.

(*. . . and two Nazis with their motorbike and sidecar, which is much faster than a Ciao, came after me and I started pedalling as hard as I could and the Germans behind were just about to catch me but suddenly I started pedalling faster and faster and the Germans were left behind and Fausto Coppi and Fausto Coppi and Fausto Coppi . . .*)

108

Pierini was incredulous. 'He's pulling away . . . Look, he's pulling away . . . Look at that! Shit! You and your crappy little Ciao.'

Dickhead had become as one with his bike and, as if a ghost had stuck a rocket up his arse, had begun to accelerate.

Pierini started thumping Flame in the ribs and shouting in his ear: 'Stop! Stop, damn it! Let me get off.'

The scooter slowed down, swerving with a squeal of brakes and tyres. When it was stationary, Pierini dismounted. 'Get off.'

Flame looked at him, puzzled.

'Don't you see? The two of us will never catch him. Get off, quick!'

'But what . . .' Flame tried to object, but then he saw his friend's face distorted with rage and understood that it was better to obey.

Pierini jumped on the scooter, twisted the throttle and zoomed off with his head down, shouting: 'Wait for me here. I'll get him and then come back for you.'

109

The Aurelia was a continuous stream of cars and trucks streaking along in both directions. And it was two hundred metres away.

Pietro kept pedalling and looked back, gasping and inhaling the fiery air.

He had pulled away from them, but only a little. They must have stopped.

Here they come again.

He was done for.

Do something then, think of something . . .

But what? What the hell could he do?

Then he had an idea. An idea which was in some ways great and heroic. An idea which wasn't exactly the most brilliant idea that anyone has ever had, and which Gloria and Mimmo and Fausto Coppi (by the way, where had Fausto Coppi got to? Didn't he have any more advice to dispense?) and any other person with a modicum of sense would have strongly advised him against, but which at that moment seemed the only chance of salvation or maybe of . . .

Don't think about it.

This is what Pietro did.

Quite simply, he didn't slow down, on the contrary, using what little strength he had left, he trod even harder on the pedals and hurled himself like a blind fury towards the Aurelia, with the insane intention of crossing it.

110

Dickhead had flipped. He was going to kill himself.

Good thinking. Federico Pierini had no objections.

Moroni must have come to the conclusion that for a pillock like him the only sensible course of action was to end it all.

Pierini pulled up and started applauding enthusiastically. 'Great! Attaboy! Go for it!'

They'd scoop him off the asphalt with a coffee spoon.

One piece here, another piece there. What about the head? Where's that head got to? Anyone seen the right foot?

'Get yourself killed! That's the way! Bravo!' he shouted, continuing to clap his hands happily.

It's always nice to watch a guy killing himself because he's scared of you.

111

Pietro didn't slow down. He just narrowed his eyes and bit his lip.

If he was killed it would mean his number was up, and if he was destined to live he would pass unscathed between the cars.

Simple.

Life or death.

White or black.

Neck or nothing.

Like a kamikaze.

Pietro didn't consider the various shades of grey that lay between the two extremes: paralysis, coma, suffering, wheelchairs, endless pain and regrets (always assuming that he was still capable of regretting) for the rest of his life.

He was too busy being scared to think about the consequences. Not even when he was only a few dozen metres from the crossing and he saw that big sign with the flashing yellow light saying SLOW, DANGEROUS CROSSING did it occur to him to squeeze the brakes, stop pedalling, look right and left. He just sailed across the Aurelia as if it wasn't there.

And Fabio Pasquali, codenamed Rambo 26, the poor trucker who saw him materialise in front of him like a nightmare, pressed his horn and slammed on his brakes and realised in a flash that from that moment on his life was going to change for the worse and that in years to come he would have to struggle against the feelings of guilt (the speedometer showed a hundred and ten and on that part of the road the limit was ninety), against the law and the lawyers and his wife who had been going on at him for ages to give up that exhausting job and he thought wistfully of the job in a pastry-shop that his son-in-law had offered him and heaved a sigh of relief when that little boy on the bike disappeared just as he had appeared, with no sounds of crushed bones and metal, and realised that he'd been lucky and hadn't killed him and whooped with joy and anger combined.

Pietro, having eluded the truck, found himself on the centre partition and in the other direction there was a red Rover hurtling towards him, horn blaring. If he'd braked it would have hit him, and if he'd accelerated it would have hit him, but the Rover swerved sharply and passed behind him, two centimetres away, and the slipstream pulled him first right and then left and when he reached the other side, on the exit to Ischiano Scalo, he was completely off balance, he braked on the gravel but the front wheel lost its purchase and Pietro skidded along, scraping his leg and hand.

He was alive.

112

Graziano emerged from Flora Palmieri's house, walked a few steps across the yard and then stopped, entranced by the beauty of the day.

The sky was the palest of blues and the air so clear that beyond the roadside cypresses and the hills you could even see the jagged peaks of the Apenines.

He closed his eyes and like an old iguana turned his face towards the warm sun. He breathed in deeply, and his olfactory terminals were assailed by the smell of the horse droppings scattered on the road.

'Now that's what I call perfume,' he murmured contentedly. An aroma that took him back in time. To when, at the age of sixteen, he had worked in Persichetti's riding school.

'That's what I must do . . .'

Why hadn't he thought of it before?

He would buy himself a horse. A beautiful bay horse. So that, when he finally settled down in Ischiano (*soon, very soon*), on fine days like this he could go out riding. Take long rides through the Acquasparta woods. With his horse he would be able to go boar-hunting. Not with a gun, though. He didn't like firearms, they weren't sporting. He'd use a crossbow. A crossbow made of carbon fibre and titanium alloy, the kind they use in Canada for hunting grizzlies. How much would a weapon like that cost? A lot, but it was a necessary expense.

He did three knee bends and a couple of neck twists to loosen up. The involuntary rafting through the rapids, the cracking of his head against the rocks and the sleep on the sofa had shattered him. He felt as if someone had removed his vertebrae one by one, shaken them up in a box and put them back in random order.

But if his body was in bad shape, the same could not be said of his mood. His mood was as radiant as that sun.

And all thanks to Flora Palmieri. To this wonderful woman he had met and who had erased Erica from his heart.

Flora had saved his life. After all, if it hadn't been for her he would certainly have been swept over the waterfall and dashed onto the rocks and it would have been curtains.

He would be indebted to her for the rest of his life. And as the Chinese monks say, if someone saves your life they will have to look after you for the rest of their days. Now the two of them were linked together for all time.

It was true, he'd been an incredible fool to try to bugger her. What the hell had got into him? Why such sexual voracity?

(*Mind you, with a bum like that you can hardly help it . . .*)

Shut up. A girl tells you she's a virgin and asks you to be gentle and before five minutes are up you're trying to sodomise her. Shame on you.

He felt the feelings of guilt paralyse his diaphragm.

113

Pierini was waiting for the road to clear when Flame caught up with him. 'Where are you going?' his friend asked him, out of breath from the long run.

'Get on, quick. He's on the other side. He's fallen off.'

Flame didn't need to be told twice. He jumped onto the saddle.

Pierini waited till there was a lull in the traffic and crossed.

Dickhead was sitting at the side of the road rubbing his thigh. The fork of his bike was twisted.

Pierini rode over and leaned his elbows on the handlebars of the Ciao. 'You've just come within a hair's breadth of killing yourself and causing a fatal accident. Now your bike's broken and you're about to get the crap beaten out of you. Just not your day, is it, my friend?'

114

Graziano, in his Uno Turbo, was driving along the Aurelia thinking hard.

He absolutely must apologise to Flora. Prove to her that he wasn't a sex maniac, just a guy with no inhibitions who was crazy about her.

'What I must do is give her a present. Something really special that will knock her sideways.' He often talked to himself in the car. 'But what? A ring? No. Too early. A Hermann Hesse novel? No. Too small. What if . . . what if I gave her a horse? Yes, why not . . . ?'

It was a great idea. A present that was original, not at all predictable, yet important at the same time. It would be a way of showing her that that night hadn't just been any old night, a matter of going through the motions, but that he was serious.

'Yes. A beautiful thoroughbred colt,' he concluded, thumping his fist on the dashboard.

I think I'm in love with her.

It was premature to say it. But if a guy feels something in his heart, how can he help it?

Flora had everything. She was beautiful, intelligent, refined. With a wide range of interests. She could paint. She liked reading. A grown woman, who could appreciate a ride on horseback, a gipsy flamenco or a quiet evening by the fireside reading a good book.

What a contrast to that air-headed bimbo Erica Trettel. If Erica was a self-centred, capricious, vain little girl, Flora was a sensitive, generous, discreet woman.

There was no doubt about it, all things considered Miss Palmieri was the ideal companion for the new Graziano Biglia.

Maybe she can even cook . . .

With a woman like that at his side he would be able to carry out all his plans. Open the jeans shop and a bookshop too and find a farmhouse near the woods to convert into a ranch with stables and she would care for him with a smile on her lips and they would . . .

(*Why not?*)

. . . have children.

He felt ready for kids. A girl (*she'll be as pretty as a picture!*), then a boy. A perfect family.

How on earth could he have thought a girl like Erica Trettel, a hysterical, spoiled bitch, the last of the showgirls, could accompany him through the years of his old age? Flora Palmieri was the soul mate he needed.

The only thing he didn't understand was why such a beautiful woman had remained a virgin for so long. What was it that had kept her away from males? She must have some problems with sex. He would have to find out what sort of problems they were, make some discreet inquiries. But actually even this idea was something he didn't at all dislike. He would be her instructor, teaching her everything there was to know. She had talent. He would make her the best of lovers.

He felt that his seven chakras had finally balanced out, redressing the equilibrium of his aura and putting him at peace with the universal soul. His anxieties and fears had flown away and he felt as light as a balloon and eager to do a whole lot of things.

Isn't it amazing what that strange feeling called love can do to a sensitive soul?

I must go and see Mama at once.

He must break it to her that he'd split up with Erica and then tell her about his new love. Then at least she'd put an end to this farce of the vow, though he felt a tinge of regret about that. This non-talking version of her wasn't at all bad.

Then he would go and look for a stud farm, and while he was about it he could drop in at a hunting and fishing shop and find out how much a crossbow would cost.

'And tonight a romantic tête-à-tête at the teacher's flat,' he concluded happily, and switched on the stereo.

Ottmart Liebart and the Black Moons struck up with a gipsy version of Umberto Tozzi's *Gloria*.

Graziano flicked the indicator and turned onto the exit for Ischiano Scalo. 'What the . . . ?'

At the side of the road two boys, one about fourteen, the other older and bigger and with an oafish face, were beating up a little boy. And they were not kidding. The small boy was on the ground, curled up in a ball, and the other two were kicking him.

On another occasion Graziano Biglia probably wouldn't have taken any notice, he would simply have looked away and driven straight on, obeying the law, always mind your own damn business. But that morning, as has already been mentioned, he felt as light as a balloon and eager to do a whole lot of things, which included defending the weak against the strong, so he braked, pulled over, lowered the window and shouted, 'Hey! You two! You two!'

The two boys turned and looked at him in bemusement.

What did this jerk want?

'Leave him alone!'

The bigger one glanced at his companion and then replied, 'Fuck off!'

Graziano gaped for a moment and then reacted angrily: 'What do you mean, fuck off?'

How dare that stupid great lout insult him? 'Listen, scumbag, you don't say fuck off to me, okay?' he barked, thrusting his hand out of the window, fingers spread.

The other, a thin, mean-faced kid with a white streak in his fringe, smirked derisively and, cool as a cucumber, retorted: 'Well, if he can't say it, I will: Fuck off!'

Graziano shook his head sadly.

They didn't understand.

They didn't understand what life was all about.

They didn't understand who they were dealing with.

They didn't understand that Graziano Biglia had for three years been the best friend of Tony the Snake Ceccherini, the Italian champion of capoiera, the Brazilian martial art. And the Snake had taught him a couple of killer moves.

And if they didn't stop laying into that poor kid and humbly apologise at once, they were going to feel the full effect of those moves on their frail little bodies. 'Apologise, both of you, right now!'

'Get lost,' the thin one retorted, then turned round and, to make his meaning clearer, gave the little boy curled up on the ground another kick.

'Right, we'll see about this.' He opened the door and got out.

War had been declared and Graziano Biglia could not but feel happy, because the day he couldn't put two little ruffians like these in their place it would be time to have himself carried off to an old people's home.

'Let's see about this, then.'

He swaggered over to them in his best orang-utan style and shoved Pierini, who fell on his backside. Then he smoothed back his hair. 'Apologise, you little git.'

Pierini got to his feet fuming with rage and gave him a scowl so full of bile and scorn that Graziano was momentarily taken aback.

'A right couple of heroes you are. Two of you agains . . .' Our paladin didn't manage to finish his sentence because he heard an 'Aaaaah!' behind him, and before he could turn round the oaf had grabbed him round the throat and was trying to throttle him. He squeezed tighter than a boa constrictor. Graziano tried to tear that alien off him, but couldn't. He was strong. The thin one stood in front of him and without more ado punched him hard in the stomach.

Graziano blew out all the air he had in his lungs and started coughing and spluttering. An explosion of colours blurred his vision and he had to tense his legs to stop himself falling on the ground like a marionette whose strings have been cut.

What the hell was going on?

Children

Once, about seven years before this story, Graziano was in Rio de Janeiro on tour with the Radio Bengals, a world-music group he had been playing with for a few months. All five of them were in a van crammed with instruments, amplifiers and loudspeakers. It was nine o'clock in the evening and at ten they were due to play in a jazz club north of the city, but had got lost.

That cursed metropolis was bigger than Los Angeles and dirtier than Calcutta.

They struggled with the map but couldn't figure it out. Where the hell were they?

They had driven off the bypass and entered an apparently uninhabited favela. Corrugated iron huts. Putrid smelly streams running down the middle of the churned-up road. Piles of burnt rubbish.

The classic shithole.

Boliwar Ram, the Indian flute-player, was quarrelling with Hassan Chemirani, the Iranian drummer, when a score of children emerged from the shacks. The youngest might have been nine years old, the oldest thirteen. They were half-naked and barefoot. Graziano had lowered the window to ask them how to get out of that place, but had immediately wound it up again.

They looked like a bunch of zombies.

Expressionless eyes staring into nothingness, gaunt faces, hollow cheeks, blue cracked lips as if they were eighty years old. Each had a rusty knife in one hand and in the other a half orange impregnated with some solvent or other. They kept holding them under their noses and sniffing. And all of them, in the same way, would close their eyes, seem on the point of falling on the ground, then recover and resume their slow advance.

'Let's get out of here. Right away. I don't like the look of these guys,' said Yvan Ledoux, the French keyboard player who was at the wheel. And he had begun a difficult manoeuvre to reverse the van.

Meanwhile the children kept slowly advancing.

'Quick! Quick!' Graziano urged him, in a panic.

'I can't, damn it!' shouted the keyboardist. Three of the kids had got in front of the van and were clinging on to the windscreen wipers and the radiator grill. 'Can't you see? If I go forward I'll run them over.'

'Go backwards, then.'

Yvan checked the rear-view mirror. 'They're behind as well. I don't know what to do.'

Roselyne Gasparian, the Armenian singer, a petite girl with a shock of coloured curls, started screaming and clutched hold of Graziano.

The boys outside banged their hands rhythmically on the bodywork and windows and for the people inside it was like being inside a drum.

The Radio Bengals screamed in terror.

The window on the driver's side shattered. An enormous rock and millions of tiny transparent cubes showered on the Frenchman, cutting his face, and a dozen little arms thrust in, grabbing him. Yvan shrieked like a madman, struggling to break free. Graziano tried to hit those tentacles with the stand of a microphone, but as soon as one withdrew another popped in, and one, longer than the rest, took the keys.

The engine stopped.

And they vanished.

They weren't there any more. In front, or behind. Anywhere.

The musicians huddled together, expecting something.

The famous multiethnic fusion that they had sought so hard to achieve during gigs without ever attaining it completely was now more present than ever.

Then there was a metallic creak.

The handle of the big side door went down. The door began to slide slowly along its runner. And as the gap widened they could see the skinny bodies of children bathed in white by the full moon and dark eyes determined to get what they wanted. When the door was fully open, they found themselves facing a group of boys with knives in their hands looking at them in silence. One of the smallest, he can't have been older than nine or ten, and one of his eye-sockets was hollow and black, motioned to them to get out. The stuff he sniffed had dried him up like an Egyptian mummy.

The musicians emerged with their hands up. Graziano helped Yvan, who was dabbing his eyebrow with the hem of his T-shirt.

And the Radio Bengals walked off into the Brazilian night without looking back.

The police, next day, said they had been lucky.

115

But Graziano was not in Rio de Janeiro now.

I'm in Ischiano Scalo, for God's sake.

A village of respectable, God-fearing people. Where the kids went to school and played soccer in Piazza XXV Aprile. At least that's what he'd thought until that moment.

Seeing the evil eyes of that small boy closing in to hit him again, he wasn't so sure.

'But now that's it, I've had enough.' He raised his leg and caught him with the heel of his boot just under the breastbone. The little thug was lifted in the air and, stiff as a Big Jim, hurled backwards onto the wet grass. He lay there for a moment with his mouth open, paralysed, but then turned over abruptly, struggled to his knees, hands on his stomach, and spewed out some red stuff.

Oh my God! It's blood! He's haemorrhaging! thought Graziano, worried and at the same time elated by his own lethal power. *Who am I? Who am I? All I gave him was a gentle kick in the midriff.*

Fortunately, what the skinny one was throwing up was not blood but tomato sauce. There were also some pieces of semi-digested pizza. The young man, before coming out to throw his weight around, had eaten some red pizza.

'He'll kill you! He'll kill you!' the oaf was yelling into his right tympanum. He was clinging to his back and trying at the same time to choke him and wrestle him to the ground.

His breath smelled disgusting. Onions and fish.

This one must have had a big slice of pizza with onions and anchovies.

It was that asphyxiating blast that gave him the strength to shake him off. Graziano bent forward, grabbed him by the hair and hauled him over his head like a heavy rucksack. The big lout did a somersault in the air and found himself lying flat on the ground. Graziano didn't give him time to move. He gave him a kick in the ribs. 'There. See how you like it.' The oaf started screaming. 'Not nice, is it? Now get out of here, the pair of you.'

Like the cat and the fox in *Pinocchio* after they get beaten by the Fire Eater, they got to their feet and, tails between their legs, limped over to the Ciao.

The oaf started up the engine and the skinny one got on behind him, but before they left he threatened Graziano. 'You'd better watch out. Don't get any big ideas. You're nobody.' Then he turned to the small boy, who had got to his feet. 'And I haven't finished with you yet. You were lucky today, you won't be next time.'

116

He had appeared out of nowhere.

Like the good guy in a western or the Man from the East or, even better, Mad Max.

The car door had opened and the avenger had stepped out, dressed in black with sunglasses, a coat that flapped in the wind and a red silk shirt. And he'd kicked their butts.

A couple of karate moves and Pierini and Flame were flattened.

Pietro knew who he was. *Big Biglia*. The one who'd gone out with a famous actress and appeared on the *Maurizio Costanzo Show*.

He was probably on his way back from the Maurizio Costanzo Show *now, and stopped to save me.*

He limped over to his hero, who was standing on the grass trying to clean his muddy boots with his hand.

'Thank you, sir.' Pietro held out his hand.

'You're welcome. I just got my boots a bit dirty,' said Biglia, shaking it. 'Did they hurt you?'

'A bit. But I'd already hurt myself when I fell off my bike.'

In fact the side of his body where they had been kicking him was very sore and he had a feeling it was going to get worse over the coming hours.

'Why were they beating you up?'

Pietro pursed his lips and tried to find an answer that would impress his saviour. But he couldn't think of one and was forced to admit: 'I sneaked.'

'You sneaked?'

'Yes, at school. But the deputy headmistress forced me to – if I hadn't she would have failed me. I know it was wrong, but I didn't want to do it.'

'I understand.' Biglia checked if his coat was dirty.

Actually he didn't seem to understand much or to be very interested in learning more. Pietro was relieved. It was a long and nasty story.

Graziano squatted down, bringing himself down to his level. 'Listen to me. Guys like that only mean trouble. If you do a bit of travelling round the world one day, as I have, you'll meet others of the same type, and much nastier than those bastards. Keep away from them, because they either want to harm you or they want to make you like them. And you're worth a thousand of them, that's what you must always tell yourself. And above all, if somebody hits you, you mustn't drop on the ground like a sack of potatoes, because that only makes things worse. And it's not manly. You must stay on your feet and face them.' He put his hands on his shoulders. 'You must look them in the eye. And even if you're scared shitless, remember that they are too, it's just that they're better at hiding it. If you're sure of yourself, they can't harm you. And another thing, you're too thin, don't you eat enough?'

Pietro shook his head.

'Get the first law into your head and obey it: treat your body like a temple. Do you understand?'

Pietro nodded.

'Is that clear?'

'Yes, sir.'

'Can you get home?'

'Yes.'

'You don't want me to give you a lift? Your bike's broken . . .'

'No, don't worry . . . Thanks. I can manage. Thanks again . . .'

Graziano gave him an affectionate pat on the back. 'Off you go, then.'

Pietro went over to his bike. He hoisted it on his back and set off.

He had been saved by Big Biglia. He hadn't entirely understood all that stuff about the body and the temple, but it didn't matter because when he grew up he wanted to be just like him. A guy who never makes mistakes, who looks the bad guys in the eye and wipes the floor with them. If he did become like Biglia, he too would help the weakest children.

Because that's what heroes are for.

117

Graziano watched the little boy walk away carrying his bicycle on his back. *I didn't even ask him what his name was . . .*

The gust of good humour that had billowed out his soul like a sail had dropped, leaving him sad and fed up. He felt terribly depressed.

It had been the boy's eyes that had changed his mood. Resignation, that's what he'd seen in them. And if there was one thing Graziano Biglia detested with every fibre of his being it was resignation.

He was like an old man. An old man who has realised that there's nothing more to be done, the war is lost and all his efforts won't change anything. How can he be like that? He has his whole life in front of him.

William Tell or someone else had said that everyone is the maker of their own destiny.

And for Graziano Biglia this, too, was a truth.

I did it, when the time came . . . I gave up the loser's life I was living, I told Mama I'd had enough of her sautéed kidneys and I travelled the world and met the most amazing people, Tibetan monks, Australian surfers, Jamaican rastas. I ate yak's milk and butter, roast opossum and hard-boiled platypus-eggs and I can tell you, Mama dear, they're a thousand times better than your sautéed kidneys with parsley and garlic. The only reason I don't tell you this is that I don't want to hurt you. And I'm in Ischiano because I want to be here. Because I need to strengthen my ties to my own land. No one forced me to come back. And if that little boy were my son, he would never have let those two thugs push him around, because I would have taught him to defend himself, I would have helped him to grow up, I would have given him . . . I . . .

From the unfathomable depths of his consciousness there arose an obscure entity, an atavistic feeling of guilt linked to our gregarious existence, which lay there, apparently placid, but ready, in favourable conditions (financial straits, girlfriend problems, crises of confidence in his own abilities, and so on) to raise its head and obliterate at a stroke all the New Age truths, Tibetan axioms, faith in the regenerative power of flamenco, William Tell, crossbows and colts, by asking one simple question.

But what have you actually achieved in your life?

And, painful though it is to admit it, there were no positive answers.

Graziano walked slowly towards his car, with his head bowed, carrying an anvil on his shoulders.

Undoubtedly he'd done a lot of things in his life. But he'd done them because he'd been bitten by the tarantula at birth, he'd come into this world afflicted with St Vitus's dance, with a never-passing restlessness that drove him to wander about in search of an obscure, unattainable happiness.

There was no plan.

There was no ultimate aim.

He opened the car door. He got in. He turned off the stereo, silencing the guitars of the Gipsy Kings.

The truth was that for forty-four years he had stuffed his brain with garbage. With beautiful films. With he-man commercials for Taverna bitters. Fantasies where he was the Tuareg and Erica Trettel the Spanish filly to be tamed in a Tunisian oasis.

Me settled, responsible, with a nice little wife, horses, a jeans shop, children. Who am I kidding? I'm just playing at happy families. I can pull three hundred woman in one summer but I can't build a permanent relationship with anyone. I'm no good.

I'm as lonely as a dog.

A diffuse pain gripped him by the stomach and made him open his mouth and utter a laboured sigh. He felt weak and limp and penniless and thriftless. In short, a failure.

(*What would Flora want with a guy like you?*)

Nothing.

Fortunately, these pessimistico-existential considerations passed through him like neutrinos, those elementary entities devoid of weight or energy which flash through the created world at the speed of light, leaving it unchanged.

Graziano Biglia, as we have already seen, was constitutionally immune to depression. And these moments of lucid vision were sporadic and fleeting and so, reverting to his habitual state of being as blind as a bat, he was able to try and try and try again. For he was sure that sooner or later he too would find some goddam peace of mind.

He turned round and took his guitar off the back seat, picked out a gentle little tune and finally started singing. 'You'll see, you'll see, you'll see, things will change, maybe not tomorrow but one day they will change. You'll see, you'll see, this is not the end for me. I don't know how or when, but things are gonna change, you'll see.'

118

Gloria Celani was in bed.

And she was watching *The Silence of the Lambs*, her favourite film, on her little TV. Beside her was a tray with her breakfast. A half-eaten croissant. A napkin soaked in spilt caffè latte.

Her parents had gone to the Boat Show in Pescara and wouldn't be back till tomorrow. So she was alone in the house, except for Francesco, the old gardener.

When Pietro entered, he found her cowering in the corner with the bedclothes pulled up to her eyes.

'Oh God, it's so scary. I can't bear to watch. Come and sit here.' She patted the mattress. 'You've taken your time. I thought you'd never get here . . .'

How many times has she seen it? Pietro wondered gloomily. *At least a hundred, and she still gets just as terrified as she did the first time.*

He took off his windproof jacket and put it on a small armchair decorated with a bright yellow-and-blue-striped material, which also covered the walls of the room.

The bedroom was the creation of a well-known Roman interior designer (as were all the other rooms and, joy of joys, the villa had been featured in *AD* and Mrs Celani had almost fainted away) and was like a kitschy little bonbonnière with those pale pink cupboards with green pommels, those curtains with pictures of cows all over them and that Wedgwood-blue carpet.

Gloria loathed it. If she'd had her way, she would have set it on fire. Pietro, more tolerant as usual, didn't think it was all that bad. True, those curtains weren't great, but he didn't at all dislike the carpet, which was soft and thick, like the fur of a raccoon.

He sat down on the bed, taking care not to put his weight on his wound.

Gloria, though glued to the television, saw him grimace out of the corner of her eye. 'What's the matter?'

'Nothing. I had a fall.'

'How did that happen?'

'I was riding my bike.'

Should he tell her? Of course he should. If you don't talk about your troubles with your best friend, who are you going to talk about them with?

He told her about being pursued by the Ciao, the Aurelia, the fall, the beating and Big Biglia's timely intervention.

'Biglia? The one who went out with that actress . . . ? What's her name?' Gloria was all excited. 'And he hit those two bastards?'

'He didn't hit them, he thrashed them. They jumped on him, but he swatted them like flies. With a couple of kung-fu kicks. Ha! Pow, pow! And they ran away.' Pietro had got really carried away.

'I love Graziano Biglia. Fantastic! Next time I see him, I don't know him, but it doesn't matter, I'm going to give him a big kiss,

I swear. Oh, I wish I'd been there.' Gloria stood up on the bed and started doing karate moves and uttering Chinese cries.

She was wearing nothing but a skimpy violet cotton T-shirt which left her stomach and navel exposed and if you looked underneath . . . plus a pair of white shorts with embroidered edges. Those long legs, that pert little bottom, that long neck, those small breasts that pushed against the cloth of the T-shirt. And that short, towselled, blonde hair.

Enough to drive any boy wild.

Gloria was the most beautiful thing Pietro had ever seen. He was sure of that. He had to lower his eyes because he was afraid she'd guess what he was thinking.

Gloria sat down cross-legged beside him and, suddenly concerned, asked him: 'Did you hurt yourself?'

'A bit. Not much,' Pietro lied, trying to put on the impassive face of a hero.

'I don't believe it. I know you. Let me see.' Gloria grabbed his trouser belt.

Pietro pulled away. 'Don't worry, it's only a scratch. It's nothing.'

'You idiot, you're embarrassed . . . What about when we're at the seaside, then?'

Sure he was embarrassed, it was different here. They were alone, on a bed, and she . . . Well, it was different, that's all. But he said: 'No, I'm not embarrassed . . .'

'Let me see, then.' She took hold of his buckle.

There was no getting out of it, when Gloria took a decision, that was the way it was going to be. Despite himself, Pietro was forced to lower his trousers.

'Goodness, look what you've done . . . We'll have to disinfect it. Take your trousers off.' She said this in a serious, motherly tone which Pietro had never heard her use before.

A bit of disinfectant was indeed called for. The outer side of his right thigh was grazed and covered with blood and drops of pus. It was throbbing slightly. He had also grazed his calf and his hand, and his ribs hurt where they had kicked him.

What a mess I'm in . . . But in spite of everything he was happy, without knowing exactly why. Maybe because Gloria was now looking after him, maybe because those two bastards had got a thrashing, maybe just because he was in that doll's room, on a bed with sheets that smelled so good.

Gloria went into the kitchen to fetch some disinfectant and cotton wool. How she loved playing nurses! She medicated him, while Pietro moaned that she was a sadist, that she was putting on far more disinfectant than necessary. She bandaged him up in rough-and-ready fashion, gave him an old pair of pyjamas and put him to bed, then drew the curtains and got into bed herself and started the video again. 'Now we'll watch the end of the film, then you can have a nap and later we'll have something to eat. Do you like tortellini with cream?'

'Yes,' said Pietro, hoping that heaven was exactly like this.

In every detail.

A warm bed. A video. The leg of the most beautiful girl in the world to brush against. And tortellini with cream.

He snuggled down under the duvet and in less than five minutes was asleep.

119

To see Mimmo Moroni from a distance, on the green hillside, sitting under a long-branched oak tree with the sheep grazing beside him and that pink-and-blue sunset gilding the woodland leaves, you felt as if you'd stepped into a painting by Juan Ortega da Fuente. But if you drew nearer you discovered that the shepherd boy was dressed like the lead singer of Metallica and that he was weeping as he munched some Mulino Bianco Crumbly Delights.

That was the pose in which Pietro found him.

'What's up?' he asked, already suspecting the answer.

'Nothing . . . I'm not feeling well.'

'Have you quarrelled with Patti?'

'No, she's . . . ditched me . . .' Mimmo whimpered, and popped into his mouth another biscuit with a rich soft centre enclosed in light flaky pastry.

Pietro snorted. 'Again?'

'Yes. But this time she means it.'

Patrizia ditched him, on average, twice a month.

'Why?'

'That's the problem, I don't know! I haven't got a clue. This morning she rang me up and broke it off without giving any explanation. Maybe she doesn't love me any more, or perhaps she's found someone else. I don't know . . .' He sniffed and sank his teeth into another biscuit.

There was a reason. And it wasn't that Patrizia didn't love him any more, let alone that a new competitor had stolen Mimmo's sceptre.

God knows why, but whenever a partner ditches us, these are the first explanations that come to our minds. She doesn't want me any more. She's found someone better than me.

If our friend Mimmo had thought more carefully about his meeting with his girlfriend the previous day, maybe, and I repeat maybe, he would have found a reason.

120

Mimmo had left the house at about five o'clock in the afternoon, got on his motorbike and gone to pick up Patti.

He was supposed to be taking her to Orbano to do some shopping, to buy some Perla tights and a cream for skin blemishes.

When Patrizia had seen him on his motorbike she'd started cursing.

How was it possible that of all her group of friends she was the only one whose boyfriend didn't have a car? Or rather, who did have a car, but whose shit of a father wouldn't let him use it?

And it was raining!

But Mimmo was unperturbed. That morning he'd gone to the market in Ischiano and bought some army capes. He assured her that with those on they'd be as dry as could be. Patrizia had sulkily donned her helmet and climbed on that hog, which was as tall as a horse, as evil-smelling as an oil refinery, as dangerous as Russian roulette and as noisy as . . . what's as noisy as a motocross bike with a broken silencer? Nothing.

And they might have reached Orbano without getting wet, because the capes did indeed do their job, but Mimmo couldn't resist swerving like a maniac through all the puddles that appeared in front of him.

They had got off the motorbike soaked to the skin. Patrizia's mood was worsening. They'd set off down the main street but after a hundred metres Mimmo had stopped short in front of the hunting and fishing shop. In the window was a titanium and carbon fibre crossbow to die for. He'd gone in, despite her protests, to ask about its price and technical specifications. It cost an arm and a leg. But among the bows, rifles and fishing rods he'd managed to find something to buy. There was no way he was leaving there empty-handed. It was a question of principle.

An air pistol on special offer.

Half an hour to look at it, half an hour to decide whether to buy it or not, and meanwhile the shops were closing.

Patrizia's mood by now was as black as pitch.

Since they hadn't been able to do any shopping (though Mimmo had eventually bought the air pistol), they'd decided to have a pizza and then go to the cinema to see *The Courage of Being Melissa*, the dramatic story of a Scandinavian woman who had been forced to live for a year in a pygmy village.

They'd sat down in the pizzeria and Mimmo had pulled up his legs and examined his boots. He was highly delighted with this purchase which he'd made earlier at the market along with the capes. He'd started explaining to Patrizia that those boots were hi-tech, identical to the ones the Americans had used in Operation Desert Storm, and that the reason they were so heavy was that, theoretically, they were proof against antipersonnel mines. And while she leafed through the menu with a bored expression on her face, to prove that he wasn't talking bullshit

Mimmo had taken the gun out of its box, inserted a pellet and shot at his foot.

He'd let out a blood-curdling scream.

The pellet had gone right through the vamp and sock and lodged in his instep, proving to him that there is often a discrepancy between theory and practice.

They'd had to run (hobble) to the emergency clinic where a doctor had taken it out and given him two stitches.

The pizza too had gone down the tubes.

They had reached the cinema at the last moment and had had to make do with seats in the front row, two centimetres away from the screen.

Patti was no longer talking.

The film had begun and Mimmo had attempted a conciliatory approach by squeezing her hand, but she had pushed him away as if he had mange. He'd tried to follow the film, but it was a total yawn. He'd felt hungry. He'd munched his popcorn, making a hell of a noise. Patrizia had confiscated it and then he'd pulled out his ace, a brand new packet of strawberry-flavoured bubble-gum. He'd put three strips in his mouth and started blowing bubbles. A glare from Patrizia had made him open his mouth and spit that huge sticky ball of gum on the floor.

When the film had finished they had mounted the motorbike (in pouring rain) and returned home. Patti had alighted and disappeared through her front door without giving him a goodnight kiss.

The next morning she had called him, curtly informed him that he could consider himself single and hung up.

Perhaps for many girlfriends all this would be quite enough to end a relationship, but for Patti no, it wasn't. She loved Mimmo unconditionally and the night would cool her rage, but what had driven her to that extreme gesture was the fact that when Mimmo had spat out the bubble-gum in the cinema it had landed right in her crash helmet. When she'd put it on, the gum had fused indissolubly with those long flowing locks treated with restructurants and extract of pig's placenta.

The hairdresser had been obliged to give her a cut which he euphemistically described as sporty.

Gorilla in the mist

But this time too, as always, Patti would let a week go by and then end up forgiving poor Mimmo.

Patrizia Ciarnò, in this sense, was a certainty. Once she'd chosen you, she would never leave you. And this was because at the age of fifteen she'd had a nasty emotional experience which she still hadn't really got over.

At that age Patrizia was already well developed. Her ovaries and secondary sexual features had undergone a massive hormonal bombardment and poor Patrizia was all tits, thighs, bum, love handles, acne and blackheads. And she was going out with Bruno Miele, the policeman, who was then twenty-two. Back then Bruno had had no thoughts of becoming a policeman, his ambition was to join the San Marco battalion and become a tough, no-nonsense commando.

Patrizia was deeply in love with him – she liked assertive boys – but there was a problem. Bruno would go and pick her up in his A112, drive her into the Acquasparta woods to boff her, take her home again when they'd finished and that was it.

One day Patrizia hadn't been able to restrain herself any longer and had burst out, 'Look, what is this? All my friends' boyfriends take them down to Rome on Saturday afternoons to look at the shop windows and the only place you ever take me is the woods. I don't like it, you know.'

Miele, who even at that time displayed a rare sensitivity, had proposed a bargain. 'Okay. Let's make a deal: I'll take you to Civitavecchia on Saturdays but you've got to wear this when we make love.' He'd opened the drawer in the dashboard and taken out a gorilla mask. One of those latex-and-fur things people wear at Carnival time.

Patrizia had turned it over in her hands and then, in bewilderment, asked him why.

How could that poor bastard Miele explain to her that if he saw Patrizia's porno-star body, that long glossy hair and those marble protuberances, his dong grew as stiff as a table leg, but if by some mischance he should catch sight of her acne-ravaged face it suddenly went as limp as an earthworm.

'Because . . . Because . . .' Then he plucked something out of the air: 'It turns me on. You see, I've never told you, but I'm a sadomasochist.'

'What's a sadomasochist?'

'Er . . . it's a person who's into kinky stuff. Being whipped, for instance . . .'

'You want me to whip you?'

'No! What are you talking about? It turns me on if you wear the mask,' Bruno had tried, unconvincingly, to explain to her.

'You like doing it with monkeys?' Patrizia was in despair.

'No! Yes! No! Look, just put on the mask and don't ask so many questions,' Bruno had snapped impatiently.

Patrizia had thought it over. As a rule she didn't approve of sexual deviations. But then she remembered what her cousin Pamela had told her: Pamela's boyfriend, Emanuele Zampacosta, known as Manu, a cashier at the Co-op in Giovignano, got off on being peed on, but despite this they had an excellent relationship and were getting married in March. She'd concluded that after all Bruno's perversion was fairly innocuous. And the game was worth the candle. He would take her to Civitavecchia and besides she loved him very much and you do anything for love.

She had accepted. And so, whenever they went into the Acquasparta woods, she'd put on the mask and they'd have sex (once when there was a thick fog, Rossano Quaranta, a sixty-eight-year-old pensioner and poacher, had passed by and found a car hidden among the oaks and being a bit of a voyeur too had crept up and seen an incredible sight. Inside the car were a young man and a large ape. He had raised his shotgun ready to intervene, but had lowered it when he had realised that that pervert was shagging the gorilla. And he had walked away shaking his head and muttering to himself that there was no limit to the disgusting things some people would do nowadays.)

Bruno Miele, however, had not kept his side of the bargain.

They'd made only one trip to Civitavecchia, then he'd started finding excuses and had finally taken her to watch him playing table football. And he even pretended he didn't know her.

Patrizia, in despair, had written a long, heartfelt letter to Dr Ilaria Rossi-Barenghi, the resident psychologist on the weekly magazine *Heart to Heart*, telling her how badly things were going between her and Bruno (she omitted the bit about the mask) and saying that despite everything she loved him to bits, but felt she was being treated like a whore.

To Patrizia's infinite surprise, Dr Rossi-Barenghi had answered her.

Dear Patti,

Once again we find ourselves up against the kind of problem our mothers faced before us. But today, having acquired a greater awareness and a little more knowledge of the human mind, we can hope to bring about a change. Love is a wonderful thing and it's good to be able to share it in a frank and equal relationship. We women are certainly more sensitive than men, and perhaps your boyfriend isn't yet capable of expressing his feelings freely. However, this doesn't mean that you shouldn't demand from him what is right. Don't let yourself be crushed by his egoism. Stand up for yourself. You're very young, but precisely for that reason you mustn't always give in to him, and if he really loves you, in time he'll learn to respect you. Today your boyfriend knows that he can easily control you, but actually it is you who are giving him this impression. In matters of the heart it pays to play hard to get, my dear Patti! Be true to your virtues and you'll see that your Bruno – who, to judge from what you tell me, is a sensitive soul underneath it all – will come to worship you. Good luck!

Patrizia had followed the doctor's advice to the letter. At their next encounter she had explained to Bruno that things were going to change. He was going to have to give her red roses and take her to dinner at the Grandfather's Barrel pub and then to the cinema in Orbano to see *Terms of Endearment 2* with her girlfriends. And she was not going to wear the ape mask when they made love any more.

Bruno had opened the car door, ushered her out and said: 'Get lost, you ugly bitch. Me go and see *Terms of Endearment 2*? What do you take me for, a poof?' And he'd driven off in high dudgeon.

Now, having learned from this nasty experience and Dr Rossi-Barenghi's advice, Patrizia had organised her relationship with Mimmo in such a way that she would never find herself abandoned like a fool and with a broken heart.

121

Pietro was seeking his brother for a very precise reason, namely to ask him if he would go and speak to the deputy headmistress. He had thought up the scheme with Gloria's help. And it seemed workable.

At first she'd tried to convince him that her mother could go. Mrs Celani adored Pietro and said he was the nicest little boy in the world. She would have been delighted to do it. But Pietro wasn't so sure. If Gloria's mother went, it would be further proof that his parents didn't care about him, that his family were all crazy.

No, it wasn't a good idea.

Finally they had come to the conclusion that the only thing for it was to send Mimmo. He was old enough, and he could say that his parents were too busy, so he had come instead.

But now, seeing him there crying like a baby underneath a tree, he wondered if it really was such a good idea. Still, he had to try, there was no alternative.

He told him he'd been given five days' suspension and that they wanted to speak to a member of the family. But Papa had refused to go and said it was nothing to do with him.

'So you're the only one left, you've got to go and tell them I'm a good boy, I won't do it again, I'm very sorry, you know the sort of thing. It's easy.'

'Send Mama,' said Mimmo, throwing a stone a good distance.

'Mama . . . ?' Pietro echoed him with an expression that meant: are you out of your mind?

Mimmo picked up another stone. 'What if nobody goes?'

'They'll fail me.'

'So?' He took a run-up and threw the stone.

'So I don't want to be failed.'

'I was failed three times . . .'

'So?'

'So what does it matter? One year more, one year less . . .'

Pietro snorted. His brother was being a bastard. As usual. 'Will you go or won't you?'

'I don't know . . . I hate that school . . . I can't go into the place. It makes me feel sick . . .'

'You won't go, then?' it was an effort for Pietro to ask him again, but if Mimmo thought he was going to get down on his knees and beg, well, he was wrong.

'I don't know. I've got a more serious problem at the moment. My girlfriend has ditched me.'

Pietro turned away and said in a flat tone: 'Well, fuck off, then!' And he started off down the hillside.

'Hey, Pietro, don't be cross, listen, I'll think about it. If I feel like it tomorrow, I'll go. If I make it up with Patti, I swear I'll go,' shouted Mimmo in that bastard's tone of his.

'Fuck off! That's all I've got to say to you.'

122

Flora Palmieri had spent the afternoon wondering what to make for dinner. She had leafed through recipe books and cooking magazines without finding anything.

What would Graziano like?

She had no idea. But she was sure he wouldn't object to pastasciutta. Linguine with zucchini and basil? A fresh dish, for all seasons. Or trenette with pesto. Although that contained garlic . . . Or no pasta and baked aubergine barchette instead. Or . . .

It's a real problem, indecision.

Finally, in desperation, she'd decided on curried chicken with raisins, hard-boiled eggs and rice. Flora had cooked this dish for herself a couple of times, following a recipe from *Annabella,* and had really enjoyed it. It was something different, an exotic dish, which would certainly appeal to a globetrotter like Graziano.

Now she was pushing a trolley among the shelves of the Co-op, looking for curry powder. She was out of it at home. But, as luck would have it, the Co-op was out of it too, it was too late to drive to Orbano and she'd already bought the chicken.

Oh well, I'll just do roast chicken with new potatoes and salad. A timeless classic.

She went to the wine section and picked a bottle of Chianti and another of Prosecco.

The idea of this intimate dinner both excited and frightened her. She had cleaned the house and got out the good tablecloth and the Vietri dinner service.

As she busied herself with all these preparations, she had tried to silence an irritating little voice which kept saying that she was making a big mistake, that this relationship would only cause her heartache, that she would fill herself with hopes only to see them dashed, that on the way back from Saturnia she had decided to do one thing but she was now doing another, that Mama would suffer . . .

But Flora's healthy side had asserted itself and locked that irritating little voice away in the cellar, at least for the time being.

I've never invited a man home, now I'm damn well going to do it. I want to do it. We'll eat the chicken, chat, watch TV, drink the wine, and that's it. No necking, no rolling about on the floor like pigs, no lechery. And if it's the last time I see him, so be it. Maybe I'll suffer. But what's a little more suffering to me . . . ? I know what's right and Mama, if she could, would tell me to go ahead.

To reassure herself, she thought of Michela Giovannini. Michela had taught physical education at the Buonarroti for a year. She was a petite girl, the same age as Flora, with brown hair and a dark complexion.

Flora had taken an instant liking to her.

During staff meetings her spontaneity came to the fore and left the old bats speechless. Michela always sided with the children. Once she had clashed violently with Miss Gatta over a question of timetables, and although in the end she hadn't got her way, at least she had told her to her face what she thought of her Fascist methods.

Something Flora had never managed to do.

They had become friends quite by chance. As often happens. Flora had asked Michela for advice about where to buy some gym shoes for walking on the beach. Next day Michela had arrived with a pair of beautiful Adidases. 'They're too big for me, someone brought me them from France but they'd chosen the wrong size. Try them on, they should fit you,' she'd said, putting them in her hands. Flora had hesitated. 'No, thank you, I couldn't possibly,' but Michela had insisted. 'What am I supposed to do with them, leave them to rot at the bottom of the wardrobe?' Finally she'd tried them on. They were a perfect fit.

Flora had invited her to go walking with her and Michela had accepted at once, enthusiastically, so every Sunday morning they would walk across the fields behind the railway and go down onto the beach for a stroll. The stroll would last a couple of hours and now and then Michela would try to persuade Flora to run a short distance and sometimes succeeded. They chatted about things.

School. Their families. Flora had talked about her mother and her illness. And Michela had talked about her boyfriend, Fulvio, who worked half-days as a building labourer in Orbano. They had been going out together for several years. He was twenty-two. Three years younger than Michela. They had rented a flat in a block near the Franceschini brothers' fish farm. She said she was in love with him (she had shown great tact in never asking Flora about her own love life).

One morning Michela had arrived on the beach, grasped her friend by both hands, looked around and said: 'Flora, I've made up my mind, I'm going to marry him.'

'How will you manage, without any money?'

'We'll get by somehow . . . We're in love, and that's the main thing, isn't it?'

Flora had given a conventional smile. 'Yes, you're right.' Then she'd hugged Michela hard and felt happy for her, but at the same time she'd felt a vice squeeze her chest.

What about me? Why do I get nothing?

She hadn't been able to hold back her tears. Michela had thought they were tears of happiness, but they were of envy. A terrible envy. Afterwards, at home, Flora had hated herself for being so selfish.

Michela had begun inundating her with phone calls. She wanted to introduce her to Fulvio and show her her little flat. And Flora, each time, would find increasingly fatuous excuses for not going. She sensed that it wouldn't be good for her. It would set painful ideas whirling in her head. But in the end, such was Michela's persistence, she'd been obliged to accept an invitation to dinner.

The flat was tiny. And Fulvio was little more than a teenager. But it was cosy, the fire was crackling merrily and Fulvio had cooked a grouper which he had caught out scuba-diving at Turtle Cliffs. It had been an excellent dinner. Fulvio was very affectionate towards his future bride (kissing her, holding her hand) and afterwards they had sat down to watch *Lawrence of Arabia* and eat cantuccini biscuits dipped in vinsanto. Flora had returned home at midnight feeling happy. No, happy is not the right word, calm.

That was what she wanted for this evening. An occasion of that sort.

The dinner with Graziano would be a bit like the one at Michela's. Except that this time she would have a man all to herself.

On her way past a long freezer she took out a tub of ice cream and was heading for the checkout when she saw Pietro Moroni appear in front of her. He was limping slightly and smiled when he saw her.

'Hallo, Pietro, what's going on?'

123

'I wanted to talk to you, Miss . . .' Pietro heaved a sigh of relief.

At last he'd found her. He had walked past Miss Palmieri's house but hadn't seen her car parked there so he had gone down to the village (a nightmare now – he had to sneak about like a spy to avoid meeting Pierini and his gang) but hadn't found her anywhere and then, just as he was about to return home, he had spotted the Y10 outside the Co-op. He had entered and there she was.

'Why are you limping, have you hurt yourself?' she asked him in a concerned tone.

'I fell off my bike, it's nothing serious,' said Pietro dismissively.

'What's going on?'

It was essential that he explain it clearly, then she would find a solution. He trusted Miss Palmieri. He looked at her and, despite his absorption with what he had to tell her, he noticed that there had been a change in her. Not an enormous one, but there was definitely something different about her. In the first place she had let her hair down, and how thick it was! Like a mane. Secondly she was wearing jeans, and that too was a novelty. He had always seen her in those long black skirts. And then . . . he didn't know how to describe it, but there was something strange about her face . . . Something . . . no, he couldn't put his finger on it. Just different.

'Well, what do want to tell me?'

His mind had wandered off as he looked at her. *Go on, tell her.* 'My parents won't come to school to speak to the deputy head and I don't think my brother will either.'

'Really? Why not?'

How can I tell her? 'My mother's not well and can't go out, and my father . . . my father . . .' *Tell her. Tell her the truth.* 'My father said it's my problem, I caused all the trouble, not him, so he won't come. And my brother . . . my brother's just an idiot.' He moved closer and asked her, ingenuously: 'Will they fail me, Miss?'

'No, they won't.' Flora crouched down to Pietro's level. 'Of course they won't. You're doing well at school, I've told you that. Why should they?'

'But . . . if my parents don't come, won't the deputy head . . . ?'

'Don't worry. I'll talk to her.'

'Will you really?'

'Yes, I will.' Flora kissed her forefingers. 'I swear.'

'And the . . . thingummies won't come?'

'The thingummies?'

'The social thingummies.'

'The social assistants?' Flora shook her head. 'No, don't worry, they won't come.'

'Thank you,' breathed Pietro, freed of an intolerable burden.

'Come here.'

He drew closer and Flora gave him a big hug. Pietro put his arms round her neck and her heart filled with a tenderness and pity that made her head spin for a moment. *This little boy should have been my son.* Her throat was stifled. *My God . . .*

She must stand up or she would burst into tears. She rose to her feet and then took an ice cream from the freezer. 'Would you like one, Pietro?'

Pietro shook his head. 'No, thanks. I must go home, it's late.'

'So must I. You're right, it's very late. See you at school on Monday, then.'

'Okay.' Pietro turned.

But before he could leave, Flora asked him: 'Tell me something, who made you such a nice boy?'

'My parents,' replied Pietro and vanished behind the pasta section.

SIX MONTHS LATER . . .

18th June

124

Gloria was trying to pull him to his feet. But Pietro wasn't collaborating.

He was on his knees, in the middle of the entrance hall of the school, with his hands over his face. 'They've failed me,' he kept saying. 'They've failed me. She swore to me. She swore to me. Why? Why?'

'Come on, Pietro, get up. Let's get out of here.'

'Leave me alone.' He shook her off brusquely, but then he stood up and dried away the tears with his hands.

All his schoolmates were looking at him in silence. In those lowered eyes and tight-lipped smiles Pietro saw a moderate dose of sympathy and a larger dose of embarrassment.

One boy, bolder than the others, came over and patted him on the back. This was the cue for the rest of the flock to start touching him and bleating. 'Don't let it get you down. What does it matter . . . ?' 'Typical of those bastards.' 'I'm really sorry.' 'It's not fair.'

Pietro kept nodding and wiping his nose.

Then he had a vision. A man who, judging from the way he was dressed, might have been his father, entered the chicken run and instead of choosing the plumpest bird (who deserved it more), grabbed one at random, from among the cluster, and said contentedly, 'We'll have this one for dinner.' And all of them, roosters and hens, were sad about their companion's fate, but only because they knew that sooner or later they were going to get it too.

The bomb that had dropped from the sky had landed on Pietro Moroni, blowing him to smithereens.

I bought it today. But sooner or later you all will. You can bet your lives on that.

'Are you coming?' Gloria implored him.

Pietro headed for the door. 'Yes, I want to get out. It's too hot in here.'

Standing by the door was Italo. He was wearing a light-blue shirt that was too short and tight for him. His belly tugged at the buttons, stretching the buttonholes. Two round patches darkened his armpits. He was shaking that round head of his, shiny with sweat. 'She told you wrong. If they failed you they should have failed Pierini, Ronca and Bacci too. It's a damn shame.' His tone was that of a funeral commemoration.

Pietro ignored him and went out followed by Gloria, who repelled the inquisitive crowd with the zeal of a bodyguard. She was the only one who was going to tend to his plight.

Meanwhile the sun, millions of kilometres away from these childish tragedies, roasted the schoolyard, the road, the tables outside the bar and everything else.

Pietro walked down the steps, went out through the gate and, without looking at anyone, mounted his bike and rode off.

125

'Where on earth has he got to?' Gloria had gone to fetch her backpack and when she had returned Pietro wasn't there anymore. She took her bike and set off in pursuit, but couldn't see him anywhere on the road ahead.

She cycled to Fig-Tree Cottage but he wasn't there either. Mimmo, bare-chested under the shed roof, was tinkering with the cylinder head of his motorbike. Gloria asked him if he'd seen his brother, but Mimmo said no and carried on loosening bolts.

Where can he have gone?

Gloria went to the villa, hoping he was there. He wasn't. So she returned to the village.

The air was still and the heat stifling. There was nobody around.

If it hadn't been for the merry twittering of the sparrows and the chirping of the cicadas, Ischiano would have been like a ghost town in the Texan desert. The scooters and motorbikes were leaned against the walls. Their stands would have sunk into the asphalt, which was as soft as butter. The shops' shutters were half down. The Persian blinds of the houses were closed. And inside the cars long white strips of cardboard had been put against the windscreens. Everyone was indoors. Those who had air conditioning were all right, but those who didn't were not.

Gloria stopped outside the Station Bar. Pietro's bike wasn't among those in the rack.

This would be the last place he'd come.

She was exhausted, hot and terribly thirsty. She entered the bar. The air conditioning, turned up to maximum, froze the sweat on her body. She bought a can of Coca-Cola and went to drink it under the parasol outside the door.

She was very worried. It was the first time Pietro hadn't waited for her. He must be feeling really bad to behave like that. And in that state he might do something drastic.

Like hanging himself.

Why not?

She had read about such things in the paper. A boy in Milan who had failed his end-of-year assessment had jumped out of a fifth-floor window in despair and, when that had failed to kill him, had crawled to the lift leaving a trail of blood behind him, gone up to the sixth and jumped out again and this time, fortunately, had killed himself.

Was Pietro capable of committing suicide?

Yes.

But why was it so damned important for him to pass? If she had failed, she would have been upset, certainly, but she wouldn't have made a big thing out of it. For Pietro, though, school had always been so important. He believed in it too much. And a disappointment like this might drive him crazy.

Where could he be? Of course . . . Why didn't I think of it before?

She downed the rest of her Coca-Cola and got back into the saddle.

Pietro's bike was hidden among the bushes, against the wire netting that separated the lagoon from the coast road.

'Found you!' Gloria exulted, and she hid her bike next to Pietro's, slipped behind a large oak and lifted the lower edge of the fence, creating an opening which, though small, was big enough for her to wriggle through on her stomach. Once she was on the other side she put it back into place. It was strictly forbidden to enter there.

And if the WWF wardens catch you you're in trouble.

One last check and she vanished into the dense vegetation.

The first two hundred metres of the narrow path that threaded between reeds and rushes more than two metres high were passable, but the further it went into the marsh, the more difficult progress became and your shoes sank into that thick green slime till the muddy water prevailed and submerged the path completely.

There was a smell in the still air, bitter and sickly-sweet at the same time, which stunned the senses. It was the water plants decaying in that warm, stagnant swill.

Clouds of mosquitoes, midges and sandflies swarmed around Gloria, feeding on her sweet blood. And there were a lot of eerie noises. The monotonous croaking of frogs on heat. The incessant buzzing of hornets and wasps. And those rustles, those swishes, those quick, suspicious whirrings among the reeds. Those plops in the water. The mournful calls of the herons.

A hellish place.

Why did Pietro love it so much?

Because he's crazy.

Now the water was over her knees. And she was finding it difficult to move forward. The plants twined round her ankles like long slimy tagliatelle. The branches and leathery leaves scratched her bare arms. And hosts of little transparent fish escorted her as she waded on like a US marine in South-East Asia.

And that wasn't all. To reach the hiding place she would have to swim across a stretch of lagoon, because the boat (boat . . . pieces of sodden wood held together by a few rusty nails) probably wouldn't be there, Pietro would certainly have taken it.

And so it proved. When she reached the edge of the marsh, covered in scratches, insect-bites and flecks of mud, she found only the thick pole sticking out of the water with no boat attached.

You bastard! You bastard! Don't ever tell me I'm not your best friend.

She steeled herself and slowly, like a lady-in-waiting reluctant to get her robes wet, she sank into the the warm water. From there the lagoon widened out into a lake where metallised dragonflies skimmed across the surface and divers and geese swam about in formation.

Swimming a slow breaststroke, so as not to disturb anything, and keeping her head well up because if one drop of that water came into contact with her mouth she would die, Gloria set off for the other shore. Her gym shoes weighed her down like ballast. She musn't at all costs think about the sunken world that lived down below. Salamanders. Fish. Disgusting creatures. Larvae. Insects. Water-rats. Snakes. Crabs. Crocodiles . . . no. Not crocodiles.

Only a hundred metres to go. On the other shore, among the reeds, she could make out the low prow of the boat.

Come on, you're almost there.

Now she only had a few dozen metres to go and was already beginning to see the longed-for dry land above her when she felt, or thought she felt, a creature, something animate, brush against her legs. She screamed and thrashed wildly towards the bank like a thing possessed. Her head went under the water and she drank that revolting liquid, re-emerged, spluttered and in four strokes reached the boat and leaped up onto it like a performing seal. She sat there gasping, picking seaweed and leaves off her body and repeating: 'Ugh! How revolting! Ugh, how disgusting! Ugh!' She waited till she got her breath back, then jumped onto a strip of land that emerged from the lagoon. She looked around.

She found herself on a tiny little island skirted partly by reeds and partly by the brown waters of the lagoon. There was nothing on the island, except a big gnarled tree whose branches shaded most of the ground and a small hut where, before this area had become a nature reserve, hunters used to come to shoot the birds.

This was 'the place'. That's what Pietro called it.

Pietro's place.

As soon as the weather turned fine in spring, and sometimes even in winter, he would spend more time here than he did at home. He had organised everything. A hammock swung from a low-hanging branch. In the hut he had left a cooling bag, in which he would put sandwiches and a bottle of water. There were also some comics, an old pair of binoculars, a gas lamp and a small radio (which you had to keep turned down very low).

Only now Pietro wasn't there.

Gloria went right round the island without finding a trace of him but then, inside the hut, she saw his T-shirt hanging on a nail. The same one that Pietro had been wearing that morning.

And as she came out again, she saw him emerge from the water in bathing trunks. He had a mask over his face and looked like the monster of the silent lagoon, covered in all that seaweed and holding . . .

'Ugh! Throw away that viper!' Gloria shrieked like a frightened child.

'Don't worry. It's not a viper. It's a grass snake. I've never caught such a long one before,' said Pietro seriously. The snake had coiled round his arm, trying desperately to escape, but Pietro's grip was firm.

'What are you going to do with it?'

'Nothing. I'll study it for a while, then I'll let it go.' He ran into the hut, picked up a fishing net and put it inside. 'What are you doing here?' he asked her, then pointed at her T-shirt, smiling.

Gloria looked at herself. The wet T-shirt was clinging to her breasts and she was practically naked. She pulled it forward. 'Pietro Moroni, you're a filthy pig . . . Give me yours at once.'

Pietro handed her his T-shirt and Gloria changed behind the tree and hung hers up to dry.

He was kneeling down by his grass snake and looking at it impassively.

'Well?' Gloria asked him, sitting on the hammock.

'Well what?'

'What's the matter with you?'

'Nothing.'

'Why didn't you wait for me at school?'

'I didn't feel like it. I wanted to be alone.'

'Would you rather I left? Am I bothering you?' asked Gloria sarcastically.

Pietro was silent for a moment, still contemplating the reptile, but then said in an earnest tone: 'No. You can stay . . .'

'Thank you so much. We are kind today.'

'Don't mention it.'

'Don't you mind about failing any more?'

Pietro shook his head. 'No. I couldn't care less. It's all the same to me.' He picked up a twig and prodded the snake.

'How come, when only a couple of hours ago you were crying your eyes out?'

'Because it had to be. I knew it. It had to be and that's that. And if I feel bad it won't change anything, I'll just feel bad.'

'Why did it have to be?'

He glanced at her just for a second. 'Because now everyone's happy. My father, because, as he puts it, I'll do something useful and start working. My mother – no, not my mother, she doesn't even remember what class I'm in. Mimmo, because now we've both failed and he's not the only dunce in the family. The deputy headmistress. The headmaster. Pierini. Miss . . .' he broke off for a moment and then added: 'Miss Palmieri. The whole world. And me too.'

Gloria swung gently to and fro and the rope tied to the branch began to creak. 'But there's one thing I don't understand, didn't Miss Palmieri promise you they wouldn't fail you?'

'Yes.' Pietro's voice cracked, breaking the fragile indifference.

'Why did they fail you, then?'

Pietro snorted. 'I don't know and I don't care. Just drop it, will you?'

'It's not fair. Miss Palmieri's a bitch. A real bitch. She didn't keep her promise.'

'No, she didn't. She's just like all the others. She's a bitch, she tricked me.' Pietro said this with an effort and then put his hand to his face to stop himself crying.

'She probably didn't even go to the teachers' meeting.'

'I don't know. I don't want to talk about it.'

During the last month and a half Miss Palmieri hadn't come to school. A supply teacher had appeared, saying that their Italian teacher was ill and that they would finish the year with her.

'No, I bet she didn't go. She didn't care. And it isn't true what the supply teacher said. She's not ill. She's fine. I've seen her lots of times around the village. The last time was only a few days ago.' Gloria was getting really worked up. 'Have you seen her?'

'Only once.'

'And . . . ?'

Why was Gloria torturing her? It was all over and done with. 'And I went up to her. I wanted to ask her how she was, if she was coming back to school. She barely said hallo to me. I assumed she had something on her mind.'

Gloria jumped to the ground. 'She's the nastiest bitch I've ever met. Nobody's worse than her. It's her fault you failed. It's not right. She's got to pay for it.' She knelt down beside Pietro. 'We must make her pay for it. We must make her pay dearly.'

Pietro didn't reply and watched the cormorants slipping into the silver waters of the lagoon like black shuttles.

'What do you say? Shall we pay her back?' she repeated.

'I don't care any more . . .' said Pietro, dejectedly, sniffing.

'That's typical of you . . . You mustn't just accept everything. You must react. You must, Pietro.' Gloria was furious now. She felt like telling him that that was why they had failed him, because he had no balls, if he'd had any balls he wouldn't have gone into the school with that bunch of idiots, but she restrained herself.

Pietro looked at her. 'How would you pay her back, then? What would you do to her?'

'I don't know.' Gloria began to pace round the island racking her brains. 'We ought to frighten her, scare her out of her wits . . . What could we do?' Suddenly she stopped and raised her eyes to the heavens as if she'd been possessed by the truth. 'I'm a genius! I'm an absolute genius!' She slipped two fingers into the net containing the grass snake and raised it in the air. 'We'll put this dear little creature in her bed. So when she goes to bye-byes she'll have a heart attack. What do you say, aren't I a genius?'

Pietro shook his head pityingly. 'Poor thing.'

'What do you mean, poor thing? She's a shit. She failed you . . .'

'No, I meant the snake. It'll die.'

'So what? Who cares? This swamp's full of lousy snakes. If one of them dies it doesn't matter a bit, do you know how many get killed on the road, run over by the cars? Anyway, it won't necessarily die. Nothing will happen at all.'

And she kept on at him until he finally gave in.

126

The plan was simple. They'd worked it out carefully on the island. It came down to a few points.

1) If Miss Palmieri's car wasn't there, it meant that she wasn't at home. In that case, you skipped to point three.
2) If Miss Palmieri's car was there, it meant that she was at home. In that case it was no go, and they would try again another day.
3) If Miss Palmieri was not there, they would climb onto the balcony and get into the house from there, put the little surprise in her bed and run away, swifter than the wind.

That was it.

Miss Palmieri's car was not there.

The sun had begun its slow, inevitable descent. It had fired its best arrows, and now the heat, though still torrid, was less than a few hours before. It was no longer that scorching heat that drives people mad and makes them capable of terrible deeds, filling the summer newspapers with gruesome murders.

The faintest breath of wind, a wish for wind, perhaps, gently stirred the scorching air. The coming night was going to be sleepless, muggy, starlit.

Our two young heroes, on their bikes, had hidden behind the laurel hedge that surrounded Miss Palmieri's house.

'Why don't we just forget it?' Pietro said for the umpteenth time.

Gloria tried to snatch away the plastic bag containing the snake, which was tied by a string to Pietro's waist. 'I see, you're shitting yourself. I'll go, you wait here . . .'

Why did everybody, good and bad, friend and foe, always end up accusing him of shitting himself? Why is it so important in life not to shit yourself? Why, in order to be considered a man, do you always have to do the last thing in the world you want to do? Why?

'All right, let's go then . . .' Pietro squeezed through the hedge and Gloria followed him.

The building was at the side of a narrow secondary road that started from Ischiano, cut across the fields, passed over a level crossing and joined up with the coast road. It was little used. Five hundred metres away, in the direction of Ischiano, were a couple of greenhouses and a garage. The house was an ugly cube covered in grey plaster, with a flat roof, green plastic blinds and two balconies full of plants. The ground floor windows were shuttered. Miss Palmieri lived on the first floor.

To climb up they chose the side facing the fields. That way, if anyone came along the road, they wouldn't see them. But who was likely to pass by? The level crossing was closed at this time of year.

The drainpipe was in the middle of the wall. It ran within a metre of the balcony. The balcony wasn't very high up. The only difficulty would be reaching out to get hold of the railing.

'Who's going first?' Gloria asked in a low voice. They were pressed flat against the wall like a pair of geckos.

Pietro shook the pipe, testing its strength. It seemed pretty solid. 'I'll go. It'll be better like that. I'll be able to help you up onto the balcony.'

He felt a sense of foreboding, but tried to suppress it.

'Okay.' Gloria stepped aside.

Pietro, with the snake wriggling in the plastic bag tied to his belt, gripped the pipe with both hands and put his feet against the wall. Plastic sandals weren't ideal for this sort of thing, but he hoisted himself up nonetheless, trying to get them on the brackets that held the pipe to the wall.

Once again he was entering where he shouldn't. But this time, according to Gloria, he had right on his side.

(*But what about you, what do you think?*)

I think I shouldn't go in but I also think that Miss Palmieri's a bitch and deserves to have this trick played on her.

The climb was proceeding without difficulty, the edge of the balcony was only a metre away, when the drainpipe, suddenly and silently, came away. Who knows, maybe the bracket had been badly cemented in or had rusted. The fact remains that it came away from the wall.

Pietro's weight pulled it outwards and if he hadn't made a sudden twist that would have done credit to a gibbon and let go just in time, he would have fallen on his back and . . . well, never mind.

He was left clinging on to the edge of the balcony.

'Oh my God . . .' he muttered frantically, and kicked out, trying to support himself with his feet on the drainpipe, but only succeeded in bending it further.

Keep calm. Don't panic. How many times have you hung from the branch of a tree? You can hang on for half and hour like this.

No, he couldn't.

The marble edge of the balcony was sawing at his fingers. He could last five, ten minutes at most. He looked down. He could let himself drop. It wasn't all that high. He shouldn't do himself too much damage. The only problem was that he would fall right on the tiled path. And tiles, as everybody knows, are renowned for their hardness.

But if I fall properly I won't get hurt.

(*Any sentence beginning with but is wrong from the outset.*) He could hear his father's voice.

Gloria was standing below, watching him anxiously.

'What shall I do?' he called out in a whisper.

'Jump down. I'll catch you.'

Now that really was a stupid idea.

That way we'll both get hurt.

'Get out of the way!'

He shut his eyes and was about to let go, when he saw himself lying on the ground with a broken leg and spending the summer in plaster. 'Like hell I'm going to jump down!' He made a big effort and with one hand grabbed hold of a bar of the railing. He strained to stretch out his leg and got his heel on the edge of the balcony, then got a grip with the other hand too, pulled himself to his feet and climbed over the railing.

What now?

The french windows were closed. He pushed at them. They were bolted.

This hadn't been foreseen in the plan. But who would have thought that in this stifling heat anyone would keep the windows shut as if it were January?

He cupped his hands against the glass and looked in.

A sitting room. There was nobody there.

He could try to force the lock, or break the glass with a flower-pot. Then find his way to the front door and get out that way. The plan would have failed (*But who cares about that?*), or he could hang down off the balcony again and drop down.

'Go in!' Gloria was calling to him and gesticulating.

'It's locked! The door's locked.'

'Hurry up, she might come back at any moment.'

It's easy to talk down there.

Just think what a fool I'd look! Miss Palmieri finding me trapped on her balcony.

He looked over to the other side. Less than a metre away there was a small window. It was open. The shutter was rolled down but not so far as to stop him getting in.

There was his escape route.

127

It was very warm.

But the water was beginning to get cold. She'd lost all feeling in her legs and bottom.

How long had she been in there? She couldn't say for sure because she'd been asleep. Half an hour? An hour? Two?

What did it matter?

She would get out in a while. But not now. All in good time. Now she must listen to her song. Her favourite song.

REW. *Srrrrrrr. Stoc.* PLAY. *Fffff.*

'What a strange man I had, with eyes as soft as velvet, I would tell him over and over I still belong to you and I floated in the air when he slumbered in my arms . . . and I remembered the days when I was innocent, when the red light of coral lit my hair, when starry-eyed and vain I would gaze into the moon and force her to tell me, You're beautiful . . . You're beautiful! Ahhh! Ahhh!'

STOP.

That song was the truth.

There was more truth in that song than in all the books and all the stupid poems about love. And to think she'd found the cassette in a newspaper. Italian pop classics. She didn't even know the singer's name. She was no expert.

But it expressed some great truths.

She should make her pupils learn that song.

'By heart,' murmured Flora Palmieri, sliding her hand across her face.

PLAY.

'You're beautiful! . . . Ahhh!' she began to sing along with the cassette, but it was like having flat batteries.

128

'You're beautiful.'

She opens her eyes. Lips kissing her.

Little kisses on her neck. Little kisses on her ear. Little kisses on her shoulders.

She runs her fingers through his hair. Hair that he'd had cut short to please her. (Well, do you like me better like this? Of course I do.)

'What did you say?' she asks him, rubbing her eyes and stretching. A ray of sun stains the dark carpet and makes the dust dance in the air.

'I said you're beautiful.'

Little kisses on her throat. Little kisses on her right breast.

'Say it again.'

Little kisses on her left breast.

'You're beautiful.'

Little kisses on her right nipple.

'Again. Say it again.'

Little kisses on her left nipple.

'You're beautiful.'

Little kisses on her stomach.

'Swear that you mean it.'

Little kisses on her navel.

'I swear. You're the most beautiful thing I know. And now, may I proceed?'

And the kisses resume.

129

Pietro slipped through head first like a fish into a barrel.

He reached out his hands, put them flat on the tiles and moved forward, taking his weight on his wrists.

The floor was wet and his T-shirt got soaked.

He found himself lying next to the bidet.

In a bathroom.

Music.

'. . . but I went out searching for you, in the streets, among the people, and I turned as in a dream, and you were there again, and the words still linger with me: You're beautiful!'

Loredana Berté.

He knew that song, Mimmo had the CD.

He got to his feet.

It was dark.

And very warm.

He began to drip with sweat.

And there was a smell . . . an unpleasant one.

For twenty seconds he was almost blind. He was in a bathroom, no doubt about it. There was a lamp but it was covered with a cloth and gave out no light. Everything else was in semi-darkness. His pupils contracted and at last he could see.

Miss Palmieri was lying in the bath.

In her hands she was clutching an old cassette recorder, one of those with a black plastic case, which was blaring out: you're beautiful. An electric wire ran right across the bathroom and ended in a socket by the door. The place was a mess. Clothes heaped on the floor. Wet linen in the washing machine. The mirror smeared with red marks.

Miss Palmieri switched off the cassette recorder and looked at him. She didn't seem surprised. As if it were the most normal thing in the world that someone should climb into her house through the window.

But she didn't look normal.

My God, she doesn't.

For one thing, her face was different, much thinner (those faces of the Jews in the concentration camps . . .), for another, floating in the water were bits of soggy bread, banana skins and a copy of *This Week on TV*.

She asked him, with the barest hint of surprise: 'What are you doing here?'

Pietro lowered his eyes.

'Don't worry. I'm past being shy. You can look at me. What do you want?'

Pietro raised his eyes and lowered them again.

'What's the matter, do I disgust you?'

'No, n . . .' he stammered in embarrassment.

'Then look at me.'

Pietro forced himself to look at her.

She was as white as a corpse. Or rather, as a wax statue. Yellowish. Her breasts were like two big scamorzas resting on the water. Her ribs stuck out. Her stomach was round and swollen. Her pubic hair red. Her arms long. And her legs long too.

She was scary.

Flora looked up at the ceiling and called out: 'Mama! We have a visitor! Pietro's come to see us.' She turned her head, as if someone were speaking to her, but no one was. The house was a tomb. 'No, don't worry, it's not the one who came before.'

She's crazy, Pietro said to himself.

130

'We're good together, aren't we?'

Flora smiles.

'Well, what do you say? Are we good together or not?' he persisted.

'Yes. We're good together.'

They are locked in an embrace on a sand dune thirty metres from the shore. In a basket there are sandwiches wrapped in tin foil and a bottle of red wine. The sea is sad, so grey, ruffled by the wind. The same colour as the sky. And the air is so clear that the tall chimneys of Civitavecchia power station seem an arm's length away.

He picks up his guitar and starts playing. One riff is difficult. He practises it a couple of times. 'It's a milonga. I composed it myself.' He stops playing and frowns. 'Ouch! What's that sticking into me?' He puts his hand in his trouser pocket and pulls out a little blue velvet box. 'Oh, that's what it was. Amazing, the things that get into your pockets.'

'What is it?' Flora shakes her head.

She's twigged.

He puts the little box in her hand.

'Are you crazy?'

'Open it.'

'Why?'

'Because otherwise I'll have to throw it to the fish. And next summer some scuba diver's going to make a lucky find.'

Flora opens it.

A ring. White gold and amethyst.

Flora puts it on her finger. A perfect fit. 'What is it?'

'A formal request for your hand in marriage.'

'Are you crazy?'

'Absolutely. If you don't like it, you only have to say so, the jeweller's a friend of mine, we can change it. There won't be any problem.'

'No, it's lovely, I like it.'

131

'Well, what have you come for?'

'Er . . .' *To play a practical joke on you, but in view of the state you're in I don't think* . . . Pietro didn't know what to say.

'So it's true that you break into other people's houses at night like a burglar? Were you planning to smash my TV? If so, go ahead. Feel free, it's in the sitting room. I haven't watched it in ages. This time, though, I don't think anyone has forced you to break in, have they?'

There's somebody downstairs who . . .

The door was there. He could get away.

'Don't even think it. You're here now and you're not leaving till I say you can. We haven't had many guests to talk to lately.' Then, addressing the ceiling: 'Have we, Mama?' She pointed to the plastic bag tied to Pietro's belt. 'What have you got in there? Something's moving . . .'

'Nothing,' said Pietro, trying to sound nonchalant. 'Nothing.'

'Let me see it.'

He moved closer. The sweat was pouring off him. Even behind his knees. He untied the plastic bag and held it out. 'There's a snake.'

'Did you want it to bite me?' she asked, interested.

'No, it's a grass snake, it won't bite,' Pietro tried to justify himself, but without sounding too convincing. It was her, she made him uneasy.

He felt her madness envelop him like a toxic cloud that could drive him crazy too. She no longer had anything of Miss Palmieri, the nice Miss Palmieri he had talked to that winter's evening in the Co-op. She was a different person and what's more she was madder than a mad cow.

I want to get out of here.

The teacher put the cassette recorder on the edge of the bath and took the plastic bag. She opened it and was about to look inside when the snake's pointed head, followed by the rest of its sinuous body, shot out, and it fell into the bath and began to swim about between her legs. Miss Palmieri kept quite still and it wasn't clear whether she was frightened, or pleased, or what.

Then the reptile slithered over the edge and flashed out through the bathroom door.

The teacher burst out laughing. Her laughter was forced and unnatural, like that of a second-rate actress. 'Now it's free to wander round the flat. I've never had a pet. It's the right one for me.'

'Can I go now?' Pietro implored.

'Not yet.' Flora stuck a wrinkled foot out of the bath. 'What can we talk about? Well, I can tell you that the last few months haven't exactly gone well for me . . .'

132

She has finished cooking. Everything's ready. The roast is in the oven. The tagliatelle is covered in sauce and is getting cold on the table. Where has he got to? He's usually so punctual. Perhaps the Milanese interior designer has kept him late. He'll soon be here. Flora has bought a video of Gone with the Wind *at the newsagent's. He gave her a video recorder.*

And at last he arrives.

But he's in a hurry. He's evasive. Strange. He barely kisses her. He tells her he's had some problems with the jeans shop (what an ugly name). That he can't stay to dinner this evening. What problems? She doesn't ask him. He says he'll call her tomorrow morning. And tomorrow evening they'll watch the film. He kisses her on (and not in) the mouth and leaves.

Flora eats the cold tagliatelle and watches Gone with the Wind.

133

'Since that evening with *Gone with the Wind* I've never seen him again,' said the schoolmistress, with a loud laugh. 'Never seen him. Or even spoken to him.'

What evening? And who? What's she talking about? Pietro didn't understand, but he certainly had no wish to inquire further.

(*Let her talk.*)

'It's funny when you think about it now. But at first you've no idea how . . . oh, forget it. The next day, not even a phone call. In the evening not a word, it seemed the day would never end. And I knew. I already knew what had happened. I tried to call him on his mobile but always got his voicemail. I left messages. I waited three days, then rang him at home. And his mother tells me he's not there. And that she has no messages for me. And then she lets slip that her son has gone away, that's all she knows. What do you mean, gone away? Gone away where? That's all she knows, can you believe it? He didn't even leave me a message.' The schoolmistress began crying quietly, then splashed some water on her face and smiled. 'No more crying. I've cried too much. And crying doesn't help. Does it?'

Pietro shook his head.

Why did I come here? What a fool I was . . . What a fool . . . If Gloria could see her, see what a state she's in. But who did she fall in love with?

'He'd left. Gone. Without a word to me, without saying goodbye. I knew he was no good. He was a buffoon, my mother said so from the start. I was well aware of it. That's what hurts so much. He'd bewitched me with his words, his music, his wonderful plans, the engagement ring. He wouldn't leave me alone. He tortured me. He made me believe in him. And now I'm going to tell you something – something amusing. You're the first person I've told, young man. You should feel honoured. Our friend left me a little souvenir.' She grasped the edge of the bath and pulled herself up.

'I'm pregnant, Pietro. I'm expecting a baby.'

And she burst out laughing again.

134

Flora puts her hand in her coat pocket and squeezes the little plastic bag which has told her the truth about those attacks of nausea, about that delay, about that lassitude which she imputed to her broken heart. She gets in the car and drives to the Biglia haberdashery. She switches off the engine. Switches it on again. Switches it off again. She gets out of the car and enters the shop.

Gina Biglia is standing behind the counter talking to two customers. When she sees Flora, she opens her mouth and signals with her eyes. The two women move into a corner, peer into the button drawer but don't leave. You bet they don't! Ears pricked up like wolves.

'Where's he gone?' gasps Flora in a broken voice. 'I must know. I'm not leaving till you tell me.'

'I don't know.' Gina Biglia fidgets. 'I'm sorry, I don't know.'

Flora sits down on the stool, covers her face with her hands and starts trembling, sobbing convulsively.

'I'm sorry,' Mrs Biglia ushers the customers out of the shop, then locks the door. She comes over to Flora. 'Don't take on so,

please. Don't cry, for the love of God. Don't cry!'

'Where's he gone?' Flora seizes her hand and holds it fast.

'All right, I'll tell you. I'll tell you all I know. Just stop, please, stop crying, calm down. He's gone to Jamaica.'

'To Jamaica? Why?'

Gina Biglia lowers her eyes. 'To get married.'

'I knew it, I knew it, I knew it, I knew . . .' Flora repeats, then takes the pregnancy test from her pocket and holds it out.

135

'Now go away. I don't want you here any more. I'm tired.' Flora picked up a floating piece of bread and began to mash it to a pulp.

Pietro turned and was about to leave when, without intending to, without wanting to, he said: 'Why did they fail me?'

'So that's why you came. Now I understand, at last.' She picked up a hairbrush to tidy her hair, but then dropped it in the water. 'Do you really want to know? Are you sure you want to know?'

Did he want to know? No, he didn't, but he turned round anyway and asked again: 'Why did they do it?'

'It was bound to happen. You don't understand. You're stupid.'

(*Don't listen to her. She's evil. She's mad. Go away. Don't listen to her.*)

'But you said I was doing well. You promised me . . .'

'You see how stupid you are? Don't you know that promises are made to be broken?'

She was a witch. With those grey eyes sunken in their purple orbits, that pointed nose, that madwoman's hair . . .

You're the wicked witch.

'That's not true.'

'It's true. It's true,' said Flora, listlessly throwing a banana skin on the floor.

Pietro shook his head. 'You say these things because you're upset. Because someone's dumped you, that's the only reason you're saying these things. You don't really think them, I know you don't.'

136

Flora is lying on the bed. She isn't angry with him any more. If he comes back she'll forgive him. Because she just can't go on like this. Graziano's mother said those things to hurt her, because she's an evil woman. They're not true. It's not true that Graziano has got married. He'll come back. Soon. She knows he will. And she'll take him back. Because without him she can't do anything, and nothing makes sense any more. Waking up in the morning. Working. Looking after Mama. Sleeping. Living. Nothing makes sense without him. She calls to him every night. She can make him come back. She knows she can. With her mind. If she can talk to her mother, who is banished to another world, with him, who is only on the other side of the ocean, it will be easy. She tells him to come back at once. Graziano, come back to me.

137

Flora opened her mouth over her set of yellow teeth and foamed: 'Be quiet! Do you know why they passed Pierini? Because the sooner they get rid of him the better. They never want to see him again. They couldn't have failed him, that boy would be quite capable of taking their precious school apart brick by brick. And I don't blame him either. They're scared. Do you know what he did to me? He set fire to my car. A little reward to me for reporting him. Now you want to know why they failed you. Well, I'll tell you. Because you're immature and infantile. Let me see now . . . How did the deputy headmistress put it? A boy with serious personality disturbances and with a problem family and difficulties of integration into the school community. In other words, because you don't react. You're shy. You don't join in. You're not like the others. Because your father is a violent alcoholic and your mother is a nervous wreck who takes too many medicines and your brother's a poor idiot who failed his school assessment three years running. You're going to become like them. And I'll tell you something, you can forget about high school, forget about university. The sooner you understand who you are, the sooner you'll get better. You've got no backbone. They failed you because you let other people make you do things you don't want to do.

(*And it was Gloria who made me come in here . . .*)

'You didn't want to break into the school, how many times did you repeat that phrase in the head's office? And every time you shot yourself in the foot, showing how weak and immature you were.' She stopped for breath for a moment, looked at him scornfully, and added: 'You're like me. You're worthless. I can't save you. I don't want to save you. Nobody saved me. And they'll walk all over you because you don't reac . . .'

A moment.

One dreadful moment.

The moment when the show-off decides to walk along the parapet.

The moment when you heave the rock off the bridge.

The moment when you reach down to get out your cigarettes, sit up again and in front of you, beyond the windscreen, there's an open-mouthed silhouette frozen on the pedestrian crossing.

The moment that never returns.

The moment that can change your life.

The moment when Pietro reacted, put his foot on the electric wire and tugged and the cassette recorder fell into the water with a simple . . .

Plop.

138

The emergency switch, by the meter, cut off with a snap.

The bathroom went dark.

Flora leaped up with a scream, perhaps thinking she'd been electrocuted, perhaps just out of instinct, at any rate she leaped up, stood for a second balancing on one foot, then another second, and another in which she realised she was going to slip and she slipped backwards and, throwing out her arms, fell back into the darkness.

Crack.

She felt a terrible blow on the back of her head. A sharp blow which jolted her jaw and the rest of her skull.

The edge.

If she had glued on to the bottom of the bath those plastic flowers she'd seen in Orbano which cost twelve thousand lire each (too much for such ugly things), she might not have died, but perhaps even they wouldn't have saved her. After three hours lying still in water your legs are like logs of wood.

She was lying in the bath again.

With one hand she felt the back of her head. She didn't understand. She felt something sticky which matted her hair. And she felt the edges of the wound swelling. And if she put her finger in she could feel that it was deep. The blow had been violent.

She didn't understand. It didn't hurt. There was no pain at all. But she told herself that serious wounds don't hurt at first.

She tried to pull herself up. She tried again.

How come she felt fine but couldn't get up? In fact she felt herself sinking gradually down into the water. That's what it was, her legs weren't obeying.

Perhaps this is how Mama felt no this is soft it's not stiff like Mama I'm gradually dissolving and the water tastes salty and metallic it tastes of blood.

The water came up to her mouth.

I can't die I simply can't it's out of the question I can't do it Mama Mam who will look after Mama if your little daughter isn't there your Flo and otherwise I'd have killed myself long ago Mama.

Mama! Mama! I'm dying! Mama!

139

A blood-curdling scream, water splashing everywhere and a hard thud against the bath.

Pietro covered his eyes, filled himself with air and didn't scream but rushed out of the bathroom searching for the front door and went straight past it without seeing it. Everything was dark. He found himself in the kitchen. A door. He opened it. A warm stench of excrement hit him like a fist. He took two steps and there was a fence, a barrier, something made of iron, something he fell over head first and landed with his mouth open on a hard body, a little body that was wheezing and panting, he started kicking and squirming and shrieking like an epilectic and climbed over whatever it was and ran back, banging against corners and falling over the telephone table and at last he saw the front door, turned the handle and fled down the stairs.

140

She was breathing through her nose.

The rest of her head was under water.

Her eyes were open. The water was warm. It tasted bitter. Red spirals whirled around her. Circles that grew wider and wider, a vortex and a noise, a muffled noise in her ears, the drone of a plane on its way from Jamaica and sitting in it was Graziano who was coming back *because I called him and there's a hill going round and round and there's Mama and Papa and Pietro and Pietro and because I Flora Palmieri born in Naples and a little boy with red hair and Graziano is playing and the koalas are coming the big silver-haired koalas and it's so easy the easiest thing in the world to follow them over the hill.*

What she saw gave her one last spasm, she smiled and, when she finally let herself go, she ceased to be pulled by the vortex.

19th June

141

Mouth half-open, hands clasped behind his head, Pietro gazed at the stars.

He didn't know their names. But he knew there was one, the Pole Star, the sailors' guide, which was brighter than the others, though tonight they all seemed equally brilliant.

His heart had stopped racing, his stomach was no longer churning, his head had ceased to spin and Pietro was dozing relaxedly on the beach. Gloria was beside him. She hadn't moved for quite a while, she was probably asleep.

They had been there for over six hours and after spending all that time agonising about what had happened, telling her the story over and over again, asking himself the same questions and debating what to do, tiredness had prevailed and now Pietro just felt drained, physically exhausted and loath to think.

He wished he could stay there like that, gazing at the sky, lying on the warm sand, for the rest of his life. But it wasn't easy, because the little psychologist sleeping within him suddenly woke up and asked him: *Well, how does it feel to have killed your Italian teacher?*

He had no reply, but what he could say was that after killing another human being you don't die, your body goes on working and so does your brain, but it's not like before. No, from that moment until the end of his life there would be a before and an after. Like with the birth of Christ. Except that in his case it would be before and after the death of Miss Palmieri. He glanced at his watch. Twenty past two on the 19th June, the first day A.F.P.

He'd electrocuted her.

For no reason. Or if there was one, Pietro didn't understand it, didn't want to understand it, it was locked away somewhere inside him and he could only feel its overwhelming power, a power capable of turning him into a madman, a murderer, a monster.

No, he didn't know why he had killed her.

(*She said those horrible things about you and your family.*)

Yes, but that wasn't why.

It had been a kind of explosion. There had been tons of TNT inside him ready to go off and he hadn't known it. The schoolmistress had touched the button that activated the detonator.

Like those bulls in the corrida that stand there in the middle of the arena and suffer agonies without moving and there's that bastard of a bullfighter torturing them and they don't react but eventually he sticks in one spear too many and the bull explodes and that guy can dance as much as he likes but he'll still get a horn in his guts and the bull will lift him up and toss him in the air with his bowels hanging out and blood trickling from his mouth and you're glad because that Spanish game of sticking spears in your back where it hurts most until you can't stand it any more is the most evil game on earth.

It might have been one reason, but it wasn't enough to justify what he had done.

I'm a murderer. 'A murderer. A murderer. Pietro Moroni is a murderer.' It had a nice ring to it.

They would find out and throw him in jail for the rest of his life. He hoped he would have a little room (a little cell) all to himself. He could read books (prisons do have libraries). He could watch TV (Gloria might give him hers) and there he would stay. He would sleep and eat. That was all he needed.

Living in peace for ever.

I must go to the police and confess.

He reached out and shook Gloria. 'Are you asleep?'

'No.' Gloria turned towards him. Her eyes glittered with stars. 'I was thinking.'

'What about?'

'About Miss Palmieri's boyfriend. Who could he be?'

'I don't know. She didn't tell me.'

'She loved him so much she went out of her mind . . .'

'She was in a very bad way. She seemed really ill, not like Mimmo when Patrizia ditches him.'

Strange. He had never thought about what Miss Palmieri did after school, whether she liked watching films or going for walks, whether she enjoyed mushrooming, whether she preferred cats or dogs. Maybe she didn't like animals at all, maybe she was scared of spiders. He had never even imagined what her home might be like. He saw the little balcony full of geraniums, the dimly lit, dirty bathroom, the hall with those posters of sunflowers and the little room with that creature in it. It was as if, for the first time, he had discovered that his teacher was also a person, a woman who lived alone and had a life of her own, not a cardboard model with nothing inside it.

But none of this mattered any more. She was dead.

Pietro sat up and crossed his legs. 'Listen, Gloria, I've been thinking, I must go to the police. I must go and tell them. If I confess it'll be easier. They always say that in films. They treat you better afterwards.'

Gloria didn't move, but snorted. 'For goodness' sake, shut up! Stop going on about it. We talked about it for two hours. Nobody saw you. Nobody knows you went there. Neither of us ever went there, do you understand? We were at the lagoon. Miss Palmieri went mad. She dropped the cassette recorder in the water and was electrocuted. End of story. When they find her, they'll think it was an accident. That's it. Now shut up. You said so yourself, you're not going to change your mind, are you?'

'I know, but I keep thinking about it. I can't stop, I just can't,' said Pietro, digging his fingers in the sand.

Gloria sat up and put her arm round his neck. 'I bet I can stop you thinking about it.'

Pietro smiled wrily. 'How?'

She took hold of his hand. 'Fancy a swim?'

'A swim? No thanks. I'm not in the mood.'

'Come on. The water must be really warm.' She grasped his arm. Finally Pietro got up and allowed himself to be led down to the waterline.

Although there was only a half moon, the night was luminous. The stars reached down into the sea, which was as flat as a table. There was no sound except the wash of the water shifting the sand. Among the dunes behind them the vegetation was a black tangle dotted with the intermittent lights of fireflies.

'I'm going in. If you don't come too, you're a bastard.' Gloria took off her T-shirt in front of Pietro. Her breasts were small, and paler than the rest of her suntanned body. She gave him a mischievous smile, then turned, took off her shorts and knickers and rushed into the sea, shrieking.

She stripped in front of me.

'It's lovely! It's really warm. Come on in! Do I have to beg you on my knees?' Gloria knelt down and put her hands together. 'Pietro, Pietro, please won't you come and swim with me?' And she said it in such a voice . . .

Are you crazy? Go on, what are you waiting for?

Pietro pulled off his T-shirt, slipped off his trousers and, in his underpants, dashed into the water.

The sea was warm, but not so warm that it didn't give him a shock which cleansed away the tiredness in his body. He took a deep breath, dived into the shallow water and started doing a vigorous breaststroke ten centimetres off the sandy bottom.

Now all he had to do was swim. Glide further and further, follow the sea-bed out to the depths, like a manta or a ray, till he was out of air, till his lungs burst like balloons. He opened his eyes. And there was the cold darkness, but he continued to swim with his eyes open and began to be aware that the need to breathe, *take no notice, keep going*, was clawing at his chest, his windpipe, his throat, five more strokes and when he had done them, he told himself he could do another five, at least seven or he was a sissy, and he was close to passing out but he must do another ten, at least ten and he did one, two, three, four, five and at that point he really felt as if a nuclear bomb had exploded inside him and he shot up to the surface gasping. He was a long way out from the shore.

But not as far as he'd thought.

He saw Gloria's blonde head turning this way and that, looking for him. 'Gl . . .' but then he broke off.

She was thrashing about anxiously. 'Pietro? Where are you? Don't be silly, please. Where are you?'

He remembered the song the schoolmistress had been singing when he'd entered the bathroom.

You're beautiful! He told me you're beautiful.

Gloria, you're beautiful. He would have liked to say it to her. But he had never had the courage. It wasn't done to say these things.

He submerged and swam a few metres. When he surfaced again, he was nearer to her.

'Pietro! Pietro, you're frightening me! Where are you?' She was panicking.

He submerged again and came up behind her.

'Pietro! Pietro!'

He grabbed her round the waist. She jumped, and turned round. 'You bastard! Damn you! You scared me out of my wits! I thought . . .'

'What?'

'Nothing. That you're a fool.' She splashed him with water, then jumped on him. They began wrestling. And it was a horribly pleasant feeling. Her breasts against his back. Her bottom. Her thighs. She pushed him under and held him down, her legs gripping his hips.

'Beg for mercy, you bastard!'

'Mercy!' he laughed. 'It was only a joke.'

'Ha ha, very funny! Let's get out, I'm freezing.'

They ran onto the beach and threw themselves down, side by side, where the sand was still warm. Gloria started to rub him down to dry him, but then put her lips to his ear and sighed: 'Will you tell me something?'

'What?'

'Do you like me?'

'. . . Yes,' replied Pietro. His heart had started pounding under his breastbone.

'How much?'

'A lot.'

'No, I mean, do you . . .' She took an embarrassed breath. 'Do you love me?'

Pause.

'Yes.'

Pause.

'Really?'

'I think so.'

'Like Miss Palmieri? Would you kill yourself for me?'

'If your life was in danger . . .'

'Let's do it, then . . .'

'Do what?'

'Make love.'

'When?'

'The day after tomorrow. My God you're stupid! Now. This minute. I've never done it, and you . . . You've never done it either . . .' she grimaced. 'Don't tell me you have. You didn't do it with that tart Caterina Marrese, did you, and then keep quiet about it?'

'I might as well ask you if you did . . .' protested Pietro.

'Yes, I'm a lesbian and I've never told you. I'm in love with Caterina Marrese.' She changed her tone, became serious. 'We must do it now. Will it be difficult?'

'I don't know. But how . . . ?'

Pause.

'How what?'

'How do we start?'

Gloria rolled her eyes up to the night sky and then said, awkwardly: 'Well, for example you could kiss me. I'm already naked.'

It was a minor tragedy the details of which are best passed over in silence. It was brief, complicated and incomplete and left them full of questions and fears, confused, incapable of talking about it and locked together like Siamese twins.

But then she said: 'You must swear an oath to me, Pietro. You must swear it on our love. Swear you'll never tell anyone about Miss Palmieri. Never. Swear to me.'

Pietro remained silent.

'Swear.'

'I swear. I swear.'

'I swear I won't either. I won't tell anybody. Not even in ten years' time. Never.'

'You must swear an oath to me, too, that we'll always be friends, that we'll never part, even if I'm in the second year and you're in the third.'

'I swear.'

142

Zagor was barking.

Obsessively, as if someone had climbed over the fence and was in the farmyard. His bark strangled by the chain. Hoarse and wheezy.

Pietro got out of bed. He put on his slippers. He pulled aside one of the curtains and peered into the darkness. There was nobody there. Only a stupid dog throttling itself and raising its blue lips over its foaming jaws.

Mimmo was asleep. Pietro went out of the room and opened the door of his parents' bedroom. They were asleep too. Their dark heads barely showing above the bedclothes.

How can they not wake up with all this noise? he thought, and the moment he thought it, Zagor stopped.

Silence. The rustle of the wind in the woods. The creak of the beams in the ceiling. The ticking of the alarm clock. The hum of the fridge downstairs in the kitchen.

Pietro held his breath and waited. Then at last he heard them. Outside the front door. So muffled, they were scarcely audible.

Tump. Tump. Tump.

Footfalls.

Footfalls on the steps.

Silence.

And there came a knocking at the door.

Pietro opened his eyes wide.

He was sweating profusely and breathing hard.

What if she's alive?

If she was alive, he would find out.

He left his bike behind the laurel hedge and cautiously approached the house.

Nothing seemed to have changed since the night before. The road was deserted. It was still early and the lowest part of the sky was tinged with light blue. The air was cool.

He looked up. The bathroom window was open. The door onto the balcony closed. The drainpipe bent over sideways. The glass front door locked. Everything as before.

How was he to get in? Could he force the front door?

No.

They would notice.

The drainpipe?

No.

He would fall down.

An idea: you climb up as far as you can go, then you drop down, hurt yourself (break your leg), then you go to the police and say your teacher phoned you to say she was ill and you rang at the door but she didn't reply so you tried to climb up the drainpipe and fell off. And you tell them to go and check.

No, wouldn't work.

One, she didn't phone you. If they question Papa and Mama they'll discover that straight away.

Two, if she's not dead, she'll tell the police it was you who tried to kill her.

He must find another way of getting in. He walked round the house, looking for a skylight, or a hole to crawl through. Behind the blackened pipes of the boiler he saw an aluminium ladder covered with leaves and cobwebs. He pulled it out.

What he was doing was very dangerous. A ladder against a window would be seen by anyone who passed by. But he had to take that risk. He couldn't live with this huge weight on his conscience a minute longer. He must climb up and see if she was alive.

(*And if she is alive?*)

I'll say I'm sorry and call an ambulance.

He carried the ladder round to the front, and with some difficulty succeeded in placing it against the wall. He scaled it quickly, took a deep breath and entered Miss Palmieri's house again.

143

The British Airways jumbo arriving from Kingston, Jamaica, via London, pitching like a huge turkey landed on the runway of Leonardo da Vinci airport in Rome, slowed down, stopped and switched off its engines.

The cabin crew opened the door and the passengers began to pour down the steps. Among the first to emerge, dressed in a safari shirt, blue Bermudas, climbing boots, a peaked cap and an enormous shoulder bag, was Graziano Biglia. He was clutching his mobile phone and when, after a couple of beeps, the Telecom Italia Mobile logo appeared on the digital display of his Nokia and he saw the five bars indicating perfect reception, he smiled.

That's more like it, home at last.

He selected Flora's memorised number from the phone book and pressed enter.

Engaged.

He made five more attempts while he was being herded with the other passengers onto the bus, but was unsuccessful.

Never mind, I'll surprise her.

He went through customs and took off the carousel his suitcase and a huge wooden sculpture of a black dancing girl.

He cursed.

Despite the packaging, the dancer had lost her head during the flight. The present for Flora. It had cost him the earth. They'd have to pay him compensation. But not now. Now he was in a hurry.

He left the arrivals lounge and went straight to the Hertz counter where he rented a car. He wanted to get to Ischiano Scalo as soon as possible, and travelling by rail was out of the question. In the car park they gave him a purple Ford with no stereo.

The usual crappy car, but for the first time in his life Graziano didn't argue till he got one that was to his liking, now he just had to rush to Ischiano to do the most important thing in his life.

144

She was dead.

Dead.

Quite dead.

As dead as dead could be.

The thing in the bath was dead. Yes, because that was no longer Miss Palmieri, but a swollen, livid thing, floating in the bath like the inner tube of a tyre. The blue mouth open. The hair plastered against the face like long seaweed. The eyes, two opaque spheres. The water was clear, but at the bottom lay a crimson carpet over which the schoolmistress's corpse seemed to be levitating. A black corner of the cassette recorder protruded like the bow of the Titanic from the red sludge.

It had been him. He had done that. With one movement of his leg. A simple movement of his leg.

He backed away till the wall stopped him.

He had really killed her. Until now he hadn't completely believed it. How could he have killed a human being? Yet he had. She was dead. And nothing could be done about it now.

It was me. It was me.

He rushed over to the toilet and vomited. He knelt there, hugging the bowl and gasping.

I must get out at once. Away. Away. Away.

He flushed the toilet and left the bathroom.

The house was dark. In the hall he replaced the table he'd knocked over when he'd run away, and put the receiver back on the telephone. He looked into the kitchen to check that everything was in the ri . . .

What about the creature in there?

Pietro hesitated in front of the door and then, driven by something that was both curiosity and need, entered the dark room.

The smell of excrement was even more penetrating and now beneath it there was another smell, if possible even more unpleasant and sickening.

He slid his hand around on the wall by the door jamb, groping for the switch. A long neon light crackled, came on, went off, came on and lit up the room. There was a bed with an aluminium frame and on it a dead, sexless creature. A mummy.

Pietro wanted to leave but couldn't take his eyes off it.

What had happened to it? It wasn't just old, it was all twisted and didn't have an ounce of flesh on it. What had reduced it to this state?

Then he remembered the ladder out there, doused the light, shut the front door behind him and went down the stairs.

The White Cliffs of Edward Beach

'There's someone to see you in the other room,' Gina Biglia had said with a smile that extended even beyond her ears.

'Who is it?' Graziano had asked, and had entered the sitting room.

Erica. Sitting on the sofa, she was sipping a coffee.

'So this is the Erica I've heard so much about?' Gina had asked.

Graziano had slowly nodded.

'Well? Aren't you going to give her a kiss? You are rude . . .'

'Grazi, aren't you going to give me a kiss?' Erica had repeated, opening her arms with a merry little giggle.

If there'd been a sexologist hidden away somewhere in that sitting room, he would have been able to explain to us that Erica Trettel, at that moment, was pursuing the most effective strategy for regaining the affections of a wounded ex-partner, namely displaying herself as the sexiest and most fuckable woman on the planet.

And in this she had succeeded to perfection.

She was wearing a pea-green miniskirt so tight and short he could have rolled it up in the palm of his hand and swallowed it like a meatball, a woollen jacket of the same colour with a single button which squeezed her wasp-like waist but left her ample cleavage exposed, a silk blouse, also green, but of a paler tone, left casually open down to the third button so as to allow, for the joy of the male universe and the envy of the female one, tantalising glimpses of a black lace wonderbra which moulded her mammary glands into firm globes. Black tights patterned her long legs with geometrical motifs. Her apparently sober black shoes concealed six-inch heels.

So much for her clothing.

As far as her coiffure was concerned, her hair was long and platinum blond. It formed soft waves which fell with studied naturalness on her shoulders and down her back in the style of the L'Oreal adverts.

As far as make-up was concerned, her lips (noticeably fuller than a few months earlier) were covered with dark, shiny lipstick. Her eyebrows were two thin arcs that crowned her green eyes, which were emphasised by a faint line of kohl. A dusting of light powder crowned the whole.

All in all, the impression she conveyed was that of a young professional woman, confident that no man whose hormones were functioning properly could fail to like her, well integrated in society and ready to devour the world in a single mouthful, with all the slick sensuality of a *Playboy* full-page spread.

You may wonder what on earth Erica was doing in Ischiano Scalo. In the sitting room of the man to whom she had said: 'I despise you, and everything you represent. The way you dress. The bullshit you talk in that know-all tone of yours. You don't know anything. You're just an ageing, failed drug dealer. Get out of my life.

If you dare call me again, if you dare come and see me, I swear to God I'll pay someone to smash your face in.'

Now we'll try to explain.

It was all because of the television. All because of those damned audience ratings.

The Tuesday evening variety show on Channel One, *You Reap What You Sow*, where Erica had made her debut as an assistant, had been such a monumental flop that it had shaken the foundations of the entire national network (in the corridors of the Italian Broadcasting Corporation malicious tongues recalled, in between guffaws, how about half an hour after the beginning of the second episode the audience monitoring system had registered zero for about twenty seconds. In other words, for about twenty seconds not a single person in Italy had been watching Channel One. Incredible!) There had been just three episodes and then the show had been jettisoned, and with it the heads of department, assistant managers, producers and writers. Only the chairman of the network had more or less survived the debacle, and even he was a marked man for ever more.

Mantovani, the presenter, had ended up making commercials for body-toning Dead Sea mud on Channel 39, and apartheid had been practised on the entire staff of the show: the comedians, the band, the telephone operators, the dancers and the showgirls, including Erica Trettel. After being thrown out by the IBC, Erica had stayed for two months at Mantovani's home, hoping to receive offers from the rival networks. Not a single phone call came.

Her relationship with Mantovani was fast deteriorating. He would come home in the evening, strip down to his underpants and slippers, gulp down some Edronax and wander around repeating: 'Why? Why me?' Then one evening Erica had caught him in the bathroom sitting on the bidet, trying to commit suicide by swallowing a 500 cc bottle of Dead Sea mud, and she'd realised that once again she'd backed a loser.

She had put on the sexiest clothes she possessed, dolled herself up like Pamela Anderson and packed her bags. Then she had headed for the station and, tail between her legs, caught the first train for Ischiano Scalo.

That is how she came to be there.

Two days later, Erica had won Graziano back and they'd left for Jamaica.

They'd got married straight away, one beautiful night under a full moon on the cliffs of Edward Beach, and had started living life the Biglia way.

Albatrosses borne on positive currents.

Beach morning and evening. Huge joints of cannabis. Swimming. Surfing. Deep-sea fishing. They had even organised a little show to make a bit of money. Two evenings a week, in a night club catering for American tourists, Graziano played the guitar and Erica danced in a bikini for the delectation of both sexes.

And yet our feathered friend was not happy.

Wasn't this what he'd always wanted?

Erica had come back, saying that she loved him, that she had made a big mistake, that television was crap, he had married her and they managed to make a living without too much difficulty and there was the intention, in a not clearly defined future, to return to Ischiano and open the jeans shop.

What more did he want, for Christ's sake?

The problem was that Graziano couldn't sleep any more. In his bungalow, under the fan, while Erica was in the land of dreams, he stayed up all night smoking.

Why? he asked himself. Why, now that his dream had come true, did he feel that it was not his dream and that Erica, now that she was his wife, was not the wife he wanted?

Deep down, somewhere in his lower belly, there lurked a feeling which made him feel like shit. One of those feelings that consume you little by little, which eat away at you like a slowly incubating disease, and which you can't tell anyone about because if you admit the truth the whole damn puppet-show will come crashing down about your ears.

He had left Flora without telling her anything. Like the meanest and sneakiest of thieves. He'd stolen her heart and run off with another woman. He'd dumped her unceremoniously. And all the fine promises, all the declarations he had made to her gnawed at his conscience more cruelly than the three Greek Furies.

. . . I asked her to marry me, can you believe that? I had the gall to ask her to marry me, I'm a shit, a shit of a man.

One night he had tried to write her a letter. And then he'd torn up the sheet of paper after two sentences. What could he say to her?

Dear Flora, I'm very sorry. You see, I'm a gipsy, it's just the way I am, I'm a . . .

(*bastard. Erica turned up and I . . . and I . . . oh, to hell with it . . .*)

And when he eventually got to sleep he always had the same dream. He dreamed that Flora was calling him. *Graziano, come back to me. Graziano.* And he was only a few metres away from her, calling out that he was there, in front of her, but she was deaf and blind. He grabbed her, but she was a cold, synthetic mannequin.

Sitting on the beach, he lost himself in memories. Their little dinners and the video recorder. The weekend in Siena, where they had made love all day long. Their plans for the jeans shop. Their walks on the beach at Castrone. He kept remembering when he had given her the ring and she had blushed bright red. He missed Flora terribly.

You fool. You've blown it. You've lost the only woman you ever succeeded in loving.

But one day Erica had arrived on the beach bubbling with excitement. 'I've been talking to an American producer. He wants to take me to Los Angeles. For a film. He says I'm just the kind of girl he needs. He'll pay our fare and give us a house at Malibu. I've made it. This time I've really made it.'

To be fair, Erica had tried hard, she'd held out for quite a while, she'd kept her resolution to have nothing more to do with show business for two whole months.

'Really?' Graziano had said, lifting his head off the sunbed.

'Yes. I'll introduce him to you this evening. I've told him about you too. He says he knows a lot of people in the music business. He's a big shot.'

Graziano had closed his eyes and, as if in a crystal ball, seen his immediate future.

Los Angeles, in one of those crappy apartments with cardboard walls next to a freeway, without any money, without any work permit, watching TV and out of his mind with boredom, no, worse, out of his skull on crack.

Everything the same. Exactly the same. Like in Rome, only worse.

This was his chance! His chance to put an end to this dismal farce.

'No thanks. You go, I'm not coming. I'm going home. This is your big break, I'm sure of it. You'll be a great success,' he had said, as he felt explode within him a happiness he had never thought he would feel again. Blessed, blessed American producer, God bless him and all his family! 'Don't worry about our marriage, it doesn't mean a thing if we don't have it rubber-stamped in Italy. Consider yourself free, as free as the air.'

She had goggled at him and asked in amazement: 'Graziano, are you angry?'

And he had put his hand on his heart. 'No, I'm not. I swear on the head of my mother. I'm perfectly happy. I'm not angry at all. You must go to Los Angeles. If you don't you'll be making a mistake you'll regret for the rest of your life. I wish you all the luck in the world. But if you'll excuse me, I've got a plane to book.' He had kissed her and dashed off to a travel agency.

And when he was in flight ten thousand metres above the Atlantic Ocean, after a while he had dozed off and dreamed of Flora.

They were on a hill with some other people and some little silver-haired bears and they were kissing and there was a little Biglia crawling on all fours. A little red-haired Biglia.

145

Pietro entered Gloria's bedroom, out of breath.

'Hi!' said Gloria, who was standing on the table trying to reach a book on the top shelf of the bookcase. 'What brings you here at this time of day?'

At first Pietro didn't notice the large suitcase open on the bed and full of clothes, but then he saw it. 'Where are you going?'

She turned and hesitated for an instant, as if she hadn't understood the question, but then explained: 'This morning my parents gave me a surprise. As a reward for pas . . . I'm leaving for England tomorrow morning. I'm going to do a horse-riding course in a village near Liverpool. It only lasts three weeks, fortunately.'

'Oh . . .' Pietro flopped down in the armchair.

'I'll come back in the middle of August. So we can spend the rest of the holidays together. Three weeks isn't long, after all.'

'No.'

Gloria grasped the book and jumped down from the table. 'I didn't want to go . . . I even quarrelled with my father. They told me I had to. They've already paid for it. But I'll soon be back, you know.'

'Yes.' Pietro picked up a yo-yo from the table.

Gloria sat on the arm of the chair. 'You will wait for me, won't you?'

'Sure.' Pietro began to spin it up and down.

'You don't mind, do you?'

'No.'

'Really?'

'No, don't worry. You'll soon be back and I've got a lot of things to do at the place, with all the fish I've put in the net . . . Actually, I'm on my way there now. Last night when we left I forgot to feed them, and if they don't get anything to eat . . .'

'Shall I come with you? I could finish packing this afternoon . . .'

Pietro gave a forced smile. 'No, better not. We made a lot of noise last night and the wardens might get suspicious. It's better if I go on my own, really. It's better. Listen, have a great time in England and don't ride so much that your legs go bandy.'

'No, I won't. But . . . won't I see you this afternoon, either?' said Gloria, disappointed.

'I can't this afternoon. I've got to help my father mend Zagor's kennel. It rotted during the winter.'

'Oh, I see. So this is the last time I'll see you?'

'Three weeks soon pass, you said so yourself.'

Gloria nodded. 'Okay. Bye, then.'

Pietro stood up. 'Bye.'

'Aren't you going to kiss me goodbye?'

Pietro briefly rested his lips on Gloria's.

They were dry.

146

Graziano drove across the main street of Ischiano and down the road that led to Flora's house.

He had no more saliva in his mouth and two waterfalls were dripping from his armpits.

The emotion and the heat.

He would go down on his knees and beg her to have pity on him. And if she refused to see him, he would stand outside her house day and night, it didn't matter how long, without eating or drinking, until she forgave him. It had taken Jamaica to show him that Flora was the woman of his life and he wasn't going to let her get away again.

There were two hundred metres to go when he saw, behind the cypresses, blue flashes in the yard in front of the house.

And now what's happened?

An ambulance.

Oh God, Flora's mother . . . Let's hope it's not serious. Well, anyway, I'm here. Flora won't be alone. I'll help her and if the old lady has died, it's probably just as well, at least Flora will be relieved of a burden and her mother will be at peace.

There was a police car too.

Graziano left the hire car at the side of the road and entered the yard.

The ambulance was parked, with its doors wide open, beside the front door. The police car, ten metres away, also had one door open. There was a blue Regata as well. Flora's Y10, however, wasn't there.

What the . . .

Bruno Miele in his police uniform emerged from the house, turned round and held the door open.

A male nurse emerged, carrying a stretcher.

On the stretcher was a body. Covered with a white sheet.

The old woman has di . . . .

But then he noticed a detail.

A detail that froze the blood in his heart.

A lock of hair. A lock of red hair. A lock of red hair stuck out. A lock of red hair stuck out from under the sheet. A lock of red hair stuck out from under the sheet and dangled down from the stretcher like a grisly paper streamer.

Graziano felt as if the ground beneath his feet were sucking away all his strength. Underneath him was a magnet which had drained him of all vital fluid and reduced him to a heap of bones devoid of energy.

He opened his mouth.

He clenched his fingers.

He thought he was going to pass out but didn't. His legs, as stiff as stilts, one step at a time, carried him over to Bruno Miele. Mechanically he asked him: 'What's happened?'

Miele, who was busy coordinating the operation of loading the body onto the ambulance, swung round irritably. But seeing Graziano appear like a ghost, he was puzzled for a moment, then exclaimed: 'Graziano! What are you doing here? Weren't you on tour with Paco de Lucia?'

'What's happened?'

Miele shook his head and in the tone of someone who has seen it all before said: 'Miss Palmieri's died. That teacher from the junior high. She was electrocuted in her bath . . . We don't know if it was an accident. The pathologist says it could have been suicide. I knew it, everyone said she was half crazy. She was out of her mind. It's strange, though, her mother died the same night. A massacre. Oh, by the way, I'm having a little party this afternoon, nothing very grand. I've been promoted, you see . . .'

Graziano turned round and walked slowly back to his car.

Bruno Miele was disconcerted for a moment, but then turned back to the nurses: 'What are you trying to do now? There isn't room for both of them in there.'

The positive currents had suddenly disappeared and the albatross, its magnificent wings numb with pain, was plummeting into a grey sea, and a black, bottomless abyss was opening up, ready to receive him.

147

Pierini was feeling good.

The teachers had bitched at him a lot during the year but in the end they'd passed him. His father was happy.

He himself couldn't give a shit.

I'm damned if I'm going back next year anyway.

Flame hadn't finished school either and he'd said that if you simply refused to take their crap, in the end they stopped going on at you.

The new development was that he had made some influential friends in Orbano. Mauro Colabazzi, aka Jawbone, and his mates. A gang of sixteen-year-olds who hung out night and day outside the Yogobar, a gelateria that specialised in yoghurt ice cream.

Jawbone, who had been around a bit, had taught him a couple of very simple tricks for getting rich. Smash a window, put two coloured wires together and bingo, the car is yours.

Child's play.

And for every car you brought him you got three whistlers (three hundred thousand lire). Only one and a half whistlers if you did the job with Flame, but what the hell, two's company.

And Ischiano Scalo, in some ways, could be seen as one big car park full of vehicles just waiting to be ripped off, and if you added the fact that the local police were a bunch of imbeciles, the whole situation could not but put him in a good mood.

That night, for example, he was intending to steal Bruno Miele's new Golf. He was sure the fool didn't even lock it, convinced as he was that nobody would dare to steal a car from a policeman. How wrong can you be!

And next day he was going with Jawbone to Genoa, where he'd heard there were rich pickings to be had.

That's why he was feeling good.

The only thing he was a bit sorry about was that he'd heard Miss Palmieri had died. Drowned in the bath. One of his favourite masturbatory fantasies had gone, because wanking over a dead woman isn't much fun and someone had even told him it brought bad luck.

After he'd set fire to her car, he had grown quite fond of the schoolmistress, his anger had cooled, he had almost come to love her, but then he had seen her with that arsehole Biglia, the guy he'd had a fight with that day when he had been beating up Moroni.

That was the kind of thing that drove him wild.

How could any woman screw a jerk like that?

The schoolmistress deserved better than some poor fool who thought he was Bruce Lee. He must be well hung, that was the only explanation.

And now she was dead.

But who cares, anyway. He caught the frisbee and threw it to Ronca, who was standing opposite him. The disc skimmed across the piazza and arrived as hard and true as a bullet, whipped through Ronca's hands and landed by the drinking fountain.

'What are your hands made of, shit?' shouted Bacci, who was standing by the palm tree.

They had been playing for half an hour, but the heat was

beginning to make itself felt and soon the piazza would be as hot as a grill. He was tired of playing with those two idiots. He would seek out Flame and go to Orbano to hear the latest news at the Yogobar.

At that moment Moroni appeared, on his bike.

Something must have changed, because he didn't feel an immediate urge to beat him up. Since he had been hanging around with Jawbone, he had lost interest in that kind of entertainment. He had tired of playing the cock on the dung-heap. A few kilometres away he felt that there were infinitely more exciting things to do and picking on a loser like Moroni was stupid.

Pathetic little jerk, he was the only one they'd failed. And he'd burst into tears in front of the noticeboards. If he could have done, he'd have given him his own place in the higher year, for all he cared about it. And what if he was going out with that little slut Gloria I'm-the-only-one-who's-got-one? Pierini cared even less about that, he had the hots for a little girl he'd met at the Yogobar, a certain Loredana, known as Lory.

I'll leave him alone.

But Ronca was not of the same opinion.

As soon as Moroni came within range, he spat at him and said: 'Hey, Dickhead, you failed and we didn't!'

148

The gob of spit hit him on the cheek.

'Hey, Dickhead! You failed and we didn't!' Ronca jeered.

Pietro braked, put his feet on the ground and wiped himself clean with his hand.

He spat in my face!

He felt his guts twist together and then a blind rage explode within him, a black fury which this time he wasn't going to suppress. Too many things had happened to him in the last twenty-four hours, and now he was getting spat on as well. No, he couldn't accept that.

'You're going to repeat the whole year, you stupid little Dickhead,' continued that odious little flea, hopping around him.

Pietro sprang off his bike, took three paces forward and slapped him in the face as hard as he could.

Ronca's head bent over leftwards like a punchball, bent slowly back over to the other side like a slack spring, then finally straightened up again.

Ronca opened his eyes wide in slow motion, passed his hand over the offended cheek and stammered, in utter amazement: 'Who did that?'

The blow had come so quickly that Ronca hadn't even realised he had been hit. Pietro saw Bacci and Pierini arriving to help their crony. He was past caring by now. 'Come on then, you bastards!' he roared, putting up his fists.

Bacci raised his hands, but Pierini grabbed him by the shoulder. 'Wait. Wait, let's see if Ronca can beat him.' Then he addressed Ronca. 'It was Moroni who hit you. Go on, hit him back, what are you waiting for? I bet you can't. I bet Moroni beats you hollow.'

For the first time since Pietro had known him, Ronca had lost that odious leer on his face. He was rubbing his cheek and looking bewildered. He glanced first at Pierini, then at Bacci, and realised that this time nobody was going to help him. He was on his own.

So he behaved like the desert dragon, that harmless non-venomous lizard, which, to frighten its adversaries, looks mean, raises its crest, swells up, hisses and goes red all over. Very often this technique works. But for Stefano Ronca it didn't.

He gnashed his teeth, tried to look fierce, jumped up and down and threatened him with: 'Now I'm going to hurt you. Really, really hurt you. You're going to suffer like hell,' then he threw himself on Pietro, shouting 'I'm going to whip your arse!'

They rolled over and over on the ground. In the middle of the piazza. Ronca seemed epileptic, but Pietro grabbed him by the wrists, pinned him to the ground, got his shins over his arms and rained punches on his face, neck and shoulders, making strange hoarse noises. And if Pierini hadn't been there to grip him by the scruff of the neck, God knows what he would have done to him.

'That's enough! That's enough, you've beaten him! Now stop it!' He pulled him away, Pietro still kicking at the air. 'You've won.'

Pietro brushed off the dust, breathing heavily. His knuckles hurt and his ears were buzzing.

Ronca had got to his feet and was crying. A trickle of blood ran down from his nose. He limped over to the drinking fountain. Bacci was laughing and clapping his hands in delight.

Pietro picked up his bike.

'It's not fair,' said Pierini, lighting a cigarette.

Pietro got on to the saddle. 'What?'

'Them failing you.'

'I don't care.'

'You're right.'

Pietro put his foot on the pedal. 'I must be going. Bye.'

But before he could move, Pierini asked him: 'Do you know Miss Palmieri's dead?'

Pietro looked him straight in the eye. And he said it: 'Yes, I know. I killed her.'

Pierini blew out a cloud of smoke. 'Don't talk crap! She drowned in the bath.'

'Who are you trying to kid?' Bacci chimed in.

'It was me who killed her,' Pietro persisted, earnestly. 'I'm not talking crap.'

'Oh yeah? Why did you kill her, then?'

Pietro shrugged. 'Because she failed me.'

Pierini nodded in agreement. 'Prove it.'

Pietro began pedalling slowly away. 'Inside the house, somewhere, there's a grass snake, I took it there. Go and see, if you don't believe me.'

149

It might even be true, Pierini said to himself, throwing away the stub. *Moroni's no bullshitter*.

150

The Miele household was celebrating. And there were good reasons for doing so.

In the first place, Bruno had been promoted and in September would be joining a special squad of plain-clothes detectives who would be investigating the links between local and organised crime. His dream was finally coming true. He had even bought a new Golf, to be paid for in fifty-six easy instalments.

In the second place, old Italo was retiring. And with permanent disability he would be getting a tidy little sum at the end of each month. From September onwards, therefore, he would no longer be spending his nights in the cottage by the school, but in his farmhouse with his wife like any normal human being, and would be able to tend to his vegetable patch and watch TV.

So, despite that African heat, father and son had organised a party in the field behind the house.

A long carpet of charcoal embers was surrounded with stones, and on top was an old bedspring, and beef offal, pork chops, sausages, scamorzas and little tunas were roasting.

Italo, in vest and sandals, was checking with a long pointed stick that the meat was done. Now and then he would wipe a damp cloth over his bald pate so as not to get sunstroke and then call out that the sausages were ready.

They had invited practically everyone they knew and there were at least three generations together. Children chasing each other round the vineyard and squirting each other with water from the pump. Pregnant mothers. Mothers with prams. Fathers stuffing themselves with tagliatelle and red wine. Fathers playing bocce with their children. Old men with their wives sheltering from that pitiless sun under the parasol and pergola and fanning themselves. A radio-cassette recorder in a corner was playing Zucchero's latest album.

Clouds of excited flies buzzed about among the smoke and the delicious food smells and settled on the trays of pastries, rice croquettes and mini-pizzas. Horse-flies were batted away with rolled-up newspapers. Inside the house there were a group of men clustered around the TV watching football and a group of women gossiping in the kitchen as they cut up bread and salami.

Everything as expected.

'Mm, this carbonara's delicious. Who made it? Was it auntie?' Bruno Miele, with his mouth full, asked Lorena Santini, his fiancée.

'How should I know who made it?' snorted Lorena, who had other problems at that moment and who, having got sunburned on the beach, was the colour of a lobster.

'Well why don't you go and ask? This is how carbonara should be made. Not that pap you make, which is practically a spaghetti omelette. You cook the eggs. I bet this is auntie's work.'

'I don't want to get up,' protested Lorena.

'And you expect me to marry you? Ah, never mind.'

Antonio Bacci, who was sitting between Lorena and his wife Antonella, stopped eating and intervened. 'It is good, I agree. But to make it really special there should have been onions in it. That's the original Roman recipe.'

Bruno Miele raised his eyes to the heavens. He felt like throttling him. Thank God he wouldn't be seeing any more of this guy from next winter, otherwise they might have come to blows one day. 'Don't you realise what nonsense you talk? I don't know why you open your mouth. You know nothing about cooking, I remember you telling me once that it spoils bass if you grill it. You don't know how to eat . . . Carbonara with onions, for goodness' sake!' He had got so worked up that little bits of pasta flew out of his mouth as he talked.

'Bruno's right. You know nothing about cooking. Onions go in amatriciana,' echoed Antonella, who never missed a chance to put the boot in on her husband.

Antonio Bacci held up his hands in surrender. 'All right, calm down. I didn't insult you. What would you have done if I'd said there should have been cream in it, killed me? Okay, there shouldn't have been any onions in it . . . What's the big deal?'

'You're always sounding off about things you know nothing

about. That's what's so annoying,' retorted Bruno, still not placated.

'I'd have liked it better if there'd been onions in it,' mumbled Andrea Bacci, who was already on his third helping. The boy was sitting next to his mother, wolfing down his food.

'Oh sure, that would have made it even more fattening.' Bruno scowled at his colleague. 'You ought to take this boy to the doctor. How much does he weigh? Eighty kilos at least. When he starts growing he's going to be a monster. Watch out, these things shouldn't be trifled with.' And to Andrea: 'Why are you so hungry, anyway?'

Andrea shrugged and began mopping up the sauce with a piece of bread.

Bruno raised his arms and stretched. 'I could do with a coffee now. By the way, didn't Graziano come?'

'Why, is he around? Is he back?' asked Antonio Bacci.

'Yes, I saw him outside Miss Palmieri's house. He asked me what had happened, I told him and he went off without even saying goodbye. Strange.'

'Do you know what Moroni said?' Andrea Bacci nudged his father.

Bacci senior ignored him. 'But wasn't he supposed to be on tour?'

'Well, maybe it's finished. I told him about the party. Perhaps he'll come.'

'Papa! Papa! Do you know what Moroni said?' Andrea persisted.

'For goodness' sake, why don't you go off and play with someone your own age and leave us in peace?'

Bruno was sceptical. 'The amount of food he's eaten, he won't even be able to stand up. You'll have to call a breakdown truck to lift him.'

'But I wanted to say something important,' the boy whimpered. 'Pietro Moroni said he killed Miss Palmieri . . .'

'Okay, now you've said it. Run along and play,' said his father, pushing him away.

'Wait a minute . . .' Bruno pricked up his antennae. The antennae thanks to which he now belonged to a special unit and wasn't going to remain an ordinary officer like that numbskull Bacci. 'And why did he say he killed her?'

'Because she failed him. He said it's the truth. And he said there's a grass snake in Miss Palmieri's house. He put it there. He said to go and see.'

151

Pietro was with his father and Mimmo in the farmyard nailing boards onto the roof of Zagor's kennel when the cars arrived. Those two, in their green Peugeot 205 with a Rome number plate, accompanied by a police car.

Mario Moroni looked up. 'What do they want now?'

'They've come for me,' said Pietro, laying down his hammer.

SIX YEARS LATER . . .

Dear Gloria,

First of all, Merry Christmas and a Happy New Year.

A few days ago I spoke to my mother and she told me you've decided to go to Bologna University. She heard from your mother. You're going to do film studies or something, is that right? Not economics after all, then. You were right to hold out against your father. It's what you wanted to do. People ought to do the things they want to do. I'm sure this film course will be very interesting and Bologna's a nice lively city. So they tell me, anyway. When I leave the institute I want to travel all round Europe by train and I'll come and see you, so you can show me around.

It won't be long now, in two months and two weeks I'll be eighteen and I'll be leaving. Amazing, isn't it? I can hardly believe it – at last I'll be able to get out of this place and do what I want. I haven't decided what that is yet. But I've heard you can study for a degree at night school and maybe I could do that. They've offered me a job here, actually, helping the new arrivals to settle in and that sort of thing. They'd pay me. The teachers say I'm good with children. I don't know, I'll have to think about it, all I want now is go on that trip. Rome, Paris, London, Spain. I'll decide about the future when I get back, there's time for that.

I must admit I wasn't sure whether to write to you, we haven't been in touch for so long. In my last letter I told you I didn't want you to come and pay me a visit. I hope you weren't upset but I couldn't bear to see you like that, after all this time, and in this place, for just a couple of hours. We wouldn't have known what to say to each other, we would have talked about the usual things people talk about in these cases and then you would have gone and I would have been miserable, I know. I'd made up my mind to phone you as soon as I got out so that we could meet in some nice place, far away from here.

In the end I decided to write because I needed to tell you something I've often thought about in all these years and which perhaps concerns you too, in a way – the reason why, that day in the piazza, I told Pierini about Miss Palmieri. If I'd kept quiet, maybe nobody would have found out and I wouldn't have been sent to the institute. The psychologists kept asking me why I'd told him and for a long time I replied that it was because I'd wanted to show Pierini and the others that I was strong too and that I didn't let people push me around and that after they failed me I was wild with rage. But that wasn't the truth, I was lying.

Then a few weeks ago something happened. A new boy arrived, a Calabrian boy who had killed his father. He's fourteen. He speaks broad dialect and when he talks – which isn't often – nobody understands a word he says. Every evening his father used to come home and beat up his wife and sister. One evening Antonio (but everyone here calls him Calabria) took the bread knife off the table and stuck it in his chest. I asked him why he'd done it, why he hadn't gone to the police to report him, why he hadn't talked to anyone about it. He didn't answer me. It was as if I didn't exist. He just sat there by the window smoking. So I told him I had killed someone too, when I was about the same age as him. And that I knew how it feels afterwards. And he asked me how it did feel and I said, awful, terrible, with something inside you that won't go away. And he shook his head and looked at me and said it wasn't true, that afterwards you feel like a king, and then he asked me if I really wanted to know why he had killed his father. I said yes. And he said: because I didn't want to become like that bastard, I'd rather be dead than like him. I've thought a lot about what Calabria said. He understood more quickly than I did. He understood at once why he had done it. In order to combat something evil which we have inside us and which grows and turns us into beasts. He cut his life in two in order to escape from that. It's true. I think the reason I told Pierini I'd killed Miss Palmieri was that I wanted to get away from my family and Ischiano. I wasn't conscious of it when I did it, nobody would do such a thing if they were conscious of it, it was something I didn't know at the time. I don't really believe in the subconscious and psychology, I think everyone is what they do. But in that particular case I think there was a hidden part of me, which took that decision.

That's why I'm writing, to tell you that when I promised you that night on the beach (how often I've thought about that night) that I'd never tell anyone, I really meant it, but then maybe the fact that you were leaving for England (but you mustn't feel guilty about that) and seeing Miss Palmieri's body again broke something inside me and I had to say it, spit it out. And I really believe I changed my own destiny. I can say that now, having spent six years in this place which they call an institute but which in so many ways is just like a prison and I've grown up and finished high school and maybe I'll go to university myself.

I didn't want to end up like Mimmo, who's still there fighting with my father (my mother tells me he's started drinking, just like him). I didn't want to stay in Ischiano Scalo. No, I didn't want to become like them, and soon I'll be eighteen and I'll be a man, ready to face the world with (hopefully!) the right attitude.

Do you know what Miss Palmieri said to me in the bathroom? She said that promises are made to be broken. I think there's some truth in that. I'll always be a murderer, even though I was only twelve, it makes no difference. There's no way of atoning for such a terrible thing, not even the death penalty. But in time you learn to live with it.

That's what I wanted to tell you. I broke our pact, but maybe it was better that way. But now I'd better stop writing, I don't want to make you sad. My mother tells me you're beautiful and I knew you would be. When we were small I was sure you'd be Miss Italy one day.

Love,
Pietro

P.S. You'd better watch out – when I come to Bologna I'm going to grab you and steal you away.

Acknowledgements

I'd like to thank Hugh and Drusilla Fraser, who gave me the tranquillity to finish the book. And I'd like to thank Orsola De Castro for standing by me and Graziano Biglia. And I'd like to thank the wonderful Roberta Melli, and Esa de Simone and Luisa Brancaccio and Carlo Guglielmi and Jaime D'Alessandro and Aldo Nove and Emanuele and Martina Trevi, Alessandra Orsi and Maurizio and Rosella Antonini and Paolo Repetti and Severino Cesari. I'd like to thank Renata Colorni and Antonio Franchini and the whole Editoria Letteraria Mondadori team for their help (Daniela, Elisabetta, Helena, Lucia, Luigi, Silvana, Mara, Cesare, Geremia, Joy). And finally I'd like to thank my whole family (including the Grancereale Gang) for being such a great support. Thank you again.